THROUGH THE STORM

DIANE GREENWOOD MUIR

Cover Design Photography: Maxim M. Muir

ISBN-13: 978-1505352405
ISBN-10: 1505352401

Don't miss the first books in
Diane Greenwood Muir's

Bellingwood Series

All Roads Lead Home – Bellingwood #1
A Big Life in a Small Town – Bellingwood #2
Treasure Uncovered – Bellingwood #3
Secrets and Revelations – Bellingwood #4
Life Between the Lines – Bellingwood #5
Room at the Inn – Bellingwood #5.5
A Season of Change – Bellingwood #6
Tomorrow's Promises – Bellingwood #7

CONTENTS

ACKNOWLEDGMENTS

This book has been waiting for me. Some of these stories have been preying on my mind for a while. I couldn't wait to finally catch up.

A writer works in solitude. Well, this writer does. When I'm deep into a story, I'm grateful for absolute silence. Fortunately, my cat is quiet. While solitude works for the writing process, there are other things that happen along the way and I couldn't do this without amazing people.

Book covers are supposed to be impossible and I'm fortunate to be married to an extraordinary photographer. Max always has something that makes me look good.

Rebecca Bauman reads while I write and ignores the horrendous errors I make in the first, very rough, draft. She encourages me and tells me I'm amazing, which gives me the courage to go after another chapter. She is also the person I trust most when designing my covers. Her eye for design and color is incredible.

My sister, Carol, has taken really good care of me through all of this. She shows up for a weekend, helps bring my world back together and then leaves so I can work again. Everyone needs a sister like that.

My beta readers are simply an amazing group. They are well read and some of the brightest folks I know. When I put my manuscript in their hands, they return it to me filled with great changes and insight into the story that I might have missed. I couldn't do this without them. Thank you to Tracy Kesterson Simpson, Linda Watson, Alice Stewart, Fran Neff, Edna Fleming, Nancy Quist, Max Muir, Carol Greenwood and Rebecca Bauman for helping me bring Bellingwood to life.

I'm always grateful to people who answer questions when I randomly drop an email into their lives. Thanks to Doug Purintun at Danda Arms for giving me wonderful information about handguns. He knows his stuff. I might have promptly forgotten it all, though, when I realized that there was no way Polly would be able to distinguish one type of gun from another. She and I ... we're useless with some of that.

CHAPTER ONE

"I'm sorry," Jason said, his chin trying to dig a hole in his chest so he could hang his head even lower.

"I'm not the one who needs to hear your apology. I'm only the taxi driver." Polly glanced over at the young man who was still just a boy, in the passenger seat of her truck. His face was blotchy and tears streaked his face. Stupid kid.

Thunder cracked, making Polly jump. The sky was grey and threatening. After another mile, a casual check in her rear view mirror showed two vehicles speeding toward her, one on each side of the road. They would be on top of her in moments.

"What in the hell?" she gasped. This was like an awful game of chicken. Neither car was slowing and she began to breathe heavily as scores of possible scenarios spun through her mind.

"What's going on?" Jason asked turning around to look out the rear window.

"Hold on." Polly wrenched the steering wheel to the side, sending her truck careening into the ditch. Somewhere in her past, someone told her that a ditch was a lot softer than hitting another car. She didn't have much time to think about it as the truck's tires dug into the soft dirt that had recently been soaked by rain, slamming her into her seatbelt. The truck bucked over the uneven surface of the ground and the steering wheel seemed to take on a life of its own. Instinctively, she knew she had to keep the wheels straight or she'd risk rolling over.

The truck was losing momentum due to the drag of the soft earth, but the ditch had funneled her so that she was headed directly toward a large metal culvert. Her only chance would be to try to drive up the other side of the ditch. She pulled the steering wheel over and the truck moved in the right direction, but the slippery slope simply pushed her back down. Polly was almost on top of the culvert and had to take quick action, so she punched the 4-hi button on the dash. Her dad had taught her not to do this when going faster than fifty miles an hour, but she really didn't have time to check the speed.

She needed more acceleration to get up the hill but the vehicle needed a moment to engage the four-wheel drive. At the last minute, Polly mashed the gas pedal to the floor and pulled the steering wheel hard to the right. Thankfully, the truck's front wheels bit in to the soil. Giant chunks of mud flew up past her window as they climbed out of the trench, narrowly missing the culvert. The truck leapt over the ridge at the top and settled down onto the edge of a corn field. Corn stalks and cobs thwacked against the hood as they broke off, while Polly sped down along the rows.

Now on level ground, it was much easier to slow down and navigate out of the farmer's field. She found a turn-out where she could rejoin the road and with her front wheels on pavement, she pulled off on the shoulder and came to a stop.

As soon as she released the steering wheel, her hands started shaking at the same speed as the racing of her heart. Polly took a breath and tried to unclench the muscles in her leg, arms and back.

"Well, that was fun," she said to Jason, who appeared to have a death grip on the handle just above his window. "You know they call that thing an oh-shit handle for a good reason?"

His blotchy face had gone pale and he looked back at her with big eyes. "That was awesome!"

"That's one word. Are you okay?"

"I'm good. That was awesome!'

"Uh huh." Polly took two more deep breaths, trying to calm her racing heart. "They're going to kill someone."

"Are you calling the cops?"

"I should. Did you see either of those cars enough to know what they were?" She couldn't tell the difference between a Ford and a Chevy. Volkswagen bugs were as specific as she could get and that's only because they were so obviously what they were.

"The blue car was a Dodge Charger and the silver one was an Infiniti. The Charger was older."

She shook her head. "How do you know these things?"

"I dunno." Jason shrugged.

Polly took out her phone and pressed Aaron Merritt's number, knowing that he was going to harass her about the call. At least she didn't have to report a dead body.

"Don't tell me," he said, without even a hello.

"No. But there is going to be a death if you don't get two idiots off the roads." She described what had just happened.

He sighed and said, "Oh Polly. I'm sorry. We've had reports on these two over the last few weeks. Are you okay?"

"I'm a little freaked out, but I think we're fine. There's a field here that looks a little worse for wear, but I know whose it is and I'll give him a call. He just saved my life."

"Who's with you?"

"Jason. Without him, I would have only been able to tell you that there were two and they were cars."

Aaron laughed. "Tell him thank you. We didn't know what the silver car was before today. That will help. Drive safely now."

"Absolutely."

The muscles in her arm were still twitching when she put the phone back down on the seat beside her. Jason had released the panic bar and was scratching his head. "Were they really going to hit us?"

"I don't know. I think so." She took another deep breath and felt tears leak from her eyes as a terrible realization hit her. What if Jason had been driving? He begged for the opportunity every time she picked him up after school in Boone. She usually handed him the keys and climbed into the passenger side of her truck.

Polly remembered the excitement of being allowed behind the wheel of her father's truck. She'd driven his tractors all over the farm, but his truck was sacred. Mary was the first person who allowed Polly behind the wheel of a car and after she assured Everett Giller that his daughter wouldn't drive off the road, he loosened up.

Eliseo had taught Jason to drive this last summer and the two years between his permit and his driver's license were going to go much too slowly for all of them. Jason took every chance he could to get behind the wheel of any vehicle around.

Polly had been annoyed with him enough today that when he came out of the high school in Boone and found her, she'd simply pointed to the passenger side and waited for him to climb in and put his seatbelt on. He'd sat there sullenly, waiting for her to yell. She'd done none of that. His mother was angry enough that his poor little life wasn't going to be worth much when he got home. It would be entertaining to watch, but Polly hadn't felt the need to pile on any more trouble.

Her breath hitched in her throat.

"What's wrong?" Jason asked.

Polly reached across and took his arm. "What if you'd been driving?"

Jason blanched. Then he glanced up at the panic bar and said, "Oh shit?"

She could hardly help herself and tears turned to laughter. They were both laughing hard when she saw flashing lights pull in behind her.

Stu Decker, one of the Aaron's deputies that she knew quite well, got out of his car and strode up to her truck. Polly rolled the window down.

"Heya Polly. I just got the call. Are you two okay?"

"We are. I'm just trying to get my courage up to drive home. They scared me to death."

He looked across her and said, "How are you doing, Jason?"

"She was awesome. You should have seen her pull this truck out of the ditch." He bobbed his head up and down. "It was awesome!"

"I guess he's fine," Polly laughed. "This has happened before?"

"Three times that we know of. They ran a stock trailer off the road. That was one pissed-off farmer. Luckily the trailer was empty or I think the old guy would have chased them down the road with a shotgun. Last week, a woman was still in her driveway when they sped by and two weeks before that, we got a call from a farmer who was mowing his ditch."

"No license plates or anything?" she asked.

"They're covered up."

"I saw that, too," Jason said.

Polly looked across at him. "I can't believe you saw anything. I was so focused on keeping the truck upright, I couldn't think about the idiots out there."

"Has your heart rate returned to normal?" Stu asked, a grin on his face.

"Yeah. I think I can make it home now. Thanks for stopping."

Stu went back to his car and Polly rolled the window up. Temperatures were all over the place lately, but today summer was well underway and it was warm. She was ready for fall weather to take hold and stay. She turned the air conditioning up and pulled back out onto the road, heading for Sycamore House.

"I really am sorry, Polly," Jason repeated. Now that the crisis was over, he was thinking back to the reason he was in trouble in the first place.

"I know you are. You're going to have to tell that to your Mom and Eliseo, though. They're the ones you've hurt."

"I didn't mean to. I just didn't think. If he ..."

Before he could go any further, Polly put her right hand up to stop him. "No apology is worthwhile if you have to make excuses. This one's all on you. You can't spread the responsibility."

Jason started to cry again and before they reached the outskirts of Bellingwood, he was sobbing. The fear of traveling through the ditch and the farmer's field couldn't have helped his emotional state, but Polly knew his heart was broken. He'd brought it on himself and facing the consequences had to be terrifying - especially when he didn't know what those would be. She wished he could understand that once he'd dealt with it in front of everyone, things would get better, but maybe this process was important, too. Worrying about what was to come would probably help him learn the lesson he needed.

It was hard for her to watch this boy, who was fast becoming a young man, fall apart like a child. He'd grown several inches this summer and his body and face were changing, as was his voice. He had grown leaner and much more muscular while working around the property with Eliseo, his features becoming more chiseled, losing their little boy softness.

"I don't want to go in," he sobbed when Polly pulled into her garage. "Can't you just go around the block or something?"

"It's best to face it and get it over with," Polly said. "Neither of them will stay mad at you forever. They love you."

"What if she never lets me ride the horses again?"

Polly knew better than that, but this was Sylvie's call. "Jason, you are going to have to deal with whatever comes your way. You made the mistake, you can't get out of the punishment."

She parked the truck and pulled her truck door open, releasing the lock on the passenger side. Jason didn't move.

"Jason," she said quietly. "You can't stay out here."

"I can't do *this*," he moaned.

His mother chose that moment to slam out of the door into the garage. Polly took a good look at her and tried not to laugh. Every bit of fury Sylvie had worked up was a sham. She'd been through all of the emotions this morning and now all she wanted to do was scare the daylights out of her son. The woman was in complete control.

Sylvie stalked over to Jason's door and pointed to the ground. "Out. Now," she said.

Jason opened the truck door and reached back in for his backpack. Sylvie took it out of his hands and flung it toward the door leading inside. She grabbed his upper arm, pushed him out of the garage, and led him across the back yard. Polly watched the two of them make their way through Eliseo's garden toward the fence leading to the barn. After she finally calmed down this morning, Sylvie had told both Polly and Eliseo that her plan was to terrify her son. She was going to make his life miserable until he knew exactly how wrong he had been. When she got finished with the fury, she was bringing out the disappointment and then she would allow repentance.

This was the fury. Polly was thankful to be far away from it and felt awful that Eliseo had to be part of this at all. His heart was as big as those immense Percheron horses he cared for and he loved Jason and Andrew as much as he would love any son of his own. He was ready to give Jason a stern talking to and let it go, but Sylvie was prepared to make a point. She'd been busy all summer, trying to finish her classes. While that happened, her oldest son had somehow found a level of cockiness and arrogance that came with the independence of having his mother too busy to pay attention.

He'd become increasingly difficult to be around at Sycamore House. Eliseo kept him in line down at the barn, but whenever he was around his younger brother, he took every opportunity to tease him, pick on him, or try to upset the boy. Polly scolded Jason, and even though he grudgingly apologized, his behavior continued to get worse.

The thing was, he wasn't a bad kid. For the most part, he was helpful and polite, but it didn't take much for him to toss out a bad attitude. Polly wanted to believe it was part of growing up. How could she know? She'd never dealt with kids this age. She wanted to believe that it was because he was building a shell before going to high school. Leaving Bellingwood's safe, little school had to be hard. School had only been in session for three weeks and he still hadn't gotten any better. In fact, it seemed like he was getting worse.

Last week, Sylvie had been called to Boone because he was part of a group of older kids that were harassing some girls. She'd grounded him, not letting him work at the barn all weekend. With this new situation, Sylvie hadn't been sure this morning what she was going to do with the boy.

Henry drove in just as Sylvie and Jason cleared the last gate to the barn. He got out of his truck and stood beside Polly. "Do you want to sneak down and listen?" he asked.

"No way! I'm so glad that I'm not involved. You have no idea."

"What do you think she's going to do?"

"I don't know that either. But I can tell you that the Sylvie who has hold of that boy right now is not someone I ever want to meet. She's calculating and quiet. All of the heat and anger she felt this morning is gone and this woman is scary."

Thunder clapped again and the sky finally opened up, pouring rain. Polly stepped further inside the garage to avoid the rain.

Henry glanced at Polly's truck. "What happened? Did you find a mud puddle somewhere?"

Her heart lurched just thinking about it. "You won't even believe what happened. It's been a long time since I've been that scared."

"What do you mean? What happened?" Henry went from calm and peaceful to worried and scared.

"Jason and I were driven off the road coming back from Boone. I don't know how I managed it, but I kept us from becoming one with a culvert and only ripped up part of Jim Dawkins's field. That reminds me, I need to call him."

"What do you mean? Are you okay? Is Jason hurt?"

"No we're fine and I called Aaron. Stu stopped by to check on us. It's all good. Just scared me to death."

"So, what happened?" Henry walked around her truck, brushing dried mud to the floor of the garage. He bent over to look under the front bumper. "You dented this on something," he said.

"Two idiots were racing down the road toward me and I had a choice to either take the ditch or get hit."

He looked up at her. "You're not kidding."

"I'm really not. Stu says this has been happening for a while. I'm only the second person they've run into the ditch. One was a farmer with a stock truck."

"And they don't know who is doing it?"

"License plates are covered up and I have to tell you, I was concentrating so hard on keeping the truck upright, I didn't pay any attention to them. Jason saw what kind of cars they were driving, but that's all."

He walked back over and took her in his arms. "You're wonderful. Thank you for driving so well today. I don't know what I'd do if something happened to you."

Polly waved her arm, encompassing Sycamore House and all of the land, and said, "You'd have to take care of all of this. That's part of the deal, you know."

"I don't want that part of the deal. I want you. So no hurting yourself in ditches."

"I'll do my best. You're home early, what's going on?"

"We came to a stopping point over at the lodge, so I thought maybe I'd come home and see if my adorable wife might want to go out with me this evening. Maybe we could even go out of town."

"I'd love to. Just us or do you want to call someone?"

He kissed her nose. "How about just us. We always do things with other people."

They went upstairs and were greeted by a very happy Obiwan, who wagged his tail until Polly thought it would fly off his body. "I was just here an hour ago," she said, ruffling the fur on his head. "You act like I've been gone for days."

They walked past him, through Henry's office and into the media room. Rebecca was at one end of the couch, leaning on the arm rest, her feet tucked under her and Andrew was at the opposite end in the same position. They both had books on their laps and their backpacks were open, with papers strewn everywhere.

"What are you two doing?" Polly asked.

"We have to do a report on Greece," Rebecca announced. "We're working together."

"That sounds interesting," Polly said. "Have you had something to eat?"

"We don't have time," Andrew said. "As soon as Mom is done yelling at Jason, I have to leave and we only have one more day to finish this. We're supposed to write about the pan ... What's it called again, Rebecca?"

"Pantheon. You know, Polly. All of the gods." She held up a drawing. "I think Poseidon is cool."

"That's terrific. Okay. You keep working."

"Did he really steal Eliseo's car?" Rebecca asked timidly. "I can't believe he'd do that. He loves Eliseo."

"Yeah, he did," Polly responded.

"Since he started hanging out with those jerks," Andrew observed, "he's gotten worse than ever. Mom told him the other night that she didn't know what she was going to do with him. He made her cry. She didn't let him see, but I heard her crying in her bedroom when I went to the bathroom. I don't like him anymore. He shouldn't make her cry." Andrew slumped a little. "I'm never going to be like that."

"He's trying to figure it all out, Andrew. You need to be patient. He's a good kid and he'll get there."

"But he's going to hurt a lot of people before he does," Andrew said. "Do you know why he took that car?"

"Not really," Polly replied. "It's not my business."

"He was trying to impress those jerks. One of them dared him to do it. He'd been bragging about how Eliseo lets him drive all the time and they called him a liar so he stole the car and drove it to school. He talked about doing it, but that was last week. I didn't think he really would."

"One of mom's old boyfriends stole cars," Rebecca said. "He had to go to jail. Jason isn't going to jail, is he?"

Andrew apparently hadn't thought of that and he looked up at Polly and Henry, his eyes huge. "Is Sheriff Merritt going to take him to jail?"

Henry walked over to the boy and put his hand on Andrew's shoulder. "Your mom and Eliseo will work this out. Don't worry. Jason will be home with you tonight."

"Maybe I want him to go to jail. He isn't very much fun to live with and now he's going to be mad. Especially after Mom punishes him. Can I stay here tonight?" Andrew asked.

Polly chuckled. "No, I think it's best if you not cross your mom much for a while."

"No kidding," he said.

"You two keep working until she calls for you, Andrew." Polly and Henry went out to the living room and she dropped into the middle of the sofa. Henry sat down beside her, then bent over and picked up a woodworking magazine.

He looked at her. "Do you want to talk?"

Polly laughed. "You're fine. Read your magazine. I'll make you talk to me at dinner."

CHAPTER TWO

Though it was Saturday morning, Polly woke up early to help in the barn. She wasn't sure whether or not Jason would be there. After the altercation with his mother last night, Polly didn't know if he'd be allowed out of their apartment at all this weekend. She slid into a pair of jeans and a t-shirt, then patted her leg for Obiwan to follow her. Henry made a noise and she stopped, standing still as a post, waiting for him to fall back to sleep.

They'd stayed out late last night, neither of them wanting to come home. After the storm passed, it had been a beautiful evening. They had dinner in Ames and then went for a drive around the countryside. Henry took her up to the Boone River and pulled into a canoe put-in site. No one else was there and they'd spent a couple of hours walking around, then sitting in his truck talking and enjoying the sounds of the river rustling by while bugs sang their songs. In the twenty minutes it took to get back to Bellingwood, Polly had been so relaxed she fell asleep, only waking up when Henry opened her car door.

Jessie Locke was still living with Polly and Henry. She was saving to get her first apartment. A job at the convenience store and taking care of Joss and Nate's twins kept her busy. They'd fallen into an easy routine around the house and Jessie was more than willing to keep an eye on Andrew and Rebecca when she was available. She helped Sylvie and Rachel in the kitchen for big events and helped in the barn most mornings during the week. Polly had never known anyone quite so driven to make a go of it. She was insistent on proving to her mother that she could live on her own and succeed.

There was still tension between Jessie and her mother. Kelly had finally accepted the fact that her daughter wasn't coming home and shipped the rest of Jessie's things to Iowa. They didn't talk on the telephone, though Jessie did talk to her father fairly regularly. He'd recovered from his heart attack and was driving his truck again. Jessie had also spent the last two months working with a counselor. Polly was grateful she wasn't responsible for the girl's mental health. There had been so much trauma in Jessie's life in such a short period of time, she really needed someone dispassionate about the situation to help her get through it.

Polly quietly closed the door behind her and wasn't at all surprised to find Jessie walking through the front room toward the door.

"Are you working this morning?" As soon as the words were out of Polly's mouth, she smiled. Jessie was dressed in cut-offs and a t-shirt. "Oh. I guess not. Heading down to the barn with us?"

"Yeah. I didn't figure Jason was going to be allowed over here again this weekend, so I thought you guys might need some help."

"Awesome. Thanks for hanging out with the kids last night."

"They weren't here very long after I got home. Sylvie texted me and told me to send Andrew down, then Rebecca and I had dinner with her mom and I came back up here and found a book. I was in bed early. I didn't even hear you and Henry come home."

"We tried to be quiet. Henry took the dog out and I was asleep before they came back."

Polly pushed the side door open and they went outside. Eliseo's car was in its normal spot at the barn. He'd already gotten started.

"How much trouble is Jason in?" Jessie asked.

"I have no idea. I haven't talked to anyone since last night. Sylvie didn't know what she was going to do yesterday."

"I just don't get why he would do something so stupid."

Polly stopped on the sidewalk and turned to the girl. "Seriously?" She chuckled. "You're the one who came out here to a place you'd never lived and then stayed."

"Well, yeah." Jessie tilted her head and smiled. "I suppose. But my mom and I don't get along at all. Sylvie's awesome. She's really good to those boys. I can't believe Jason doesn't get that."

"It's got to be hard growing up without a Dad. He feels like he has to be the man of the house and at this age, everything confuses him."

"But he has Eliseo. Those two are great together. I hope he figures this out before he screws it up. He's got a good life." Jessie took Polly's arm. "By the way, I don't say it very often, but I have a good life now, too, thanks to you. Not that living with my parents was the worst thing in the world, but I don't know what I'd have done if you weren't the one who showed up in Oelwein that day. Emily says that I'm lucky. She's right."

Emily Smith was Jessie's counselor. She was in her late twenties - not that much older than Jessie - but they made it work.

"I'm glad you're here. You've gotten involved in a lot of things at Sycamore House and we all appreciate your help." Polly pushed the first gate open and waited for Obiwan and Jessie to walk through.

"You pay really well. I love working the receptions and parties. See, that's what I don't get with Jason. His mom is great."

They went through the next gate. The door to the barn was already open. "Sylvie is pretty terrific. They'll get through this," Polly said.

Jason was in the barn. When they entered the door, he was carrying a bale of hay from the back.

"Hey Jason," Polly said.

"Hey," he replied. He didn't look up and didn't say anything more, just took the bale into Nat's stall.

"Where's Eliseo?" she asked as they watched him break it up.

He motioned with his head and said, "Back there."

"Great," she muttered as she walked away. "Happy boy."

Eliseo came out of the feed room with a bucket of water. "We've got a problem with the plumbing down here. I've already called about it. I'm carrying water this morning, though."

"What do you mean?"

"Something's wrong with the pipes on this side of the barn. Demi and Daisy aren't getting water. I could tear into it, but I thought maybe you'd rather pay for a little bit of work than have me wreck it." He grinned at her. "Who knows what happened."

"Jessie and I are here to help and we're early. You guys got going fast this morning."

He nodded, looking around the place. "Yep. Jason and I were up early so we decided to come on in and start working. We have a very long day today."

Polly glanced around. "Errr, what?"

"Mom kicked me out," Jason said in a grumble as he went past them.

"She what?"

"She didn't kick him out," Eliseo interrupted, "but he's going to be staying out at my place on the weekends. We're putting new siding on the house this weekend and if the weather holds, we'll also put on a new roof this fall. Jason is now my sidekick. Every minute that he's not in school or doing homework, I have work for him to do."

Polly gulped back laughter. Sylvie was one of the smartest women she'd ever known. There was going to be no more time for Jason to get in trouble, and with someone who worked as hard as Eliseo, the poor boy wouldn't know up from down before he finally fell into bed each night.

Eliseo continued, "That old farmstead is going to get a lot of attention this fall. There is a garden to clean up so that we can plant next spring, the yard needs work and there are some fences that need to be repaired. Betty is going to teach Jason how to take care of the chickens and I'm about to add a few goats to my life."

Jason walked back through with another bale of hay and went into Nan's stall.

"It sounds like this is going to be an interesting season for both of you," Polly said, keeping an eye on Jason. He was doing his best to avoid looking at her.

Eliseo chuckled. "I knew that my list of things to get done was pretty big, but now that I have some good help, I might actually finish it all." He took a step to the side and called out, "Jason, when you're done with the stalls, you can start working on the tack. It's been a while since it's been cleaned and oiled. I'm going up to the garden." He walked over to the stall. "If I'm not back when you're finished in the tack room, sweep out the alley and then come find me."

Polly didn't hear anything and watched as Eliseo waited by the stall. "Did you hear me, Jason?"

"Yes sir," came the grunted response.

"Terrific. I'll see you in a bit."

"Unless you ladies really want to spend time with the horses, I think we've got it. In fact, why don't you both sleep in tomorrow morning, too." He winked. "We'll take care of things down here."

Polly and Jessie followed Eliseo out of the barn and when they cleared the last gate, Polly asked, "Do you suppose he's happier working than being banned from the barn?"

"No question about it. He might sulk, but that's to be expected. I kept him working late into the evening last night and woke him up early this morning. But I promise you that by tomorrow morning, he will be back to his normal self. We'll work through this. He's a good kid and I love him."

"I know you do. We all do," Polly said. "I hope someday he realizes how lucky he is to have you in his life."

Eliseo stopped with her just before she opened the side door. "I'm the one who is lucky, Polly. I never thought I'd get the opportunity to raise a son. He and his brother are as precious to me as if they were my own. I hope their mama knows that."

"She trusts you with him. I'd say she knows that," Polly said, reaching out to touch his hand. "We all do."

She waited for Obiwan to catch up and then went inside while Eliseo walked around back to the garden. It had been a wonderful season for fresh vegetables.

"What's up for you today?" she asked Jessie as they hit the stairway.

"I have to work at ten and then I'm working the reception tonight."

"You have a busy day."

"I love it. I don't want to stay at the convenience store forever, but it's fine for now."

Polly opened the door and smelled bacon. "He's cooking!" she said. "What's up with that?"

Obiwan ran for the kitchen and Henry came around the corner. He was wearing a purple with pink lace apron that Polly had received as a wedding gift. She rarely wore it, but it made her laugh to see her macho husband comfortable in it. "You girls are back early. I hoped to have everything ready and on the table."

"We weren't needed. Jason and Eliseo got here early Apparently Jason is Eliseo's lackey for the next several months - spending weekends out at the farm, helping with construction and everything else."

Henry laughed. "It serves him right and what a terrific way to deal with this. He'll be too tired to get into trouble. Breakfast won't be ready for another half hour though."

"Then I'm taking a shower," Polly said. "Will you put food down for the dog?"

"Already done. The cats are fat and happy and your Saturday is about to begin. Take your time. I'll ring a bell when it's ready."

He spun around and went back into the kitchen. Jessie was trying her best not to giggle.

"Go ahead, laugh," Polly said. "I can't believe he's wearing it either."

"It's really purple."

Polly chuckled. "You don't know the story about that, do you?"

"There's a story? About a purple apron?"

"Oh no, not an apron. A pair of purple panties with hot pink bows on them. I hadn't been here very long and was carrying my laundry down the front steps one Saturday morning. Sycamore House wasn't even Sycamore House yet. We were still in the middle of a mess. Doug Randall had come in early to pick up a tool that he needed out on a worksite and I didn't know he was here. When he startled me, I dumped my entire basket of laundry down the stairs and the first thing he saw was my purple panties. I'm not sure who was more embarrassed, me or him, but word got around and those panties were the subject of a lot of teasing. It was all in good fun. I still can't believe it escalated."

"People in town really like you."

"They're just good folks. All you have to do is treat people well and they'll return the favor. You go on and get ready. I'll meet you in the kitchen for breakfast."

Polly went into her room and found both cats sleeping on the bed. "Did you two get up too early this morning?" She reached down and picked Luke up and sat where he'd been sleeping, then kicked her boots off. Luke jumped out of her arms and padded to the other end of the bed and curled up on her pillow.

"That's telling me," Polly said.

~~~

Breakfast was a bacon and sausage breakfast casserole with sausage gravy. Henry had been working on Polly's recipe. He'd told her that she wasn't allowed to be the only good cook in the family. He could learn. And he was. She often wondered how she'd been fortunate enough to land on his radar. The man was pretty close to perfect.

Jessie left for work and Polly helped Henry finish cleaning the kitchen. Since he'd moved in, the place was in much better shape on a regular basis. Honestly, as Polly looked around, she realized that it was both Henry and Jessie who helped keep this place clean. She'd quietly worked harder at picking up her belongings, but when she got distracted by too many things, cleaning was the last thing on her mind. The one household chore she managed to
~~~

keep up with was laundry. Especially since Henry installed a small washer and dryer in the bathroom across from his office. Things suddenly became much easier.

"I want to run over to the lodge this morning," Henry said. "Do you want to go with me? It won't be long. The guys had some trouble installing the tile on the backsplash behind the bar and they wanted me to check it before Monday morning."

"Sure. Then what are we going to do?"

"Are you telling me you don't have any plans for today?"

"I guess I could hang out here with Andrew and Rebecca, but I'd rather be with you."

"No shopping with Sal or snuggling babies with Joss?"

Polly sidled up to him and tickled his neck. "Are you feeling left out?"

"Stop that," he shook his head and brushed her hand away. "You know how I hate it when you play with my neck. No, I'm not feeling left out, but you're not around very often on Saturdays."

"I am today."

He looked at her suspiciously. "Everyone else has things to do, right?"

"No!" Polly clapped both of her hands against her cheeks, opening her mouth into a surprise "O" shape. "Why would you think that?"

"You're so transparent. Well, whatever. I'd love to have you come with me."

"Maybe we could go look for a new car for me?" Polly twisted the ring on her finger and looked at the floor.

"You really want a new car?"

"We've talked about this. I can't put more than two other people in my truck. There isn't room. And I can't really put two other adults up there. I have to have something different."

He shrugged. "Then let's go. That sounds like fun. It's been ages since I've looked at cars. You really want something new?"

"I don't care. Used is fine. I just need to haul people and animals and stuff."

"Well, let's get going. This should be fun!"

They went downstairs and got in his truck. Polly looked at her father's pickup a little forlornly. It was still a mess from yesterday's encounter with the ditch. She wasn't prepared to get rid of it. "I can't sell Dad's truck," she said quietly.

"Oh honey, you don't have to. We'll figure something out. It's still in really good shape and extremely useful. Eliseo and I will find a place to park it."

"Thank you. I just can't bear to part with it."

"I know. It's fine."

He drove past Sycamore Inn. There were a few cars in front. Jeff was easing them into being hoteliers. They hadn't hired someone to manage the Inn, so reservations were still being made out of the office at Sycamore House.

Henry pulled into a parking place in front of the lodge. The outside was beautiful and the landscaping was beginning to take hold. They had opened just before school started, even though there was still work to be done.

"Do you want to wait out here or come inside?" he asked.

"I'm fine here. How long?"

"Just a few minutes. I want to look over their work and I'll be right back."

"I can keep myself occupied."

Henry gave a visible shudder. "Please don't get into trouble. You make me nervous when you say things like that."

"I've never found a body in the same place twice." Polly winked at him. "Go on. I'll be good and stay right here in the truck."

"Don't you move." He got out and ran up the sidewalk to the front door, unlocked it and went inside.

Polly chuckled. He was so darned cute. She took out her phone and started flipping through apps, checking email and social networks. There was nothing interesting going on, so she texted Sal. *"Hey bright eyes. What 'cha doing?"*

"Go away. I'm writing." Sal came right back.

"What 'cha writing?"

"Go away! I'm working."

"You're no fun. Where's your boyfriend?"

"He's working. Am I going to have to lose this thought or are you going to be good?"

Polly sighed. This wasn't any fun. *"I'm going to be good. You're a meanie."*

"I love you too. Talk to you later."

She wasn't going to text Joss or Sylvie. Joss was busy with babies and Sylvie was probably trying to get herself to Sycamore House for work. Who else could she bother?

Lydia was in Dayton all weekend taking care of her grandkids while her daughter and son-in-law were at a wedding in Colorado. Beryl was in Boston until Monday and Len and Andy were in Wisconsin doing some sort of happy couple thing.

Henry opened the truck door and she looked up in surprise. "I didn't see you come out."

"I came out the side door. What have you been doing to keep yourself busy?"

"Nothing. No one's around."

"I knew it. That's why you had time for me today. Well, I just got a call from Nate."

Polly perked up, "Do they want to do something?"

"Well, yes, but it's more of a Nate thing than a Joss and Nate thing. Do you mind tagging along?"

"What are we doing?"

"An old lady who comes into the pharmacy was telling him about her late husband's cars. It seems he has a couple of old cars in their barn and she wants to know if Nate would be interested."

Polly grimaced and rolled her eyes. "Old cars?"

"We have plenty of time to get to the new cars. I promise. It won't take long."

"He's got babies at home."

"You and Joss can play with babies while we work on cars. Please?"

"Of course," she said and chuckled at him. "Let's go look at your old cars."

CHAPTER THREE

"See, I told you he'd be here already," Henry said, pulling in behind Nate's Impala.

Polly glanced around and asked, "Front or back door?"

He shrugged. "I dunno. Let's see what happens."

"You know I hate this stuff."

"We'll hope Nate rescues you."

They got out of the truck and sure enough, Nate came out of the back door of the big, white farmhouse with a huge sweet roll in one hand and a mug in the other.

"Man you have to try this. This roll melts in your mouth." He took another step toward them. "I'm not kidding you. Mrs. Willard can cook!"

Mrs. Willard came out of the back door, smiled and waved. "Come on in!" she said. "I made these especially for you."

"We just had breakfast," Henry protested.

"Don't give me that. There is always room for something sweet. And you need coffee to jumpstart your day, don't you?"

Henry slid a look to Polly and she smiled and shrugged. "This is your party," she said.

"I can't eat a roll that big," he said as they followed Nate and Mrs. Willard back into the house.

"Sit here and I'll bring the coffee pot over. Help yourselves to the rolls on the plate. Mr. Mikkels has been telling me all about his little babies. When are the two of you going to start filling that old school with children?"

Polly waited until Mrs. Willard turned her back and reached out to squeeze Henry's thigh. "What?" she mouthed at him.

He gave her an evil grin and then said, "We're really not in any hurry, Mrs. Willard. We've only been married for a few months."

"But you two aren't getting any younger. I told my Damon and his wife Gina that it is good to have your babies when you're young and have the energy to keep up with them. If you two wait much longer, you're going to be too tired to do all of the things that little kiddos need to do. You have to wear them out, you know. It's the only way to stay on top of things. Make them so tired that they can't wait to go to bed."

She poured two cups of coffee and placed them in front of Polly and Henry. "Drink up. This is the good stuff. I drink it until noon and then I only drink water until I go to bed. I need my coffee to get started, but when I turned fifty-five, I had to start drinking more water instead of coffee so I could sleep at night. And that pop stuff that you kids drink? I won't have that in the house. All of that sugar in a can? What were they thinking? My kids grew up with only homemade food. None of that processed junk. My friends thought those TV dinners were the best thing since sliced bread. But I knew better. Those aren't natural. And who buys sliced bread? Any woman worth her salt can make better bread than that stuff you buy off the shelves. I still make bread every Saturday morning. That's why I have such strong arms and hands. A little hard work is good for the soul."

While she talked, Mrs. Willard strode back across the kitchen floor and opened the refrigerator. She pulled out two loaves wrapped in aluminum foil.

"I was up at five thirty this morning making my bread for the week. I find that since it is just me, I don't need quite as much.

Would you like to each take a loaf home?" She put the bread down on the table, a loaf in front of Henry and one in front of Nate and then went back to her cabinets. "I have two jars of blueberry jam in here. Please take those with you, too. If you don't have a big breakfast planned for tomorrow morning, you could at least have toast and jam."

Henry opened his mouth to speak, but before he could take a breath, Mrs. Willard continued. "I don't know how young people today are able to do all that they do eating such horrible food. All of those preservatives and chemicals. No wonder you are sleep deprived. It's screwing up your metabolism. That's what I always told my John and Damon. Gina won't let me cook for them but a couple of times a week. Damon says she's a gourmet cook, but I've seen the boxed mixes in her pantry. She doesn't do any canning either. I wish she'd put in a garden."

"Do they live around here?" Polly asked quickly, before the woman could start again.

"Damon and Gina live over by Ogden. He's a letter carrier and John lives in Slater."

"What does John do?" Polly hoped to keep Mrs. Willard talking about her sons.

"He's in between jobs right now, but when he was here the other day, he said he had a lead on a couple of things. You know how boys are, especially when they're your babies. He has his mama wrapped around his little finger. I think he comes over just so I'll pack up enough food for him for a week. He's had a rough patch, but he'll be okay. I just know it.

Polly nodded and took another bite of the sweet roll. Nate was absolutely right, it was the lightest, sweetest thing she'd ever eaten, but she was going to die if she ate too much more. She managed to get through half of it and pushed it in front of Henry. He looked at her in panic. He'd finished his, but his eyes told her there was too much food in his belly.

"If you can't eat the whole thing, that's fine, Miss Polly. A sweet young thing like you shouldn't be packing in the calories. You never know when they're going to start attaching themselves to your hips. I'll just put it into a bag here and split the rest of these up so that you can take them home. Does that sound okay, Mr. Mikkels?"

Nate nodded and took another drink of coffee. "My wife would love to taste your sweet rolls." He took a breath as she crossed the kitchen to another cupboard. "Are the cars out in the barn? Maybe we could go look at them. I know that Henry and Polly have quite a bit to do today and I don't want to leave my wife alone for too long. I try to help her out on Saturdays."

"Of course, of course. You kids go on out to the barn. I'll make you a couple of care packages. I have some things in the cellar you might like. It's right out there." She pointed out the back door. "If you'd like to stay inside, Polly, you don't have to go with them."

Henry took one look at Polly and, after seeing her face, said, "I might be buying one for Polly, so I'd like her to see them."

"Fine, fine. You kids go on. Come back in and tell me what you think before you leave."

The three of them thanked her and filed out the back door. They walked silently to the barn, not wanting to laugh or say anything until they were well out of hearing.

Nate opened the barn door and waited until Polly and Henry were inside before laughing. "She's a hoot! I've never heard her talk quite like that at the store, but oh how she must miss her husband."

Polly shook her head. "And dear heavens, but she has opinions on food. She's probably not wrong, but wow."

"Stop talking and look," Henry said. "Look at this."

Polly looked. All she saw were two rusted out hulks of old vehicles. That wasn't what Nate and Henry saw. They each took off after a different car, talking to themselves and to each other.

"Can you believe this?" Henry asked. "Do you think we can fix these?"

"They'll take a lot of work. A lot of work," Nate responded.

"But think how much fun they'd be to drive around town when they're finished. Are they the same year?"

"I wonder if they were purchased as a matching set."

Polly was bored. This was better than sitting inside with Mrs. Willard, but not by much. She had no idea why they were so excited. The barn was fairly large, with several different rooms. The two vehicles were parked in one of the side rooms.

She wandered into a room with newer pieces of equipment. She pulled back tarps from a snow blower and riding lawn mower. Rakes, hoes and other hand equipment were hanging from racks on the wall.

Henry and Nate were still jabbering and going back and forth between the two vehicles, so she wandered into another room. She recognized some horse tack. Funny, Mrs. Willard hadn't said anything about owning horses.

Another large room was filled with junk. She recognized an old wringer washer amid bed springs and frames. An old clawfoot tub was on the floor. She'd seen some used as gardens and wondered if it wouldn't be something fun they could put out front at Sycamore House. Actually, Joss might even love having this in her yard. She was really eclectic when it came to gardening and decorating.

Polly wandered over to look at the tub, wondering how much work it would take to clean it up. Surely Henry would know how to do that. She pulled a piece of plywood away from the top and peered in. It was dark in the room, so she swiped her phone open and turned on the flashlight app. Pulling the plywood away again, she peered in again and let out a squeak, dropping the plywood.

"Henry! Nate! Come here!" she yelled. "Right now!"

Both men came running in and Henry asked, "What? Are you okay?"

"I'm going to curse," she said and pointed to the tub. "But damn it. I did it again."

"No. You did not." Henry said.

"What?" Nate asked. "What did she do?"

"In there?" Henry asked.

Polly nodded her head. "You're going to make me call him, aren't you?"

"Call who? What did she do?" Nate picked the piece of plywood off the tub and pushed it away. "Oh. That's not good."

"I should have known. I brought Polly to a strange location and of course she was going to find a body." Henry looked into the tub. "This one's been here a long time. I can't believe no animals got to it."

"Do you recognize who it is?" Nate asked. "I don't."

Henry looked in again. "Nope. I can't tell." He took Nate's arm and led him away from the tub. "I can't believe that I'm so damned nonchalant about this. Polly, what have you done to me? I can look at a dead body now and not fall completely apart."

"How did he die?" she asked quietly.

"Looks like a gunshot to the head," Nate said.

"Okay. I'll make the call. But you two have to tell Mrs. Willard why the Sheriff is coming. I'm not going back in there and face her after this."

Polly walked out of the barn and took a deep breath. All she smelled was grass and dirt. Thank goodness. Then she did what she knew she had to do and made the call.

"Polly Giller, you have got to be kidding me," Aaron Merritt said without even a hello.

"You're going to have to get better about your greetings. Now, do you think that I wanted to call you?" she asked. "Not on your life."

"Whose life then?"

"I don't know."

"You're serious."

"I'd like to say 'as a heart attack,' but Nate tells me that it's a gunshot to the head that did the poor guy in."

"Nate Mikkels? Is this at his place?"

"No, we're out at Mrs. Willard's house. He and Henry came out to look at some old rusted out pieces of junk in her barn. They think they can restore these cars. I wandered around and found the body in an old tub."

"Cars? Two cars?"

"Yeah. Why?"

"They're rusted out? That's too bad. That will take a lot of work."

"What's so special about two cars?"

"Those were beautiful classic Woodies, Polly. Mr. Willard bought a pair of them. They drove them for years. One was red and the other was blue. He must have just put them in the barn and gave up on them."

"Uh huh. So, what are you doing about the body?"

"I'm on my way. As soon as I hang up, I'll call Stu and have him pull a team together. Don't go anywhere. I'll be there in less than ten minutes."

Polly turned around and found Nate and Henry back at the two cars. "He's going to be here in less than ten minutes and we aren't supposed to go anywhere. Which one of you is telling Mrs. Willard that she's about to have company?"

The two men looked at her and then at each other.

"You know her best," Henry said to Nate. "You go tell her."

Nate shook his head. "I think I'll just let the Sheriff do it. I can't imagine what she'll have to say."

"You guys are chickens. I called Aaron. One of you should do this."

They looked at each other again and Nate said, "Nope. I'm fine with the chicken moniker."

"Aaron said these were Woodies. What does that mean?" she asked. "He said that Mr. Willard bought two of them - one for him and one for his wife. One was blue and the other was red."

"Really," Nate said. He bent over and rubbed his finger on one of the doors. "This was the red one."

"Woodies are classic vehicles that had wood panels on the doors," Henry explained to Polly.

"Oh, like those station wagons you see in movies from the seventies?"

"Sort of, but not really. These aren't anything like those Ford Country Squires." Henry said.

Nate looked up. "No. These are nothing like that. These are probably 1949 or 1950," Nate ran his hand along the rusty hood.

"If you don't want one of them, I'm buying them both from her. I can't let them go to someone else."

Henry looked up at Polly, trying to make a decision.

"Just do it," she said. "I'm trying to see it all fixed up with new upholstery and fresh paint. I think it would be fun to drive one around town."

"You do?" he asked. "Really?"

"Sure!"

"You know this means we're rescuing a car now, right?"

Polly pointed at him. "You're rescuing the car. Not me. Get that straight. I have enough rescues in my life. This one's on you."

The crunching of tires on rock announced Aaron Merritt's arrival and the three of them left the barn in time to see Mrs. Willard come out of the back door, drying her hands on a towel tucked into her apron.

"Sheriff Merritt, what are you doing here?" she asked. "Is something wrong? Has something happened to Damon or Gina or their kids?"

"No, no, no, Mrs. Willard. But Polly found something in your barn and she called me. Could we go inside and talk for a minute?"

"What did she find?" Mrs. Willard started walking across the driveway to the barn. "Is there something wrong out here with the cars?"

All of a sudden she stopped in her tracks. Her brows wrinkled into a frown. "You find dead bodies," she said accusingly. "Are you trying to tell me you found a dead body in my barn?"

Polly took a step back. "I'm sorry," she said.

"Now Mrs. Willard. It isn't Polly's fault. I believe that when she finds a body, it's her way of setting the universe straight. That poor person needed to be found and Polly's just the one to do it. Let's not get upset."

The woman had brought her hand up to point at Polly in accusation and then she seemed to wilt. "You don't think I had anything to do with killing someone, do you?" she asked Aaron.

"I'm not going to accuse anyone of anything yet. But I do have a team of people who will arrive in just a little bit to start investigating." He took her by the arm and steered her back to the house. "Have you seen anyone out here who doesn't belong?"

"Certainly not. I wouldn't be afraid to run them off with a shotgun. You know I scared a couple of kids out of here last year. They thought they were going to mess with me. A couple of blasts over their heads and they were running for their cars. Calling me all sorts of terrible things. But I never saw them again. They'll learn to mess with an old lady with a gun."

They got to the door and Aaron turned around. "You three wait right there. Stu will be here in a few minutes. If I'm not out by then, would you show him where to go?"

"Wait a minute," Mrs. Willard said. "You boys. What do you think about those hunks of junk? Are they of interest to you? Because if they're not, Damon said he'll help me find a buyer from one of the cities. I'm doing you a favor by letting you have first crack at them. And you, missy. Don't you leave before you come in and take these care packages. One for you and one for the new mama. She probably needs all the strength she can get. You hear me?"

Polly could only nod. "Yes ma'am," she finally said.

Mrs. Willard waited at the door. "Well? What about it boys? Do you want those old cars?"

"Yes ma'am," Henry said. "Both of them."

"We'll work out payment and how you're going to haul them out of here after all of this mess is taken care of." Mrs. Willard flung her right hand toward the barn. "What a mess. I'm going to have to make something for these people for lunch. You come in here, Sheriff, and tell me what you need to tell me. Ask me what you need to ask. But you can do it while I'm cooking. How many do you think you're bringing out?"

Polly chuckled as she watched the woman take over. Aaron Merritt might have met his match.

CHAPTER FOUR

Nate and Henry made arrangements with Mrs. Willard to pick up the cars later in the week, so once the rest of Sheriff Merritt's teams arrived at the Willard farm, Henry, Polly and Nate were free to go. The two men were as giddy as kids in a candy store. Polly finally offered to take Henry's truck back to Sycamore House so they could make plans.

"What about looking for a car for you?" Henry asked.

"Seriously?" she said, with her hands on her hips. "You think I'm crazy enough to believe you'll be any good for me today? Go play with your friend. I'm not in that much of a hurry. And besides, I'll just spend time online looking at the most expensive vehicle I can find."

"This is really okay with you?"

Polly kissed his cheek. "It's really okay. Enjoy your afternoon. Maybe I'll call Joss and see what she's up to."

"Up to her eyes in alligators and diapers," Nate said. "There are always diapers. Diapers never end. Our lives are all about diapers. Buying new diapers, changing diapers, dealing with dirty diapers." He clutched Henry's arm. "I'm so tired of diapers. Every time we buy formula, I realize that we're just setting in supplies that will provide ammunition for more diapers."

"You're only a few months into this. It's not going to get any better for a few years," Henry said.

"Joss seems to think that watching me change a diaper is cute." He flared his nostrils. "She still thinks it's cute. What is wrong with that woman? There's nothing cute about it. It's toxic waste and it's never ending."

"Take him to your shop or the diner or something," Polly said. "I think the poor man needs to get out more often."

"But the diapers will still be there tonight," Nate said. "And tomorrow morning. And the day after that. It will go on into infinity."

Polly shook her head and walked over to Henry's truck, then beckoned for the keys. He tossed them and she missed the catch, watching as they plowed into the gravel at her feet.

"That's my girl," he said, laughing. "I can always count on your hand-to-eye coordination."

"Shut up, you. It was your toss that missed me." Polly bent over and snatched up the keys, then climbed up in his truck.

He strode across to her and when she bent over to hug him, he whispered at her, "I like the idea of bringing older children into our lives. I don't ever want to sound like Nate. I don't want to face an infinity of diapers."

"Sounds good to me. Distract him for a while and maybe he'll quit thinking about them. I'm going to spend some time with Joss. Do you want me to take your truck home and use my own or can I go straight over?"

"I know where to find you. I'll let you know when I'll be home. I love you and I'm sorry you had to face another body this morning."

Polly shrugged. "It's so sad that it barely even registers any more for me. All I have to do is look at them once and then Aaron comes in and takes care of everything. I hate to say it, but I think I'm beginning to take it in stride. You've always said that if someone was going to die in three counties, I'd be the one to find it. I just wish I knew who was in that tub and how long he'd been there. Is someone missing him? How horrible that would be - not knowing where your husband or boyfriend, or even where your son was and then finding out that he'd been killed and no one knew it. What if I'd never wandered in there? What if you and Nate hadn't come out here to look at those cars? How long could that person have been there with no one ever knowing?"

"You don't get it, do you sweetie?"

"What do you mean?"

"Of course all of those things came together so that you would be out here today. It's the universe's plan for your life. You had to find that person today, so you did. I'm not surprised and even the Sheriff isn't surprised by it anymore. It's just how it is."

"Nate was a little surprised."

"He doesn't know you as well as the rest of us do. He'll get past it."

Polly kissed his forehead. "Okay, you take care of him and figure out how you're going to rescue those cars and I'll find something to occupy myself today."

"I love you."

"I know," she said, winking at him. Polly pulled the door shut and turned the key in the ignition, then backed up and out of the driveway, doing her best to avoid all of the emergency vehicles spread across the lawn. She let out a deep sigh when she turned onto the gravel road leading back toward town. What a morning.

Polly switched the blinker on and waited for several cars to go past before turning onto the Mikkels' street. Maybe she should have called Joss first. Oh well, if her friend wanted her to leave, then that would be fine. Polly pulled into their driveway and went to the front door and rang the doorbell.

The front door opened and she was assaulted by sounds of screaming and crying babies. Joss took one look at her, opened the screen door, grabbed Polly's hand and said, "Help me!"

"What's going on?"

"I don't know. I've tried everything and they're just mad. I carry Sophie around and get her settled and then Cooper starts up, so I put her down and pick him up. I'm about to go out of my mind."

"Tell me what to do. But how do you think with all of this noise?"

"Think? Think about what? There's no thinking." Joss picked Sophie up and put her in Polly's arms. "Move with her. Sway. Bounce. Do something."

The child was so startled to be handed to a stranger that she gurgled a little and smiled at Polly, forgetting that she'd been angry. That lasted for a brief second until she heard her brother crying, then her face contorted and Polly could feel her building up for a caterwaul. "It's okay, Sophie. You don't have to cry right now, do you?"

Joss jammed a pacifier in Polly's hand. "Try that with her. Maybe if we both do this, they will settle down."

Polly took the pacifier and teased Sophie's lips with it, kissing the baby's head. She walked out of the room and down the steps to the basement rec room, humming in her throat. Sophie took the pacifier and tried to cry around it, but finally settled into Polly's arms. Cooper's sounds had started to die down as well and when she felt like it was safe, she went back up the steps into the living room.

"You're a lifesaver," Joss said. "I don't know what got into them, but I thought I was going to lose my mind. Nate just called to tell me that he and Henry were going to be gone for a while and I told him it was fine. Then all hell broke loose."

Polly stood in the middle of the room and stared at her friend. "Ummm, do you see what you just did to me?"

Joss wasn't paying any attention as she paced back and forth, rocking Cooper in her arms. "No, what do you mean?"

"I thought we had a deal. I wasn't holding babies."

Joss turned around with a mischievous grin on her face. "Oh. Oops. Look what kind of wonderful friend you are. You saved me in my hour of need."

"Not only am I holding a baby, but I'm comforting her, too. What kind of insanity is this? I'm not a baby person."

"You said you would love my babies."

Polly sighed and smiled down at the little girl in her arms. Sophie's brown eyes began to relax and the tension in her little body ebbed away.

"Here, sit." Joss said, moving a blanket out of one of the rocking chairs. "I'm sorry the place isn't very clean. I just haven't had time to put everything away."

The living room wasn't at all messy. There were extra blankets and baby toys around. Joss and Nate had purchased two rocking recliners so they could relax with the babies and Polly dropped into one of those, pushing back and forth with her feet.

"Did Nate tell you what else happened this morning?"

Joss grinned. "You found another body? He was a little shook up. I think it's hilarious that he got to experience a Polly Giller moment. Do they know anything yet?"

"Not yet. I'll call Aaron tomorrow and see what he knows." She ran her finger over Sophia's upturned nose, causing the baby to giggle, then touched the child's ears. "This little one is so sweet when she's relaxed."

"That's what my dad always used to say to us when we were kids. He told us we were sweet when we were asleep." Joss shrugged. "We didn't sit still very often. He and Mom were chasing us down all the time."

Polly slipped her finger in Sophia's hand again. "Did you ever find out what their background is? They have really unique features."

Joss nodded. "They are unique. Their mother is Korean and American Indian and their father is African American and Caucasian."

"Have you heard anything more from the parents?"

"No. Not really. We offered to send pictures through our lawyers, but they don't seem interested right now. Maybe when they do some more growing up, they'll want to know what happened to their children, but they weren't much more than kids themselves." Joss stroked her son's brown hair. "I met their father. He was a good kid. He didn't have to be there through the birth, but he was. Even though they'd broken up, he made a point to be there. I think he wanted to know that his kids were going to be in a happy home. He asked Nate a lot of questions that first day in the hospital."

"It really takes a lot of courage to do this, doesn't it?"

"For them? Yes. All they can do is hope that their babies are placed with loving parents."

"But for you, too."

"I suppose. But look at what we have. I've never been so happy."

"Even with the screaming and the diapers?"

Joss laughed. "Did Nate start on that again? He is obsessed with diapers. I found a piece of paper with marks on it taped to the inside of one of the cupboards. He counts them."

"Why?"

"I have no idea. For some reason, this is his obsession."

"That's weird."

"Tell me about it. But at least he helps. When we were at the hospital and the nurses were trying to make sure we knew what we had to do, one of them kept insisting that Nate understand how important it was for him to be an equal partner. She was almost rude about it. I couldn't tell her often enough that Nate was a good husband and would be a good father - that I wasn't at all worried. She just ignored me and started in on him again. Polly, it's not like we're 20 years old and just starting out!"

"I know!" Polly said, laughing. She felt her phone buzz in her pocket and shifted Sophia around so she could reach it.

"Do you mind?" she asked when she realized it was a call from Sylvie.

Joss nodded and Polly answered, "Hi Sylvie, what's up?"

"I hate to bother you, but can you come home?"

"I suppose. I'm just over at Joss's holding Sophia. What's going on?"

"Andrew just came downstairs and Polly, he smells like weed."

"Marijuana?" Polly did her best to maintain her composure so as not to upset the baby in her arms. "In my house?"

"Uhh, yep."

"Let me hang up and say goodbye here. I'll be right there." She swiped her phone to end the call and looked at Joss. "I have to go home."

"Marijuana?"

"I have no idea, but someone's head might be rolling down the street in a few minutes. In my house!"

Joss put Cooper down in the playpen and took Sophia from Polly. "Go on and call me later to tell me what's going on. Thank you for stopping by, though."

"You know you can always call me if you need help, don't you?"

"I know, I know. Generally I just ride it out, but I was sure glad to see you today."

Polly reached around Sophia and gave her friend a hug. "I'm sorry to run away, but I really have to deal with this."

"Don't worry. We'll talk later."

Polly ran out to the truck and drove home, trying not to be angry, but the closer she got, the more furious she became. There was only one person she knew that would be in her apartment smoking marijuana and that was just out of line.

They hadn't had much trouble with Jessie since she was so busy trying to save money. At least she told Polly she was saving money. But right now, Polly didn't know what to think.

She pulled in the driveway, opened the garage door and was out of the truck before it opened enough to let her through. Polly ran in the back door, flung the door to the stairs open and ran up the back steps and into Henry's office. Sure enough, there was a distinct smell in the house. What was this stupid girl thinking?

Polly took a breath when she reached the media room and looked at the kitchen. Yep, telltale signs. Bags of potato chips were open on the peninsula, a jar of peanut butter was out with its lid askew. Bread and lunchmeat were still out on the counter. No one had bothered to clean up after themselves. She walked into the living room and gritted her teeth.

Of course.

"What in the hell are you doing in my house?" she demanded.

Jessie jumped up from the sofa. "Polly! I didn't think you'd be home until later."

"That's patently obvious. Do you want to explain yourself?"

"Oh god," the girl said. "I'm so sorry. This is all my fault."

"I don't think you're alone in this." Polly pointed to a young man with his feet up on her coffee table and a joint hanging out of his mouth. "Get your damned feet off my table and put that out right now."

"Oh come on," he said. "Loosen up."

"Seriously? That's the tone you're taking with me? In my own house?"

"Troy, don't." Jessie pleaded.

Troy Kandle had rented both rooms of the second floor of the addition for himself and a bandmate. They'd come to Bellingwood after hearing about what a perfect place it was to jumpstart their creativity. When Polly first met him, his face had been caked with makeup, having just come off a Midwestern tour, but the next morning, he'd come down fresh-faced and young looking. He was quite a charming young man and apparently, their band was hot on the indie charts.

He sighed and dropped his feet to the floor, then nonchalantly put the joint into a beer can on the table. "Is that better?" he asked.

"Not really," Polly said. "I want all of you out of here immediately and you have until Monday morning to find another place to stay. You aren't welcome here any longer."

"We have a contract, doll," he sneered at her.

"Check it again, you moron. Any illegal infraction nullifies it immediately. You're lucky I'm giving you until Monday. Now get the hell out of my house."

He settled back in the chair. "That doesn't really work for me. I'm comfortable here."

Polly walked across the room and grabbed his shirt collar, pulling him upward. "I said get out of my house. I can call the Sheriff or the Police Chief to have your ass escorted out the door if that's what you'd prefer, but one way or the other you're gone."

She pushed him off balance and he fell to the floor.

His buddy scrambled across the room and took Troy's arm, helping him to stand up. "I'm sorry. He's been drinking all day. We'll get out of your hair. I'll make sure we're out of here by tomorrow."

"Out of here, my ass. We paid to stay here and we're not done writing." Troy wrenched his arm free. "And I didn't get nearly enough time to play with little Miss Jessie here. She wants me. You can see that, can't you?"

"Well, I don't want you. I think you're a filthy pig. Are you leaving or am I calling the police?" Polly asked.

"Yeah, yeah, yeah. Don't get yourself in an twist. I'm going. But you can't get rid of me that easily. I'll be back." He winked at Jessie. "We'll find our time together, little girl. I'll show you what the real world is all about - not this backward town."

He stumbled for the door and swung it open. "Thanks for the party," he said. "It's been grand."

When the door shut behind him, Polly spun on Jessie. "What in the hell were you thinking? In my house and with Andrew up here. I expected better of you than that!"

"You sound like my mom. I don't need this shit. I'm sorry that you had to see this, but I'm not sorry for anything else." Jessie stomped into her bedroom and slammed the door.

"What just happened here?" Polly asked herself, trying to quell her fury. She wanted nothing more than to follow the girl and then kick her out, too. That didn't seem to be the best way to fix this, though, so she took a deep breath and looked around. The living room was a mess. There were empty beer cans and plates strewn all over the floor and the table. How long had they been up here?

No, she wasn't cleaning this. It wasn't her mess. Polly walked over to Jessie's room and knocked. There was no answer.

"I'm not going to fight with you about this right now. We will discuss it, but later, when you aren't high and I'm not furious. I'm going downstairs and when I get back, I expect that the mess out here will be cleaned up and things in the kitchen put away. This isn't over. You can't get away with disrespecting me and my home."

Polly went back through the media room and, calling Obiwan, went down the steps with him following her. Andrew was at his desk under the stairway when she emerged from her back door.

"Hey Andrew. I'm sorry about that," she said.

"Jessie got weird when I went upstairs. I told her you didn't smoke and wouldn't want her to be doing that in your house. I was going to go get Rebecca so we could play games, but I didn't want her to see Jessie like that. She was mean."

"I know and I'm sorry."

"I don't like that Troy guy. He's creepy. He was drinking beer and told me that if I was going to hang around, I had to get him more out of the refrigerator. That's when I came downstairs."

"That was the right thing to do. I've sent him back over to his rooms and told him that he had to leave by Monday. We aren't going to have that going on here. Especially when you're around. You are too important to me." She ruffled his hair.

"Do you want me to take Obiwan out for a walk? I was going to do that when I went to get Rebecca."

"Why don't both of you take him for a walk. I'll bet she wouldn't mind getting out for a while."

"Cool! Then can we go into the conference room and draw on the big table?"

"Absolutely." Polly bent over and hugged him in his chair. "Thanks for being such a good kid. You know I love you, right?"

"Yeah." He pushed his chair back, obviously a little embarrassed, then took the leash that Polly handed to him and followed her into the kitchen.

"Rebecca and I are taking Obiwan for a walk, Mom. Then we'll be in the conference room."

"Sounds good," Sylvie said. When he was out of the room, she took Polly's hand. "What happened up there?"

"Jessie was stupid and those two punks living in the top floor of the addition were hanging out with her, drinking and smoking."

"What are you going to do?"

"Well, they've gone back to their rooms and I've told them to be out of here by Monday. Jessie stomped off to her room, telling me that I was just like her mom. I told her to clean the place up and we would have the discussion later. I needed to calm down. My first reaction was to boot her to the curb."

"That wouldn't do anyone any good."

"I know. That's why I walked away. But when I realized that she put Andrew in harm's way, I could hardly see straight, I was so angry."

"And that's why I love you. You are fierce when you're protecting people you care about. I didn't have any authority up there, but I knew that once you got in the building it would be just fine. I'm sorry I interrupted your afternoon, though."

"Oh Sylvie, it's just been another one of those days and I'm guessing this is only the beginning of the insanity. Once it starts for me, it doesn't stop for a couple of weeks. All I can do is take a deep breath and hold on for the ride."

CHAPTER FIVE

Each website supplied a little different information, but Polly finally decided she needed to give Jessie another hour or so before the girl would come down off that high. If Jessie was smart, she'd put the time to good use. What in the world was she thinking, smoking pot in front of Andrew? Polly was just thankful that Rebecca hadn't been upstairs. That little girl worshiped Jessie and right now, she didn't need anything else falling apart in her life.

Polly took a stack of papers out of her top desk drawer and looked through them once again. One day she would sign these in order to become Rebecca's guardian and then to fully adopt her. The papers were a reminder that death hovered and change was coming to Sycamore House.

Sarah Heater's cancer was still progressing. The doctors had hoped for remission, but it wasn't going to happen. There was one more experimental therapy they wanted to try, but after that, Sarah had made the decision to stop everything to have a full life without things battering her down every time she got her strength back. She would die on her own terms. That conversation was one Polly never wanted to repeat again in her life.

Sylvie had taken Rebecca and Andrew to a movie in Ames and Polly sat with Sarah in her room while the two of them held each other and sobbed their way through difficult decisions. Actually, none of the decisions were all that difficult. It was just nearly impossible to say the words out loud. Yes, Sarah could stay at Sycamore House and Polly would make sure her life was comfortable and happy and her death would be as painless as possible. And yes, Polly wanted nothing more than to raise Rebecca as her own daughter. Adoption papers were drawn up, but Polly couldn't sign them right now. She promised Sarah that when nothing more could be done, she would sign them and make Rebecca part of her family. The lawyer agreed that it was abnormal, but no one was ready to separate Rebecca from her mother. The knowledge that she still had a daughter to raise had given Sarah a great deal of strength. She was determined to spend as much time as possible with Rebecca.

Polly knew the day that Sarah had told Rebecca what was going to happen. The little girl refused to look Polly in the eyes. She'd stayed away from Andrew, Polly and Henry for the entire weekend, her anger readily apparent on her face. Whenever she emerged from their room to get food from the kitchen, she stomped past the three of them, daring them to speak to her. Andrew had been confused until Polly explained what happened. Even then, he couldn't understand why his best friend was angry with him.

It had been Jessie who ended up breaking the impasse. She'd been sitting at the big table in the downstairs kitchen, playing a guitar Eliseo had uncovered. Rebecca had come in for something to drink and was drawn to the music, so she sat down across the table and before long, her tears began to flow. The two girls had talked and talked. Neither of them told anyone else what they'd discussed, but the next morning, Rebecca came into Polly's office when it was time to go to school and gave her a hug, holding on for a few extra seconds.

For that alone, Polly was willing to give Jessie some leeway today. She slid the papers back into her desk drawer when

Obiwan came running in to see her. "Hey bud, are your friends here, too?" Polly asked.

"He knew where you were." Andrew was panting and red-faced and Rebecca came running in right behind him, her hair a mess.

"What were you three doing out there?" Polly asked.

"We ran around Sycamore House three times," Andrew said. "Every time we got close to him, he took off again. What did you feed him this morning?"

Polly grinned at the two kids. "Nothing special. The poor dog probably had a lot of extra energy from being inside too long today."

"You don't suppose ..." Andrew asked, looking pointedly upstairs.

"No," she said. "That wouldn't affect him. He'd be sick, not running you two around."

"What?" Rebecca asked.

Andrew looked at her, then at Polly and then back at Rebecca. "Nothing. I just wondered if ..."

"He was afraid Obiwan might have gotten into something."

"Oh. Do you want us to take him upstairs?" Rebecca asked.

"No, you two go on into the conference room. You know where to find blank paper."

"Maybe Jessie will come in when she gets back from work," Rebecca said. "I haven't seen her for a couple of days."

Andrew looked at Polly again. She shrugged. "Maybe."

Why wasn't Jessie at work? Man, she did not want to have this conversation with the girl. For the most part, they had an easygoing relationship. It wasn't like she was difficult to live with. She worked or spent time in her room on her phone. What had happened?

Jeff Lyndsay came in the front door and waved at Polly through her office window.

"What are you doing down here today?" He glanced into the conference room. "Everything okay?"

"A little trouble upstairs. I'm kicking your rockers out of here by Monday morning, just so you know. If they give us any trouble, I'm calling Ken Wallers."

He pushed her door shut and sat down. "So, everything isn't okay. What happened?"

"I walked into my apartment and found them upstairs with Jessie, smoking and drinking. When I told them to leave, that Troy character got belligerent and aggressive."

"Okay." Jeff licked his lips and breathed through his teeth. "Well, that's not good. I'm sorry."

"It was worse because Andrew had been up there, too. Troy got a little pushy and Andrew was smart enough to just leave. Sylvie called me while I was at Joss's house."

"Stupid kids. They will spoil everything they put their hands on." Jeff clenched his teeth again and slammed his fist on the arm of the chair. "Damned entitled brats. Why do they think they have a right to anything?"

"Money and power. It's always about one or the other."

"I'll take care of it later today. I'm sorry you had to deal with that in your own home. What are you going to do about Jessie?"

Polly looked at the time. "I'm about to figure that out. Hopefully she has cleaned up the mess and can have a conversation with me. Otherwise, I'll wait until she's ready."

"You aren't kicking her out?"

"Not yet. I know this is a biggie, but it's really the first screwup she's had. Coming from what she lived with, I'm surprised there haven't been more in the last few months. We'll see what this is about."

"You're calmer about it than I would be."

Polly chuckled. "I wasn't when I stormed out of there, but you know what? There are bigger things to deal with than a little pot and some beer." She nodded to the conference room. "I started thinking about what Rebecca is going to face and then about the family who will find out someone they love has been killed and it just isn't that big of a deal."

He perked up, and tilted his head at her. "Someone was killed? Are you telling me ..."

"Shaddup," Polly said. "Yes, that's what I'm telling you. I haven't told Sylvie either. We were out looking at some old rusted out cars that Nate and Henry want to restore and I went poking around."

"Of course you did." Jeff shut his eyes and shook his head back and forth. "It's never going to end, is it?"

"I'd like to say no, but that would be foolish of me."

He leaned forward, propped his elbow on the table and rubbed his forehead. Then, he started to chuckle. "At least I have a theme for this year's Halloween party."

"We're having a party this year? More than just the haunted hallway for trick or treaters?"

"Halloween is on a Friday night, so we can have more fun. Trick or treating will end by seven and then we're going to have a dance starting around nine. We talked about doing more of those after last year's hoe-down and just haven't had an open night. I've already hired the band so you can't talk me out of it. But, I think a great theme might be "Polly's Ghosts."

"You wouldn't."

"I'm going to have to do something that has to do with your predilection for finding dead bodies. Everyone knows about it. We might as well own it and just put it out there."

Polly shuddered. "That sounds awful."

"But you aren't going to give me any trouble about it?"

"Like I could stop you."

"Uh huh. Okay, I need to get busy. I'll take care of your punks upstairs and let you know when they're gone."

"Don't put them up at Sycamore Inn either. They can just get the heck out of town."

He put his hand on the door handle. "I know, I know. We don't need that kind of trouble around here."

Polly got up and waved at the kids as she left the office. She didn't want to go upstairs and face Jessie, but the problem wouldn't solve itself. When she got to the top of the steps, she could still smell it. They were going to have to open every window in the place just to clean it out.

Bracing herself, Polly opened the door and was pleasantly surprised to find that the living room was back to normal. She heard sounds coming from the kitchen. Obiwan took off at a trot and she followed him.

"Jessie?" she said to the girl's back.

Jessie turned around from the sink, her hands covered in suds.

"I'm sorry, Polly. I don't know what I was thinking. It just got out of control. They wanted a place to hang out and before I knew it ..." She flung the suds off her hands into the sink and bent over, her shoulders shaking. "I'm sorry. It's my fault."

"I don't know about fault. But it is your responsibility. Thank you for cleaning things up. We need to open all of the windows and air the place out. I'll start in Henry's office. You get these and then open up your room and the middle room. There are two fans in the back closet. You should pull those out, too."

Polly walked across the media room and started opening windows, welcoming the fresh, crisp air. She was going to need a sweatshirt before the afternoon was over.

She opened the windows in her bedroom and in all of the bathrooms, hoping most of the smell would clear out before Henry got home. It was one thing to tell him what had happened, but having him experience it wasn't something she wanted to deal with.

When they both came back into the living room, Polly pointed to a chair and said, "We still need to talk about this."

Jessie nodded, "I know. This has been a horrible day and it really is all my fault."

"Do you want to tell me why you aren't at work? I thought you had a full shift."

"They fired me." Tears filled her eyes.

Polly rubbed her temples with the thumb and middle finger of her right hand. "What happened?"

Tears turned to sobs and Polly waited. These weren't tears of sorrow, they were guilt and shame. Whatever had happened was of the girl's own doing. So ... she sat back and waited for the drama to end.

When the crying jag slowed, Polly asked again. "What happened?"

"It's not all my fault. Everyone else gets away with it. But not me. I don't know why I'm the one who got fired."

"What's not your fault?"

"Well, it's not like they don't throw out a lot of food and pop anyway."

"What did you do?"

"I didn't do anything," Jessie's left nostril went up in the beginning of a sneer.

"Okay, then why did they fire you?"

"I just didn't charge everybody for refills on pop. And some of that pizza had been sitting in the warmer for a long time anyway."

"So, you made a decision to give things away."

"Well, it's no big deal."

"Who says it isn't a big deal?"

"It's just not. They throw food away after shifts all the time. So what if someone takes some?"

"I see. So you're the authority on whether things should be free or not? It's your store and you are responsible for the sales numbers?"

"Whatever."

"Don't get snotty with me. I didn't just get fired from a job."

"Everybody else does it. They didn't fire Kirsten. She does it more than me."

Polly shook her head. "I don't get it. Why do you think that because someone else does something wrong, you should be allowed to do the same thing? It's wrong."

Jessie dropped her head. "The kids yelled at me and made fun of me when I didn't."

"You could have dealt with that any number of ways, but you chose to let them steal from the store and now you want to tell me that it's no big deal. Jessie, you don't have the right to make that decision. It means you aren't trustworthy. If you make the easy decision now, what will you do when something really difficult comes up?"

"I don't know." Jessie's shoulders drooped and her lower lip started to quiver again.

"Oh, for Pete's sake, don't cry again. You have to figure this out. Now you don't have a job and you can't even use this job as a reference for your next one because you were irresponsible."

"I made a mistake."

"How long has this mistake been going on? It couldn't have happened just once."

"No. It didn't. It's been a while."

"Did they warn you?"

"Brian might have said something once, but it wasn't like he told me that I couldn't ever give food away."

"You're trying to place the blame for your actions on him? It's his fault?"

"No. It's my fault."

A shiver went down Polly's back when the fan blew at her. Even though it had been warm yesterday, it was too chilly today for open windows. The world was upside down.

"What did you say when you left there this morning."

"Nothing. He handed me my check when I walked in and told me I was fired. I just came back here."

"Then what happened? How did those guys get up here?"

"We were sitting outside. I was pissed about the job and Troy asked if I'd ever smoked a joint. I used to back in Colorado. It's no big deal. When we got cold, he invited me back to his room, but I didn't think that was a good idea so we came up here. I didn't know his buddy was bringing beer. It wasn't even lunch time yet. Then the next thing I knew we were smoking and they were drinking and then Andrew came up."

"So ... one mistake just led to another and another. What did you think I was going to say?"

Jessie looked down. "I thought you'd be gone all day. You said you were going to look at cars. I hoped they'd be gone before you got home and I could clean up."

"Seriously." Polly looked around. "And how exactly did you plan to get rid of the smell so I wouldn't notice."

"Just like this." Jessie met Polly's eyes. "Are you going to tell Henry?"

"Uhhh. Yeah. This is his house, too and he's going to know that something happened here. The smell won't be gone by the time he gets home. I don't lie to him." Polly said.

"Is he going to kick me out?"

Polly thought about that. This would make him as angry as she was, but he wouldn't do anything other than what she'd already decided. "Always remember that Henry and I are a team. We're responsible for all of this together. So no, that's not in the plan. One mistake ... well, several mistakes all in one day ... don't equate to you having to leave. I hope this behavior won't continue. If it does, you and I will be having a different conversation."

"It won't. I promise. What about Rebecca? Does she have to know that I screwed up?"

"That's up to you. Andrew and I didn't tell her anything, but if she hears it from someone other than you, it will probably be bad. She loves you, Jessie. Be honest with her. She needs to know that you're human and that you're honest. That's something we all need from you."

"What about everyone else. Can I still help Sylvie and Eliseo?"

"Of course. Nothing changes there, Jessie. You screwed up and I hope you learned something from it. You can't blame anyone else, no matter what they did or didn't do. It's all on you. This is your life and your responsibility. You either deal with it or you don't. If you choose not to and make it everyone else's problem, then you're going to have a tough time out there and I won't be able to help you."

"Are you really kicking Troy and Austin out on Monday?"

"Jeff is talking to them right now."

"I didn't mean for them to get in trouble."

"They have to own their mistakes. You are still under twenty-one and I could have them arrested for supplying you with any of this. He tried to get Andrew to serve him. That was foolish. Those are their mistakes to deal with. You have to deal with your own choices."

Jessie had pulled her legs up to her chest and was trying to huddle in on herself. Polly realized the poor girl was probably as cold as she was. "Go on in your room and pull on sweats and a sweatshirt. You're going to clean the bathrooms up here before you go down to help Sylvie with the reception."

Polly stood up and waited for Jessie to crawl out of the chair. "Tomorrow will be another day. I won't forget any of this, but as time passes, I will start trusting you again. Don't screw it up. You've got a big future in front of you and every choice you make impacts which doors open and which close for you."

Jessie had pulled her shirt sleeves around her hands, but reached out tentatively to hug Polly. "I'm really sorry. Thanks for not kicking me out and for talking to me like an adult. You aren't like my mom. I'm sorry for saying that, too. I'll look for another job on Monday and I promise to do better."

Polly watched the girl go into her room and then went into her own, pulling out her phone. She shut the door and sat down on her bed to call Henry. He might as well know what to expect when he got home. He didn't need another surprise today.

CHAPTER SIX

Venting with her friends would definitely take some of the pressure off. Sunday evenings had become a tradition. The first few weeks after the babies arrived, things had been haphazard, but now that Sal lived in Bellingwood and Jessie was in place to care for the twins, a regular table at Pizzazz had become theirs. In just a few weeks, every waitress in the place knew their standard orders and Polly had taken to calling when they weren't going to show up.

She was ready for an evening with the girls. Henry was going back to the garage to spend the evening with Nate. They'd already started tracking down parts for the two Woodies and were clearing space to bring them in.

He'd been quite a bit more upset about the drinking and marijuana episode than Polly expected. When she called him yesterday, he hadn't said much, but by the time he got home, he was pretty worked up. She was glad Jessie had to work the wedding reception because he really was ready to kick her out.

The thing that had infuriated him the most was the complete disrespect the girl had for Polly after all she'd done. Polly didn't see it that way. Jessie had screwed up. It wasn't about Polly, it wasn't intentional. It was just poor decision making. Every young person made those awful decisions. Sometimes they needed a safe place to screw up so they could figure out a different paradigm without the world collapsing around them. She didn't want to remind Henry that he'd made his own mistakes while he was in college and his parents might have been angry, but they didn't kick him out.

Jessie was already out on her own and she hadn't even turned twenty-one yet. Her parents wouldn't provide a safe landing for her if things fell apart. Polly wasn't about to take away the little bit of safety she had left.

They'd driven over to Ogden for dinner and after some onion rings and a beer, he'd come around, though things had been strained around the house today. He didn't say anything to Jessie and wasn't his normal, easy-going self. He usually got up and made breakfast on Sunday mornings while Polly joined Eliseo, Jason and Rachel for their regular trail-ride. When she left this morning, he told her he was going over to the shop and talk his mom into feeding him.

The rest of the afternoon was quiet. Henry spent time in his office and Jessie hid in her room. By four o'clock, Polly was wound tighter than a ten dollar watch. She wanted to go out that evening with her girlfriends, but didn't want to leave the two of them alone in the house, so she decided to step in and make a scene.

It took her a few moments of thinking to decide how to do it, but she ended up sitting in the doorway between the living room and her old apartment, wailing loudly. Obiwan was the first to try to help. He crawled up on her lap and licked her face, trying to stop the noise. Within moments, though, both Jessie and Henry were standing over her. Henry was bemused, Jessie confused - exactly where Polly wanted them.

She pushed the dog off her lap, stood up and pointed at the dining room table and said, "Both of you. Sit. We're hashing this out now. I can't take the uncomfortable silence any longer."

Surprisingly, they obeyed with no protest. Polly took a container of brownies and a carton of milk out of the fridge, then grabbed three glasses, placed everything on the table, and sat down. Without a word, she poured the milk and passed around the glasses, then popped the top off the container of brownies.

"Eat. I don't care whether or not you want a brownie. Everyone has to eat one. Now."

Jessie gave a timid chuckle and reached for a brownie at the same time Henry put his hand out to take one. They smiled at each other and looked at Polly.

"Nope. No talking until you've finished your brownie. Eat it." She took one out and took a bite, looking back and forth at the two of them. "I'm waiting," she said.

Henry grinned across the table at their young housemate and jammed the whole brownie into his mouth. Jessie followed suit.

While they were trying to swallow the yummy goodness, Polly took another dainty bite of hers, then said, "That's fine. But since I'm not finished with mine yet, you must each take another. You might want to go more slowly this time."

Henry scowled at her.

"My meeting. My rules," she said and pushed the brownies in front of him.

Once he finished swallowing, he opened his mouth to say something, but Polly put her hand up.

"Nope. Not yet. Eat your brownie."

He huffed and took another brownie, then nibbled at one corner of it.

"Drink your milk, too. I don't want either of you to mess up the chocolate to milk ratio."

The mood in the room had considerably lightened when brownies were eaten and milk glasses were empty.

"Now," Polly said. "Does anyone have any messy stuff they feel the need to toss out on the table?"

Henry shook his head.

Polly turned to Jessie. "Do you have anything you need to say?"

"I'm sorry, Henry. I screwed up bad and it won't happen again.

I appreciate everything you and Polly have done for me and I didn't act that way yesterday. Will you forgive me?"

Henry reached under the table and squeezed Polly's knee. "Absolutely. It isn't easy trying to get your life together. You're safe here."

"Thanks." Jessie rolled her eyes. "It looks like I have some free time until I get another job. Is there anything I can help you with?"

Henry sat back, stretching his legs out under the table. "You know what? I think there is. Mom says that she's worried about heading south this year because there's been so much office work and no one else has learned how to do it. What would you think about working at the shop and learning what she does?"

Polly just shook her head and laughed. "You're pathetic," she said to him.

"What?"

"Nothing, but I love you."

"Well, that conversation just happened this morning."

"I know. Jessie, what do you think?"

"I'd love it! Your mom is awesome."

"We'll pay you a dollar more than you were making at the convenience store. How many hours were you working?"

"About twenty-four or twenty-five. If I wasn't living here, I couldn't do it."

"We'll guarantee twenty-five hours a week. Mom works more than that and I think she'd like to get back to being retired. Once you learn the ropes, you'll slowly move to full time work and she'll be your backup. Does that sound fair?"

Jessie jumped up, ran around the table and hugged his shoulders, then jumped back. "I won't do that ever again. I promise. But thank you." She headed for the living room. "What time do you want me there tomorrow and what should I wear?"

"It's construction. Wear jeans. But you're working with a bunch of guys and we're pigs, so be modest, okay? Be there by nine. You can have an hour for lunch and be out by three."

She tore out of the room and pretty soon, her bedroom door opened and closed.

"Well, aren't you just the tyrant," Polly said.

"Shut up. It's a good idea. Mom was complaining this morning that we were so busy she didn't have time for any of her friends. She really doesn't want to do that job, but she knows it better than anyone else."

"So you're going to train our juvenile delinquent to work for you and ask her to hang out with your parents."

He grinned, "They raised me. A little Marie Sturtz influence couldn't hurt and besides, at least I know where she is during the day. How much trouble can she get into at the shop?"

"Well, I love you. You're a pretty amazing man."

"Whatever. You think you're pretty cute with this whole brownie episode, don't you."

"It worked."

"Where in the world did you come up with it?"

Polly shrugged. "I don't know. It just came to me as it played out. I decided that food generally makes people feel better and if I could get you two facing each other without thinking about how mad you were, life would work itself out."

"You just wanted us to play nice so you could go out with your friends tonight."

"Did it work?"

He leaned over and she met him for a kiss. "Of course it did. I'll take Jessie with me over to the Mikkels's house and you go have pizza with the girls."

~~~

Polly walked uptown. It was another beautiful evening and people were driving around, chatting with each other after pulling into parking spots along the strip and others were out walking their dogs. This was home now. She couldn't imagine ever living somewhere else. How had she ever gotten along in the city?

The front door of Pizzazz opened and she smiled at people who were leaving. The smell of pizza greeted her like a long lost friend. The hard wood floor creaked as she made her way back to
~~~

their normal table. Polly was the first to arrive, so she positioned herself to watch the door. Before she'd settled in a chair, a glass of iced tea was in front of her and plates were on the table.

"Hi Bri," she said. "You know it's a little embarrassing that you're always ready for me."

The girl laughed. "It would be even more embarrassing if you decided to change your order."

"No worries. I plan to be boring for a long time."

Bri walked away and came back with a diet cola, then waited as Joss found her seat.

"You're barely in the door and she's ready for you," Polly said as Bri set the drink down in front of Joss. She looked up. "You might as well bring the other two. They'll be here any minute."

The girl smiled and came back with two more drinks and two baskets of cheese bread. "I've already turned the pizza order in. I'll bring it out when it's ready."

"Thanks."

Polly turned to Joss. "Do you remember that show 'Cheers'?"

"Yeah. Why?"

"I always thought I wanted a neighborhood bar. A place where I could go and everyone would know me."

"That's what we have here, isn't it."

"Yeah. I like it. This is our table. She knows our orders. People say hello."

"What's up, sassy girls?" Sal asked, sitting down beside Joss.

"We're just talking about how we like being here every week."

Sylvie slid into the last seat, her face white.

"What's wrong?" Sal asked.

"I can't stay."

"Why not? What happened? Are the boys okay? Did something happen with Jason?"

"No, he's fine. They're both fine. For now." She took a drink from the glass in front of her, then beckoned Bri over. "I need a beer. Whatever you have on tap."

Bri nodded and scurried away.

"You're scaring me," Polly said. "What's going on?"

Sylvie took another sip of her soft drink and breathed deeply. "You won't believe who is in town. I can't believe he's here."

"Who?"

Bri put a chilled glass of beer in front of Sylvie and the woman took a long drink. "I have to take a breath and quit being so dramatic about this. But I just saw him outside. I don't think he came in. I don't know if he saw me."

"Who?" Joss pressed.

"My ex. Anthony Donovan is in town. Why in the hell is he here? He doesn't have any family in Bellingwood."

"Except for the boys," Sal said quietly, reaching out to put her hand on Sylvie's arm.

"That's what I'm afraid of. What does he want with us?"

"Maybe it's nothing like that," Polly tried to sound reassuring. "Maybe he's just on a run through the area and stopped in to see what Bellingwood was like after all these years."

"Yeah. Right." Sylvie drained the glass and caught Bri's eye, then pointed at it.

"Whoa. Slow down, girl," Polly said.

"Not happening."

"Are you planning to stay and eat some pizza?"

"Yeah. I was being overdramatic. That one helped. The next one will help even more. I'll calm down and then I'll figure out what I'm going to do."

Sal sat straight up. "What you're going to do? You're going to let your friends deal with him. You don't have to face that jackass. He lost all rights of seeing your pretty self years ago. We'll take him out."

"He's two hundred fifty pounds of mean muscle."

"Okay, then," Sal slumped back into the chair. "I'll let the Sheriff take him out. He has guns."

Sylvie chuckled. "I love you. Thanks. I don't feel quite as sick to my stomach as I did when I walked in here tonight."

Bri slid the pizza onto the table and turned around, taking a second glass of beer from another waitress and replacing the glass in front of Sylvie. "Anything else, ladies?"

"I'm going to want one more of these when this one is gone and then I'll be done," Sylvie said. "Thanks."

"Got it."

"I'm so glad I can walk home. I can drink until I'm stupid if I need to." Sylvie drank from the second glass while Polly served pizza around the table.

"Are you sure it was him?" Joss asked.

Sylvie shuddered. "I'd know that face anywhere. It still haunts my nightmares." She took a bite of pizza, then dropped it back onto the plate in front of her and pushed it away. "I'm sorry. My stomach is still too upset to eat pizza."

Sal reached over and rubbed Sylvie's back. "I'm so sorry. Tell us how we can help." With her other hand, she pushed the basket of cheese bread in front of the woman.

"I don't know. I wish I knew why he was here. What does he want?" Sylvie took a bite out of a slice of cheese bread, then another. "I can't let him hurt my boys. I won't let him hurt me."

She started to breathe heavily, panic filling her eyes. "I can't do this. I can't go through this again. Why in the hell is he here?"

Joss reached across and started rubbing her back as well. Sylvie gulped down a bite of bread and dropped her head into her hands on the table. Her shoulders shook and soon quiet sobbing began.

"Honey, do you want some help tonight? You can stay with me," Polly said. "I have that middle bedroom and the boys can sleep on my couches."

"I'm so scared," came a pitiful sound from the table. "I haven't been this scared in years. I don't want Jason and Andrew to see me like this. I thought I was strong enough to handle anything."

Both Sal and Joss had tears in their eyes.

"He terrorized you," Sal said. "I'm so sorry."

"Sometimes the nightmares are so bad that I don't think I'll live through them." Sylvie brought her head up. "If it weren't for my boys, I don't think I'd still be alive. What am I going to do?"

"I'm going to say a couple of things and you can tell me yes or no," Polly said. "I know that this goes against everything you are, but you shouldn't have to deal with this alone."

"I can't believe how helpless I feel," Sylvie said. "I hate what he's done to me."

"Let me call Aaron and tell him that your ex is in town and then let me call Eliseo. Jason can spend more time with him this week and you and Andrew can come to Sycamore House. Be honest with your boys and tell them what's going on. I've spent the last two years stressing how important it is that we rely on friends when bad things happen."

Sylvie nodded. "And I've appreciated that. But I don't want to involve everyone in my mess. I don't even know for sure that he is here for us."

"What if he is and you wait too long to ask for help?" Sal said.

"How about I call Aaron first, just to alert him. He's the one who dealt with Anthony the last time, right?"

Sylvie nodded again. "Okay. He's a friend. Call him. He gets this more than anyone else."

Polly took out her phone and dialed Aaron's number.

"Oh good heavens, Polly Sturtz, please tell me you are safe somewhere and not calling me with another body."

"No, not this time. It's something different."

His voice changed immediately. "What's up?"

"Sylvie just saw her ex. We're all here at Pizzazz. He's in town."

"Damn it." Aaron breathed in and out twice and said, "Does she need me to come up? Lydia and I can be there in just a few minutes."

Polly pulled the phone away from her cheek and said, "Sylvie, would you like Aaron and Lydia to come up here?"

"No, that's fine. It's enough that he knows."

"Did you hear that, Aaron?"

"Tell our girl that all she has to do is call. One of us will be wherever she needs us to be immediately. She's not alone this time."

"I'll tell her. Thanks."

Polly put her phone down on the table and reached across to Sylvie's hand. "Do you have his phone number programmed?"

Sylvie shook her head.

"Give your phone to me and I'll put it in. You're supposed to call him any time. Whatever you need. He says that you aren't alone this time. That's the truth. You know it, don't you?"

"I feel like such a little fool," Sylvie said. "I'm a grown woman. Why am I reacting like this?"

Joss took the phone from Sylvie and passed it to Polly. "You know, everything I know tells me that you probably are facing the same type of thing that Eliseo faces with post-traumatic stress."

Sylvie huffed. "That man fought in a war. It makes sense that he deals with it. He's a hero."

"You fought in a war, too, sweetie," Sal said. "Yours was inside your house. You never got to choose which battles you would fight. Don't think for a minute that what you faced wasn't horrific and life threatening. Just because you lived through it and got out of it doesn't mean you weren't damaged by what that man did to you. It's okay to admit it."

Sylvie began crying again and dropped her head back down into her hands. She looked up. "Things were just starting to go so well for us. What if he decides to move back to Bellingwood? I can't live here with him in town."

"Don't worry about that," Polly said. "Can you see him living here peacefully once Aaron and Ken Wallers decide that he needs to move on? We don't know his reason for coming into town, but we definitely know his reason for leaving again. You are going to be safe in your home. We promise you that. Now, do you want me to call Eliseo and deal with your oldest boy or do all three of you want to come to Sycamore House?"

Sylvie sat back up, wiped her eyes and blew her nose, then said. "Okay. Fine. Let me call Eliseo. It's probably better that Jason stay with him anyway. Once he knows his dad is in town, he's going to erupt. It will be awful. Eliseo will handle him better than I do."

She took her phone back from Polly. "Do you mind if I make the call from here? I'm not ready to go back outside, just in case he's still around."

"Go ahead," Polly said.

Sylvie dialed her phone. "Hi," she said quietly. "No, he's fine. But I have a huge favor to ask of you. Would you mind if he spent the week on the farm with you?"

After a pause, she said. "No. We haven't had another fight. He's really okay. Oh, Eliseo." Sylvie started to cry again and handed the phone over to Polly.

"Hey," she said.

"What happened?" he asked. "Is Sylvie okay?"

Polly looked across the table at her friend, her eyebrows raised in a question. Sylvie waved her hand and Polly said, "Eliseo, Sylvie's ex is in town and she's scared that he's here for the boys for some reason. She saw him and can't figure out any good reason why he'd be here."

"Oh. If Jason is with me, what is she planning to do with Andrew?"

"I've invited them to stay at my house for a few days."

"Nonsense. They can all come out to the farm. I have those three bedrooms upstairs and there's plenty of room to move around."

"Seriously?"

"Put her back on the phone."

Polly handed the phone across the table. "Just listen to him. You don't have to say anything."

Sylvie put the phone back to her ear and said, "Yes?" She listened and nodded. "You're right. It's a good idea. I have plenty of sheets. No. That's fine. Really? Tonight? But it will be late." Another pause. "Okay. That's true." A hint of a smile passed across her lips. "Thank you. We'll be out later."

She swiped to end the call, her face softened. "We're going out tonight. I just need to go home and get the boys. I guess we don't have to pack a lot of things. We can do that tomorrow. I feel a little silly about being so dramatic."

"You've said that already," Polly remarked. "You aren't being dramatic. We'll probably all sleep better knowing that you are somewhere safe. Now, why don't we take you home and make sure you get out to Eliseo's house safely."

"He said I should eat something else and stay here for just a little while longer before I go home to talk to the boys."

"More bread?" Sal asked.

"I can't stomach the idea of pizza," Sylvie responded. "So yes. Bread is fine." She pushed the beer away from her. "Okay, three was ridiculous. I can't get through two of them."

Everyone around the table took a deep breath and tried to eat the pizza in front of them. Polly didn't have the energy. "Who wants to take this home tonight?" she asked. When there was no response, she said. "Sylvie, will your boys eat this?"

"Of course they will."

"Then one box it is." Polly turned around. "Bri? Could you box this up and skip Sylvie's other beer? I think she's done."

Bri took the pizza off the table. Polly looked up and started to laugh. "Your white knight is here," she said.

"What? Who?" Sylvie turned around and stood up.

Eliseo folded her into his arms. "I'm sorry that you have to face this, but you don't have to do it alone. Shall we go get the boys?"

Polly's eyes filled with tears and she smiled at her friends. Holy cow, something was going on with those two. Bri put the pizza box back on the table and Polly didn't even have time to catch Sylvie before she walked out the front door with Eliseo's arms around her shoulders.

"What in the world?" Joss asked. "Did you know about that?"

"I didn't know anything," Polly said. "Do you think it's really something?"

Sal chuckled. "If it wasn't before, it's about to be. He's got it bad for her and she just figured it out."

CHAPTER SEVEN

"Except for coming to work," Sylvie said as she dropped into a chair in front of Polly's desk, "This was a weird morning."

"You look like hell. No sleep?"

"Thanks." Sylvie tried to pat her hair into place and gave up. "No sleep. Two really upset boys and to top it off, Jason has to go back to school today and face those kids. He was just awful this morning. I could have kissed Eliseo when he offered to drive him to Boone." She shook her head. "I'm really sorry about my behavior last night. Looking back at it now, I blew it way out of proportion. There's nothing that man can do to hurt me. I shouldn't have been so overdramatic."

"Stop it. You had a terrible shock and we handled it the best way we knew how. You also got everyone into a safe place and now you can deal with whatever comes next."

"I suppose. But I erupted all over you and then Eliseo come into town to take care of us and then we were at his house. Aaron is all worried about me and that's just too many people."

Polly smiled. "Uh huh. You're talking to me, you know. The entire town knows when I'm in the middle of something."

"Yeah. We didn't even get to talk about your newest body find. Do you know who it was?"

"I haven't talked to Aaron yet. I hope he'll tell me something."

"I have a huge favor to ask," Sylvie said.

"Anything. You know that."

"Do you care if I use your shower? I suppose I could go home, but I promised Eliseo I wouldn't without someone with me and I didn't have time this morning."

"I can either take you to your apartment or you can absolutely use my shower. Henry's gone and the one back by his office is never used. It's really nice, too. There are towels in the cabinet and I think it's fully stocked with soap and shampoo."

Sylvie lifted her bag. "I have what I need in here. It was easier just to keep carrying it." She slumped back in her seat. "I wish I knew why Anthony was in town. I'm going to have to confront him at some point, just so I can make some plans for myself. I can't hide at Eliseo's forever."

"Well, you could ..." Polly said, grinning.

"What?"

"Are you really that blind?"

Sylvie wrinkled her forehead, squishing her eyebrows together. "What in the world do you mean?"

"Oh, good heavens, you are that blind. Sal and Joss even noticed it last night."

"Noticed what? There wasn't anything to notice."

"You keep telling yourself that. Eliseo is smitten with you."

"That's ridiculous. He's just helping out a friend."

"You can say whatever you want, but you need to pay attention. He loves your boys and Sylvie, he's fallen for you."

Sylvie sat forward and crossed her arms. "Don't do this to me. I don't need to worry about some man wanting me to fall in love with him now. My ex is in town for god knows what, I'm trying to get an owly freshman settled in high school, my ...," she glared at Polly "... *our* catering business is just taking off. I have to think about employees and family and where I'm living. I can't be thinking about him and I certainly don't have time to fall in love."

"You just keep telling yourself that. We watched you in his arms as you two left last night. You fit perfectly."

"That's just horse crap."

"No, that's what I shoveled this morning while you were trying to manage all of the people in your life."

"Sorry about that. We have to figure out a better schedule. He was really antsy when he couldn't get to the barn to help you."

"All I had to do was put feed out and open the doors. I cleaned up the big chunks and Jason and Eliseo can do the rest tonight. Don't worry about it."

Sylvie reached down, picked up her bag again, and stood up. "I'm not talking about this with you. It's ridiculous."

"You already said that."

"Well, it is. I'm in my forties and don't need to be hooking up with a man. I like my life and my boys need me."

She turned to the door and threw up a hand. "Don't say it. I'm not that stupid."

"Good, because I wouldn't want to have to remind you how much your boys need Eliseo."

"I told you not to say it. Now I'm going up to take a shower. I have a meeting at ten." She left as Jeff came in the front door shaking himself like a dog. Another round of thunderstorms was passing through. Polly hoped it wasn't a portent for the day.

He sat down in the seat Sylvie vacated. "What was up with her? She looked terrible. Is everything okay?"

"She's going upstairs to take a shower. I think she had a rough night, but I'll let her tell you about it."

"The boys are okay?"

"Yeah. Everyone's okay. I will tell you that her ex-husband is in town and she's pretty freaked out."

"I wonder what he wants."

"So does she. What's up this morning around here?"

"I'm sorry I'm late. I had a breakfast meeting downtown. Then we got to talking and before I knew it, too much time had passed."

"Why would you ever apologize to me about being late?" Polly asked.

"Well, I should tell you where I am. Is Sarah coming in this morning?"

Polly shook her head. "I don't think so. She's in pretty bad shape right now. Rebecca didn't even want to go to school. I'm pretty sure that Sarah has several more months, but it terrifies Rebecca that she'll be away from her mom when she needs her."

"Poor little girl."

"Yeah. She's handling a lot right now. I'm just glad that she's here and that Andrew is around to distract her."

"What would you think about spending some time at the hotel this afternoon? I have a group coming in. I'd go if Sarah was going to be here, but ..."

"No, that would be fine. We really need to find someone to manage that place, don't we?"

"We're not quite there yet. I'd like to see at least a regular sixty percent occupancy before we hire."

Polly ran her hand through her hair. "I just keep thinking that there has to be someone who would like to live on-site."

"That would be great. When you're there, you need to walk through the apartment. Len Specek has done a beautiful job with the woodwork. Henry said something about finishing the basement this winter. That would make it really nice."

"Maybe you should move in," Polly said, teasingly.

"Not happ'nin. Bellingwood isn't ready to have me around full-time." He huffed a chuckle out. "It's enough that I live in Ames. Sometimes I think it would be easier to commute from Chicago."

"Did something happen?"

"Nah. Prejudice is everywhere. It's just not so obvious in a city the size of Chicago."

"Oh Jeff. Why didn't you tell me that something was going on?"

"Nothing's going on, Polly. Nothing has happened to me. I promise."

"You know I love you and it would destroy me if anyone hurt you."

"You old softie you," he said. "I love my job here and I love working with everyone. I have a great life and good friends.

Changing attitudes don't come easily to people. Bellingwood does right by me most all the time. I shouldn't have said anything."

"Well, please talk to me ... about any of it. I'm serious. Any of it."

He stood up and tapped the corner of her desk, then winked at her. "You're a good person, Polly Giller. I wouldn't want to work for anyone else." When he got to her door, he turned back around, "If you see Sylvie before I do, let her know that I'll do what I can to help."

He walked into his own office and Polly took a deep breath, then picked up her phone and called Henry.

"Hey sweet thing, how are you?" he asked.

"I think that one's acceptable," she responded. "I just wanted to hear your voice. Some days I feel like you are the only sane person I know. What are you doing this morning?"

"I'm up at Bennett's house. We'll finish here this week and then it's interior work over at Chubby Dean's place."

A tornado last spring had destroyed some homes completely and others had been in various states of upheaval. Slowly but surely, the town was re-building all that had come down. Sturtz Family Construction was gaining a terrific reputation for work well-done and on-time. Henry's employees worked hard and it showed with all of the new construction bids he was taking in. They were trying to plan through the winter as much as possible, in order to allow Bill and Marie to leave before the snow came.

"Do you want me to go over to the shop with Jessie?"

"Nah. I think she's got it. Mom's going to keep an eye out."

"I appreciate you doing this."

"It's no big thing, Polly. Mom needs the help and Jessie needs a job. If it doesn't work out, we'll do something else. Have you seen Sylvie yet?"

"Yeah. She's here. I think she's a little embarrassed that she got everyone worked up last night."

"That's foolish. If Anthony Donovan is in town, something is going on. That man is a piece of work."

"You remember him?"

"Sure. Everyone does. It was only seven or eight years ago. He wasn't smart enough to hide his beatings. Her bruises were obvious, even though she tried to cover them."

"I just can't imagine."

"It was pretty awful."

"Well, she's here and taking a shower right now. I'm going to be over at the hotel later today. Jeff needs me to check a big group in. He tells me we're not ready to hire someone full-time over there yet."

"Well, that's why he's your assistant. He knows his stuff."

"Okay. You're normal and I feel better."

Henry laughed. "That's me. Normal. I love you."

"Love you, too." Polly put the phone back down on her desk. What a weekend. As long as Henry was stable, she could get through all of the other ups and downs in the lives of people around her, but sometimes it was nearly too much.

Polly was neck deep in paperwork when her phone rang. She didn't even look to see who it was, just swiped to answer and said, "Hello?"

"Hi Polly, Marie Sturtz here. Have you seen my new helper this morning?"

She wrenched her mind away from what she was doing and looked at the time - ten thirty.

"No. Let me check upstairs. I'll call you back."

"Maybe she didn't realize we were starting this morning."

"No, she knew. I'll let you know."

Polly stuck her head in Jeff's office. "I need to run upstairs. Have you seen Jessie?"

"Ummm, no, but I haven't been paying attention to much."

"Thanks." She left the office and ran up the steps to her apartment.

"Jessie? Are you here? Is everything okay?"

Other than the animals who were always glad to see her, there was no other sound in the place.

"Jessie?" Polly checked the kitchen and media room. "Jessie?" She went into Jessie's bathroom. No one was there, so she walked across the living room to the girl's bedroom door and knocked. "Jessie? Are you in here?"

With no answer, Polly opened the door to an empty room. The bed had been made and things were cleaner than she was used to seeing them. She stepped all the way in and opened the wardrobe. Some of Jessie's things were gone. Durango, Jessie's stuffed purple horse wasn't in its regular place of honor, hanging around the headboard post.

What had the girl done this time? Henry was going to be furious. Polly sat down on Jessie's bed and called Marie.

"Hey," she said.

"Did you find her?"

"I don't think she'll be in to work this morning. I think she left."

"She left? Did she take everything?"

"No, but it looks like she took some things that were important to her."

"Oh Polly. I'm sorry."

"Me too. I don't know whether to be furious or heartbroken."

"Well, she's in an awkward place in life. Her parents have cut ties with her and she's trying to figure out how to be an adult. There really isn't anyone that she feels responsible to."

"I guess I'd hoped that she would feel responsible enough to herself to cut through some of that. She's been fine for the last three months."

"Can I ask a crazy question?"

"Sure."

"When is the trial for that boy in Oelwein coming up? Could she be running away from that?"

"A couple of weeks. Oh, Marie, you're right. That's exactly what's going on. But why didn't she talk to me?"

"Who ever knows what goes on in their heads. The only thing you can do is keep loving them and try to make life strong and safe while they leave childhood behind."

"Henry is going to be furious that she screwed this up. He was so pleased that he'd figured out something so great for her."

"Well, let's not discount this job for her yet. I'm in no hurry.

There is still plenty of time before I go south. And sometimes kids need another chance."

"We already gave her a second chance. It's kind of difficult to think about risking another one."

"Isn't everyone worth more than one additional chance?" Marie asked softly.

Polly took a deep breath and smiled. "Sometimes you remind me so much of Mary. Thank you."

"Well, that's high praise. I know how much you love her. This will work out as it is supposed to. You have to have a little faith."

"Can I send Henry over to talk to you when he tells me we're finished with her?"

"Sweetie, who do you think talked Henry through that year he waited for you to realize how much you loved him?"

"Oh, Marie," Polly laughed. "Was I really that much of a problem?"

"You were a little stubborn. I just had to tell him that love could be more stubborn than fear." Marie was chuckling on the other end of the phone. "He'll be fine. Just like his dad, he needs a little time to deal with his disappointment, but then he'll stand beside you and do the right thing. Never fear."

"Thank you for your time this morning," Polly said. "I'm glad I talked to you before I spent energy getting angry."

"Do you have any idea where she's gone?"

"I have an idea, but I need to do some research. If I'm right, should I go after her?"

"Not right now. Let the girl have some space. Tell her that she's welcome to come back and that you know what she's done. She won't be able to confront this without some help from you. Make it okay for her to return and then you can upend her comfortable, self-centered, bratty self. There have to be consequences, but not until she's safe."

"This is why your kids are so wonderful. Thank you."

"You're a wonderful young woman, Polly. I'm awfully glad you are part of the family."

"I love you, Marie."

"I love you too, sweetheart. Now go figure out where your girl is … and Polly?"

"Yes?"

"You don't have to tell Henry about this until you know for sure what is going on. No sense giving him fuel for a fire that doesn't need to burn."

Polly nodded and grinned. "Thanks, Marie. I'll talk to you later."

She left the bedroom and pulled the door shut, then went back downstairs and into Jeff's office.

"Did you find her?" he asked.

"No. She's gone. I haven't looked, but I'd guess her car is gone too."

He leaned back in his chair and looked out into the parking lot. "It's not where she usually parks it. So, what are you thinking?"

"What do you know about Troy Kandle?"

"The punk kid? He's a peach. They're gone. Don't worry." Then his eyes lit with realization. "You think she went with him?"

"I do. When did they leave?"

Jeff shrugged, "I'm not sure. They were supposed to be out of here by noon today and I know they're gone. Rachel has already started cleaning the rooms."

"Did he give you any clue as to where he was going?"

"He said something about Minneapolis. But here, his band has a Facebook page. Let's see what that will tell us." Jeff clicked and typed and brought up the band's page.

Polly growled under her breath when she saw it. He had changed his profile picture to a hand with the middle finger up. The description was not unexpected. "Screw you, Bellingwood. Uptight assholes."

"Well, there's a five-star review if I've ever seen one," she said.

"He posted that at eleven o'clock last night. I'm guessing that's when they left."

"I was sound asleep - didn't even hear her go."

"Apparently she didn't want you to hear her. What are you going to do?"

"I'm going to send her a message on Facebook and tell her that she's welcome to come back any time. When and if she does, we'll deal with the consequences at that point."

"That's kind of open minded."

"I had a talk with Henry's mom this morning. She's a smart lady. She also reminded me that Jessie is probably panicked about the trial that is supposed to happen in two weeks. That's how long I have to help her get her head on straight or there is going to be a prosecutor who is very upset."

Jeff had been clicking through things on the band's page. "It looks like they have a couple of gigs in Minneapolis this week and then they're heading for South Dakota before ending up in Omaha."

"That's close enough to track her down if I have to. Thanks." Polly braced her hands on the armrests of the chair and pushed herself up. "I really didn't want to be a mom, Jeff."

"This is what happens when you try to help someone who was raised quite differently than you. You are aware that when you take responsibility for Rebecca, you will run into unknowns like this all the time."

"I suppose you're right. But at least Rebecca has always been confident that her mother loves her."

"And that's a big deal. Let me know if I can do anything to help you."

"Thanks. What time do I need to be over at the hotel?"

"They're coming in between two and four."

"So one o'clock?"

"Thanks, Polly. The computers are all hooked up. You shouldn't have any trouble signing them in."

"I'm on it. No worries." She left and went back into her own office and logged onto Facebook to send a quick message to Jessie. If the girl didn't respond, Polly would take other actions, but she had to start somewhere.

CHAPTER EIGHT

Running her fingers across the top of the counter, Polly mused that spending time at the hotel was actually quite pleasant. She'd brought a plate of cookies from Sylvie's kitchen, along with several thermoses of coffee and iced tea. They were expecting a group of bikers who were enjoying a week's vacation at wineries in the state, beginning with Secret Woods this evening. Henry's crew still had a few small projects left at the lodge, but the winery had opened its doors just before school started and the boys were giddy with excitement.

A newspaper article about the damage done to Bellingwood during the tornado and how the vineyard had remained intact garnered some interest. The fact that there had been a death on the property and the victim's wife had been part of the murder had also attracted attention. The Terrible Trio had capitalized on the stories, their grand opening had been a success and so far, they were doing as well as could be expected.

She sat down in an overstuffed chair to wait. Dark wood on the walls and floor, white stone around the fireplace and heavy pewter sconces on the walls gave the room a Victorian feeling.

Henry was planning to add glass fronted bookshelves to several of the walls above the cabinets that were already in place. He and Jeff had designed the lower cabinetry to hide a kitchen space and other storage.

It would be quite easy to get used to working here every day. Polly leaned back and shut her eyes. This was nice.

The roar of engines woke her and she jumped out of the chair. Patting her hair and straightening her shirt, she went to the front door and pulled it open, then watched as different colors and makes of motorcycles filled her parking lot. This was what she lived for. There was nothing better than meeting new people and inviting them to be part of her world.

Helmets and rain gear came off and men and women stretched before coming toward her. The first man to reach her stuck his hand out and said, "I'm Dino, are you the mistress of the castle?"

Polly chuckled. "I am Polly Giller. Welcome to Bellingwood. Come in and we'll get you all set up."

He poked his head inside and then called out, "She has cookies and you gotta see this place."

He followed her to the counter and soon the room filled with people, laughing and chatting while milling around.

"This is some beautiful work," he said. "Local?"

"My husband. He and I own Sycamore Inn and he's the cabinet maker."

"You're a fortunate woman. My wife better not find out about this or I'm going to be ..." he turned and looked around. "Too late. She's taking pictures." He pointed to a blond woman who was snapping pictures of the woodwork. "I'm going to be busy this winter. I can tell." The woman came up to the counter and showed him a picture on her phone, then spun him around so that Polly's face was between their shoulders and snapped a picture.

"Do you mind if it's on Facebook?" she asked, grinning a wide smile.

"That's fine," Polly said, chuckling.

"Your manager said we could have the rooms in the back, facing the woods. Is that still okay?"

"Absolutely. It looks as if Jeff has everything taken care of here. All I need to do is show you where things are."

Polly walked back outside with them, around to the back rooms. Two by two and one by one, the rooms filled as people left the crowd following her. At the corner, she pointed to a shelter and said, "Ice machines, pop machines and snacks. Your key will get you inside. If you need anything else, you know how to reach us. We'll be here in a minute."

"What if we find a dead body?" Dino asked, winking at Polly. His wife just laughed.

"That's my job," Polly retorted. "But if you do, let me know. I have an in with the Sheriff. Can you think of anything else you need?"

"Where can we get a good breakfast in the morning?"

"If you want to come over to Sycamore House, you just need to tell me what time you'll be there so I can get our chef busy. Otherwise, there's a diner up town that serves a great breakfast."

Dino looked at his wife and she gave a slight shrug. "We'll hit the diner. They won't have a problem with all of us?"

A dozen more people on a weekday morning probably wouldn't tip them over the edge, so she smiled and said. "How about I call Joe so he knows you might show up."

"Thanks. Then I think we've got it from here."

"The main building will be open until eleven if you need anything in there. I'll have coffee on by six tomorrow morning. How does that sound?"

"That sounds perfect. Thanks, Mrs. Giller."

She smiled and wondered what Henry would think of being Mr. Giller.

Polly got back in her truck and checked her phone. There were two texts, the first from Sylvie.

"I need to scream. Where are you?"

The second was from Jason. *"Is Mom going to kill me?"*

What had happened this time? She called Sylvie.

"I'm sorry I missed your text. I was busy with guests at the hotel," she said as soon as Sylvie picked up.

"Polly what am I going to do with him?"

"With Jason?" It was only a guess, but it seemed like a good guess.

"That little shit is suspended for a week."

"He's what?"

"He got in a fight. He hit two kids and gave one of them a bloody nose. The other one is going to have a black eye. Then when the principal tried to break it up, he flipped him off and told him to go to hell - that it wasn't his fault. Polly, whose kid is this and what's happened to my son?"

Polly's stomach roiled. She wanted to be sick. What was going on with Jason?

"Where are you?"

"I'm driving to Boone to pick him up."

"Have you talked to him yet? Tried to find out what's going on?"

"No, the vice principal called me and told me that I could come get him. What am I supposed to say to my own personal rotten kid? I'm so angry right now I want to make him walk back to Bellingwood, but I'm afraid he'd do something stupid. I don't trust him anymore at all."

"Before you completely freak out on him ..."

"Don't give me any namby pamby parental, child-raising crap right now. He has no right to touch anyone and absolutely no right to talk to his principal that way. I thought we had this dealt with the last time."

Polly took a deep breath. Sylvie really didn't want to hear her and that made sense, but Jason wasn't a bully. If he hit someone, they'd worked him up to it.

"The last time he got into a fight, it was to protect his little brother, right?"

"Yes, but that wasn't a good reason to fight. I didn't raise my son to use his fists. I raised him to use his head. Polly, he can't turn out like his father. He just can't! What am I going to do if he was born this way and there is nothing I can do to make him better?"

There wasn't much Polly could say at this point. Sylvie was off the deep end. She'd had so much stress in the last few days and Jason was about to be the recipient of her fury.

"What are you planning to do?" Polly asked quietly.

"I don't know!" Sylvie was yelling into the phone. "I'm so far out of my depth right now. I thought I knew my son, but this boy is unrecognizable to me. I'm going to be stuck paying for hospital bills, I just know it. I thought that the last time would be the last time, but it's happened again. What if it keeps happening and he really hurts someone bad. I couldn't stand to have him end up in Eldora.

Polly hadn't thought about the Boys Training School in Eldora for years. When she was in high school, it was a huge threat that teachers held over a boy's head when he acted out. It was only about forty-five minutes away and one year, the youth group took a day off from school and went over to see what it was like. She wasn't sure if it scared anyone straight, but it certainly gave her something to think about.

"That's not going to happen, Sylvie, and you know it. You need to get your head on straight. This is your son and you're acting like it's the end of the world." If handling Sylvie with kid gloves wasn't going to startle her into sanity, then Polly figured she'd try a firm hand.

"Did you just yell at me?"

"I think so. Did it work?" Polly let out a small chuckle.

"You're right. I'm embarrassed and I'm worried that he's going to be like his dad. But this isn't about me, is it?"

"Not at all. There's something going on with Jason and he isn't able to tell you what it is."

"It's those damned boys he's hanging out with. I'm just sure of it. I don't know how to fix that."

"Are they older or his age?"

"Oh, they're older."

"And you told him last night that his dad was in town."

Sylvie was quiet, then she said, "Yes. I told him. He didn't say anything and it was late, so I just let him go to bed."

"He was in a strange house, not knowing what was going to happen, but knowing that you were scared enough to leave your apartment."

"This is my fault."

"No, come on. Don't go down that path either. It's not about fault. But I think you need to talk before you wig out on him."

"But I get to wig out on him soon, right?"

Polly laughed. She had no idea when she'd turned into the reasonable parental type.

"I think wigging out is an appropriate measure at some point. Maybe you ought to get him home first."

"Can I do this at Sycamore House? I'm really not ready to be at the apartment yet."

"Of course you can. How long is his suspension?"

"All week."

"Well, it seems like Eliseo has a dedicated helper for the week. I'm guessing a lot of work will get done at Sycamore House and out on the farm."

"Okay, I'm pulling into the school. I have to go in and talk to Jason and his counselor. Thanks for talking me down."

"I love you, Sylvie Donovan. You are a great mom and just because things are a little messy doesn't change that, right?"

"I'll work on believing that tomorrow, okay?"

"Okay. I'll see you after a while."

Polly dropped the phone on the seat beside her. She'd been in her driveway for the last of the conversation. All of this drama with young people was ridiculous. Had someone spiked the water in town? What was it going to take for them to get their heads out of their back ends and take responsibility for life?

Man, she was frustrated.

She got out of the truck, slammed the door and went inside. Rachel was in the kitchen when Polly walked through and didn't say anything when she saw the look on her boss's face. Jeff stepped out to say something, took one look at Polly, then grinned and went back into his office.

"What's up?" she asked.

"It'll keep. Did everything go well over at the hotel?"

"It was great. Easiest job in the universe. I think they'll be fine."

"Thanks for doing that."

Polly went into her office and quickly checked to see if Jessie might have responded. There was nothing. She growled at the computer and sat back in her seat, looking out the window. A strange man came in the front door and her heart sank. It had to be him. This was not what Sylvie needed right now. Before he could get to the office, she darted into Jeff's and shut the door.

"Call Sylvie, don't let her come here. Tell her that her ex has shown up and she needs to go straight to Eliseo's. I'll call her later."

She opened the door and, putting on her most pleasant face, went into the main office to greet the man.

"Hi, can I help you?"

"I'm looking for Sylvie Donovan." He was a big man and wearing work clothes - jeans and a red shirt under a khaki jacket. He'd taken off his ball cap, exposing thinning brown hair. His voice was low and rough and his hands were calloused and rougher. Not someone she wanted to mess with.

"She's not here right now. Is there anything I can do for you?"

"I know she's here. People around town told me where she works." He glanced around the office and started to walk away.

"But she isn't here today. Can I tell her who is looking for her?"

"She knows. I know she knows." He stepped out of the main office and looked around some more, trying to get his bearings. "The place is different. Kitchen still back here?" He walked away from Polly.

"It is, but I've told you that she isn't working here today."

"Why don't I just look for myself?" He didn't even turn around, just kept walking toward the kitchen with Polly tripping to keep up with him.

He stopped at the window and peered in, trying to see around the corners of the equipment. Rachel had been bent over, putting pans away under the prep table and let out a small gasp when she stood up and saw him.

"Can I help you?" she asked, looking desperately at Polly. Polly gave her a slight head shake.

"I'm looking for Sylvie. Where is she?"

"Uhh. I don't know. She's not here right now." Rachel's face had turned bright red.

"Is she coming back?"

Polly shook her head as imperceptibly as possible, hoping Rachel would get it.

"I don't think so. She's done for the day."

"Fine. Tell her Anthony wants to talk to her and she'd better quit ducking out on me."

"What did you want to talk to her about?" Polly barely squeaked out, ashamed that he'd caused her to sound like that.

"None of your business. Best to just stay out of it, if you know what I mean." He sauntered toward her, then brushed past her and headed for the front door.

Polly followed to make sure he was gone and then felt a cold sweat break out all over her body.

"Is he gone?" Jeff came out of the office.

"For now. That man terrifies me," she said. "I wasn't as scared when those idiots had me trapped in the barn last year. This guy could fold me into a taco and serve me for lunch." Polly put her hand out to take Jeff's forearm. She needed a little contact to maintain her stability. "Did you reach Sylvie and wave her off?"

"Yeah. And I called Eliseo, too. I thought he should know."

"I'm going to go back and check on Rachel. I think he terrified her, too."

"I know this sounds a little melodramatic, but are you going to call the Sheriff?"

"I don't want to sound like a baby," Polly protested.

"You'd rather be a taco?"

She chuckled, then took a deep cleansing breath. "Okay. Thanks. I'm better. We'll see."

Rachel was standing at the sink, her hands under running water, when Polly walked back in. "Are you okay?" Polly asked.

"Was that her ex-husband? He's huge."

"Yeah. That was him. Thanks for backing me up."

"At least I didn't have to lie. But you know Andrew is upstairs, don't you?"

"Oh, for heaven's sake. I didn't even think about that. I'm so glad he didn't come down. Is Rebecca with him?"

"Yeah. I thought Jessie was around, but he said she's not. Are they okay alone up there?"

"They'll be fine. Now that I'm breathing again, I'll figure out what is happening around here. Sylvie can't come back until she's ready to face this. Do you need any help?"

Rachel thought about it. "I need to go out and help clean rooms tomorrow after that group leaves, but I think we're fine. Ask Sylvie if I should call Hannah. I'm sure she can come help if necessary."

"I'll do that. Thanks for everything."

Polly was nearly out the door when Rachel said, "Polly? Have you thought about doing something for Sylvie getting her certificate?"

"What a horrible friend I am," Polly said as she turned around. "I know Sylvie was just so glad to be done with classes, I didn't even think about celebrating. But we can't do it here because she'd think she has to do all of the work."

"Hannah and I were talking about it. I think we could come up with something fun."

"Let's get through this and then yes, I want to congratulate the heck out of her. Thanks for reminding me. Don't let me forget again, okay?"

Rachel smiled, "Okay. I'll say something to Jeff, too."

"Perfect. He never lets me forget things."

CHAPTER NINE

A rather upset Eliseo was waiting for Polly in her office.

"Hey," she said and walked around her desk.

"You okay?" he asked, waiting to sit down until she'd taken a seat.

"I suppose. Have you talked to Sylvie?"

"Not yet. I want to find out from you how bad you think this is going to get?"

Polly slowly shook her head. "I don't know. He's scary and he's pretty intent on getting to her. I wish I knew what he wanted."

"Everybody does. Now that he's figured out where she works, it makes sense that he knows where she lives."

"But he doesn't know about you. That gives her a little breathing room."

Eliseo leaned forward and put his hands on her desk. "Do you think we're making more out of this than it is? Maybe he's in town for something inconsequential." Every once in a while Eliseo's accent broke through. Polly loved it when he did. Rather than the 'ch' sound at the end of the word, she heard the "tee-ahl" and smiled.

"Maybe. She's going to have to face him sooner or later, but I'd like there to be plenty of people around. I've known her for a couple of years and always thought of her as a warrior. Last night, just thinking about him turned her into a wounded puppy. It was awful. That man messed with her."

Eliseo remained quiet, but his fists clenched in front of her.

"Do you know about Jason?" Polly asked.

He clenched his fists again and through gritted teeth, asked, "What happened now?"

"Crap. I don't want to be the one to tell you this. I have to believe he has more sense than to make a stupid mistake but he's been suspended for a week for fighting. He beat two kids up this afternoon. That's why Sylvie was gone. She had to go get him."

"That poor woman." Eliseo deliberately unclenched his muscles and leaned back in the chair. "I thought we were handling this."

"I know. She did too."

"I've failed her."

"Oh come on, Eliseo. Jason is capable of making bad decisions all on his own."

"I thought he and I had come to an understanding. We had a really successful weekend."

"And it all fell apart last night when he found out his father was in town. He's fourteen years old and is powerless to protect Sylvie against that man. Of course he did something stupid."

"If you don't mind, I'm going out to the farm to check on them. Jason and I will come back tonight to bring the horses in. He'll probably need to get out of the house, so don't worry about trying to do the work yourself."

"Are you sure? I've done it before." It had been over a year and a half ago since she'd had to do all of the work by herself. It was a little intimidating, but it could be done.

"I'm sure. Thanks for telling me." He was up and out of the chair, then out of the office before Polly could say anything else.

She put her head down on her desk and shut her eyes. This day sucked so far.

"Polly?"

She lifted her head slightly and opened one eye when she heard Rachel's voice in her doorway.

"What's up?"

"I think something's wrong with Sarah. I just took some juice in to her and she looks terrible."

Polly jumped up from the desk and the split second that it took Rachel to move out of the way seemed like an eternity. No. Not now! She bolted out of the office and into the addition to the room Sarah and Rebecca were sharing. She didn't bother to knock, just rushed in and found Sarah Heater lying limply in her bed, barely responsive.

"Sarah? Sarah? Can you hear me?"

"Yes," she said weakly.

Polly dialed 9-1-1 and gave the information to the dispatcher.

"Sarah, we need to take you to the hospital. Something is dreadfully wrong."

"Rebecca," came the response.

"You know I'll take care of her. Don't worry."

Jeff had come into the room and said, "You go upstairs and get Rebecca. I'll wait for the squad."

"Are you sure?"

"Absolutely." He pulled a chair up beside Sarah's bed and took her hand. "You're going to be just fine, right? Now is not the time for you to leave us. Got that?" He turned back and said, "Go ahead, Polly. We'll be right here."

Polly ran back through Sycamore House and up the steps to her home. When she rushed in the front door, she stopped and took a breath before heading into the media room where she could hear Andrew and Rebecca chattering.

What about Andrew? He needed someone to take him to Eliseo's house. They'd completely forgotten about him. Polly had to shut her eyes to think. Too much information was spinning through her mind and she didn't know what to do first.

Which meant that she knew exactly what to do. She pulled the phone out of her pocket and swiped the number of the one person who would help her think straight.

"Hey, sweet thing, what's up?"

Polly slipped back outside her front door and closed it softly, ignoring Obiwan's attempt to follow her. "Henry, I need your help. Every single thing that could fall apart today has fallen apart and now Sarah needs to go to the hospital. The EMTs are on their way and I have to tell Rebecca. Sylvie had to pick Jason up at school because he was in a fight and Eliseo has gone out to his house because that's where she is because her ex-husband showed up here and I need to get Andrew there too. Obiwan needs to be walked and I don't know what to do next."

"Breathe honey. We can do this."

"How? Tell me what to do. My brain is running on high and I can't make it make sense."

"Tell Rebecca about her mom and that you and she are going to Boone. Then, tell Andrew that I'm going to come get him and take him out to Eliseo's house, but first he needs walk the dog. Have Rachel and Jeff keep an eye on him and the place until I get there. After we are both where we're going to be, we'll talk and figure the rest of this out. How does that sound?"

That was all it took. A sane, calm voice in the middle of her panic. "Thank you. That's perfect. I didn't know how to ask you to do this. I know you're busy."

"The day is almost over. I can leave in a few minutes. You can always ask me for help. If I can't do something right away, there is somebody close who can. You're never alone, Polly."

"I know," she said. "I just forget. I love you."

"I love you too. Now go take care of your little girl."

Polly felt much calmer when she opened the door to the apartment again. Now if she could just keep Rebecca from panicking and feeling guilty because she was upstairs rather than sitting by her mother.

"Rebecca?" Polly said, walking into the media room.

"Just a sec," Andrew said without looking up. "We're almost done. I'm going to beat her!" In a second, he dropped the game control and threw his hands up in the air. "I win! I never win!" He jumped up and danced around the table. "I win! I win!"

Sirens cut through his chant.

Rebecca dropped her controller when she saw Polly's face. "Mom!"

Polly put her hand out to stop Rebecca from bolting. "We've called the ambulance for your mother. She's very sick and needs to go to the hospital. But you and I will go down to Boone, too."

"Is she going to die?" Rebecca burst into tears.

Polly didn't know what to say. She felt like she had a relationship with these kids based on truth, and promising that Sarah would be okay seemed like the wrong thing to do.

Andrew sat back down on the sofa, "I'm sorry," he said.

"Here's the deal," Polly said. "Things are really wacky in Sycamore House world today. Jessie is gone and your mom had to pick Jason up from school this afternoon. They're already out at Eliseo's house and as a matter of fact, so is Eliseo. I was going to take you out there later, but now I want to be able to take Rebecca to Boone to spend time with her mother. So I need your help, Andrew."

His entire body had crumpled in on itself, but he looked up. "What?" He looked at Rebecca again. "I'm sorry for beating you and dancing around."

Rebecca paid no attention to him, she just cried where she sat.

"I'm sure she's not upset with you," Polly said. "I need you to take Obiwan out for a walk for me. Rachel and Jeff are downstairs and you have to tell them when you go outside and when you come back in. Got it?"

"Why?" he asked.

"Because otherwise no one will know where you are. Henry is going to come home in a little bit and I want you to be ready to go because he'll take you out to Eliseo's house. Will you do things my way?"

"I can't believe they left me."

Polly chuckled. "I know it feels that way, but honestly, Andrew, today it seems like everybody has a whole lot of stuff going on. You are about the only person who doesn't have some big crisis."

"Did you know my dad is in town? Mom's scared and Jason's mad. I don't even remember what Dad looks like."

"I do know that. It's going to be okay. We just have to figure out how to get through it. Now, will you check in with Rachel and Jeff and take Obiwan out?"

"Sure." He touched Rebecca's arm. "If Polly lets you, will you call me later and tell me about your mom?"

Rebecca nodded and then stood and walked to the front door. She didn't wait for Polly, just walked out and left.

"I'd better follow her," Polly said. "Thanks for everything. You're a really good kid."

Polly trotted off to catch up to Rebecca and did so at the bottom of the steps. Rebecca hesitantly tried to approach the gurney the EMTs were wheeling out and Polly took her hand and led her over to her mother.

"Mom?" Rebecca asked.

"I'll be okay," Sarah said. "I promise. This isn't it."

Whew. At least Polly didn't have to worry about that conversation. Rebecca pulled her hand away, crossed her arms tightly in front of her and nodded to the EMT, dismissing him.

"We'll be right behind you," Polly said.

They watched the back door of the ambulance close and Rebecca turned to head for the addition.

"Don't you want to leave now?" Polly asked.

"Not without her robe and her book." Rebecca was resolute. Gone was the whimpering child who had desperately needed Polly when Sarah had first been diagnosed. This sickness was hardening something in the little girl. Polly hated to see it happen, but tried to understand that she was doing whatever she could to protect herself from the pain that was coming. She waited for Rebecca to return.

"Are you okay? You've had a rough day," Jeff said.

"I don't know. Things are falling apart around me and all I can do is react. Will you keep an eye on Andrew? He's taking Obiwan outside for me and then Henry will take him out to Eliseo's house."

"Sure. No problem. We're living in interesting times, aren't we," he dead-panned.

"No kidding."

Rebecca came back with a small travel bag and her backpack. "I'm ready," she said and continued past them to the kitchen.

"I guess I'm leaving now. Thanks for taking care of things," Polly said, and once again, followed Rebecca.

The ride out of town was silent except for the whoosh of wiper blades on the windshield. Rebecca kept her arms clasped tightly around the bags she carried and didn't say a word.

"Do you want to talk about this?" Polly asked.

"No," came the response.

"Are you angry?"

Rebecca set her jaw and then looked at Polly, her eyes flashing. "Of course I am. My mom is dying and there's nothing I can do about it. I'm supposed to be happy and sweet and go to school and play with my friends and be nice and I can't cry because it upsets her and it freaks you out and ..." She punched the bag. "I'm just a girl. Why is this happening to us?"

"I don't know, sweetie. Those are questions that have no answers." Polly reached across the seat to try to touch Rebecca, but the girl pulled back and scooted closer to the door.

"I know you're going to be my guardian when she dies, but I'd rather have her take care of me." Rebecca realized what she had just said and grimaced. "That's not what I mean."

"I know. It's okay. I'd rather have her take care of you too. And that's not what I mean." Polly gave the girl a little smile. "I think everyone would rather have your mom stick around for a long time, but if that can't happen, what will you do about it?"

"I'm going to be really mad."

"That's a normal place to start. You're going to hurt like crazy when it happens. You're going to ask God to undo it and bring her back. You're going to feel things that you've never felt before. And, Rebecca, I promise you that all of those feelings are okay. No one will be upset with you for having them."

The girl's voice was very small, "Even if I hate you?"

"Why do you hate me, sweetie?"

"Because you made my mom go to the hospital in the first place. If you had never taken me home that day ..." Rebecca dropped her head. "I know," she said.

"I know you do. It's okay to hate me right now. I get it."

"I'm sorry, Polly. I don't really hate you."

"Sweetie, your feelings are going to be all over the place for a while. Here's what I can promise you. No matter what happens, no matter how angry or scared or hateful or freaked out you get, I will still love you. So will your mom. So will Henry and I'm pretty sure, so will Andrew."

"I let him win today," Rebecca said, looking up with a gleam in her eye.

"You what?"

"Don't tell him. He was really scared because of his dad showing up. I've never seen him like that before. He said his mom was crying last night and Jason got mad. I think that Jason scared him more than anything. Jason talked about killing his dad so that he wouldn't hurt anybody again."

"Really?"

"Andrew said Jason was just mouthing off because he was mad, but he's never been like this before."

"Jason's having a rough time right now."

"Because he is in high school?"

"I think that's part of it."

"Andrew said that he's hanging out with bad kids. Jason wanted to be cool and isn't talking to his friends from Bellingwood. It's like Bellingwood kids are stupid or something."

"Growing up is really difficult."

"I know," Rebecca said. "Jason should live my life for a couple of weeks. At least his mom isn't going to die." She huffed out a breath. "That was mean."

Polly turned to drive down Story Street. "It's probably going to take them a little while to check your mom into the hospital. Do you want to get something to eat first?"

"McDonalds?" Rebecca asked with a shy smile.

"Are you sure? We could go to a real restaurant."

"Please?"

"Okay. Fine. You're certainly a cheap date."

"Do you really think Mom is going to be okay?"

Polly could tell Rebecca was starting to relax around her again. She'd put the backpack on the seat beside her and had dropped the overnight bag to the floor.

"I'd guess that your mom knows what is happening in her body better than anyone else. If she tells you that this isn't her time yet, then you should believe her."

"What do you think is wrong? I knew she was getting weaker, but ..."

"I have no idea, but they'll figure it out. Do you want to go inside or eat in the truck?"

"Can we just eat in the truck?"

"Absolutely."

Polly went through the drive-thru and when they had their food, she pulled into a parking place under a tree. She had just unwrapped her sandwich when her phone rang. She was so glad to see that the call was from Henry.

"Hi there, husband of mine," she said. "Rebecca and I are trying to relax a little in the McDonalds parking lot before we go up to see her mom at the hospital. What are you planning to do?"

"Polly, are you parked?" His voice was low and quiet.

"Oh no, what's wrong."

"When I got here, Obiwan was sitting in front of the back door. Andrew is gone."

"You've checked everywhere? Upstairs? The barn?"

"Polly," his tone was measured.

"Of course you have. And Aaron and Ken? Are they there?"

"They're here."

"Have you guys talked to Sylvie?"

"Aaron is taking Lydia out to Eliseo's house."

"She can't take anymore."

"I needed you to hear this from me. Can you deal with what you have to deal with or do you want Jeff to bring me down?"

"I'm empty right now. It's like there's a black hole in my mind."

"You're in the McDonalds parking lot?"

Polly looked around, having completely forgotten where she was. "I think so."

"Don't move. Don't go anywhere. Do you promise?"

"I can't breathe." The sandwich fell out of her hand and on to the floor of the truck.

"Polly?"

"Come get me," she squeaked and started to cry.

CHAPTER TEN

Polly was shaken back to reality by a small, soft voice asking, "What happened?"

She shut her eyes and tried to get her bearings. Andrew had to be okay. God wouldn't do this to Sylvie. He just wouldn't.

"Polly?"

"What?" she responded and then realized that she wasn't alone in the truck. "Oh, I'm sorry, Rebecca. I went away for a moment."

"What happened?"

The little girl had enough to deal with right now. But Polly couldn't lie to her. It would be worse later.

"Andrew's missing."

"What do you mean, missing? He was just at your house."

"I know, but when Henry got there, Obiwan was sitting in front of the back door and Andrew was gone."

"Was he upstairs? Maybe he fell down in the creek. Maybe Obiwan just got away from him?"

"I'm sure they've checked the creek. They've been through the house and the barn."

"Where would he go and why wouldn't he take Obiwan?"

Polly turned in her seat and reached over to take Rebecca's hand. "I don't know where he is. We're afraid that someone has taken him."

The little girl's eyes grew big.

It hadn't been that long ago that she had been the victim of a kidnapping. Why in the world did people think it was appropriate to involve children in their conflicts?

"Someone crazy like that woman who kidnapped me?"

"I hope not, sweetie."

Rebecca pointed to the floor. "You dropped your sandwich."

"I really did, didn't I." Polly bent over and picked it up and then dropped it in the empty sack.

"Do you want some of mine?" Rebecca started to pull her sandwich apart.

"No, no, no. That's fine. I'm really not hungry right now."

"Neither am I." She tucked the wrapper back around the sandwich and dropped it in the sack on top of Polly's. "If you hadn't brought me down here, would Andrew still be safe? Is this my fault?"

"It's no one's fault except for the person who took him."

"It's his dad, isn't it?" Rebecca looked Polly squarely in the eye. "He's a bad man, isn't he?"

"We don't know that for sure."

Rebecca pulled her hands into her lap and sat quietly, then turned back to Polly and said, "I'm going to be strong for you now. You have too many people to worry about. Jessie ran away and Andrew is missing. My mom is going to be okay this time and I'm not going to be mean any more. You can count on me."

"Come here," Polly unbuckled Rebecca's belt, pushed the backpack to the floor and pulled the girl across the seat and into her arms. "I'm so glad you're here with me," Polly sobbed into Rebecca's hair. While they held each other, Polly looked out the front windshield to see sun peeking through the clouds.

Rebecca held on to her for a while and then backed up and said, "This is becoming a thing."

Polly chuckled. "A thing?"

"Yeah. You and me crying in the front seat of your truck in Boone. Is it always going to be like this?"

"Ummm," Polly laughed from her belly. "Oh, Rebecca. You're wonderful. Thank you."

"They're here," Rebecca scooted back across the seat.

"Who?" Polly asked.

"Jeff and Henry." Rebecca touched Polly's shoulder and pointed across her.

Sure enough Jeff's car was parked in the next space and Henry got out, looking very worried. Polly brushed away her tears and gave him a weak grin, then opened the truck door and climbed down into his arms.

"You've had a lot happen in one day," he whispered into her ear. "Mom told me about Jessie. I'm guessing you've risen above it all."

"Until now." She leaned back enough to kiss him. "I'm sorry I'm so sloppy. If you had just given me some time, I would have processed it all and managed."

"I don't know when you're going to figure out that you don't have to manage this all by yourself. I'm here now."

Polly rested her head on his chest and let him hold her.

"I'm so sorry, Polly. Andrew told me he was going outside. I checked the time. He wasn't gone five minutes before Henry came in with Obiwan," Jeff said.

"It isn't your fault, Jeff."

"Rachel and I both feel horrible. We should have gone out with him. I just can't believe this happened."

"Stop it." She gave him a sly grin. "Tell me you didn't unhook the cameras around the building."

"Well, Polly Giller, whatever do you mean? I thought you hated that invasion of privacy."

Polly pulled away from Henry and put her hands on her hips. "Jeff Lyndsay, you are a brat. Did you or did you not get this on video?"

"We did. And Aaron has it. It was Anthony Donovan. He didn't hurt Andrew or anything, just opened his car door and said something to the boy. Andrew sent Obiwan to the back door and got in. Polly, it was in your driveway."

"Of course it was. Where else would it be? At least I know he didn't dump Andrew in the creek."

"Polly," Henry scolded, nodding his head toward Rebecca.

"What? She's the one who thought of it."

Jeff took Polly's arm and drew her aside. "If you want to go back to Bellingwood, I can take Rebecca to the hospital. I'll bring her back later this evening."

Polly glanced into the cab of her truck. Rebecca was watching them intently. "No, that's okay. If Henry doesn't mind spending some time up there with us, we'll stop in and see Sarah, then head back to town. I think I need to be with her right now. Sylvie has Lydia and Eliseo. They'll take care of her."

"Call me if you need anything tonight, then," he said. "Anything. I can be back in Bellingwood in a half hour. And when Andrew is found, call me with that, too."

"I promise." Polly pulled him into a hug. "Do not feel guilty about this. It was going to happen. I'm sorry that it happened on your watch, but it was going to happen."

"Okay. I'll call Rachel and let her know. She's pretty upset."

"Thanks, Jeff. I'll see you in the morning."

Henry held the truck door open so Polly could get back in. She slid into the middle and pulled the lap belt on while he shifted the seat back and turned the truck on. Polly put her arm around Rebecca's shoulder. "How are you doing, sweetie? I know you've waited a long time to get to see your mom."

"That's okay. They're probably running tests and junk." Rebecca craned her neck around Polly. "We don't have to stay too long, Henry."

"We'll stay as long as it takes, Rebecca. Don't you worry." He drove out of the parking lot and headed down the street for the hospital. "You definitely need a new vehicle, Polly."

"I've never sat on the hump before." She looked down at Rebecca. "Why didn't you tell me it was so uncomfortable to sit here?"

"I dunno. Didn't think about it."

"Well you're getting taller - this is not fun. My legs don't fit here, my butt doesn't fit."

Rebecca giggled. "I'm still a little girl."

"Yeah. Whatever. I'm changing things this week."

"What are you going to do with the truck?" Rebecca asked.

"Nothing yet. It was my dad's and I can't get rid of it. But it's not practical any longer. We need comfort."

Henry pulled up in front of the hospital. "I'll be in the main waiting room when you come down. I have some calls to make and work to do. Don't worry about me."

"Thanks, Henry." Polly kissed his cheek. "Thank you for rescuing me and for being patient."

"Both of those things come standard with being married to you," he said, smiling. "Now go, take care of Rebecca and her mom."

They asked questions at the front desk and found that Sarah was still in the emergency room. When they got down there, the receptionist told them that it would be several hours until she would be in a room.

"Can her daughter see her quickly and tell her goodnight? We'll come back tomorrow," Polly asked.

"Let me check."

In a few moments, a nurse came out to get Rebecca. "It will have to be quick. We're doing more tests to see what is wrong with your mother. But, if you want to say hello and give her a hug, let's do that first."

Polly nodded her thanks and sat down to wait. She called Henry.

"Is everything okay?" he asked tentatively.

"Don't get too comfortable. We aren't going to stay long. She's still down here in emergency and it's going to be a while before they put her in a room. Rebecca is telling her good night and then we'll be ready to go home."

"Cool. I'm still in the truck. I'll drive around to the emergency room parking area. Come on out when you're ready."

"How did you know that I needed you to come down?"

"Because I wouldn't want to deal with everything you've faced today by myself. You're an amazing woman, but you should only have to handle so much."

"I thought I was going to be sick when you told me Andrew was gone."

"You know he won't hurt his own son, right?"

"I don't know that. He threatened Jason once and Sylvie said that he got worse after Andrew was born. Who knows what he's thinking?"

"Anthony Donovan is a bully and a jackass, but he's not stupid. He's trying to get Sylvie's attention and if he hurts one of her sons, that will only make things very bad for him."

"I hope you're right."

"Andrew is a smart little boy."

"But he's so danged innocent. He isn't even aware when people are bullying him."

"We'll hope that he treats his dad like he does everyone else and then he'll be just fine."

"He has to be so scared right now."

"Don't borrow trouble, sweet thing. You don't know what's going on."

Polly shuddered. "You're right. I just wanted to let you know where we were. I'll be out soon."

"I love you, Polly."

"I love you too."

Rebecca came through the large white swinging doors. She looked so small with that cavernous space behind her. Polly stood and walked to greet her. Rebecca reached up and took her hand.

"Mom's going to sleep tonight, but they said she'll start getting better tomorrow. She has to start giving herself shots."

"What?" Polly stopped as they were crossing the threshold of the building. "Shots? Why?"

"She has diabetes."

"After all of this, she has diabetes too?"

"That's what she said. But she smiled at me and told me this wouldn't kill her." Rebecca looked up at Polly in all seriousness. "My mom's weird."

"It's a good weird, right?"

"Yeah."

They got back in the truck and Henry asked, "Anything else while we're here?"

"Are you hungry, Rebecca?"

"Not really."

"Me either. Let's just go back to Bellingwood."

Polly took her phone out and typed in a text to Lydia. *"Leaving the hospital. How's our girl? Has Aaron heard anything yet about Andrew?"*

"She's completely finished with victim-Sylvie and is on the warpath. I think Anthony Donovan better run for the hills ... after he drops Andrew off."

"Ask if she needs me tonight."

"She says that everything is fine here and she'll be in tomorrow morning. You're supposed to sleep well."

"Tell her I love her."

"Done. She loves you back. And sweetheart, I love you too. The sun rises tomorrow and we get another chance at it. Remember that."

"Thanks, Lydia. I love you back."

"Okay," Polly announced. "Sylvie is back to normal. That's one stressor off my back."

"Nothing about Andrew?" Henry asked.

"Not yet. But Sylvie is pissed off." Polly glanced down at Rebecca and said, "Oops, sorry."

"Yeah. Because no one has ever said that in front of me before."

"Well, I shouldn't."

"Polly, I have a serious question," Rebecca said.

"Okay, ask away."

"Do I have to go to school tomorrow?"

Polly looked at Henry. He nodded.

"Well, I think you should get a day off. Between your mom in the hospital and your best friend in trouble, it makes sense that you want to stay close. I'll email your teacher when we get home."

They fell silent during the rest of the trip to Bellingwood. When it became uncomfortable, Polly finally spoke up, "I feel like we should be doing something more to find Andrew tonight."

"Me too," Henry said. "But what?"

"Do you know who any of Anthony's old buddies in town were? Maybe they'd know where he is."

"We already went through that list with Aaron. He was going to reach out to them."

"Oh. Okay."

"Everyone is really trying, Polly."

"I know. I just think that I should be too."

Henry turned onto the road leading into Bellingwood. "Let law enforcement do their thing tonight and tomorrow you can stir them up and drive 'em crazy. But first, some supper and a good night's sleep for both of you girls."

"That's Andrew!" Rebecca shouted, pointing to someone walking along the side of the highway.

"What?" With dusk approaching, the figure was still too far away for Polly to see clearly.

"That's his walk. Hurry, Henry."

Henry pulled over just behind Andrew, and Rebecca jumped out of the truck as soon as it stopped, with Polly right behind her.

"Andrew! Are you okay?"

The boy turned around and a big grin split his face. "I knew someone would find me," he said and ran back to them.

Polly caught him up and lifted him in a hug. "We've been so worried about you."

"Oomph," he said. "You're squeezing me. I can't breathe."

"Darn right," she responded and gave another squeeze before putting him down.

"I was just going to walk to Sycamore House. It wasn't very much farther. I'm just glad the rain stopped."

"How long have you been walking?"

"I don't know. He dropped me off at the corner. Maybe fifteen minutes." They'd just turned that corner. It was a two mile walk into Bellingwood and they were right on the edge of town.

"Come back to the truck," Henry said. "You need to call your mom right away. I'll call Aaron."

Andrew climbed into the truck and Polly swiped her phone to Sylvie's number, then handed it to him.

"No Mom, it's me. I'm with Polly," Andrew said.

He waited a moment and gave a sly grin to Polly and Rebecca. "I'm fine. No, I'm not hurt at all. We just talked."

Another moment passed and Polly could hear the sound of Sylvie's voice in the background, but not with enough clarity to distinguish words.

"I'm really fine, Mom. I promise." A few more sounds from Sylvie and Andrew pushed the phone at Polly. "She doesn't believe me and wants to talk to you."

"Hi Sylvie, I think he's fine."

"Are you at Sycamore House?"

"No, we were coming back from the hospital with Rebecca and saw him walking down the highway. Apparently, Anthony dropped him out at the Boone corner."

"What a jackass, making him walk. Was he afraid of being caught?"

"I know, right?"

"Did you hug him?"

"I squeezed him pretty tight."

"Will you bring him out here?"

"We're going to Sycamore House to change vehicles and then we'll be out. He's in good shape, Sylvie."

"You know I won't believe that until I see him. What happened today? I feel like everything is spinning out of control."

"It does feel that way. But you're about to have all of your chicks back in one nest."

"I'm so glad it was you who found him. Polly, what if something awful had happened?"

Polly knew where this could spiral. "Lydia told me earlier that tough Sylvie was back. Don't let her go. We'll be out in just a few minutes." She climbed into the passenger seat beside Rebecca and then pulled the girl onto her lap. They were within two blocks of her driveway. Tomorrow she was getting a new vehicle. This was ridiculous.

Henry stopped in front of the garage and everyone piled out of the truck.

"Can we take Obiwan with us?" Andrew asked. "He didn't get a very long walk."

The two adults looked at each other. "I don't see why not," Polly said.

"I'll get him." Andrew ran inside and Rebecca was close behind him.

"Kids are more resilient than we are," Henry said, shaking his head. "I wonder what happened."

"I want to ask, but his mom should probably hear the story first. What did Aaron say?"

"He's going back out to Eliseo's house and will meet us there."

The kids and dog came rushing out of the back door and Obiwan ran for Polly. She knelt down to hug him. "You're a good boy. Next time, bite the guy's ankle or something, okay?"

"Everyone in," Henry called, opening the back door of his truck.

Polly waited for the kids to belt in, smiled at them chattering at the dog and each other, then climbed into the passenger seat. She pulled her belt on and held her hand out for Henry, winking at him as he squeezed it.

"Do you want to know where we went?" Andrew asked, leaning forward to get Polly's attention.

"It's killing me not to ask, but I think your mom should be the first to hear about your adventure."

"I wasn't scared or anything. I knew right away who he was, but he wouldn't let me put Obiwan inside the house. He told me we didn't have time."

Henry took Polly's hand again. "I was there within a few minutes after you left. Obiwan was sitting at the back door waiting for me."

"I told him to stay. Then I told ..." Andrew didn't know what to say. "Dad, I guess, that it was wrong to not let me put him inside.

He said Obiwan was just a dog." The boy sat back in his seat and looked out the window, then put his hand on Obiwan's back. "He's one of my friends. That made me mad."

"Everything worked out," Polly said. "Obiwan is fine and you're back where you belong."

"Polly says I don't have to go to school tomorrow because of what happened to you and because my mom went to the hospital. Do you think you can get out of school too?" Rebecca asked.

"Can I?" Andrew asked. "Do you think Mom will let me stay home for one day? That would be so cool."

"Let's wait and see," Polly responded. "And Rebecca, if Sylvie says Andrew is going to school, you should go too. Friends stick together. We'll see your mom at the hospital after school."

"I'm going to beg her, Rebecca."

Henry grinned at Polly, then said, "You two know the homework stays the same."

"And we have band tomorrow," Rebecca said. "That's always fun."

"I'm still going to beg her. We never get to take a day off," Andrew announced.

Henry pulled into the driveway. Polly hadn't seen the place since his uncle's death. The yard was cleared of junk and grass was starting to grow again. New siding completely changed the look of the house.

"Wow," she said.

"He's doing a nice job. Dad and Aunt Betty are thrilled. They've cleared all of Grandma's little stuff out, but haven't dealt with all of the furniture."

The front door opened and Sylvie came barreling out, off the porch, and to the truck. Andrew hadn't gotten his seatbelt off when she threw open the door and grabbed him, pulling him out of the truck.

"Mom! I'm caught," he said.

"Too bad," she said, sobbing into his shoulder. "I'll buy you a new jacket."

CHAPTER ELEVEN

Polly wandered through the rooms of her empty apartment, making sure windows were closed and finally went into the bedroom. Henry was already in bed, reading.

"I should be ecstatic we're finally alone," she said.

"But everything feels upside down, doesn't it?" he responded.

"Yeah. Upside down. At least Andrew is home and safe."

Henry drew back the comforter on her side of the bed and she slipped in beside him.

He kissed the top of her head after she snuggled under his arm and laid her head on his chest. "It's been a long day. I'm glad this one is over," he said.

"Me too. That was a lot of chaos for one twelve hour period. I'm sorry I fell apart on you."

"It was nice to know you need me." He put the book on the bedside table and wrapped his arms around her. "You manage your life pretty well."

"It's funny. The only reason I do is that I know you've got my back. All the time." Her muscles relaxed as he rubbed her back. "Sylvie is terrified of coming in to work tomorrow."

"You know she's going to have to face this guy sooner or later. If it were you, what would you want to do?"

Polly looked up and grinned, "Make you do it."

"That's funny. Not even I believe that. You confront things and people all the time, just so it doesn't haunt your dreams."

"I suppose. He made me nervous today. He's a scary man."

"At least none of you will be alone here tomorrow if he shows up again."

"Yeah." Polly shut her eyes. She was much more comfortable with bad things happening to her rather than Sylvie. This was just not the time for that poor woman to have to deal with one more problem. Sylvie had practically carried Andrew inside and refused to let him out of her sight. Polly wasn't sure that the poor boy would be allowed to sleep tonight without his mother in the room.

Anthony Donovan had picked his son up at Sycamore House and driven straight to Boone. He'd not threatened or harmed Andrew in any way, just asked questions about his life and school, his friends and his brother and mother. He asked where they were staying; knowing they weren't in the apartment. But Andrew had kept his wits and knew that this man scared his mother. If she didn't want him to know where they were living, he wasn't about to tell him.

Andrew had been quite proud of himself ... for playing dumb. Since Anthony had never really known his son, Andrew figured he could get away with acting like a much younger child. He told the man that he didn't know how to get where they were going and said they were staying with a friend, never identifying Eliseo.

Polly couldn't have been more proud of the boy. Sylvie just clung to him, alternating between sobbing and sniffling.

When Sheriff Merritt arrived, he asked specific questions about Anthony and the little trip they'd taken. Andrew pointed out that he knew who Anthony was when he got in the car and that he'd done so, with assurances he'd be returned to Sycamore House. It hadn't felt like a kidnapping, but Aaron nodded at Sylvie. If need be, they'd make those charges stick.

Lydia had bustled around the house, raiding Eliseo's kitchen. While Andrew told his story and Sylvie held onto her son, she prepared a feast, serving mashed potatoes and gravy, roasted vegetables and oven-baked chicken. Polly didn't know how the woman pulled off the things she did, feeding nine people with as much ease as Polly served two or three.

Jason and Eliseo left in the middle of the Sheriff's interview to bring the animals in and close up the barn, returning in time for dinner. Jason was sullen throughout the evening and Polly knew Sylvie was at a loss as to how to deal with the kid.

Now that Polly had met his father, she realized how much Jason looked like him. His hair was dark and thick. One of these days poor Sylvie was going to have to discuss the unibrow that was going to always be a problem. He had the same square jaw and thin lips; his hands were going to be big and strong. While she'd thought that his shoulders were filling out because of the hard work he was doing with Eliseo, she realized that some of that girth was genetic. Jason's torso was thick and tall; his height not just from his legs. He could be a football player or maybe a wrestler. Once he gained some self-confidence, girls would always be attracted to his dark features.

Andrew had the same lips and his eyes were similar to his father's, but the rest of his features came from Sylvie. There might be a chance that his body's build would be similar to Anthony's, but he had long, slender fingers like his mother and his legs were long and lean. He would soon catch up to his brother's height and his sandy brown hair showed no sign of darkening.

After dinner, Polly insisted on cleaning the kitchen. Lydia tried to help, but Polly pushed the older woman back into the living room, telling her that old ladies needed to rest after a long day's work. Lydia had swatted Polly's behind, but grinned and tossed the towel at her.

Eliseo came out to help and Polly tried to send him away too, but he'd insisted.

"How is it, having all of this drama in your home?" Polly asked.

"I feel so badly for Sylvie," he responded. "She works hard to make a good life for herself and her boys and doesn't deserve any of this."

"I still wish we knew why Anthony was in town."

"Maybe it's as simple as seeing his boys. You never know."

Polly dropped a handful of silverware in the dish strainer and looked up at him. "Do you really believe that?"

Eliseo's eyes grew dark and menacing. "I hope so, because if he tries to hurt Sylvie or those boys, his life won't be worth much."

"You really like her, don't you?" Polly asked, trying to lighten the mood.

"She's a wonderful woman. No man deserves someone like that if he can't find a way to tell her every single day how terrific she is."

"There aren't a lot of men out there who know how to do that."

"No ma'am, there aren't. But that's what she deserves. I'm proud of her. She took a dream and made it come true." He pushed the silverware drawer shut with extra force and chuckled. "Sorry. I will stop anyone from taking that away from her."

"Have you told her how much you care for her, Eliseo?" Polly asked quietly, turning to look him in the eyes.

Shock passed across his face quickly and then he gave her a slight smile, his eyes twinkling. "You don't miss much, do you?"

"Does she know?"

"No she doesn't, and you aren't going to say anything."

"I won't, but you should."

"She's not ready, especially not right now. Her oldest boy is giving her fits, her youngest nearly scared her to insanity and she has an ex-husband who has a hold over her psyche like nothing I've ever seen. Sylvie doesn't frighten easily and that man takes away all of her confidence."

"I met him today, Eliseo and he scared me witless. There is something about him that is terrifying. Rachel felt it too. I don't think it's just because we know what he did to her, it's his presence."

"A truly strong man doesn't frighten or intimidate people to get his way. Look at the Sheriff. He carries a gun, but you don't see him lose control or get mean. People in this county think the world of him and that's how he gets things done around here."

"That kind of describes you."

"I just take care of the animals. But, you're right. Of course, they will respond to intimidation and fear, but it won't ever be a healthy response and before you know it, you have animals that won't do anything that's asked of them."

"That's how you're dealing with Jason."

Eliseo shook his head. "That boy is going to take some work. If all of this hadn't happened with Andrew today, I would certainly have asked permission to paddle his behind."

Polly chuckled. "Oh, that would have been so humiliating for him. And it probably would have worked."

"Well, I haven't completely taken it off the table."

"Has he told you or Sylvie yet what caused the fight?"

"He won't talk about it. Says it's better that we don't know. But again, there wasn't enough time to really get into it with him, what with Andrew being taken. Once Sylvie heard that, she forgot everything else."

"Has he said anything about Anthony?"

"No. Last night he was pretty shook up. I asked him tonight if that was why he'd gotten into a fight at school and he said it wasn't. I don't know whether to believe him or not, but it can't have helped."

"As long as I've known him," Polly said, "he's worried about protecting his mother. Now that he's face to face with the reality of his father in town, it's probably scaring him."

"I want to tell him that we will protect him and his mother, but that's not what he wants to hear. He wants to feel confident that he can do that and that there is nothing Anthony can do to harm her."

"I can't imagine feeling so helpless." She thought about it and then said, "Well, yes I can, but I lived through it and he will too. He just doesn't know that yet."

"I guess it's hard to be a kid and not have the capacity to look back over years of living and know that things will work out. For him, right now is the worst thing he's ever faced and he has no idea that the sun will rise tomorrow and life will continue to move on until trouble passes."

Polly wiped the last counter down and tossed the wet dishcloth to Eliseo. "Don't wait too long to tell Sylvie how you feel. She needs to know that a good man can love her, not just that horrible monster who is frightening her family."

"That's easier said than done," Eliseo responded.

"Say it and do it," Polly said. "You're worth it and so is she."

She had walked out of the kitchen before he could protest anymore and cornered Aaron as he was trying to leave. "Do you know anything more about that body we found at the Willard farm on Saturday?"

"I know that Mrs. Willard has a new respect for you. She talked about hiring you out to all of the farmers in the area, checking their barns for bodies."

"She did not. You stop that," Polly said, swatting his arm. "Seriously. Have you found out anything yet?"

"We're pretty sure he was killed the same night as Henry's Uncle Loren, which is why Mrs. Willard didn't hear it happen. She was in her basement and said she had the radio on. Then she fell asleep. Her husband made her fix up a room for one of their farmhands years ago and then it was their storm shelter. It's tucked way into the dirt, so she wouldn't have heard the shot. And she hasn't been in that barn since old Daryl died. Her boy wants to pull it down, says it's a danger. That's why she's getting rid of the cars."

"I can't believe she didn't notice the smell or think anything was strange out there. Animals didn't bother it. Nothing," Polly said. "Do you know who it was yet?"

"No. We're looking through missing persons. It's no one from around here, unless there's a wife out there who finally killed her husband and just hasn't told anyone he's gone missing."

"Has that ever happened?" Polly asked, aghast.

"Not here. Well, not that I know of," he chuckled. "But it would be a good story. Can't you just imagine some poor woman finally getting fed up with her jerk of a husband, decking him with a cast iron pan, dragging him to the basement and burying him?"

"You're horrible!" she said.

"I am. All in a day's work." Aaron turned to where his wife was sitting on the sofa with Sylvie and Andrew. "Come on Lydia, it's time to let these people finish their day. You need to take me home and tuck me in."

Lydia smiled seductively at him and walked over to take his arm. She whispered to Polly, "You know what 'tuck me in' means, don't you?"

"Get out of here, both of you," Polly said. "I'm never going to be able to un-hear what you just said."

Aaron shook his head and drew his wife to the front door. "If you need me for anything else, Sylvie, do not hesitate to call. No matter what time, day or night. Promise?"

Sylvie touched Andrew's shoulder, then joined them at the front door. "I promise. Thank you for everything."

Lydia hugged her and said, "Call me even if all you need to do is cry or talk. You're going to be fine and this will end."

"I know," Sylvie said. "I just wish it were finished now instead of beginning, though."

"We should probably go too," Polly said. "What are you planning to do with Andrew and school tomorrow? Rebecca's plans are going to be based on yours."

Sylvie looked back at the two kids on the sofa. "I think he can have the day off and it sounds like Rebecca could use some downtime, too. What if she stayed out here with us tonight? She'll be perfectly safe and both of them will be good for each other. Friends and distractions always help when things feel like they're falling apart."

"Why not?" Polly asked.

"She's tall enough to fit into a pair of my sweats and a t-shirt tonight and we'll have her back to Sycamore House in the morning."

Rebecca and Andrew jumped at the opportunity to spend the night at Eliseo's. Jason made a point of dramatically rolling his eyes at their glee, but settled back and watched as they took paper and colored pencils out and began drawing at the coffee table.

"We'll take good care of her," Eliseo said, joining Sylvie at the front door. He and Henry shook hands and Polly reached out to hug Sylvie to her.

"It really is going to be fine," Polly said.

"I know."

Henry stepped out onto the porch. "You've done good work out here, Eliseo. It's going to be nice to see this place transformed into your home. It spent too many years as a dump. I thought the memories would make it difficult for me to see it change, but this is really good. I hope you enjoy it for a long time."

Polly didn't say anything as she watched Eliseo touch Sylvie's back. "It has good bones. It will make a good home."

Henry was on his way to the truck with Obiwan when Jason slipped past his mom. "I need to ask Polly something, okay, mom?"

"Sure, honey," Sylvie said, giving Polly a questioning look. But she stepped back inside as he closed the door on her.

"What's up, Jason?" Polly asked, waving at Henry to wait.

"Can we talk tomorrow?" he asked.

"Sure, what about?"

"I just need to talk to you."

"Something you can't tell your mom or Eliseo?"

He took a deep, long breath and his face crumpled. "Don't tell her I want to talk to you."

"She's going to know. You're out here right now."

Jason dropped his head. "You're the only person who gets it."

"Of course we can talk tomorrow," Polly said, reaching out to touch him. "I didn't mean to imply otherwise. Is it about what's going on at school?"

"Yeah." He didn't lift his head. "I screwed up. I know that, but I want someone to know why I did it."

"Tell me what you want to do. Your mom will be around at Sycamore House, the kids will be upstairs and Eliseo will be down at the barn."

"Maybe we could go to lunch?" he asked, bringing his head up to look at her.

"Jason, that sounds wonderful. I don't think you and I have ever done that together."

"Thanks, Polly. I know I'm in trouble and I'm going to deal with that. I just need you to know."

"We'll talk tomorrow."

His face lit up with a smile. "Thank you! I don't want you to be angry at me."

"It's going to work out, Jason. Just wait and see."

He turned around and ran back inside, standing at the door to watch as she got in Henry's truck, then shut the door.

"What was that about?" Henry asked.

"He wants to tell me why he got in the fight at school. This is going to make Sylvie crazy."

They had barely gotten onto the main road into town when Polly's phone buzzed with a text.

"Is everything okay with Jason?" Sylvie asked.

"Do I tell her?" Polly asked Henry.

"Yes. She's his mom. She needs to know something."

"He wants to tell me something. Can we talk about this in the morning?"

"I'm glad he has you. I love you, Polly. Don't worry. I just wanted to make sure he was okay. If he's not, will you help him talk to me?"

"I love you too, Sylvie. I'll do what I can to make this all be fine."

"Thanks so much for everything today."

"Good night."

When she and Henry got home, they took Obiwan for a short walk and then went upstairs. She needed to email Rebecca's teacher, so she did that while Henry got settled into bed.

"Polly?" Henry said, shifting his body out from under hers.

"Hmmmm?" Polly snuggled in closer to him as he slid down in the bed, pulling the blankets over the top of them.

"I love you, sweet thing."

"Love you too. G'nite."

He wrapped himself around her. "Goodnight.

CHAPTER TWELVE

Restful sleep was a thing of the past. Polly came fully awake and felt a clench in her gut. Today had the potential to be disastrous. If ... no, when ... Anthony Donovan showed up, Sylvie and her boys had to face that problem. And more than likely it was going to happen right here in Sycamore House. That just made her feel sick. Lunch with Jason was an unknown as well. There was every probability it was nothing. Jason had a tendency to make things bigger in his mind than they really were, but there was something going on with him and he asked her to be part of it.

It would be easy to say that all of this bad behavior of his was out of character, but it really wasn't. He'd been more difficult to get along with all summer. He was sullen with his mother, belligerent with his brother and pretty much just ignored everyone else. The only person who had really maintained any sound contact with the boy was Eliseo. Thank goodness for him.

Now that Sylvie was finished with school and back in Bellingwood, she had expected to regain some control of her family. Andrew was no big deal. That kid was so easygoing. He didn't get angry at his older brother when Jason acted out, he just shrugged it off. He was Rebecca's true north. No matter what was happening with her mother, Andrew just let it flow over him. He kept her distracted when she needed it and knew enough to step away and let Polly handle Rebecca's emotional needs when those came up.

She took her phone off the table and swiped it open to check the time. It was still early, so she put it back and smiled to herself. Andrew was a lot like Henry. He just did what he needed to do and had a good time with the rest of his life.

"You're doing it again," Henry whispered.

"What?"

"Thinking loudly. I can practically hear the wheels in your brain turning."

Polly turned over to face him. "I'm worried about Anthony Donovan showing up here today."

"He isn't going to hurt Sylvie in front of everyone."

"Even if he doesn't physically hurt her, he can do a lot of damage. Henry, I've never seen her like she was Sunday night. Sylvie doesn't let fear control her life and he triggered all of her fears. She faces down the toughest, bitchiest wedding moms while stirring up a light soufflé and when she's finished, both turn out perfectly. But this man is really frightening."

"Do you want me here today?"

Polly thought about it. She really did. Everything was better when Henry was around, but that was ridiculous. It wasn't like she had any work that he needed to do and he had plenty of job sites to deal with.

"No. That's okay. We'll be fine. Jeff will be here, Eliseo is just down at the barn and you're right. He isn't going to do anything to her in public."

"I'm in town this week. You know it will take less than five or ten minutes for me to get here. Just call if you need me, promise?"

"I'd probably call Aaron first. If anyone is going to wrangle Sylvie's ex into submission it will be him. He's done it before."

"Then call me after that happens. I'll be here with a huge crew of men, if necessary." He chuckled. "There isn't a one of them who wouldn't enjoy a good opportunity to manhandle a jerk to the ground."

"You're pretty wonderful." Polly slid her leg between his and nestled her head into his shoulder.

Henry pushed her hair away from her face and wrapping the palm of his hand around the back of her neck, pulled her closer to kiss her. "Wonderful enough to be late to the barn and maybe even skip breakfast?"

"I'm not going to the barn this morning and who cares about breakfast," she said.

~~~

Polly was in her office when she looked up and saw Beryl, Andy and Lydia come in the front door. They waved at her through the window and pranced in. Beryl was carrying an easel and an immense tote bag, Andy had her office supplies on wheels and Lydia had a basket covered with pretty kitchen towels. She snagged a chair from the outer office and the three of them descended on Polly.

"What are you three doing here?" Polly asked. "You look as if you're moving in."

"We are," Lydia announced. "At least for today."

"Why?"

Beryl leaned forward. "If our Sylvie is worried about facing a jerk of an ex-husband, we're going to be the gauntlet he has to go through to get to her. And she can't tell us to go away. We have things to do."

Polly let out a chuckle. "You do! What kind of things are you doing around here today?"

Jeff came in from his office. "Oh good, you're here. Andy, let me show you what I need and you can use Sarah's desk while she's in the hospital."

"I have muffins," Lydia said, pulling back a towel.

He moaned and took the proffered napkin and a muffin. "You're killing me."
~~~

"Who planned this?" Polly asked.

Jeff grinned at her. "Lydia texted me last night and asked if I had work for them to do here. I always have things for people to do."

"I love you," Polly said. "What are you painting today, Beryl?"

"I'm not sure yet. Something will come up. I'm going to sit right there in that hallway and dare anyone to threaten our Sylvie girl."

"Does she know you all are here today?"

Andy grinned, "What do you think?"

"Okay, got it. Have I told you that I love you?"

"Let's get to work, girls. We have things to do. And thank you Jeff, for letting me host the women's group in the auditorium today," Lydia said.

"You're what?" Polly gasped. "When did this happen?"

"Oh, it's been on the calendar for weeks. They are putting new carpet in at church this week. I've been dying to bring them here and this was the perfect opportunity."

"What are they going to say about Beryl sitting in the middle of all of the activity?"

"Hmm," Beryl mused. "Maybe I'll imagine Sylvie as a nude. I can put clothes on her this afternoon."

"You wouldn't."

"Damn straight I would if it were anybody but our Sylvie." She reached into the tote and pulled out a stack of canvas panels. "But I could do a random nude just for their entertainment." Beryl grinned evilly up at Lydia.

Lydia shrugged, "It's fine with me. They all think you're going to hell anyway. It might just garner you some extra prayers during the meeting."

Sylvie, Andrew and Rebecca came in the front door. She took one look at the crowd in Polly's office and gave them a weak smile, then came around the corner to the office.

"What are you three doing here today?" she asked.

"We're working," Lydia said. "It's going to be a busy day at Sycamore House. Now don't you have some food to start cooking? I have a group of ladies coming in today who can't wait to taste food by the new chef in town." She held the basket up to Sylvie. "Muffin?"

"I don't know what to say. Are you here to protect me?"

"We're here to work. If protection is part of our racket, then that's what we'll do," Beryl announced. Then she laughed and pointed at Sal and Joss coming in the front door, both of them carrying a baby in its car seat.

"Are all of you here because of me?" Sylvie asked, her eyes filling with tears.

"Well, this is quite the crowd," Sal announced as she poked her head in the office.

"What's your excuse for being here?" Polly asked.

"The internet isn't working at home and I need to do some writing. I thought maybe I could use the conference room," Sal said and glanced around at everyone. "Will you buy that?"

Sylvie hugged her and turned to Joss. "And what are you doing here?"

"We were bored at home. I just don't get enough adult interaction, so I thought maybe I could find some friends here who would like to spend time with me and the babies."

"See," Lydia said. "Now we all have plenty to do. There are babies in the house." She turned back to Polly. "Do you still have that portable crib?"

"It's in the basement," Polly said. "I'll go get it. Where do you want me to set it up?" She stood from her desk and waited while the rest of the women made their way out into the main hallway.

"Why don't I get one of those big fluffy blankets and we can put it on the floor right here in the middle of everything," Lydia said. "That way they'll be surrounded by friends and their mama can relax in one of the comfortable sofas in the lounge.

Jeff stood up a little taller, then put his hands out in front of him. "Come on, ladies. We're a team. Give me a little love here."

One by one, they caught on to what he was asking for and put their hands in on top of each other.

"Who's the team that can't be beat?" he chanted.

Everyone stared at him. Beryl finally said, "That's lame."

"Fine," he laughed and then said, "Let's go!"

They left the office, all laughing. Polly went to the basement and returned with the portable crib, setting it up just at the edge of the large opening to the lounge across the hallway from the office.

"Where did Andrew and Rebecca go?" she asked, hoping someone would answer her.

"They went upstairs," Joss said. "When the office was filling up with women, Andrew took her by the arm and dragged her out."

"I should talk to Rebecca. But first, I'll call the hospital to make sure her mom is doing okay."

Lydia waved Polly away. "You do whatever you need to do. If I had known Cooper and Sophie were planning to be here today I might even have canceled the women's meeting." She unbuckled Cooper and took him up in her arms. "You are a beautiful little boy. All of those dark curls and those beautiful cheekbones. Joss, do you know what their heritage is? I don't know that I ever asked."

"They are such an amalgam of America," Joss said. "Their mother's parents are Asian and American Indian and the father's dad is African American and I think his mother is Irish. It's like these kids represent the best of all of us."

"They're both gorgeous," Lydia said, stroking Cooper's hair. "You are so lucky. Are they sleeping?"

Joss blinked at her, "Uh huh. Just not all night long. It's getting better, but I've just decided that I'll sleep when they go to school."

Lydia chuckled. "It will get better soon, I promise. And then it will get bad again and then it will get better."

"I'm trusting you on that."

"You just tell me when you want me to come over and take care of these beautiful little babies so you can take a nap. I want them to get to know their Aunt Lydia very well."

"I'll do that," Joss said, holding Sophia. She dropped down into an overstuffed chair and sighed. "This is nice. I'm not moving."

The little girl wriggled to get out of her arms, reaching for her brother. "Oh no you don't," Joss said. "I've got you now." She snuggled her face into Sophia's neck and gave her a raspberry, causing the child to giggle.

Polly shook her head and walked away and into her office. Babies were a lot of work. Oh please, dear God in heaven above, never let it happen to her. She sat down and dialed the Boone hospital, asking for the nurse's station on Sarah Heater's floor. This had to be good news. No one here needed any more bad news. The nurse she spoke with assured Polly that Sarah was stabilizing, but that it was going to take quite some time for them to get her healthy enough to return home. Her blood sugar was all over the place right now and until they got that normalized, she was going nowhere. It was too dangerous.

The worst part was that they had to stop chemotherapy while they were doing this. Once they got things evened out, they could re-start chemo, so Polly wasn't to worry. And yes, Rebecca was welcome to come down and see her any time.

Worry, hah. Now to figure out how to tell Rebecca what was going on. She took a deep breath and headed out. Everyone really was working quietly. Andy was sorting through filing cabinets, Sal was typing away in the conference room, Lydia and Joss were chattering over the babies and Beryl had planted herself right in the middle of everything, her canvas on an easel and a palette in her hand.

"You're really doing this, aren't you?" Polly asked.

"I am, but I chose a different subject," Beryl whispered. "Tell me there isn't anything more beautiful here today than that young mother and her babies."

"You are such an old softie."

"Shhh, don't tell anyone. It's a secret."

Polly ran up the steps to her apartment and opened the door to the sounds of squealing tires and laughter. She missed having the kids around all day when they were back in school. She gave herself a small chuckle. Babies weren't anything she was interested in, but kids? That was a different story. She loved them.

"Hey," she said when she went into the media room.

"Shhh," Andrew replied, not taking his eyes off the screen.

Then he threw his hands up in the air, dropping the controller. "She always wins."

"Rebecca, I called the hospital," Polly started.

Rebecca jumped off the sofa, "Is she okay. Can we go see her?"

"She's okay and yes, we'll see her today. I think she'll be in the hospital for a while so they can get her stabilized. Her blood sugar is all out of whack and that's what was making her so sick."

The girl dropped back down on the sofa. "Thank you. I was so worried." She looked back and forth from Polly to Andrew, then exhaled loudly. "I don't want her to die."

Andrew looked at Polly in panic and she smiled back at him, then said. "I know you don't, sweetie. This isn't her time yet. It may take some time before she comes home, but when she does we'll make sure she is in good hands."

"Sometimes she cries at night. I know she thinks I'm asleep and can't hear her. She's really quiet. Do you think she's scared?"

Polly knelt down in front of Rebecca and took her hands. "I think she's scared. Wouldn't you be if you were her?"

"I'm scared and I'm me," Rebecca said.

"This is an awful lot for the two of you to handle, but you know what? You have each other. Do you tell her when you're scared?"

Rebecca looked at her in shock. "No. I don't want her to worry about me."

"I can almost promise that she wants you to talk to her. Your mama loves you very much and would rather hold you while you cry than think about you crying all alone."

"Should I go hold her when she cries?"

"Oh honey, of course you should. If she isn't hurting physically, you should crawl right up in bed with her if that's what you want. Didn't you used to do that when you had a bad dream?"

"She always told me that the purple pillow was mine and I could either put it on my bed or on hers. It was the traveling pillow."

"Where is that pillow now?"

"I got too old for that. We got rid of it when we moved to Bellingwood."

"Why don't we look for a purple pillow," Polly said. "I think the two of you need to have another one of those in your lives right now. What do you think about that?"

"There are fuzzy purple pillows at the Dollar Store," Andrew said quietly.

"Seriously?" Polly chuckled. "How do you know that?"

"I dunno. I just saw it there. They have these square pillows in lots of colors."

"We'll get one of those before your mom comes home."

Andrew took a deep breath. "I have one."

Rebecca looked at him, her eyes scrunched up in disbelief. "Why do you have a purple pillow?"

"I was going to give it to you for Christmas. Mom said you'd like it, so I bought it. She told me that we were Christmas shopping early this year because we had so many more people in our lives. It used to just be us. And now there are a lot of people."

Polly thought she was going to fall apart right there, but she rocked back on her heels and stood up. "You're a wonderful kid, Andrew." She bent over and hugged him tight.

"Mrumph," he said.

"What?"

"Can't breathe."

"Yeah. Whatever. You just don't like being hugged."

Rebecca was still staring at her friend. "You bought me a purple pillow?"

"It's no big deal. It's just ... it's no big deal."

"You two start another game and Rebecca, you be nice to him. Let him win once in a while or something," Polly pointed at the screen.

"She can't let me win. It's not fair," Andrew protested. "I want to beat her fair and square."

Polly headed for the front door, then turned around. "I'll be back for Obiwan later. You don't have to worry about taking him outside today."

"You're just worried that my dad will show up and take me away again. He's not going to do that, you know," Andrew said.

"Why's that?"

"Because he already talked to me."

"Why do you think he's here, Andrew?" Polly asked.

"Everybody asked me that last night. I don't know. He said he wanted to meet me and that he had to talk to Mom and Jason. Do you think he's going to apologize for beating them up?"

"Beating them up?"

"Yeah. Jason told me a long time ago that he got hit once. I'm glad he didn't hit me."

"I'm glad too. Well, anyway, I'm still going to take Obiwan out. Did you get the classwork you're missing out on?"

"Mom's going to the school to get it. She said we have to work all afternoon, but we could play this morning."

"Okay. We'll go to Boone after you're finished with your work, Rebecca."

The girl nodded at her, scrolling through the game screen for the next match.

"I love you two," Polly said and left the apartment.

CHAPTER THIRTEEN

Once she said checked on her friends who were scattered through the building, Polly went into the kitchen where Sylvie and Rachel were working.

"Good morning again," she said.

"Hi Polly." Rachel smiled at her while mixing something at the prep table.

"Sylvie, do you want me to go over to the school and pick up books and homework for the kids?" Polly asked, craning her neck to see Sylvie. The woman was under one of the counters, twisted into a pretzel. "What are you doing?"

"She dropped a spatula and then kicked it. It went flying," Rachel said.

"Hush you," Sylvie said, crawling back out and brushing herself off. "Don't be telling the boss that I'm a klutz." She straightened her hair and stood up. "That would be great. Mrs. Hastings said she'd have it ready after ten o'clock."

"I was a little afraid to leave this place when I woke up this morning, but it looks like you are in safe hands around here."

"It's the most ridiculous thing I've ever seen," Sylvie said, laughing. "Can you imagine that five people have enough free time in their lives to disrupt themselves and come hang out here so that I don't have to worry about my idiot ex-husband?"

Polly nodded. "That first year I was here, I was always so surprised that they could just uproot themselves at a moment's notice for me. Who does that?"

"You do that," Sylvie chided her. "All the time."

Polly pursed her lips, then said, "Duh. Exactly. And so do you. They're all doing what they would normally be doing, they're just doing it here and with friends. Beryl found two new subjects for a painting, Joss has extra help with the babies, Sal can write anywhere and Andy is helping Jeff organize files. Lydia? Well, she's at home wherever her friends have taken root."

"Did I hear my name?" Lydia asked, coming into the kitchen, carrying Sophia. "Little Miss Cutie-Pie needs a long walk. She was getting fussy and her mama fell asleep on the couch with her baby boy in her arms. Can you imagine sleeping here? That poor woman must be exhausted." She turned to Polly. "Whatever happened with her babysitter, the young girl you have staying here? Joss said that she was gone."

"I don't know," Polly said, shaking her head. "How do you get a girl to figure out what the right thing to do is? I'm not her mother and she's an adult. But the poor, stupid girl is going to mess her life up if she doesn't figure this out."

"If she comes back are you kicking her out?" Rachel asked.

"I don't know. It seems like the wrong message. How many chances did we have to screw up? Over and over and over again and our parents punished us and then let us learn our lesson and move on. But I don't know how many times I let her get away with being an idiot. I thought we had everything figured out after the incident on Saturday, but I guess bad boys carry more weight with her than good sense."

"What does Henry say?" Lydia asked, bouncing the baby in her arms.

"We really haven't talked about this one much, what with everything else falling apart yesterday. His mother told me to be patient, that sometimes we need more than one extra chance in life."

"She's a wise woman. It's all going to work out just the way it's supposed to. Now will someone explain why little ones always fight so hard to go to sleep? This little girl is so tired, but it's the last thing she wants to do. I'm going to keep walking. You girls take care." Lydia left the kitchen, cooing and talking to the baby.

"Does this town know how lucky it is to have her in it?" Sylvie asked.

"They can't possibly." Polly turned for the door. "I'll be in my office if you need anything. And by the way? I really like having both of you here during the day. This place is a lot more fun."

She'd barely settled back at her desk when Aaron Merritt dropped into a chair across from her.

"This is Grand Central Station today," she said. "Are you here to keep an eye on Sylvie, too?"

Aaron grinned across at her. "No, I think the girls have that well in hand. And you have a couple of extras here, too."

"Can you even believe it? I think they're all a little nuts, but if a group of Sylvie's friends can't intimidate big, scary Anthony Donovan, I don't know who can." She smiled. "Unless, of course, it's you with a gun."

"We'll hope it doesn't get to that."

"What can I do for you, then?"

"I know that Henry's on-site somewhere and I've already talked to Betty and Bill, but I thought I'd let you know that the fellow you found on Saturday out at Mrs. Willard's place has been identified."

"Wow, that was fast. How did you do that?"

"A little more digging and some legwork. He's from Fort Dodge. Name's Jim Todd."

"Who is he?"

"Just some guy as far as we know. An old guy, about Loren's age. No relatives here in Iowa. He worked for the railroad and just stayed out here. We've contacted his family. They're all in Illinois. Say they wouldn't have started worrying until Thanksgiving when he was supposed to show up for dinner. They see him once or twice a year. No kids, wife died about five years ago."

"I can't imagine not having people wonder where I was every day," Polly said.

"It's surprising the number of people who don't have a big network. It's harder to get away with that in a little town like Bellingwood, but there are a good number of folks who don't have any family except maybe their wife or husband. And then there are all of those people who just don't like their families much."

"Again, that seems so alien to me. There's no one they talk to every other day or so?"

"I know. Ken Wallers and I try to keep an eye on people, but it's not easy. Too many slip through the cracks."

"Do any of these people ever use the senior center?" she asked.

"Would you when you get to be that age?"

"Well, probably not, but ..."

"There are plenty of folks who do and it's great for them, but there are still too many who won't admit they need those services or even admit they need companionship."

"Okay, is there anything I can do?"

"No. Not really."

"So you just came over to tell me this so Henry would know?"

Aaron glanced around. "Maybe I came by to check on things and make sure that somebody saw my vehicle out front."

"So I should expect to see Ken later on today, too? Or maybe Stu will be stopping by for coffee?"

He chuckled and stood up, heading for the door. "You caught us. We have plenty of other places to be today, but we'll be driving through every once in a while. You call us if you need anything. And tell your posse to do the same."

"I promise."

Polly checked the time. It was a little after ten o'clock. She had enough extra energy that a quick trip to the elementary school might help burn some of it off.

"I'll be back in a while," she said, poking her head into Jeff's office.

"Okay. Your friends are all cool?"

"I think they can take care of themselves. What are you working on?"

"Pulling things together for a Chamber of Commerce meeting this afternoon."

"Need anything from me?"

Jeff looked up at her and laughed, "Who do you think you're talking to?"

"Well, I thought I'd ask. Good heavens, I would never be able to do everything you're doing."

"I know that and so does everyone else around here. I'm just glad that you're aware."

"Always. Thank you."

She poked her head into the conference room and Sal barely looked up at her, typing like mad. A quick wave to Andy and she headed for the side door. Joss was still sound asleep with Cooper on her shoulder and Beryl was quietly painting the scene. Lydia had put Sophie down to sleep. Polly thought that there couldn't be anything more beautiful happening in her home right now.

There was so much happening today, she hoped to steal Jason and maybe take this time to talk to him. Lunch promised to be a carnival ride with everyone at Sycamore House and he deserved whatever peace and quiet she could offer for the conversation.

"Good morning, Polly," Eliseo said as she walked in the barn. "How are things up at the main house?"

"Main house," she laughed. "It sounds like I have a plantation here."

"Pretty close, but no cotton or tobacco fields, so ... "

"Is Jason around? He said he needed to talk to me. I have to go over to the elementary school to pick up work for Andrew and Rebecca and wondered if he wanted to take a ride."

"He's back in the feed room working on his own homework. I'm sure he'd like a break." Eliseo turned his head and yelled, "Jason, you've been rescued. Come on out."

"What's up, Eliseo?" Jason asked, coming into the alley. "Oh hi, Polly. It's not lunchtime yet, is it?"

"No. I have to run an errand. Lunch is going to be crazy busy and I thought maybe we could go now."

He looked up to Eliseo. "Is it really okay?"

Eliseo nodded. "You can finish your homework later. You and I are heading out to the house after lunch to work on the siding, but there will be plenty of time for all of it."

"Thanks," he said.

Polly put her hand on Jason's back as they walked out of the barn. "I'm going to pick up homework for Andrew and Rebecca and then I thought we might go to Boone and look at cars. I want to be back by noon."

"Okay."

They walked around the back of Sycamore House to her garage. Eliseo's garden was still producing vegetables and he had planted pumpkins and squash, so those were beginning to fill out. She opened the garage door and they climbed in the truck. She waited until he was belted in before backing out and heading down the highway.

"How is your week off going?" she asked.

"Yesterday was pretty bad. It just kept getting worse, too. Mom was as crazy as I've ever seen her. She wasn't even that bad when she picked me up from school."

"It was scary."

"I wish I knew why he was here."

"We all do. That would make it a lot easier on your mom."

"I don't want to see him."

"Did you tell your mom that?"

"No."

"Why not?"

"It just wasn't the right time. Everything is such a mess. And I'm the one who screwed most of it up."

"You've certainly made a mess of things, but I don't think you screwed *most* of it up. Yours is only a small part. It was a big deal when Andrew was taken. Heck, having your dad show up in Bellingwood is a pretty big deal. Let's just say that you screwed one third of it up. See, that's not most of it."

He looked at her and wrinkled his nose. "You're really strange."

"I know. Look, you sit here while I run into the school. I'll be right back. You can listen to the radio or whatever. But you'd better be here when I get back."

"Where would I go?" he asked.

"I'm just saying. I hate it when kids go missing."

"I'll be here."

Polly ran in and stopped in the office. They sent her to Andrew and Rebecca's classroom and called to let the teacher know she was coming. When she arrived, Mrs. Hastings met her outside the door with notebooks and textbooks.

"I've marked the pages they should read and the problems they need to work on today. It's all in there." She slipped everything into a plastic grocery bag and handed it to Polly. "How are the kids doing today?"

"I think they're fine. It just feels like a lot of chaos hit all at once," Polly said.

Mrs. Hastings took her elbow and guided her away from the doorway. "How is Mrs. Heater? I mean, how is she really doing?"

Polly took a breath. "This was diabetes. It isn't going to help her body deal with the chemo and the cancer, adding one more issue. It sounds so callous, but it really is a matter of time. We were hoping to get Rebecca through this school year, but I don't know."

"I worry about that little girl. The only friend she has is Andrew. I put her into groups with other girls so she'll get to know them, but she does her work and shuts down. I know that grades haven't come out yet, but she isn't doing as well this year as she did last year. It's all really hard on her. I'm trying my best to help her out as much as I can, but I don't know what else to do."

"How big of a difference is there in her grades?"

"Last year she was in the top of the class and this year she's doing all she can to hold on to the middle. And she isn't drawing as much anymore. I have some of the things she drew last year. Her teacher said that she was sketching every time she had a free minute. Right now all she does is stare off into space unless I refocus her. She'll do the work I ask her to do, but nothing else."

"Thank you for saying something. We might just have to tough it out this year. She's not getting into trouble or anything, right?"

"No, she'd have to engage with other kids to get in trouble. I've caught some of the girls saying mean things to her and even that doesn't get a reaction."

"Mean things?"

"You know how girls can be. She doesn't have a dad, her mother can't be here to help in the classroom, her best friend is a boy, she doesn't live in a house like other girls do, she wears old clothes."

"That breaks my heart," Polly said. "I can fix the clothes and I can certainly come help in the classroom. Please let me know if something like that comes up. I'll talk to Sarah and maybe we can ease some of this for her. Are there any girls that she communicates with?"

"No," Mrs. Hastings shook her head. "I didn't want to land all of this on her mother, and I probably shouldn't say anything to you, but since you're a big part of her life, I wondered if you might be able to talk to Rebecca."

"Thanks for telling me. I'll see what I can do."

"I'd better get back in there. Who knows what those little hel ... angels are up to." The woman smiled at Polly and patted her arm. "Thank you for taking care of those kids. Tell them I'm looking forward to seeing them tomorrow morning."

"Thanks a lot," Polly said and walked back down the hallway. It never failed - every time she was in an elementary school, the scents and images took her back to her own childhood.

She dropped the bag behind her seat and buckled in. "I'm glad to see you're still here," she said to Jason.

"Do we have to go to Boone?" he asked.

"Why?"

"Because what if someone sees me down there. It's bad enough I'm not in school."

"If someone sees you, they're not in school either. Did you think of that? We're just going to drive around a few car lots. I won't even get out."

"There's really only one."

"One what?"

"One car lot."

"Then we'll go to Ames."

He relaxed as soon as she changed her mind, so she turned east rather than south and headed for Ames.

"Okay, what's going on," she finally asked.

"It's hard to talk about."

"Is this the reason you got in a fight yesterday?"

"Yeah." He spoke quietly, his head bowed down.

"You want to tell me about it?"

"Yeah, but it's hard."

"Okay. Do you want me to change the subject or shut up?"

"I know that I'm not supposed to fight and I get it that I screwed up, but it wasn't my fault," he said.

"Yeah. It was your fault. You chose to use your fists. You had a million other choices."

"But they wouldn't have ever stopped. It would have gone on and on. And they said really bad things."

"About you?"

"No."

She waited for him to continue, but got nothing. "Then who?"

"Mom."

"What would they say about your mother?"

"And Eliseo."

There it was. Of course they did.

"And you've told no one about this?"

"What am I supposed to say to Mom and Eliseo? That those guys were saying some half-baked spic was ... you know ... the f word with my mom because she couldn't do any better? I can't say that to them. It's so gross."

"Why didn't you just ignore it?"

"Polly, I tried. I really did. When Eliseo dropped me off at school, they were waiting for me. They laughed at him because of the way he looks. I told them to shut up and they kept asking if he'd fallen into a vat of acid or maybe someone dumped gasoline on him because he was so ugly. It was all day long. Every time I came out of class, someone else was talking about how he was effing my mom and how could I let that happen. One kid said that if she had his babies, they'd come out looking like Hellboy with horns and everything. Then they said that I was a pussy because I let him eff my mom."

"Oh, Jason."

"I just put up with it all day until finally two of them - Rudy and Logan - caught me and started spinning me around, telling me that if I let the half-baked monster eff her, they knew a smelly homeless guy who could at least take a shower first. If I was so desperate for a dad that I'd let anyone eff her, maybe one of them could come over and show her a good time."

Polly took a shuddering breath, pulled into a field entrance and stopped the truck. She unbuckled her belt and slid across the seat and pulled Jason into her arms. "I'm so sorry, Jason."

"I'm not like my dad," he said before breaking into tears.

"What do you mean by that?" Polly asked, pushing him back so she could see his face.

"I heard Mom say that she was worried I was just like dad, using my fists to handle any situation. I'm not like that. I promise."

"Oh baby, I'm sorry." She held him while he sobbed and sobbed.

Jason finally took a few shuddering breaths of his own and opened the glove compartment to look for paper napkins. Polly kept a pretty good supply of them in there. She slid away from him while he blew his nose and regained his composure.

He looked at her and said, "I need to tell you one more thing."

"Okay?"

"This is kind of serious and I should have told Mom last week."

"What is it, Jason?"

"Dad sent me a letter and told me he was coming to Bellingwood."

"He what?"

"It came last week. I always get the mail after school and it was addressed to me. I don't know why I didn't tell anyone. I wanted to see him first and tell him to go away, but then everything got weird and I was grounded and out at Eliseo's and ..."

"Oh sweetie. You aren't supposed to have to deal with any of this by yourself."

"Who else is going to?"

"Any of us. You could have told me. You could have told Eliseo. You could have told your mom."

"It just would have upset her. You saw how she was Sunday night. It's my job to take care of her, not to make things worse for her."

"So that's why you stole Eliseo's car and that's why you got in a fight at school, to make things better for her?" Polly felt terrible for pointing it out to him when he was feeling so badly, but damn, the boy was making some really bad decisions.

"I know. I screwed this up. Those ..." he screwed his mouth up and around, trying to come up with the right adjective to describe something. Finally, he just said, "Those kids I've been hanging around with aren't really my friends. I figured that out yesterday."

"Then why were you with them?"

"They like cars and one of them works in his dad's garage. They're cool."

"Uh, not so much."

"Yeah. Crap, Polly. How am I ever going to get any normal friends?"

Polly scooted back into the driver's seat. "I know that this sounds impossible to believe right now, but everything changes all the time. You're going to have to deal with the embarrassment of all that you've done, but time will pass and people will let it go. Other people will have things happen to them and the focus will change away from you and before you know it, you'll be walking down the hall one day and you'll realize that no one is thinking about any of this any longer."

"It doesn't feel like that."

"I know it. But you're tougher than this. You can come home every day from school and talk to the horses and play with the donkeys and hold the cats and remember that you have family and friends who love you very much and think you're pretty special. Then you go deal with another day and come back and do the same thing and pretty soon it gets easier and easier."

"I don't know."

"You're going to find something at school to get involved with. Something that is far away from those guys. Maybe FFA or 4H. You know a lot of the 4H kids in Bellingwood already. Most of them would die to get a chance to come work with the Percherons.

"But their meetings are at weird times."

"We can figure it out, Jason. Be proactive about this. Make the right kind of friends and figure out how to keep your nose clean."

He absentmindedly brushed his nose. "Are you going to tell Mom and Eliseo about this?"

"I think someone should, don't you?"

"Maybe."

"Are you asking me not to tell them?"

"No."

"Is it less embarrassing for me to talk to them than for you to say the words?"

He looked up at her and then back at the floor. "Yes."

"Then I'll talk to them. Thank you for telling me."

"You're always cool about these things and you aren't my mom. She flips out really fast."

"I get that. She's got a lot to worry about trying to get the two of you boys all grown up."

"Andrew's easy. He never does anything wrong."

"Give him time. Nobody gets out of life without doing something wrong."

"Promise?"

"Promise." She chuckled. If it made him feel better to know that his little brother was going to screw up someday, then she'd let that be real.

CHAPTER FOURTEEN

Polly and Jason had driven around car lots in Ames and she'd seen nothing that really called to her. Sedans were too boring, mini vans were out - they were too soccer mom and she just wasn't a soccer mom. The SUVs weren't bad, but what had happened to the sharp lines that defined a vehicle's profile? Everything was either square and boxy or round like a bubble.

Jason hadn't said much, but pointed out a few things he thought she might like. When they turned onto the highway leading into Bellingwood, he finally spoke up again.

"Polly?"

"Yeah, Jason?"

"Do you think Eliseo and my mom are ... " his voice trailed off.

"No, Jason. I don't think they are right now, but don't you think that's their business?"

"Well, yeah. I like him and everything."

"You like him a lot. Don't kid yourself."

"You're right. I do. But what if he marries Mom?"

"Jason, where is this coming from? They've never even been out on a date."

"But we're living at his house now."

"Temporarily. Just until things settle down with your dad being in town. Your mom got really nervous about that and Eliseo gave her a safe place to stay until the situation could be handled. Right?"

"But she made breakfast for him and last night I heard her running a load of laundry in his washing machine."

"Jason, let me ask you a question. Has your mother ever lied to you or withheld things from you and Andrew?"

"Well ..." he thought about it for a moment. "No. I don't think so. But then if she did, I probably wouldn't know about it, right?"

"Okay, you've got me there. But your mom has always been really up front with you two. And so has Eliseo. If they were going to do something drastic like get married, don't you think that you and Andrew would know before anyone else?"

"I'm being dumb, aren't I?" he said.

"You're worrying about things that haven't happened yet." Polly pulled into the driveway and stopped the truck, then turned and looked at him, taking his hand. "The world is filled with changes that happen every day. Worrying just makes it difficult to enjoy life."

He gave her a little chuckle and pulled his hand back. "You're getting all preachy now."

"Okay, whatever. You go on down to the barn."

Jason opened the truck door and jumped to the ground. Turning back to her, he said. "Thanks for listening to me. I know that I've been a brat lately and I know that I deserved this suspension."

"New friends, new life rules and you'll get this thing licked. I have a lot of confidence in you. And by the way, Jason. Thanks for trusting me."

He nodded and shut the door, then jogged around the back of the house, heading for the barn.

Polly waited for some spark of inspiration on how to tell Sylvie and Eliseo what was going on. What she wanted to do was round up the biggest of Aaron's deputies, march into the school building and drag those rotten kids out by the greasy hair on their heads, then threaten them with their lives. Yeah. That wasn't going to work.

She took a deep breath and went inside to a cacophony of noise in the auditorium. Polly stepped into the kitchen and laughed at Rachel and Sylvie who were sitting at the back table, both of them with their heads in their hands.

"Did the ladies kill you?" Polly asked.

Sylvie looked up, "You have no idea. 'Cook for the church group,' she said. 'You'll get great references,' she said. 'It will be easy. Everyone will pitch in and help.'" She gestured at the kitchen, which looked worse than Polly had ever seen it. "Help? No. They didn't want to help. They wanted to tell me how to plate the food and how to drain the vegetables. I think every single one of those women walked in while we were serving with a little bit of advice. If it wasn't about the food, it was about how to clean pans or how to get more business."

"So ... ?"

"I need a stiff drink." Sylvie dropped her head back into her hands.

"Okay, so no drama in here." Polly took an apron off the hook behind the door and put it on. "Tell me where to start and I'll be your cleanup girl."

"It's okay. We'll get back to it. At least we don't have to clear tables. Lydia is making them bring their own plates into the kitchen when they're finished. Desserts and drinks are already out there. They are having a program right now, so we have plenty of time to clean."

"Really. I want to help."

"Did you get their homework?"

"Yeah. I just need to take it upstairs to them."

"Go ahead and do that. Are you taking Jason out for lunch?"

"He went for a ride with me. We need to talk."

Sylvie looked up again. "Do I need to worry?"

"No. Well, yes. But no. He's a good kid and there is another side to the story. It's not something you want me to tell you in a hurry, or where ladies from the church group might come in and hear. I think Eliseo should hear it as well."

"So I can quit being sick to my stomach about this?"

"About your boy being out of control? Absolutely. Let me run the books upstairs. Mrs. Hastings made notes for the kids. They should be able to figure it out. Then I'm taking Obiwan out."

"It's killing me, you know," Sylvie said. She followed Polly into the hallway and whispered, "Just tell me what happened."

"He spent all day yesterday listening to those supposed friends of his taunt him about you and the half-breed monster screwing. He took it until it finally got to be too much. Two of them were spinning him back and forth, saying horrible things and he lost it."

Sylvie wilted. "That's why he couldn't say anything. Does he know you're telling me?"

"I think he wanted me to. But Eliseo needs to know, too."

"Why don't we all sit down at the end of the day," Sylvie said. "And then it sounds like I'm going to make a call to the school and turn into bitch-mom-from-hell."

"You might want to ask Jason about that first," Polly said and then she stopped. "No, I'm sorry. That's not my business."

"Of course it is. Jason and I have made it your business." Sylvie hugged Polly. "Thank you for listening to him. You're right. I'll talk to him. Did he have any ideas about how to deal with this?"

"I think his biggest concern is how to make different friends. I'm not sure why or how he got caught up in this crowd, but we talked about FFA. Is he part of the Bellingwood 4H group?"

"He really should be," Sylvie said. "Those kids all go to school in Boone."

"You guys will figure it out. And Sylvie, he's wondering about you and Eliseo."

Sylvie got defensive, "There's nothing there. Why does this keep coming up?"

"Maybe because there's more than you think and you just haven't admitted it yet?" Polly knew she needed to tread lightly, but she couldn't help herself.

"There's nothing there," Sylvie protested again.

"Do you think there could ever be anything there?"

"I don't know. He's great with the boys and he's so kind and gentle. Nothing at all like Anthony. He's generous and ... " She stuck her tongue out at Polly. "I'm an idiot."

"I wouldn't go that far."

"He and I need to talk, don't we?"

"That would make sense to me. No reason to let it fester."

"I don't know how you do it. Everything is just right out there for you. If you think there's going to be a problem, you face it down and expose it. The rest of us aren't like that. It's much easier to ignore these things."

"Not really and I think you know that."

Sylvie pushed Polly's arm. "You go put the kids to work and take your dog for a walk. I'm about to become a cleaning hurricane. Way too many things going on in my head."

Polly ran upstairs with the bag of homework and found Andrew and Rebecca sitting at the dining room table, their empty plates pushed away from them and papers strewn everywhere.

"What happened here?" she asked.

"I told Rebecca that she should draw something for her mom's room in the hospital."

"That's a great idea. What are you working on?"

Rebecca pushed a piece of paper toward Polly. "Mom likes watching the horses in the morning, so I'm trying to draw them. So far they don't look very good."

"Maybe you should look at them rather than try to draw them from memory," Polly advised.

Andrew slapped his forehead. "Duh."

"I tell you what. I have your homework here. Why don't you work on this and then whatever time we have before Rebecca and I head to Boone to see her mom, you can spend in the barn with the animals. You'll have to be careful, though. Jason and Eliseo are going out to the house to work on siding."

"I can do something different. We can go down tomorrow," Rebecca said quietly, pulling the paper back in front of her. "I'll just draw a rainbow or something."

Polly bent over and kissed the top of the little girl's forehead. "Your mom will be happy to have lots of pictures from you. We'll make time for you with the horses. I promise."

"Polly?"

"Yes, sweetie."

"Do you think I can be an artist someday?"

"You have a lot of talent and if you want to, then go for it."

Polly turned around and put her hand on Obiwan's head. "Come on bud, we're going for a walk." She opened a drawer by the front door and drew out a leash. "We're going to make a quick stop first and you need to be on leash. Be good, okay?"

They went down the front steps and Beryl looked up from her easel. "There you are. People have been looking for you."

"I had a couple of errands to run. Are things still good here?"

"Joss and her babies got absorbed by the women in there," Beryl threw her head back to the auditorium. "And Sal mumbled something about leaving before they descended. She said she'd talk to you later."

"Okay. Say, I have a question for you. Maybe a favor."

"You never need anything from me. I feel a little honored."

"Oh stop it, you," Polly grinned. "Rebecca loves art. She loves to draw and I think she's pretty good. Her teacher says that with everything that has been happening to her, she's starting to get withdrawn unless Andrew is around. And, she's quit drawing whenever she has a spare minute. What would you think about spending time with her on a regular basis?"

"Is this something she wants?" Beryl asked. "I don't want to scare the little pumpkin."

"I haven't talked to her about you. I don't even know if she fully understands who you are."

Beryl laughed and struck a pose, with her hand behind her head and her chest jutted out.

"Okay, whatever," Polly said. "She wanted to draw some horses for her mom, but was frustrated because she was trying to do it from memory. The poor thing doesn't know where to go next and right now her little mind is so caught up in all of this mess with her mother that she can't express herself."

"You know that helping kids find their true potential is a passion of mine. Of course I'd like to spend time with her."

"I'll pay you. Just like other students you have."

"Stop it."

"No. Seriously. If this is something that she really wants, I want her to learn from you." Polly knelt so she wasn't looking down at Beryl. "The papers for becoming her guardian are in my desk. I'm not going to sign them until I have to, but Rebecca is going to be part of my family. You aren't going to be giving Sarah and Rebecca charity, you're going to be hired by me."

"I tell you what," Beryl said plainly. "Rebecca and I will have ... let's say ... five sessions together. No cost to anyone. If she enjoys it and really wants to dig in and learn, then you and I can talk about money. Does that sound fair?"

Polly hugged her, "That sounds more than fair. When I get back from this walk with Obiwan and she gets her homework done, I'm going to send her down to spend a few minutes with you. Will that be okay?"

"Perfect."

"Oh, and by the way," Polly said, pointing to the canvas, "You missed a spot."

"Get out of here, you brat." Beryl turned her back on them and Polly went out the front door with her dog. The parking lot was filled with cars. It still thrilled her to see so many people use her home. She hoped she never got tired of that.

Obiwan knew where they were going and picked up the pace once they crossed the highway. Since it was the middle of the day, there weren't many others on the trail and she released him to run. He took off, stopping to sniff and mark his territory. They made their way through the woods behind the swimming pool and then she turned and they walked slowly down Pierce Street.

They were getting to know some of the folks on these streets, walking through the neighborhoods as often as they did. Before getting to Walnut, there was always an elderly couple sitting out on their front porch. She knew them as Sam and Jean, but had no idea what their last name was. Their old basset hound roused up when Obiwan came into view, but the gate across their porch kept the two apart. He would woof and bark and Polly always had to make sure Obiwan was leashed, or he would be up the steps trying to make a new friend.

She waved as they approached and Sam stood up. "Miss Giller," he called out.

"Hello there," she said back.

"Do you have a moment?"

Polly stopped at their sidewalk and said, "Of course I do. How are you today?"

"We're very good," Jean said, stepping around her dog and opening the latch on the gate. The two came down the sidewalk.

"Sit," Polly commanded Obiwan. "Stay."

He sat down, his tail wagging in the grass behind him.

"We'd like to invite you and your husband over for dinner one of these evenings. We don't have a lot of company anymore and our kids have all taken off. Mother here is a pretty good cook and she misses feeding hungry young people. We could play cards after dinner, if you have time for that."

The invitation took Polly aback. Sam and Jean both looked at her, almost pleading with her to say yes.

"Of course. We would enjoy that," she said, then bit her lip. Henry wouldn't care if she agreed to this.

"If you need to speak to Henry first, we understand," Jean jumped in, trying to assure her.

"No, no. It's okay. He'd love to. I'm sure."

Jean looked down at Obiwan and said, "We'd invite you in more often, but I don't know how Sebastian and your Obiwan would get along. You seem like such a friendly girl."

"Thank you. When would you like us to come over?"

"Well, I know how you kids like to go out and party on the weekends and we promise not to keep you up too late, so would tomorrow work for you? About six thirty? You don't have to bring anything at all. Jean makes a good apple pie and I'll go up to the store and buy some ice cream," Sam said.

"Wednesday at six thirty." Polly took out her phone. "I have to put everything in my calendar or I forget myself. We'll be here. I'll call Henry when I get home just to make sure. If he has made other plans, I'll let you know right away." She started to put her phone back in her pocket. "Wait. Could I get your phone number?"

"Two six two oh," Sam said. "Call us any time. We're always here and no one ever stops by, so we're free."

"Thank you very much for the invitation," Polly still wasn't used to everyone in town having the same exchange and only needing to share the last four numbers. "I look forward to dinner."

"We do too. Maybe we can do this more often if we have fun."

Polly nodded. She wasn't sucking Henry into that. One dinner at a time. "Are you sure that I can't bring anything?"

"No, not a thing. Just come over and wear comfortable clothing. You don't need to dress up for us," Jean said.

"We'll be here. Thanks again."

The two waved as she and Obiwan started back down the street toward Sycamore House. She turned around at the highway and waved back, then crossed and jogged to the front steps.

"Well, that was interesting," she said to the dog. "Those poor people must not have anyone else around to talk to." They always had something to say to her when she walked by. More often than not, she stopped for a few minutes in front of their house to discuss something they had heard on the news or maybe the weather. How lonely it would be to live like that.

She sat down on the cold concrete step and took her phone back out of her pocket, swiped it and waited.

"Hey sweet stuff," Henry said. "Everything still okay over there?"

"If you're asking if Anthony Donovan has shown up, the answer is no, so things are okay. But it's been a morning."

"Anything you need help with?"

"Nope. But I hope you aren't mad at me, I just agreed to go over to this old couple's house for dinner tomorrow night."

"You what?"

"It's an old couple I see on Pierce Street whenever Obiwan and I walk that way. They came off their porch today and asked if we would come to dinner. She's making apple pie and he's buying ice cream. Are you mad that I said yes without asking you?"

He laughed, "Of course not. That should be interesting. Do you even know who they are?"

"It's Sam and Jean something. Oh, and we're playing cards after dinner."

"We are, are we?"

"And they want to do this often."

"What did you say to that?"

"Not a word. I just let it float away. I thought I should talk to you before agreeing to a lifetime of dinner and cards."

"Well, thanks for that."

"Do you know what their last name is?" Polly asked, giggling a little.

"No. I have no idea who this is. I'll ask Mom when I get back to the shop. You said they're on Pierce?"

"Yeah. I didn't look at the house number, though. I can walk right to it."

"I love you, Polly Giller."

"Well, thank you for not getting mad at me. I think maybe they really need friends or something."

"Now you're rescuing old people. At least this time there's a good meal in it for me."

"I can't guarantee the good meal, but he guaranteed pie and ice cream."

"That will do. I love you and I'll be home later."

"Rebecca and I are going to Boone, but we'll be back for dinner."

"I'll make something."

"Really?"

"Yeah. I can do that."

"I love you."

CHAPTER FIFTEEN

Relaxing on the sofa with her legs tucked underneath her, Polly waited for Henry to get out of the shower. He'd called his mother and learned that they were planning to visit Sam and Jean Gardner this evening. Polly felt much better about having a last name to go with the couple she'd grown to know this last year. She wasn't sure how she possibly could have rectified that oversight without embarrassing herself or them.

After visiting her mother in the hospital in Boone, Rebecca went out to Eliseo's with Sylvie and Andrew for the night. Polly gave a slight smile. She really did enjoy being alone with Henry. Hopefully they wouldn't stay out too late tonight and have some time to themselves.

The last two days had flown by. Anthony Donovan hadn't shown up yet and it was driving Sylvie nuts. She jumped out of her skin every time someone startled her and looked up at every sound. After his short conversation with Andrew Monday night, there hadn't been another peep out of the man.

The conversation with Sylvie and Eliseo had been uncomfortable to say the least, but it was over and both of them had a better understanding of what had happened to Jason. Sylvie had scheduled a meeting with the school counselor ... once she calmed down. She wasn't sure what good it would do, but she would insist that documentation be entered into his file regarding the harassment he had suffered. Polly had no idea what was going to happen between Eliseo and Sylvie, but at least Sylvie wasn't fleeing from his home. That had to be positive. Either that, or she weighed the fear of her ex-husband against the fear of starting a new relationship and made a decision based on the lesser of two evils.

Polly sent a text and one more Facebook message to Jessie, wanting the girl to know that she was concerned. No response to any of it yet. That frustrated Polly to no end. If you're going to run away, just be up front about it and admit that you want something different than what you have. The other stuff was just idiocy.

"Dress up nice or dress up casual?" Henry asked.

Polly turned around. He was framed in the door in just his shorts.

"Um, skip the whole dressing thing completely and I'll call in sick?" she said.

He ducked behind the door and poked his head out. "You just want me for my body. I feel so objectified."

"Whatever. Dress nice casual. Your black jeans look good with a casual shirt."

"So you're not helping."

"Did you lose your head when we got married? I have to dress you now?" Polly shook her head. Sometimes men were just dopes.

"Should we take something with us?" he called out from the bedroom.

"Don't worry. I've got it covered."

"Wine?"

"I don't know if they drink or not. No, I'm taking a couple of Sycamore House t-shirts and a mason jar candle."

Henry walked out, fully dressed except for his shoes and socks and sat down on the couch. "Those mason jars have been used a couple of times, isn't that a little tacky?"

"The jar is clean and I re-made the candle. It's pretty and she'll like it, so there."

He grinned up at her. "I'm just poking at ya. That sounds nice. Are we walking over?"

"It's only a couple of blocks and it's a nice evening. Don't you think?"

"Sure." He slid his foot into a shoe. "This feels weird."

"Maybe it's on the wrong foot."

"No, you dope, going to someone's house I don't know. Whenever we go out, it's with our friends."

"It looks like we're making new friends. Are you nervous?"

"That's not it. It just feels ... different." He stood up and shook out his pant legs. "Well, shall we? Do you think we need jackets?"

"Who are you?" Polly asked, laughing. "Why would we need jackets? It's in the seventies outside."

"I don't know. We always take the truck whenever we go places. I feel ..."

"Weird, I know. It's a good thing you're taking me with you."

Henry kissed her nose. "You always make things easier."

Polly laughed and snorted through her nose. "Yeah. Uh huh. That sounds like me. I have never made life easier for you."

"You're right. I was exaggerating. But it is a lot more fun when you're around."

"I'll buy that." She turned around to check the animals. The cats were on the cat tree in the bedroom and Obiwan was curled up where she'd left him on the sofa. "We'll be back in a while. Hold down the fort," she said to him. He thumped his tail.

The front door of the Gardner home opened as they walked up the sidewalk and Sam came out onto the porch. "Welcome, welcome!" he said. "I was just telling Sebastian that we should be seeing you come down the street any minute now. Come in and make yourselves at home."

"Who's Sebastian?" Henry whispered.

"The dog. Be good."

The basset hound harrumphed a couple of times and Sam shushed him, but smiled proudly as Sebastian wagged his tail nearly off his body, waiting for someone to pat his head. "He's very friendly. We just don't let him loose or he might never come home. Especially if he started chasing a dog the likes of your Obiwan."

"I'm sure Sebastian wouldn't stay away very long. It looks as if he has a good thing going here," Polly said, pointing to a corner of the living room that was obviously where the dog resided. A large beanbag chair was covered with a couple of blankets, there was a basket of dog toys and the shades on the corner windows were pulled up just enough so the dog had a clear view of the world outside.

"He likes to greet the mailman. Well, the mail woman. She always has a treat for him and he loves her."

"Smart mail person," Henry acknowledged.

"Get in your bed, Sebastian," Sam ordered and pointed to the beanbag. The dog finally waddled over and clambered into it, rustling around until he had made himself completely comfortable.

"Come on into the dining room. Jean is nearly ready. Can I get you a beer, Henry? A soda or juice, Polly?"

"I'll just have water," Polly said.

"That sounds great." Henry sat down beside Polly.

Jean stuck her head out of the kitchen door. "We'll be right there. Don't move. Just be comfortable. We don't have guests very often and I've had a wonderful day making dinner. I'm so glad you're here."

"They just want water, Jean. Let me in and I'll pour that for them."

When he was out of earshot, Polly turned to Henry. "How come he didn't offer me a beer?"

"Because you're a delicate flower and delicate flowers don't drink things as common as beer," Henry replied, laughing. "Here, let me take the gift. I'll put it under my chair."

"Seriously. I can do that, too. I feel like you all are desperately trying to remind me that I'm a girl. I can take care of myself." She swatted his leg. "You be good."

Sam returned with the glasses of water and took a seat across from Polly. "How was your day?" he asked.

"It was a good day. How about you?" Polly responded.

"Jean had me running around all day cleaning. I put my foot down and made her do the vacuuming. I'm not very good at that."

His wife carried in two covered platters and put them in the middle of the table, then returned to the kitchen, to return with another dish. When she left the room again, Henry jumped up.

"I'll help you, Mrs. Gardner."

"Oh leave her to it. She loves to serve," Sam said, shaking out his napkin and placing it in his lap.

Henry ignored him and followed Jean into the kitchen, returning with a basket of rolls and a bowl filled with salad. They made two more trips and Jean patted him on the back.

"You are such a good helper, Henry. Thank you."

He held her chair for her and then took a seat.

"Henry enjoys cooking," Polly said. "He's better about finding time to do that than I am. I'm much more apt to order a pizza. And he is so much better at cleaning up than me. I'd let the dishes sit for a day, but he cleans all the time."

"I can't let Sam clean. He is forever putting the dishes in the wrong rack in the dishwasher."

"After all these years, I'll bet he puts them in the wrong place just so he won't have to help," Polly said and winked at Sam.

He looked at her in shock, recognizing that he'd just been called out, but asked, "What did you make for us tonight, mother?"

Jean began uncovering dishes and placing the lids on a dresser beside her. There was chicken noodle soup, a tossed salad, bread and rolls, mashed potatoes, green bean casserole, a squash casserole, sliced ham and an orangey fluffy salad.

"You're going to kill me," Henry said.

"Be sure to save room for dessert. I've made apple pie and rhubarb cobbler."

Polly started to chuckle and pretty soon she was laughing out loud.

"What is it, dear?" Jean asked.

"You're amazing. I haven't had a meal like this in years, except for those that Sylvie cooks at Sycamore House." She turned to Sam. "Do you eat like this all the time?"

"No, not all the time. It's just the two of us, but she never fails to put out a good meal."

"Eat up," Jean said. "Don't let it get cold."

They dug in and listened as Sam told stories of his days teaching at Iowa State. Polly gulped back surprise upon learning that he had quite a few articles published in horticulture and ecology. Retirement had been difficult for him, but after ten years, he was content to let that part of his life be in the past.

"What do you think of the garden at Sycamore House?" Polly asked.

"The ladies have done a nice job with it. It's very attractive," he said.

"I'm surprised you weren't involved."

"No one asked and I don't like to horn in. They did just fine."

"Are you involved with the garden club or anything?"

"No. It's not something I'm interested in. There's more to a garden than pretty flowers."

Polly started to open her mouth and Henry gently laid his hand on her knee. She brushed it aside and went on. "Have you met Eliseo Aquila?"

"The man who cares for your grounds? No, I haven't."

"I'll bet he would love your input. Did you see the garden he has behind Sycamore House?"

"We walked past it once or twice."

"He wants to expand it. You know he uses a horse to pull the plow. Next year he's thinking of putting more into that rough pasture land we bought on the other side of the creek."

"You bought that?" Sam perked up. "I'd be glad to talk to him. You really should do some things to help stop erosion of those creek walls. I could draw up some plans."

"Let me talk to him and we'll set up a time for the two of you to meet. I'm sure he'd love input."

Jean interrupted. "We were very sorry to hear of your uncle's death, Henry. He was a good man."

"You knew Uncle Loren?"

"Of course we did," she said. "And that poor Jim Todd."

"Wait. You knew both of those men?" Polly asked.

"Certainly. They were part of a card club we belong to."

"Uncle Loren played cards?" Henry sat back. "In a club?"

"Twice a month on Friday nights."

"Uncle Loren played cards with people? That just doesn't sound like him."

"Sometimes you kids don't know everything there is to know about your elders."

"I don't think Mom and Dad or Aunt Betty even know about this."

"He was there every week."

"Where did you play?" Polly asked.

"We meet in different places. It's all on a schedule. Community halls, churches, restaurants. None of us want to admit we're senior citizens, but we all like to do the same things. Not everyone comes every time, but it gives us a good opportunity to get to know people from around the area"

"I had no idea," Henry muttered.

Polly patted his hand. "Can you think of any reason why Loren and Jim were killed? It seems strange that both of them were involved in the same activity."

Sam and Jean Gardner looked at each other, trying to imagine any dark purpose behind their deaths. Sam spoke first, "I can't think of anything right offhand. How long ago was that?"

Jean responded. "It was during the tornado, wasn't it?"

Henry and Polly both nodded.

"We played that Friday night. Where was that?" Jean asked her husband. "Never mind. Let me get the schedule. I can tell you for sure."

She went into the front room and when she sat down at her desk, Sebastian slid off his chair and thumped his tail on the floor, looking for attention.

"Yes, old man, I will put you outside. Give me a minute." She spoke loudly to those in the dining room. "I have the schedule memorized for the rest of the year, and that means I've tucked this away somewhere so I won't lose it." She continued to riffle the papers and sort through stacks on top of the desk.

"Here it is. Come on, Sebastian. I'll give you a cookie before you go. Outside?"

He ran his big old body across the floor to the kitchen.

"He'll do anything for a cookie."

"He's why I don't have a garden out back," Sam grumped. "He digs everything up."

Jean put the schedule down in front of Polly. "I'll be right back," she said.

When she returned to the table, Sam passed the dishes of food around again. Polly tried not to groan. She hurt by this point. How she was ever going to get through dessert was beyond her.

"It looks as if you were in Stanhope that night," Polly said, passing the paper back to Jean.

Sam intercepted it and scanned through the listing. "That's right, remember? That was the night the group from Ames joined us. We had a big bridge club battle."

"A battle?"

"It was just a large tournament," Jean said. "They promoted it as the Big Bridge Battle. There were prizes and everything."

"Did Loren and Jim Todd play on the same team?" Polly asked.

The two looked at each other again, trying to remember details of that evening.

"I can't say for sure," Jean finally said. "They weren't a regular team, but everything was out of kilter that evening and so many people were there, it was hard to pay attention to everyone. We came home with a basket of fruit and a gift certificate to Hickory Park. Each person's entrance fee was a door prize. There were some pretty nice prizes, too. We took a certificate for a live tree from ISU's tree farm and I gave a lap blanket that I quilted. There were computers and televisions, some jewelry and other gift certificates. It was quite a lively event."

"It sounds like it," Polly said. "Oh, I almost forgot. I have something for you."

"We told you not to bring anything," Jean said.

"It's not much, but I thought you might like something from Sycamore House." She handed the box over to Jean, who opened it.

"These are wonderful," she exclaimed. "Sam, will you look at this. We'll fit right in with the kids now."

Henry chuckled. "I'm guessing you could fit in with the kids no matter what you wore."

"Oh you, you're such a smooth talker. Now how about some dessert?"

Polly groaned and put her hand on her belly. "I don't know how I can eat anything else. This was all so wonderful."

"Surely there's room for a little piece of pie or maybe some cobbler?"

She looked at Henry and he smiled back at her, and then said, "I was more careful than you. I'd love pie and maybe a bite of the cobbler."

"I like this one, Sam. He knows how to make a woman happy. Does he make you happy, Polly?"

"All the time. Even when he drives me crazy."

Jean looked at her husband, "Driving you crazy is what takes you into old age together. Don't ever stop doing that. When you stop it, you get old and boring and then it's just no fun anymore."

"We certainly have fun, don't we?" Sam said. He handed his plate to her.

"Let me help you clear the table," Henry said.

Polly stood up. "I can, too."

Sam took her arm. "Let them. If he wants to help her clean up, that's fine. You tell me more about the gardens over at Sycamore House."

She watched helplessly as Henry began gathering dishes and followed Jean into the kitchen. "I don't know very much at all, I'm afraid. Without Eliseo, there would be no gardens."

"What's his background?"

They continued to talk about Eliseo and the ideas Sam had for the grounds. Polly knew that she had just set her friend up for more help than he needed, but maybe since he had so easily befriended Ralph Bedford, he wouldn't protest too much when she gave him another helpful old man to play with.

"Polly, are you sure you won't have some dessert?" Henry asked, poking his head out of the kitchen door.

"A very little bit," she said, "of each. And I mean it. A very little bit. With a very little bit of ice cream."

"Sam?"

"Cobbler. She makes apple pie for me a lot, but I never get rhubarb cobbler. This is a treat," he responded.

Henry delivered dessert and sat back down beside Polly. When Jean didn't join them, he got up and went back into the kitchen and then immediately returned.

"She said she'll be here in just a minute. She kicked me out."

"Eat up," Jean called. "I'll be right there."

"A couple of years ago, your uncle told us that your sister was going to grad school in Michigan," Sam said to Henry. "How is she doing?"

"He told you that, did he? We didn't think he knew anything that was happening in the family. He certainly didn't want us around," Henry said. "Oh, and she's doing fine. She took his dog back to Michigan with her. I think they're both very happy with that arrangement."

"He loved that dog. If it was a nice evening, he would bring her with him and she'd sleep in the back of his truck while he played cards. He didn't go out too often without her."

Henry shook his head. "I wish we had known that side of him."

Jean came back into the dining room with two large shopping bags and set them beside Henry. "I packed the leftovers for you."

"You didn't have to do that," Polly protested. "What will Sam eat?"

The old man grinned and patted his own belly. "Don't you worry about me. She feeds me so well that I have to chase the dog around the block to work it all off."

"I saved some of the cobbler for you, you old liar," Jean said and handed a laminated piece of paper to Polly. "When you finish the pie, do me a favor and make another someday in the pie plate and give it to a friend with this."

Polly read the note, which said:

"This pie is a treat, the plate is a gift.
Its beautiful design, a sight to uplift.
Food and love are only a part
Of friendship, a gift that comes from the heart.
The gift of this plate is but a point in a line
That stretches beyond us, oh friend of mine."

"This is lovely," Polly said. "And what a beautiful sentiment. I've never heard of doing anything like this."

"I had the idea years ago and had a dozen of these pie plates designed. Every once in a while I start another one and hope that it makes people smile along the way."

"I'll be sure to pass it along. Thank you."

They heard a low bark.

"Oh!" Jean said, "I forgot about Sebastian. Poor boy. I'm going to have to give him a couple of cookies." She winked at them. "And maybe a little piece of ham."

"We really should be getting home," Polly said. "I'm sorry we can't stay to play cards."

"Of course," Sam said, standing with them. "We'll do this another time."

"And next time you will let us bring food," she said.

Jean waved them off as she ran through the kitchen for the back door. "If I can't cook for friends, what fun is it?" She came back, following Sebastian who was very happy to see everyone. He sniffed at the bags of food on the floor and Henry bent over to pick them up and place them on the table.

"Thank you for your hospitality and thank you for telling me a little more about my Uncle Loren. I'm glad that he had some people that knew him, even when his family didn't."

"We'll see if we can't come up with some more stories," Jean said. "Maybe when you come over again sometime, we'll be able to tell you something else that you don't know about him."

They said their good nights and Henry carried the bags as he walked home with Polly.

"Do you think I should call Aaron?" she asked.

"About Loren and Jim Todd knowing each other? Yes," he said. "What a strange little bit of information to pick up on a night like this. I wonder if something happened at the card games that night."

They waited for a car to pass on the highway before walking across into the Sycamore House driveway. "It's strange to realize that if I had never talked to them while I was out walking Obiwan, we never would have found out about this. The universe hands us information in the weirdest ways."

"Polly, there is enough food in here to feed us for the next two weeks. I can't believe she made all of that and then sent it home with us."

"At least I'll be able to enjoy it again. I was so overwhelmed by it that all I could think about was not filling up. And then I did."

She held the door open to their apartment and he went in and headed for the kitchen. "Do you want to walk the dog or put the food away?" she asked.

He looked at the happy dog, wagging his tail between them. "You walk. I'll put things away."

"Cool. I need to get rid of some of that food." Polly reached up and kissed him. "Thanks for going with me tonight. That was fun. We'll invite them over here sometime."

"Of course we will," he said with a smile. "Now go. Last one in bed has to ..." He gave her a wicked grin.

"Come on, Obiwan! We must hurry!" She ran to the back of the apartment and down the stairs with her dog.

CHAPTER SIXTEEN

"I can't take it any longer," Sylvie said. She looked at the chair in front of Polly's desk. "I seem to drop in here a lot. Maybe we should put my name on this one." Sylvie flopped down in it, her face grim.

"What's up?"

"I am about ready to crawl out of my skin. That man is destroying my sanity."

"What man? What are you talking about?" Polly pushed back the stack of papers that were scattered in front of her and leaned on the desk.

"Anthony. He scared me to death Sunday night, he shows up here and kidnaps my son on Monday and now, here it is Friday morning and nothing. I haven't seen him or heard from him. What the hell is he trying to prove? I'm so tired of hiding out at Eliseo's house. I want my own bed and my own stuff. But that man won't let us leave. What am I supposed to do?"

Polly grinned. "He won't let you leave? Girlfriend, you're a big girl. I thought you weren't going to let men push you around any longer."

"You know what I mean. Eliseo's been so nice about this and he knows how scared I was and that I want to keep the boys safe." Sylvie unclenched her hands and thrust them into her lap. "I'm going crazy. I just want this whole thing to be over so I can get back to normal and do you and Henry want to come out for dinner tonight?"

"Okay." Polly drew the word out as she tilted her head. "Are you sure? You don't have an event happening here at Sycamore House?"

"You will never check your calendar, will you?" Sylvie said, with a slight chuckle. "Jeff teases you about it, but I thought he was kidding."

"No. If I have to be here for something, one of you will tell me."

"What do you think about tonight?"

"I can't believe you have a Friday night open and you want to cook for us."

"It's no big deal. On top of it all, I have to go down to school to talk to Jason's counselor and the vice-principal this morning. I feel sick to my stomach. I have to sit in front of two strangers and tell them about all of the horrible things those kids said to Jason about me."

"Do you want me to go with you?"

Sylvie sat back. "You'd do that?"

"Sure," Polly said, shrugging. "No one has told me that I have to be here this morning, so I must be free. Just a sec." She got up and went over to poke her head in Jeff's office.

"Hey there," he said.

"Is there any reason I need to be around this morning?"

"No? Why?"

"Just checking. Back to work with you, now."

"I'm always working, you slacker."

"Uh huh, whatever. Sylvie tells me you have the night off. What are you going to do with that?"

Jeff gave her an evil smile and said, "I'm going out on a date."

"Someone you know or a first date?"

"I'm not telling."

"Well, I hope you have fun. I won't ask any more questions."

"That doesn't sound like you, but thanks. Are you leaving me this morning?"

"Yeah. I'm going to Boone with Sylvie. She has to talk to Jason's counselor and is pretty wigged out about all of the chaos in her life right now."

He ducked his head forward and whispered, "Nothing from her ex yet?"

"No, can you believe it? She's a mess."

"I would be too. Okay. Have fun. I'm leaving early so I won't see you until tomorrow."

"Gotta get yourself all dolled up, eh?"

"Shut up and get out." Jeff scrunched a piece of paper and threw it at her. It lost its arc before clearing his desk.

"That was pathetic."

"Go."

"I'm free," Polly said when she got back into her own office. "Should we make a day of it and have lunch somewhere?"

"You're asking me a question and expecting me to give you a cogent answer," Sylvie said with a sigh.

"You just came up with the word cogent. You're doing fine."

"I'm glad you're coming out tonight. Eliseo wants to show Henry something he found in a hidden cubby hole in the house."

"What did he find?"

"It's nothing important. But it was fun, so we thought maybe Henry might want to have it."

"You aren't going to tell me what it is, are you?"

Sylvie grinned across the desk. "Nope. You have to come out and eat with us to find out."

"You're a horrible friend." Polly took out her phone. "Let me ask Henry. Can we make it a little late though, so I can take Rebecca down to see her mom?"

"Just tell me what time." Sylvie lifted herself off the chair and then dropped back down. "When is Sarah coming home?"

"I don't know," Polly said. "I'm really worried this time. I don't have anything in place to take care of her if she gets sicker. I can't do it. Rachel did fine when Sarah was able to do most of her own care, but Rachel isn't a nurse or even a registered caregiver. If we have to do more serious care, I need someone here."

"For once *I* can help *you*." Sylvie flipped her own phone open and then said, "Here, take this number. Evelyn Morrow lives next door to us in the apartment building. She's a retired nurse and a wonderful person. She's done hospice care before and I know she'll help you. She was telling me a few weeks ago that she was either going to have to take a cruise or find another client."

"Why wouldn't she just take a cruise?" Polly giggled.

"She was kidding. After her husband died, she went on several cruises and traveled around the world. She says she got it all out of her system and is tired of being alone. So she helps people who need her."

"And today when I need the information, here you sit, ready to tell me about her."

"Well, kind of," Sylvie said. "I've been thinking about this for a while, but Sarah was doing well enough she didn't need any extra help. Now you tell me she does and I know someone."

"I'll talk to Sarah this afternoon and then call your friend so they can meet each other."

"If Sarah isn't coming back for a while, Evelyn can go down to the hospital. She does that sometimes to meet her clients. That gives her a chance to talk to doctors and nurses and find out what they need before going home."

"Wow. She's quite the deal."

Sylvie smiled. "I'm going to the kitchen. My appointment is at eleven. We'll leave at ten thirty, okay?"

"Gotcha. No running away before ten thirty."

"And lunch is on me."

"McDonalds it is."

"You pay me better than that. I can afford KFC." Sylvie made it all the way out of her seat this time and left the office.

Polly looked at the phone on her desk and couldn't for the life of her remember why she'd pulled it out. She was supposed to call someone ... oh, right. Henry.

"Hey there, sweet stuff," he said, answering after the first ring.

"Hey yourself. Sylvie was just in my office. I'm going to Boone with her so she can meet with Jason's counselor."

"Awww, I was going to come home and beg you for some nookie at noon."

"I can tell her she has to go alone. That's no problem."

"Hoisted by my own petard. I was kidding. What's up?"

"People are using all sorts of great words around me this morning. I think that means it will be a great day." Polly waited for his chuckle and went on. "Anyway, she's invited us out to Eliseo's house tonight for dinner. He found something in a cubby hole and thinks you should have it."

"What is it?"

"She wouldn't tell me. So do you want to go?"

"Two meals out in one week? We're becoming quite popular."

"I know. That's a yes?"

"At least this time I don't have to get all dressed up."

"You have to get kind of dressed up."

"I'm kidding. That sounds great. I'm curious as to what Eliseo found."

"Me too." She looked up and saw Aaron Merritt come in the front door. "I have to go, the Sheriff is here."

"Uh oh. Better hide your stash."

"No kidding. See you later."

"Love you, sweetie pie."

"Nope, not it."

"Darn."

Aaron walked in and grinned down at her before sitting across from her.

"Henry said I was supposed to hide my stash. It's all put away now," Polly said. "What can I do for you?"

"I wondered if you and Henry would want to do some undercover work for me."

Polly couldn't help herself and laughed out loud. "I thought there was an agreement in place and I was always the one who reneged on it. You won't let me do any investigating."

"Well, this time it's easy. You and Henry play cards, don't you?"

"Uh, yes, but oh, no you don't."

"What do you mean by that?"

"You want me to call Sam and Jean Gardner and ask if they'll take us to their card club. That's tonight, isn't it?"

"Well. Yes. You know them and they like you. That means you'd fit in really well."

"Sorry, Charlie. We already have plans."

He dropped his head. "I was afraid of that. Nobody wants this gig. I tried to talk a couple of my boys into it and they laughed at me. I didn't feel like officially assigning it to someone. I try not to be that mean."

"What do you think you're going to find out while you're playing cards?"

"It's too much of a coincidence that both men attended that night and then died two nights later. I was kind of hoping that you could nonchalantly ... you know, like you do ... get to know some folks and ask crazy questions until you stirred the murderer up and they attacked you."

She cackled into a snort. "You're horrible! Henry would kill you if he knew that you were trying to set me up with that."

"Puhleeze, Polly. You and I both know that these are old people. No one would really attack you. They'd probably tip over on their walkers trying to get to you. Then you'd have to call the ambulance and it would be such a mess."

"I'm not going to even dignify that with a response. I don't think these people are who you think they are."

"I know. I know. They aren't that old and decrepit. But you were my last hope. Now I have to take Lydia and make it semi-official. They'll all know why I'm there."

"Maybe that's a good thing. Maybe the murderer will have a heart attack and while you're reviving him or her, they'll confess with their last words because they're afraid of going to hell once they die."

"Now who's being horrible? If we have to go play cards, I had better make sure Lydia knows about this. She's a lot nicer to me than you are."

"That's her job. Mine is to find dead bodies and make you crazy with worry."

"You're a success at that, for sure." He heaved a huge sigh and stood up. "It was worth a shot. Do you know if we're supposed to take snacks or anything?"

Polly glared. "You're kidding me, right? I had dinner one time with the Gardners. I did not plan to ever attend one of these card nights. I didn't ask questions. I didn't make any plans. I don't know anything."

"But you could ask?"

She put one hand out, palm up.

"What's that?" he asked.

"I've been told by my local sheriff that I can't investigate or get involved in any of these murders. Now you're asking for my help. Either give me a badge or start paying me."

Aaron took out his wallet and drew a dollar bill from it, then placed it in her palm. "Would you please call Jean Gardner and ask her if we would be welcome this evening and what we should bring?"

"Of course I will." Polly slipped the bill into her top desk drawer. "Oh. Do you want me to do that right now?"

He shook his head. "No, you're being impossible this morning. I have things to do and people to see. Would you call my wife when you get the information?"

"So does this mean that now you're amenable to me setting up an investigative agency and employing her as well? Because that could be a lot of fun. Andy would organize all of us and we'd send Beryl out to ask questions of the perps. She'd have them turning themselves in just to escape her insanity."

Aaron left, continuing to shake his head.

Polly dialed the Gardner home and within moments was greeted by Sam's cheery voice.

"Hello there, Polly," he said. "What can the Gardners do for you?"

"Good morning, Sam. Are you and Jean planning to play cards tonight?"

"We certainly are." He obviously turned away. "Jean? Where are we playing cards tonight?"

A muffled sound came through the phone and he returned. "She says we're in Lehigh. Would you and Henry like to come along?"

"No, we can't, but Sheriff Merritt was just here and he would like to join you all this evening. He'll bring his wife, Lydia. It's too much of a coincidence that Loren and Jim Todd were both killed two days after being at the same game night."

"We would love to host the Sheriff and his wife," Sam said. "I've never met them, but Jean knows Lydia, so we'll make them feel at home."

"Thank you. Is there something they should bring? A snack or anything?"

"Tell them not to worry. Jean would be glad to take care of it and if they're coming as our guests, it is our responsibility to provide for them."

"You don't know Lydia Merritt very well, do you?"

"Not as well as I know my Jean. But we insist. Please tell her that. Does this mean that one of us might be the murderer? That sounds quite intriguing."

Polly chuckled. "I don't know. I suspect that Aaron simply wants to ask some questions to see what people might remember."

"I'll be sure to introduce him around. Does he know that there was another group with us as well?"

"I told him. But, this is a good place for him to start."

"Well, we look forward to getting to know them better. Please assure Mrs. Merritt that they need to bring nothing else."

"Thank you Sam. I'll let her know. Thank you again for the wonderful evening and the terrific leftovers. We enjoyed your wife's cooking again last night."

"You're a sweet girl. I already got your thank you note from the post office this morning. That wasn't necessary."

"I was taught as a very young child to write thank you notes.

The woman who raised me would have my head if I didn't express my appreciation for such generosity."

"Tell the Sheriff we look forward to seeing him and his wife."

"Thanks again, Sam."

Polly hung up. If he wasn't such a nice man, she'd be greatly put off by his chauvinism. Jean hadn't seemed too terribly bothered by it the other night. That reminded Polly. She'd never said anything to Henry about how great he was helping Jean in the kitchen. Sam had ignored the entire thing, never offering to help. Polly had gotten herself tucked into a corner so she couldn't, but Henry ... wonderful Henry ... had dug right in and taken care of things.

"I think you're wonderful," she texted to him.

"Well, thank you. I couldn't agree more. Why do you say that today?"

"You're not a chauvinist pig."

"Well! I have no idea where this has come from, but thank you again!"

"I love you and will see you tonight."

"I love you too. If you need me to clean or do laundry or something to keep up appearances, just let me know."

Polly texted back a smiley face and dialed Lydia.

"Good morning sweet girl," Lydia said. "My husband says that we're bailing you out tonight."

"He did not."

"Yes, that is what he said until I pinned him down."

"He's a brat."

"And that's why I love him. Did you talk to Jean?"

"I talked to her husband. He says that you and Jean know each other so you'll be able to find them tonight."

"Sure. We've been on committees together in the past. I know who she is. Am I supposed to take anything?"

"No, apparently they're going to be your hosts and Jean would be upset if you didn't allow her to take care of it."

"Then I'll let her do just that. I'm in Dayton today with the twins while Marilyn takes the baby to the doctor."

"Is everything okay?"

"Oh yes. Just a regular checkup. When they get back, we're all going to ..." The pitch of her voice went up a register and Polly could tell she was speaking to one of the kids. "take a walk to the park and have a picnic. Doesn't that sound like fun?"

"It sounds like fun and you sound busy."

"I'm never too busy for you, dear. But thank you for calling."

The phone went dead before Polly could say goodbye, so she just smiled and put it back on her desk. What a strange morning. No, if she thought about it, this was par for the course.

Sylvie came back into her office. "Are you ready to go?"

"It's ten thirty already?"

"I'm a little early, but I have to get out of here. I'm so nervous, I can't get anything done in the kitchen."

Polly swiped her phone and looked at the time. "You know that we're going to be really early. It's only ten o'clock."

"We'll have coffee or something. I can't sit still."

CHAPTER SEVENTEEN

"Are you up there, Polly?" Henry's voice called up from the bottom of the back stairs. "Polly, what's going on?"

"I don't know what you mean," she responded sweetly. She turned to Rebecca. "Whatever could he possibly mean?"

Rebecca giggled. "I don't know. Maybe he just wants to tell you that he loves you."

"Polly!" Henry crested the stairs and his footsteps across the office and the media room were filled with purpose. "Polly. What have you done?"

The two girls looked up at him from the sofa.

"Why, whatever are you talking about?" Polly asked.

"You know what I'm talking about. Where is your dad's truck?"

"Oh, it's in Boone. We'll need to pick it up on Monday."

"Okay. That answers that. But were you going to tell me about the new truck in the garage?"

"New truck? It's not a new truck. I would never buy a new truck without talking to you first."

"But you'd buy a used truck."

Polly coyly batted her eyes at him and winked at Rebecca.

"Well, maybe. Are you planning to get all macho and yell at me in front of these innocent ears?" She placed her hands over Rebecca's ears and the little girl giggled again.

"No, I'm not going to yell at you. But did you really buy a used truck without talking to me?"

"Kinda and not really." Polly pulled her hands back into her lap. "I have it for the weekend. I thought you and Nate could look at it and test drive it and if we like it, then I'm buying it."

"I thought you were going to buy something more mom-like."

"Mom-like?" She raised her eyebrows at him.

"Not a truck. You already have a truck."

"But my truck only holds three people and that's only if one of those people is a little people. This truck has a big extended cab. I can put lots of people in there. And stuff. Look at all of the stuff I can put in it."

"You really want a truck?"

"Sit," she said. He sat.

"I really do. I thought about it and I'm not ready to give up my truck. It's a 2012 and it's a great deal and low mileage and," Polly poked her lower lip out at him, "can I have this truck, daddy? I'll let you drive it sometimes."

"Stop it," he laughed. "Are you sure this is what you want?"

"I am. When you and Nate finish with those Woodies in two or three years, they will be fun to drive around town, but I want something comfortable for long trips. And something that I can put kids into with seatbelts in every seat. You should see all of the fun stuff. Heated and cooled seats, a DVD player in the back seat and all sorts of other things I haven't figured out yet."

She reached behind her back and pulled out the manual. "I brought this up so I could read all about it and learn what I'm supposed to do and everything."

"You're going to read the manual?"

"Yes. Out loud to you at night before we go to sleep. Doesn't that sound romantic?"

"I'm swooning. What are you going to do with your dad's truck?"

Polly took a breath. "I don't know. I can't sell it. Maybe Eliseo would like to use it around here. It would be great for hauling things and it has enough horsepower to pull a horse trailer if we ever get one of those."

"Because we're taking horses on trips now?"

"You never know. I just think I'd like there to be an extra truck on site."

"You're crazy and I love you. You're going to try to sell that truck to Eliseo for a dollar, aren't you?"

"That would be a lousy business decision, wouldn't it?" She poked Rebecca. "I think maybe ten dollars is a better deal, don't you?"

Rebecca giggled again, her eyes going back and forth between the two adults as they discussed Polly's purchase.

"How did you make this happen so fast?" Henry asked.

"I made Sylvie drive through the lot with me before she met with the people at school, and then I found the one I wanted. It was right there. Almost as if it was waiting for me. So, she dropped me off and I sat down with them and made a deal. Rebecca and I picked it up after we saw her mom."

"So you were in on this, little girl?" Henry spun on Rebecca, his eyes laughing, his tone quite serious.

"I'm sorry, Mr. Meanie. She told me to protect her from you."

"Wait. How did that happen?"

"What do you mean?" Polly asked as innocently as possible.

"How did she figure out I wasn't scary?"

Polly stood up and hugged him. "Because you're about as scary as Jessie's stuffed purple horse."

Her face fell and when she looked at Rebecca, the girl's shoulders drooped.

"I'm sorry. I shouldn't have said anything about her. I'm sure she's fine. She'll let us know where she is when it's the right time."

"I wish she would call," Rebecca said.

"So do I." Polly turned back to Henry. "Are you taking a shower before we go out tonight or were you a lazy boy today and still fresh as a daisy?"

He started to raise his arm over her head and glanced down at Rebecca. "I'll take a shower. You two be good and don't buy anything else like a boat or mobile home while I'm gone."

"Whew, we lived through that one," Polly said, dropping back down on the sofa beside Rebecca. "Thanks for standing up for me. I was worried."

"No you weren't."

Polly chuckled. "You're right. I wasn't. Do you have everything you need for your sleepover at Eliseo's?"

"Right here." She patted her backpack.

"And you have your sketches and drawings for tomorrow morning?"

"In here, too. I'm nervous."

"About Beryl?"

"What if she doesn't think I'm any good?"

"Honey, you are eleven years old. I've seen how you draw and you are very good. Beryl is going to teach you things that will make you better."

"She's kind of crazy."

"She's a lot crazy, but she will love you and you'll love her."

"Maybe I should take Andrew. He can sit and read while I'm there."

Polly turned to face Rebecca. "There is nothing to be afraid of with Beryl. You've seen her plenty of times and though she's a little eccentric, she is a wonderful woman and she is going to be lots of fun. I promise that she won't wear a big black hat on the top of her head or ride a broom around the building or anything like that. She doesn't put children in the oven and cook them for later and she doesn't turn children into cats or mice or anything else."

"No Andrew?"

"No Andrew. This one is all yours. All by yourself. You're going to have a blast. Okay?"

Rebecca blew out a dramatic sigh. "Okay, fine. I'm still nervous."

"Here's what I'll do. Andrew and I will show up early in my

new truck. If you hate it and have to leave, we'll be sitting in Beryl's driveway, ready to haul you away."

"Really?"

"Of course. But I'll bet that's the last time I have to show up early. That's how confident I am that you are going to have a great time."

"Thanks."

Henry came back out, dressed and ready to go. "So, are we taking your truck?"

"And I'll even let you drive."

"Oh, goody, goody," he said flatly. "I've never driven a truck before."

"Fine then. You don't get to if you're going to be a poop about it. Come on Rebecca. We'll make him sit in the back seat."

She glanced up at Polly. "Airbags, remember?"

"Well, both of you can sit in the back seat, then."

Polly scooped up her keys and led the procession down the back steps into the garage. When Henry tried to take the keys from her, she snatched them and pointed to the back door. "You heard me. Back seat for bad boys."

Henry lifted Rebecca in and handed her backpack to her, then trotted around the truck to the back seat of the driver's side. "You know I can torment Polly from here, don't you?" he said to the girl.

"But she's driving and you have to be safe."

"The two of you are no fun at all. I don't think I like having girls gang up on me."

Polly looked in the rear view mirror and stuck her tongue out at him.

Jason was in Eliseo's front yard when Polly drove in and walked over to her truck as nonchalantly as possible. "New truck?" he asked, when she opened the door.

Henry got out and went around to open Rebecca's door.

"You want to sit in it?" Polly asked.

"Can I?"

"It's not mine yet, so I can't let you drive it, but if Henry and

Nate check it out and tell me it's a good buy, it's mine on Monday." She held the door while he climbed in.

He ran his hand across the dashboard and flicked the turn signal. "This is really nice. What are you going to do with the red truck?"

"I think it will be a Sycamore House truck for now. We'll see what happens to it after that."

"Maybe Mom would let me buy it when I can drive."

"That's a couple of years away. Who knows, you might find something even better. And maybe you shouldn't push your luck right now."

He looked at her in shock. "I wasn't going to say anything to her now. Do you think I'm crazy?" He put his hand on the keys. "Can I at least turn it on?"

"I promise, next week you can drive it."

"Okay fine." He handed her the keys and climbed back down.

Andrew and Eliseo came outside and Jason said, "Look at her cool new truck!"

Andrew nodded and ran over to Rebecca. "Put your bag on the front porch and come out to see the chickens."

"I just saw them yesterday," she said.

"But come on!"

Rebecca gave Polly an eyeroll and followed him behind the house.

"What do you think, Eliseo?" Polly asked.

"Nice truck. Couldn't bear the thought of being short to the ground again, huh?"

"I really couldn't and come on, it isn't just men who drive trucks around here, is it?"

"Usually," Henry laughed. "But not my wife. She'll push 'em all off the road." He put his hand on Eliseo's back. "My truck is still bigger though." He turned around and stuck his tongue out at Polly. "Now let's go inside and you can show me what you found in the cubby hole."

This left Polly and Jason alone and all of a sudden he began acting awkward, his head down, a slow shuffle in his step.

"What's up, Jason?"

"Mom talked to the school today."

"Yeah. I went with her. That's when I got my truck."

"Everybody knows what happened."

"It's not easy to have these things out in the open, is it?"

"They're going to bring those guys in to talk to them. Something about bullying and harassment."

"You don't want them to, do you?"

He looked at her. It struck her that they were the same height now and my goodness, but he was getting big. "Now I'm going to have to listen to them call me a tattle tale and whiny kid."

"Jason, look at yourself." She put her hands on his shoulders. "You aren't a little kid any longer. You've already proven that you can take them down and that you're willing to take responsibility for your actions. Who cares what that single group of kids thinks or says?"

"But everyone else hears them say it."

"So?"

"Then everyone will think I'm a tattle tale."

"So?"

"I'll never have any friends."

Polly let her hands fall and took his hand in hers, drawing him toward the front porch. "Is that the worst case scenario?"

"I suppose," he said, a little sullenly.

"Do you really believe that's going to happen or do you think that you might be blowing things a little out of proportion."

"You just don't know what it's like in high school."

"Yeah. That's right. Because I jumped right from elementary school to adulthood."

"You know what I mean."

She stepped up onto the first step and looked down at him. "Here's what I'm going to tell you and it's going to sound harsh, but you need to listen to me. You can't stop those kids from saying things to you. But you can stop your reaction to them. You are not their victim. You can laugh along with them, you can take the high road, you can know that you are better than their behavior.

You can stand up for others who are being bullied by them. You can stand in front of them and let them wail on you as much as they want and take it, because Jason, they can't really hurt you. What happened on Monday hurt you, but only because you gave into them and lowered yourself to their behavior. I promise that they will get tired of it at some point. It might take all year long, but every day when you come home and talk to your mom or to me or to Eliseo, or dare I even say it, to your little brother who adores you, you will hear from us that we love you and think you are wonderful. You have to remember that."

Polly winked at him, "Because if you look like you are starting to forget it, I'm going to start sending little happy post-it notes in your school work telling you how wonderful you are."

"You wouldn't!" Jason looked up at her in shock.

"Of course I wouldn't. That would be horrible now, wouldn't it!"

"Do you really think I can do this?"

She took his arm and drew him up to the next step. "You have such great compassion inside of you. There are going to be kids who need you to stand up for them as you go through these next four years. I'm going to ask you to watch out for them. Show your brother and all of those kids that it doesn't take a bully to stand up to a bully. Be the wall for them. Don't react. Don't take it personally. Just be solid and strong. You're already those things. Now you just have to stop reacting every time something falls apart."

"That's what Mom said. But she didn't say it like you."

"Now let's go inside and see what Eliseo found for Henry."

"It's pretty cool." He opened the front door for her. "Andrew always says that you're willing to talk about things, no matter how weird. He's right."

"You could be a little nicer to him."

"Not likely. I don't want him getting a big head or anything."

"Got it." She laughed and went into the front room.

Henry was sitting on the couch, surrounded by a pile of comic books.

"What in the world?" she asked.

"Look at these. Uncle Loren actually took the time to put them into plastic sleeves and everything."

Sylvie was sitting beside him. "I told Andrew he couldn't touch these until you saw them. I have no idea what they're worth, but they look old."

"Let me see one of those," Polly said.

Henry handed her a comic book from the pile. "See, this is the premiere issue of *Silver Surfer*."

Polly took out her phone and entered the text, then turned it back to Henry. "I have no idea how they determine the quality, but this one is up for auction at more than five hundred dollars."

Sylvie put the comic she was holding back on the stack and took a breath. 'You have to get these out of here. I just about had a heart attack. How much money is this worth?"

"Some of these are pretty beat up," Polly said. "But if they're early comics, those guys are rabid. I wonder where Loren got them."

"There were always comics here at the house when Grandma and Grandpa were alive," Henry said. "Maybe he was smarter about this than I realized." He pointed at the bookshelf on one of the walls leading to the dining room. "When we were little, there were piles of comics that all of us cousins would pull out and read while the adults were talking. I don't know if any of those are in this stack or not."

"Well, they're yours," Eliseo said. "I certainly don't want to be responsible for them. I haven't bought the house yet, and who knows what else I'll find here."

"Where was this cubby hole?" Polly asked.

"It was up in the bedroom where I'm staying," Sylvie said. "In the closet. I told Eliseo the other morning that I thought something looked odd with the wallpaper in there. He checked it out and found that Loren had cut the wall out and made a door. I wonder if he did that when he was a kid. That front room was his bedroom, wasn't it?" She looked at Henry.

"Yeah. It was." He shook his head. "The things you learn after someone has died. I wish I'd known him better when he was normal."

"Dinner's going to be ready in a few minutes," Sylvie said. "Jason, would you help me put things on the table?"

He started to huff, but thought better of it after looking around the room at the other adults and got up, following his mom into the kitchen.

"I'll get Andrew and Rebecca," Eliseo said and went out the front door.

"If we sell these and there is a lot of money here, I have to let Eliseo in on that," Henry said.

"I know. We'll talk to your dad and Betty and decide what the best thing is to do." Polly sat down beside him.

"If these are really worth so much money, I'm not comfortable with them sitting around the apartment."

She started to pick one up, then drew her hand back. "We can always put them back in the cubby hole."

"That might be a little strange. I'll take them over to Dad. He's got plenty of hiding places between the house and the shop. If you go up to their attic, you could stow these in a corner and no one would ever know they're there. So much stuff it's easy to lose things."

Andrew and Rebecca came running in, followed by Eliseo. "Aren't those cool? Mom wouldn't let me open any of them. She said they are really old."

"They are. And she's very smart. They might be worth some money."

"Not worth much if you can't read them," he grumped.

"You are a very smart kid, Andrew Donovan," Polly said, laughing. "That's exactly how I feel about them too. But, since not everyone is as smart as we are, I guess we'll have to abide by their rules."

"I was afraid you'd say that. I love comic books."

"Have you ever spent much time with comics, Rebecca?" Polly asked.

"No. We couldn't afford them."

"Really. The way you draw, you'd be great at doing something like this."

"Rebecca!" Andrew shouted, getting the attention of everyone in the house. "Oops, sorry."

"Andrew," Sylvie scolded from the dining room. "Inside voice."

"I said I'm sorry," he muttered.

"What did you want?" Rebecca asked quietly.

"That's what we should do. Make a comic book together. I could tell the story and you could draw the pictures."

Her face lit up. "That would be fun."

Polly looked at Henry and smiled, shaking her head. "I love watching little brains get all creative."

"You're going to have to buy a lot of paper."

"Anything to keep them doing things like this."

CHAPTER EIGHTEEN

Turning over in bed, Polly said, "I like having Jason live with Eliseo. I don't have to get up as early in the morning."

"When's the last time we got to sleep in?" Henry asked.

"No kids until later, nobody else in the place. I could get used to this." She jostled a cat, who yawned, stretched and curled back into the warm spot she'd left behind.

"That seems dangerous."

"What do you mean?"

"Getting used to this."

"What are you doing today?"

"I'm going to take the comics over to Dad. He needs to know about them. Nate borrowed a flatbed and we're going out to Mrs. Willard's to pick up those cars."

"I can't believe the two of you think you're going to bring those shells back to life. You're insane."

Henry tucked his arm under her shoulders and drew her in close. "I wouldn't do it if Nate wasn't sure of himself. It does seem pretty overwhelming. After that, though, I don't know what else is happening. What about you?"

"Nothing much, actually. Rebecca is spending time with Beryl this morning. Sylvie's dropping her off. Andrew and I will pick her up and then we'll head down to Boone. That probably means a stop at the bookstore."

"Do you ever think about those days when we didn't have anyone else in our lives and we spent entire days watching movies and eating pizza?"

"That was just last year," Polly said.

"It seems like forever ago."

Obiwan's head popped up and he jumped to the floor. Standing in front of the door with his tail wagging, he turned back to look at Polly.

"There isn't anyone out there," Polly said, "and I'm not ready to take you for a walk. Come back to bed, you stupid dog."

He let out a bark.

"What?" she asked. "That's just not right." Polly nestled back into Henry's arms. "What's up with him, anyway?"

"Shhh. Do you hear that?" he asked.

"I don't hear anything. No one is getting me out of bed this morning. Stop it, both of you."

"Polly, someone is out there."

She sat up and scooted up against the headboard. "Oh come on. Unless they have a key to get into Sycamore House and then into the apartment, no one is there. I don't hear anything."

"If you'd be quiet long enough to pay attention, you'd hear something."

Obiwan barked again, three times.

"You stay here," Henry said. "I'll see what's going on."

"Like I want you to be the one who gets shot?" Polly sat forward and took a deep breath. "Who's out there? You're bothering my Saturday morning sleep."

She nearly leaped out of her skin when there was a knock at their bedroom door.

"Polly? Henry? I'm sorry, it's me. Jessie."

Polly glared at Henry. "I nearly wet the bed," she said softly, then broke into hysterical laughter. "You'd be shot and I'd wet the bed. What a pair we'd be."

"I'll be right there, Jessie," she called out. "Just let me get my wits about me."

"What in the hell do you think she wants?" Henry asked disgustedly.

"You stop it. We don't know what's been going on."

"She runs out on you, she runs out on Mom and now she sneaks back here in the dark of night and scares us to death. Does the girl have no sense?"

"It's seven o'clock in the morning. The sun has been up for half an hour. Dark of night left a long time ago. Get over yourself and put some clothes on. I'm going to start the coffee and you're going to take Obiwan for a walk. Then we're calmly going to find out what she's been doing this last week and we're calmly going to figure out what comes next. Got it?"

"Don't calmly me. I was nearly shot." He threw the blankets back and swung his legs to the floor. "I told you not to get used to being alone here. You did this to us. You jinxed our lazy morning, so I'm going to be mad at you."

"I need coffee," Polly said. "Lots and lots of coffee. My heart is racing so fast it seems to have missed the checkered flag."

"No more Sunday afternoon Nascar racing for you."

"It's great for naps. Varoom, varoom ... wonderful white noise."

"Get out and deal with the girl."

Polly pulled on her robe and opened the door. Obiwan dashed to the sofa and jumped up on Jessie's lap.

"It looks like someone's glad to see you're back," Polly said, walking through to the kitchen. "Come on out while I make coffee."

She filled the pot with water and the filter with coffee and flipped the switch, then leaned back on the counter to wait for Jessie. When it didn't happen immediately, Polly opened the refrigerator and stared at the shelves, hoping for breakfast inspiration. Finally, she took out milk, eggs, and a loaf of bread. French toast seemed easier than pancakes this morning. She was whisking the egg mixture when Henry and Obiwan walked through to the back door. The dog was wagging excitedly. Henry scowled as he went past.

"Jessie?" Polly called out. "Come on in. No one will bite you."

The cats were meowing and weaving through her feet, so she filled their food dishes and then went ahead and put food in Obiwan's dish as well.

"I'm so sorry, Polly. I should have called. I should have messaged you. I should never have left." Jessie poked her head around the corner of the door and walked across the room.

"Yep. You're right. Okay, you're sorry. I accept that. When's the last time you had anything to eat."

Jessie looked at the floor. "I don't know. I ate something yesterday at a gas station."

"You haven't eaten except for food at a gas station?"

"I only had money for gas."

Polly dropped two slices of bread into the toaster, opened the refrigerator and took out milk and orange juice, pouring a glass of each and putting them on the peninsula. "Sit. Start drinking. We'll deal with this past week after you've had something to eat and taken a shower."

"I'm so sorry."

"No apologies yet. Just deal with what is coming next. I don't want you to talk about any of this until you're ready to face every bit of it."

"But ... "

"Nope. No buts. First food, then shower, then talking. In that order, so we aren't interrupted. Then we start fixing things."

"Can it be fixed?"

Polly leaned over the counter and looked at Jessie. "Tell me that you are okay. That you haven't been hurt, that you don't need a doctor or something like that."

Jessie pulled her shirtsleeves down over the back of her hands. "I'll be okay."

"What?" Polly asked and reached out to touch her.

The girl drew back suddenly and turned her head so that her hair fell in front of her face.

"Jessie. Have you been hurt?"

"It's fine."

"Is something broken?"

"No." Jessie looked up at Polly, silently pleading. "I'm fine."

"Do you promise that there is no need to see a doctor?"

"It's okay."

"That's not a promise, but as long as nothing is broken, we'll deal with that later, too."

The toast popped up. Polly buttered it and took out two jars of jelly and put it all in front of Jessie. "Start eating. French toast and coffee will be up in just a few minutes."

No sooner had she started dipping bread, than Jessie was finished with the first piece of toast and slathering jelly on the second. Polly refilled her milk glass and then the orange juice.

"This is so good," Jessie said. "Thank you."

"How long did it take you to get here?" Polly asked.

"I was stupid. I went to Omaha."

"From where?"

"I left him in Rapid City."

Polly slowly nodded her head. "When did you leave?"

"I snuck out yesterday morning. I drove all day, well, I had to stop several times to sleep. I don't think I slept all week. I fell asleep last night in a truck stop and then came here and slept in the parking lot."

"Oh sweetie, you should have called me and come up when you got here."

"I don't have my phone and I didn't want to scare you in the middle of the night."

"I see. Okay. More about that later."

"I want to tell you."

Polly flipped the four slices of French toast on her griddle. "I know you do. And you'll have plenty of time to do that. Just let me ask one question. Is anyone chasing you? Am I going to have to deal with something else?"

Jessie shook her head, "No, he doesn't give a shit about me." She looked up. "Oops, sorry."

"That's okay, there's no one else around to hear it."

"No, I have to get used to being around the kids again."

Polly put two pieces of French toast on her plate and pushed the syrup toward her.

"Do I get to be around the kids again?"

"It's going to be okay. One way or the other it's going to be okay. Rebecca missed you. It's been a rough week around here."

"What happened? Is her mom okay?"

"She will be, but Sarah went back into the hospital this week. This time because she's diabetic. She was getting really lethargic and went downhill pretty quickly."

"Oh, poor Rebecca."

"And, Andrew was taken by his father Monday night."

"What?"

"Yeah. It's been a little rough. I think we're getting through it, though. Rebecca was worried about you."

"I missed her."

"She'll be here later today. She's at Beryl's this morning."

"Doing art? That's so cool. That little girl is so good."

"Yes she is. Now eat. More milk?"

"No, I'm fine. Thanks."

Obiwan dashed across the floor, stopped to sniff Jessie's leg, then ran to his food dish. Henry came through and turned to head back to their bedroom.

"I'll be right back. Eat those other two pieces if you want. I have plenty." Polly left and followed Henry.

"So. Has she sowed her wild oats again?" Henry asked once the door was shut.

"I don't know anything yet. She hasn't eaten since yesterday afternoon and she's starving. She's been on the road from Rapid City since yesterday morning and I think she's been hurt. Nothing is broken, but she isn't ready to tell me what's wrong. You have to be nice until we know the whole story, please?"

He set his lips into a flat line. "I'll be nice. This girl is trouble, Polly. I can't believe you want her here and influencing Rebecca and Andrew."

"Henry, please don't do this."

"Do what? She ran away from her parents and now she's run away from us. Who's to say she won't run again?"

"She came back. Can't we at least wait until we know everything?"

"You rescue people and you take care of them. My job is to take care of you. When people abuse your good will, that infuriates me. She's a stupid kid and you're going to bend over backwards to make sure that she's okay. She'll hurt you again and what if she hurts those kids?"

"I don't want to fight with you about this."

"I don't want to fight either, but I'm pissed."

"Are you mad enough that you don't want to eat breakfast? I'm making French toast."

He took her by the arms and then wrapping them around his waist, he hugged her. "I'm mad enough that I don't want to eat breakfast. Will it make you angry if I take a shower and head over to the shop? If I sit with her and she tries to make me feel sad for her, I don't know what I'll say."

"I won't make you put up with young girl angst," Polly said, tilting her head up to kiss his cheek. "Go hang out with your parents, get rid of your comic books and call your buddy to pick up your cars."

Henry stepped back from her. "You just made me sound like a teenager."

"Oh I did? Come on, now." Polly let a burble of laughter escape her lips. "You have it pretty good, big boy. Do you really think it's a bad thing for me to try to help someone who didn't grow up with parents like yours?"

"Now you're just being mean." He brushed his index finger down her nose. "I'll go away and calm down and when you've found out all of her dirty little secrets and gotten her all fixed up, then you can tell me about it and I'll feel sorry for her."

"I'm probably going to let her sleep the day away here. Are you sure you'll be gone all day?"

"I am now. I'll pack a lunch."

"I love you, you big, gruff bear."

"Maybe you should call me Sugarbear."

"Uh huh. Go take a shower. I'll talk to you later."

"Are you still taking Andrew and Rebecca to Boone?"

"Yeah. Do you need something?"

"No, that's fine. Just be careful."

Polly moved in closer and kissed him, feeling his arms wrap around her again. "I'm sorry we didn't get our lazy morning," he said.

"We can try again some other time."

She went back out to the kitchen and turned the heat on under the griddle again. Jessie had finished all four slices of French toast. "Do you want any more?" Polly asked.

"No, I think I'm going to die."

"Well, I'm going to cook all of this up and we can toast it later on. I thought I was cooking for a crowd, but Henry is going over to his parent's house."

"Is he really mad at me?"

"He's kind of mad," Polly said, matter-of-factly. "He went out of his way for you with his mom and feels like you stiffed him."

"I know. I should have called."

"Yes, you should have. It's going to take a while before he trusts you again." She reached up and took out a box of parchment paper. "Here, tear this up in bread size pieces."

After they finished cooking and packing the French toast, Polly sent Jessie to take a shower. Henry had slipped out the front door, not bothering to say goodbye. Polly cleaned the kitchen, poured another cup of coffee and sat down at the dining room table. She put her hand on Obiwan's head when he nudged her leg.

"I know. It's a weird house we live in. Where did all of these strange people come from?"

She listened as Jessie made her way back across the living room to her bedroom. Polly took her coffee into the living room and dropped onto the sofa, pulling her legs up underneath her. The dog climbed up and lay down beside her, his head as close to her lap as he could get it. Polly rubbed his ears.

After what seemed like an eternity, Jessie re-emerged, dressed in baggy sweats, and a t-shirt underneath a long sleeve, sloppy sweater.

"If you want coffee, help yourself," Polly said, nodding back to the kitchen.

"No, I'm fine."

"Are you ready to talk about this week?"

"I want to tell you."

Polly waited while the girl got comfortable in a chair across from her. "Just start whenever you're ready."

"I feel like I've really got a messy life. Everything is falling apart."

"Chaos can do that to a person."

"Can I ask you a question?"

"Sure, go ahead."

"Are you going to make me go over to Oelwein by myself next week?"

Polly had completely forgotten about that. "Wow, that's not where I thought we were going with this right now."

"I know, but I just want to know how badly I screwed this up."

"Jessie, if you want me there, of course I'll go with you."

"Okay, I just wanted to check. Now do you want me to tell you what happened?"

"Of course. Tell me whatever you want me to know."

Jessie pulled the sleeves of her sweater up to reveal red welts on her arms.

"What is that?" Polly asked.

"Cigarette burns."

"I'm sorry, what? Where did those come from?"

"Okay, so we left Sunday night and met up with the rest of the band in Minneapolis. Troy told me to bring my car because they had to return the rental. He said there was good money in it for me, that I could be like a roadie. All I had to do was drive. I didn't have to haul equipment, just drive. They had a pickup for the gear, but only two people could ride in that and the other three had to ride with me."

"A lot of money. Got it," Polly said.

"I know, I should have talked to you. But it was really last minute and he told me we were in a hurry."

"Go ahead."

"We met up with the others in Minneapolis and they had a couple of gigs planned and then we went to South Dakota. There was a gig on Wednesday night. I had to do all the driving. They smoked weed and got high all the time I was driving."

"But they paid for hotels and gas and food, right?" Polly asked.

"Well, yeah. Kinda. The first two shows in Minneapolis didn't pay much and they were going to get paid this weekend for the stuff in South Dakota. I was going to get money then."

"Got it."

"Well, I pissed him off when we got to South Dakota. I knew I was running out of money for gas and the only thing we ate was crap from gas stations and fast food places. I wanted to eat somewhere decent. And then things got weird. The drummer said he should be able to sleep with me. I was the only girl there. And then they all started coming on to me. I didn't know what was going to happen. If Austin hadn't been there, it could have been bad. That's when Troy got pissed. I was driving and all of a sudden he was yelling at me and he jammed his cigarette into my arm and told me that I was just a stupid little girl and if the guys wanted to sleep with me, it was my job."

Polly stayed quiet and kept her eyes on Jessie while the girl told her story. She wasn't going to reveal her inner fury. If she ever got her hands on that boy he would be ... well ... not dead, but definitely in great amounts of pain.

"Austin told him to shut up and Troy threw a full bottle of coke at him, nearly knocking him out. I pulled over, I was shaking so hard I couldn't drive. Troy told me to get out, that he would drive, but I didn't trust him. He'd been drinking and smoking and tons of other stuff. And I was worried that he'd drive off without me, so I kept the keys. He started yelling that it was his band and that I was his whore and whatever he said was what was going to happen. Then he lit up another cigarette and jammed it into my arm again and told me that I'd better learn my place if I was going to travel with them."

"I'm sorry," Polly said. "Go on."

"That was Thursday. They played that night and I thought about leaving, but I didn't know how mad you'd be at me and I was scared to come back here. I could have gone home, but how would I ever tell my mom that I screwed up a second time."

"You should have called."

"Well, yeah. Except that when we got to Minneapolis, Troy started going through my purse and he thought he was being funny and threw the whole thing except my wallet out the window while I was in the middle of morning rush hour traffic. I didn't have a phone."

"So what made you decide to leave?"

"Austin saved me. He took me to his room Thursday night and locked the door. He didn't try anything, but all night long Troy and the others kept knocking and calling and bugging us, trying to get in. Troy thought it would be lots of fun to have some big party with me and some other girls they picked up. Finally everybody fell asleep and Austin told me to leave. He only had a little money and he gave it to me for gas. He told me to just get out and come back here. It would be better to face you than to put up with anymore crap from Troy."

"He was right."

"So are you going to kick me out because I screwed this all up?"

"Jessie, I'm not going to kick you out. I'm sorry that this happened again to you. Can I tell you that you make really poor choices with men?"

"I know. What am I doing wrong?"

"I don't know. Have you been talking to the therapist about this stuff?"

"I suppose," Jessie shrugged. "Yeah. A little."

"Well, I think you need to talk about it a little more. Now, let me look at that arm. Did you do anything to clean it up or put anything on it?"

"I washed it when I was in the bathroom."

"Does it hurt?"

"Like a son of a bitch," the girl said. "I'm so sorry. Every conversation this week was bad words. I forgot."

"Again, no worries. We're all alone. Come into my bathroom. I have some aloe vera in there. You need to put it on a lot and then you're going to want to keep that skin soft while it heals. There are going to be scars, but maybe we can reduce them some."

"I'm sorry I let you down, Polly. You've been so nice to me."

"Sweetie, the only person you really let down was yourself. You have got to start believing that you're worth more than these jerks you keep hooking up with. You're sweet, kind, good with kids, and other than making bad decisions about men, you're very bright. You don't need to do this."

Jessie let Polly clean her arm and then relaxed as the aloe vera gel hit the burns. "Thank you."

"Take this to your room and use it whenever you need to. Did you sleep much in your car?"

"I suppose."

"Can you sleep in your bed here?"

"Yes, but can I watch TV for a while with the animals?"

"Henry is going to be gone all day. Andrew and I are planning to pick Rebecca up and go to Boone. You'll have the house to yourself. Eat whatever you like, sleep when you want, watch television. Maybe you could take Obiwan outside later on."

"I can do that."

"Everything can be fixed later. You're here. You're safe. We'll deal with your phone on Monday."

"I'll get another job as fast as I can."

Polly put her arm around Jessie's shoulders and nearly wept when the girl slumped against her, holding on. She drew her in for a full hug. "You know," Polly said into Jessie's ear, "the person who talked to me about giving someone lots of chances was Henry's mom. Why don't we go see her on Monday."

"Really?"

"Really."

CHAPTER NINETEEN

"Exhaustion makes sense for me," Joss said, "Those babies have decided that they're going to double team me. Sleep and I no longer have a relationship, but what's up with the rest of you?"

The girls were all back at Pizzazz since it was Sunday evening.

Sal took a drink of her iced tea. "I'm not so much exhausted as I am dreading the trip back to Boston this week."

"Why are you going back?" Sylvie asked.

"My father is having knee surgery and Mom insists that I be there, just in case he dies. I wouldn't want to miss out on that, would I?"

"I think that's sweet. You love your dad," Polly said.

"Of course I love him, but Mom is turning this into a huge production. She's hired an entire staff of nurses and physical therapists to be on hand the moment he comes out of surgery. The poor man can't just suffer through this alone. No, he has to have an immense audience of highly paid professionals watching his every movement. I swear, one of them is only there to wipe his ass when he goes to the bathroom."

Sylvie smiled. "Has he ever been sick before?"

"No. Not ever."

"Then she's in a panic. She's never known him to be weak and probably can't bear the thought of losing him."

"It's knee surgery, for heaven's sake. The man is as healthy as a horse. He'll be fine."

"Wouldn't you feel horrible if ..." Sylvie stopped. "I'll shut up."

"Yes, I would feel horrible, but why in the world is she turning this into such a big deal? I'd get it if it was something incapacitating or long-term, but this is going to make him feel better. The woman is insane. She always has been and I promise you, from here on out, it is only going to get worse. I don't know why it couldn't be her going through this. Dad would just manage through it and do whatever she needed."

Polly patted Sal's arm. "But you get to come back to Iowa when it's all over, don't you?"

"Oh hell, I'd better. You can't believe what she has planned for me. While Dad is recuperating in the hospital, I have to host a tea with her friends. Mom won't be able to make it, because, you know, she'll be sitting at his bedside every moment of the day. So, all of these little old ladies with sticks up their behinds are going to come to her home and expect me to be gracious."

"You've been well trained. I know that for a fact," Polly said. "You'll be charming and wonderful and they won't even miss her."

"I should make you come with me. You're the one they all like. That sweet little Iowa girl who has such terrific manners. Who would have expected such a thing?"

Joss chuckled. "You're kidding, right?"

"No," Polly said. "She's not kidding. She invited me to tea and it seems that I was the sweetest thing they'd ever met. They all wanted me to meet their sons and grandsons. Blech. That's one part of society I never aspired to."

"So, to wrap up. I'm not tired yet. But I'm dreading this next week," Sal said. "Your turn, Sylvie."

"I want to sleep in my own bed."

"You aren't back there yet?" Sal asked.

"No. Eliseo insists that we stay at his place until we know what

Anthony is doing in town. But at this point, I don't even know if he is in town. I haven't seen him all week. I keep waiting for him to show up at the kitchen. I'm terrified there is going to be some big confrontation, but so far, nothing."

"How are things with Jason?" Joss asked quietly. "That can't have been easy this week."

"Did you tell them?" Sylvie asked Polly, who shook her head no. "The school is going to keep an eye on the boys who set him up. They went at him all day long, talking trash about me and Eliseo. He finally snapped. I've talked to him this week about blowing it off and not letting them get to him. But honestly, I don't know if I'd have the patience to put up with that."

"Can't he tell someone while it's going on?" Sal asked.

"That boy never wants to be known as a snitch," Polly said. "It would just kill him."

"No," Sylvie said. "He needs to learn how to deal with this and he needs to learn that violence is an unacceptable way to deal with anything."

"He's getting big," Joss said. "Working with those horses has done wonders for his muscles."

"He looks so much like his dad. I'm just glad he smiles every once in a while. When he does the whole sullen teenager thing, I want to slap it right off his face."

"So much for non-violence," Sal said, laughing.

"I know! I think he'll do better now that he's found out what a bad thing this was," Polly said. "He wants so badly to be a good kid. It's going to take a while, but he'll figure out a better class of friends and it will get easier."

"Nate was bullied when he was in high school. He was smart and a little overweight and he hated sports," Joss said. "His Mom didn't help. She made him dress in stupid little dress pants and sweater vests when he was young, so that didn't help his cred. By the time he was in high school, it was really tough. That's why he started working on cars. He could escape down to the industrial arts wing and hide. The teacher figured it out pretty fast and spent a lot of time with him. It was the only thing that saved him."

"If they had horses down there, Jason would be fine," Sylvie said.

Polly smiled. "At least he has them when he comes home."

"What about you?" Sal said. "I haven't spent any time with you this week."

"Oh, things are fine. I bought a new truck. Henry's taking me down to Boone tomorrow. I'll sign papers and then bring Dad's truck back to Sycamore House. I'm not sure what I'll do with it, but I can't bear the thought of trading it in and having some stranger drive it."

"You get awfully attached to weird things, Polly Giller," Sal said. She looked around the table. "This girl still has the silk corsage from our freshman winter ball."

"It brings back memories. You shut up," Polly protested.

"So you're just parking it ... where?" Sylvie asked.

"I don't know. Maybe down by the barn. Eliseo needs a truck every once in a while to haul things, so rather than borrowing mine, he can just use Dad's whenever he needs it."

"So rather than buy a car or a van or even an SUV, you bought another truck?" Sal pressed forward, taunting her friend.

"Yes, I bought a truck."

"You've really gotten into this whole Iowa farm girl thing, haven't you?"

"The back has doors and room for three people. That means I can strap all of the kids in and everyone can quit worrying. Now leave me alone. I love my truck."

Joss shook her head. "I don't see you driving around in a little sedan. A truck fits you."

"Exactly," Polly said. "And now that Nate and Henry have given it their final approval, I can be done with this process."

"How's Sarah Heater? Did you set anything up with Evelyn?" Sylvie asked.

"Yeah. She went down to meet Sarah yesterday. It's going to work out just fine. She was quite ... ummm ... organized about the whole thing."

Sylvie chuckled. "She is that, but she's really sweet. Sarah will be in good hands once she comes home. When is that supposed to happen?"

"Sometime this week. We don't know exactly when, yet."

"How's Rebecca handling all of this?" Joss asked. "She's such a sweet little girl. This has to be really hard on her."

"It is. But Jessie came back yesterday and having that commotion settle down in Rebecca's life was a good thing."

"Where did she go?" Sal's voice was flat, her eyes narrowed. "She really gets herself in trouble, doesn't she?"

"Yes she does. But we're going to be nice about this. That poor girl hasn't had all of the benefits we had growing up. She's got a lot to learn about life yet ..." Polly's mouth dropped open as she quit talking. Then she said, "Ummm, Sylvie?"

"What?" Sylvie turned around to see what Polly was looking at. Then she turned back to the table and said, "Shit. Not here."

Sal raised her eyebrows at Sylvie's curse word. "Well, well, our Sylvie has a potty mouth."

"That's her ex-husband, Anthony," Polly whispered.

"Oh."

"Sylvie Donovan, there you are! I have looked all over for you and I can't believe I find you here, of all places. I thought you were a certified chef now. Why are you slumming it in a joint like this?" Anthony's loud voice carried across the room and he loomed over the tables as he made his way back to where Sylvie was seated.

She seemed to shrink as he approached. He snagged an empty chair as he passed a table and planted it beside Sylvie, straddling it as he lowered his frame.

"How you been, little woman? I haven't seen you in years. Life's been good to you and look at all of these pretty young ladies you're hanging out with. You never had time for friends when I was around. I was too much man for you, wasn't I?"

Polly gulped. He was everything that Sylvie had been scared of and more.

A waitress approached, "Can I get you something to drink, sir?"

"Whatever you have on tap and keep 'em coming." He took out his wallet, drew out a pile of twenty dollar bills and slammed them on the table. "It's all on me tonight. I have great news."

"What's your news, Anthony?" Sylvie finally spoke.

"I got a job. That's where I've been this week. I had an interview and found a place to live. I'm back in Iowa, baby. Now I can spend time with the boys and make sure that you've been doing right by my kids."

"In Iowa?" she squeaked. "Where?"

"I'm driving for a company up in Fort Dodge. I'll be on the road a lot of the time, but when I'm home, I'm going to want to be spending time with those boys of mine."

"Are you going to introduce us, Sylvie?" Sal asked. "No? Well, I'll take care of that. Hi, I'm Sal Kahane. You are?"

"You didn't tell them about me?" he demanded.

"I'm Joss Mikkels."

Since Anthony had dropped down between her and Sylvie, he reached a large paw out to take her hand. "You're a pretty little thing. You married?"

"Yes, with twins," she said.

"Lucky man." He looked at Polly, "You must be the school marm, fixing up that old building and making it all fancy. I've been hearing about you and how you stick your nose into everybody's business. After I saw you last week, I did some asking. Seems not everyone thinks you're as popular as you think you are."

"Stop it, Anthony," Sylvie said.

"Oh, pardon me," he said dramatically, "I forgot, she's your boss."

"Why are you here?"

"I came into town to see some of my buddies. We get together on Sunday nights. You know, try to forget that we have to go to work on Monday mornings? I was over at the Alehouse when someone said you were here. So I thought I'd drop in and see your pretty little face." He brought his hand up and grasped her chin, turning her to face him. "It's always been a pretty little face."

Sylvie pushed his hand away. "You're hurting me."

"Oh, that ain't nothing and you know it. You're a tough girl. You can take it. Speaking of tough. What in the hell are you doing with Andy. What a little sissy boy he turned out to be."

"He's smart and witty and a really good kid," Sylvie said.

"I'll fix him right up. And how's Jason? Did you screw him up too?"

"Jason is fine. He's just fine."

"We'll see about that."

"Anthony, I don't want to have this conversation here."

"Where in the hell do you want to have it? I come into town and find that you've ducked out of your apartment. Don't tell me you're hiding from me, or did you find some other man to move in with. Someone else who can take care of you." He turned to the rest of the table. "She's always needed someone to take care of her. A lot of pretty in the face, not a lot of stuff in her brain, you know."

Polly opened her mouth to speak, but Sylvie gave a slight shake of her head.

"Where's that beer?" he called out. "How long does it take to pour something into a glass?"

"You've been drinking all night, haven't you," Sylvie asked.

"What's it to you? You gonna call your cop friend again? I ain't hurt you none tonight." He winked at Polly. "Not yet, anyway. She likes it sometimes when I hurt her, don't ya baby." Anthony put his arm around Sylvie's shoulders and pulled her close to him.

She pushed him away. "Stop that, you don't have any right."

"Any right? Right? I don't need a right. I'm just being friendly."

The waitress came back with his beer and put it down in front of him, scurrying away before he could say anything else to her.

"Go back to your friends, Anthony. We don't want you here tonight."

"I'm not going anywhere until I'm ready to go. And I haven't spent nearly enough time with all you pretty ladies."

Sylvie shifted her chair away from him and turned to face him. "Anthony Donovan, you're a big, nasty bully. I'm done being afraid of you. You can hurt me, you can bloody me, you can insult me, but you can no longer control me. You're drunk and you are being loud and rude. Either leave now, or you know what? I will call my cop friend. In fact, I will call all of my friends, the Sheriff, the Chief of Police, deputies and anyone else that needs to show up to tell you to get away from me. You can't intimidate me any longer."

She stood up and looked down at him. "And you lost all rights to Jason and Andrew. You will not talk to them or have anything to do with them. The custody agreement is still in force and you screwed up when you took Andrew last Monday. If I wanted to have you arrested for that, there's nothing you could do about it. So get the hell out of here before it is me that makes trouble for you."

He scooted his chair back and stood up. Sylvie planted her feet and put her hands on her waist and stared him down. "I. Said. Leave," she said flatly. Her voice never rose in pitch. Now that didn't mean that her face hadn't gone fully flush. Polly watched as her hands trembled at her waist, realizing that there wasn't much time before the poor girl was going to fall apart.

Polly slowly stood up and before she realized it, both Sal and Joss were standing as well.

Anthony shoved the chair and said, "We're not done, you and me. This conversation has a long ways to go before we're done."

"Oh, we're done. Come near me again and I'll show you how much we're done," Sylvie said. She grabbed her chair, pulled it out and sat down, showing him her back. He took one more look at her and walked out of the restaurant.

Sal, Polly and Joss sat back down.

"My knees are a little weak," Sal said. "And I'm pretty sure I might have peed my pants, but there's no sensation down there right now, so I can't be certain."

Sylvie looked at her and started to laugh. Soon there were tears streaming down her face as she lost control of her laughter. It was contagious and Polly and Joss found themselves out of control as well. It didn't take long for Sylvie to begin sobbing.

"I'm so sorry. I don't know why I'm crying. I did it. I finally stood up to that asshole and I made him leave."

"It's just release," Polly said. "Let it out."

She looked up to see Dylan Foster, the owner of Pizzazz and the husband of Mark Ogden's sister, come to their table. He put his hand on Sylvie's back and she jumped.

"I'm sorry, Sylvie," he said. "Are you okay?"

"I'm fine, now. Thanks."

"I called Mark. He's on his way over. There might be a posse with him," Dylan said. "He was going to call the Sheriff and Henry and your husband, too, Joss."

Polly started laughing again. "We're so sorry this happened in your restaurant," she said. "And now all of our knights are showing up to keep us safe. After we dealt with it."

She stood up and held her right hand out, "High five, ladies. Our Sylvie girl rocked!" They stood and clapped their hands together, raising them as one, when Mark and Henry strode in the front door.

"You're a little late, fellas," Sal said. "Sylvie got her mean-girl on. She took out the bully and didn't even have to shoot him in the kneecap or anything."

"Are you girls really okay?" Henry asked.

"We're fine. And look," Polly pointed at the money on the table. "He left money to pay for our dinner tonight. Do you want to join us?"

Aaron Merritt came rushing in the front door, Lydia close behind him. "What happened?" he asked.

Lydia grabbed Sylvie and pulled her in for a hug. Sylvie turned in her arms and looked up at Aaron. "I did it. I told him to leave and I meant it. And he left."

"I'm proud of you. I knew you'd get there," he said. "What's he doing in town?"

"He got a job in Fort Dodge. He thinks he's going to be involved in Jason and Andrew's lives. He's wrong, but I'll deal with that tomorrow. Tonight, I think I'll just pass out."

"Pull up another table and bring some chairs," Sal said. "We have some celebrating to do. It isn't every day we get to see a bully stripped to his knees."

Sylvie dropped into a chair as Lydia turned the chair Anthony had appropriated and sat down beside her. "Are you sure you're okay?" Lydia asked.

"I'm positive. I didn't know if my legs were going to keep me upright, but I made it. I finally realized that the physical crap he did to me didn't have to make me weak. If he hurts me, I'll heal. And I don't give a crap what he says to me anymore. He's nothing."

She leaned forward on the table, "At least I no longer feel like I'm going to puke."

"You did great, girlfriend," Polly said. "I'm proud of you."

"I'm a little proud of me, too."

CHAPTER TWENTY

Turning to go into the dealership after Henry and Rebecca drove away in her new truck, Polly felt a little wistful. A few last things to sign and she would take the keys to her dad's truck and go home. She'd asked Henry to take Rebecca with him back to Bellingwood after they'd stopped to see Sarah at the hospital. She couldn't believe that she was feeling so attached to a vehicle, but she wanted a few more minutes with her dad before finally parking his truck and moving on.

A young man held the door for her and pointed to the desk where her salesperson was waiting. It had been years since she'd actually had to go through the process and Polly was more than a little surprised at the fact that with all the technology available to humanity, buying a car still took forever and frustrated her to no end. Most of it had been completed last Friday, the check had cleared and yet here she sat. Finally, the girl came back, handed Polly an extra key fob and a folio with paperwork in it.

They walked to the front door, commented on the thunder sounding nearby and Polly broke away and got into her truck. Today was a good day to take the long way home. She drove back through Boone and turned left. There was a road to the west of town that she hadn't explored yet. She was in no hurry, there was plenty of gas in the tank and she was taking a farewell tour.

Polly thought back to the first time she'd driven a pickup truck. She had to have been about twelve and barely reached the pedals. She kept insisting that all of the other farm kids were running errands for their parents who were working in the fields. Mary had finally convinced Polly's dad to relent. The first time she put her foot on the gas pedal, she'd nearly wet her pants. The truck had gone ripping down their long driveway and her Dad had quickly slid over beside her, put his hand on the wheel and lifted her leg away from the gas. It had taken a while for her to build up the courage for that again.

But over the years, driving her dad's trucks had become as comfortable as driving anything else. They were part of him. And it was going to be strange not having this one around any longer. She bent over to the glove compartment and flipped it open, then looked up quickly and placed both hands back on the wheel as she approached a bend in the road. There were more bends and curves and hills and valleys than she was used to driving. It might be important to pay a little better attention.

A vehicle passed her and she realized that even though the road was twisty, forty miles an hour might be a little slow. She hadn't been paying enough attention to her speed. Yes, she could pick it up a little. She glanced once more at the glove compartment. She'd kept a pair of her dad's work gloves in there, just like he always did. They smelled like him, sweat and cologne ingrained in the leather. Polly wanted to remember to take those out when she got home. They could just as easily reside in the new truck as they did in here. She couldn't stand it, so reached over to grab them when she was startled by a bump. It felt as if someone had run into her from behind. She sat back up and looked into the rear view mirror. A large, black SUV was right behind her, just a few feet from her bumper.

What in the world? The SUV dropped back and Polly flipped her turn signal on and slowed down to pull off on the shoulder.

Damned kids. The poor truck was already damaged from the last altercation with a ditch.

Annoyance quickly turned to fear as the all-black vehicle with a large brush guard on front, lunged at her instead of slowing down. She was already pulling onto the shoulder and jerked her truck back onto the road. She had absolutely no desire to take a ride into the ditch again, and besides these were deeper. The vehicle slammed into her bumper again and she lurched forward.

Polly's mind reeled. What did he want? It had to be a mistake.

When he rammed her a third time, she knew she had to take action. It wasn't a random accident, this guy was trying to hurt her. She stepped on the gas as she saw him taking another run at the truck. She lurched forward, but the SUV kept pace with her. There was no way to outrun him.

In her mirror, Polly caught a glimpse of a silver car coming up behind the truck and breathed a sigh of relief. The idiot would surely stop harassing her if there was a witness. She pulled her foot back off the accelerator and was grateful the SUV didn't take advantage of it by hitting her bumper again. If she could just stop and pull over, she could call for help.

They'd come up to one of several sharp bends in the road and Polly was shocked when the silver sedan pulled around her pursuer. They were only going thirty-five miles per hour, but this corner was completely blind. As the sedan came even with her truck, she broke out into a cold sweat. It was the same silver sedan from last time. She looked at the driver - a kid with long, greasy black hair and a bit of a beard coming in. He reached his arm out and flipped a finger up at her.

Her truck lurched again. Polly had no idea what kind of sick prank this was, but she was terrified and her terror was giving way to fury. Even at thirty-five on these roads, someone was going to get hurt if they kept this up. Apparently, they'd moved past simple racing and leaving accidents in their wake, to deliberately causing damage by terrorizing drivers. She and Jason had been collateral damage the last time, this time it looked as if she was their target.

She stepped on the brake, lightly at first, not wanting the SUV to hit her too hard. If she could, she'd use her brakes to slow down both vehicles. The expected impact came, harder than before. This time, instead of dropping back, the SUV stayed on Polly's bumper. She pressed harder on the brakes, but with his power and speed, they weren't working like she wanted them to work. He was also causing her truck to weave on the road. She was losing control.

They entered the curve and since she couldn't afford to let him stay in control, she let up on the brakes and was horrified when the truck accelerated. The silver car was still driving beside her and when she looked, the greasy-haired kid was rocking wildly back and forth in his seat, with one arm circling.

Coming out of the curve, to her continuing horror, she saw a third vehicle, the blue Dodge Charger, sitting across her lane about forty yards ahead. They were herding her. All Polly wanted to do was come to a stop and call someone for help, but there was no time and she couldn't afford to take her hands off the wheel.

Polly had to make a decision. She either rammed the Charger or flew off the sharp embankment. The ditch was too deep and at this speed, that was a horrible idea. She gulped and took a breath, then jammed both feet onto her brakes, pulling on the steering wheel to give her more leverage. She'd heard brakes screaming on asphalt when she lived in Boston as cars careened into each other, but in all her life, she'd never been in anything like this. The slide toward the Charger began and apparently this wasn't what the kids had planned for. The silver sedan accelerated, opening up the lane on the left. Polly desperately wanted to jump over there, but the SUV chose that moment to switch lanes and was overtaking her.

What in the hell were they doing? Why would kids be so bent on such destruction? Had she done something to piss them off?

There wasn't going to be enough room to stop. The kid in the Charger saw it too, and he'd finally figured out that Polly wasn't going into the ditch like they'd planned.

"Get out of the way," she screamed. For a moment, she thought he'd do the right thing and all she would have to do was keep moving forward, but they were out of time. She didn't want to hit him head on, so at the last minute, Polly released the brakes and cranked the steering wheel to the left.

That might have worked, if the idiot in the Charger had known what she was doing. But, he chose to move forward and they were moving together. Her truck struck the front end of his vehicle, going way too fast. Metal joined with metal and the vehicles became intertwined for a moment. For a few surreal seconds, Polly had a perfect moment of clarity. The back end of her truck lifted when they collided and it cartwheeled.

The black SUV and the silver sedan drove on down the road, leaving their friend and Polly. Her truck slid upside down on the pavement, and it occurred to Polly that her father had just given her one last moment of protection. When it finally came to rest, Polly was hanging upside down, her head sideways on the crushed roof of the cab, still held in by the seat belt.

Polly tried to reach the release with her right hand, but pain ripped through her shoulder. After a moment of struggling, she reached across her body with her left hand and triggered the catch, then fell into a heap. Pain jolted through her body. This was worse than anything she'd ever experienced.

The windshield had broken out and Polly crawled toward the opening. She saw her Dad's gloves lying beside a pool of blood, but couldn't bring herself to reach for them. Everything hurt. She half-crawled, half-slithered through the windshield, glass biting into her left hand and knees as she cradled her right arm close to her body.

When she was finally clear, she tasted blood in her mouth, reached up to her head and felt more at her scalp line. The adrenaline finally left her body and she took a look at her hand, now covered with blood. Big drops of rain started falling on her head. It was too much.

~~~

"Gloves," she murmured.
~~~

"What's that, Polly?"

"Dad's gloves. Blood."

"Shh. Go back to sleep. You're safe and you're going to be okay."

The voice was familiar, but it was going to take too much effort to put a name to it. Her eyes wouldn't even open so she could try to put a face to the voice. Sleep was fine. She didn't fight it.

~~~

"Why can't I move?" she asked. Her eyes still felt heavy, but Polly knew she had to figure out what was going on. She hoped she wasn't paralyzed. No, she'd managed to crawl out of the truck. She was being ridiculous.

"You were thrashing and you needed to stay calm." The voice. She knew who that was. It was Henry. "As soon as you are back with us fully, you'll be okay," he said.

Polly opened one eye. "Hospital?" It seemed obvious. Lots of light, beeping sounds, people moving back and forth, curtains hanging around the bed. She closed the eye again.

"Yes."

"What time is it?"

"It's about seven o'clock."

"Morning?"

"No, it's still Monday."

"Thank God."

"Do you have big plans for tomorrow?"

"No. Just didn't want to lose a whole day. I'm going to live?"

She felt his hand stroking her arm. "You're going to be just fine."

"Other kid?"

"I'm going to kill him, but until then, he's alive."

"Why?"

"We don't know that yet. Stu Decker is with him."

"Two other vehicles. Scared me to death."

"Polly?"
~~~

She recognized Aaron Merritt's voice and started to cry. "I couldn't call you. I was scared and I wanted you to come help me, and I couldn't even call. All I could do was keep driving."

"Oh honey," he said. His voice quavered. "I'm so sorry."

"Will you catch them now?" she asked.

"We're closer. The kid in the Charger isn't able to talk yet. He's in surgery."

"Oh god, no," she said. "I didn't want to hurt him. I wanted him to get out of the way."

She tried to shift in the bed and pain rushed through her torso. "Ohhhh," she moaned. "Did I break something?"

"We'll take care of the pain for now, your clavicle has been broken and you've got a few bruised ribs. Just lie back and we'll get you doped back up."

A nurse appeared in front of Polly's face and before she could say anything, everything went grey.

~~~

"Henry?" Polly asked, finding herself coming awake again. When there was no response, she panicked. "Henry?"

"I'm right here," he said, rushing in through the door. "I was just in the hallway."

"Is it morning yet?"

He stood over her and smiled down. "It's the middle of the night. About one o'clock."

"I'm thirsty."

"I can't give you much. You're having surgery in the morning."

"What? Why?"

"They're going to fix your clavicle. You're about to get some metal in your body."

"Crap. I was perfect before."

"You're still perfect, sweetie."

"Tell me what happened?"

He chuckled.

"Why are you laughing?"
~~~

"I've told you the story three times so far. We'll see if this one takes."

"Don't laugh at me. I'm damaged."

"Yes you are."

Polly could finally turn her head and she watched as Henry sat down beside her. "If I ask you to hold my hand, does it sound like I'm whining?"

He took hold with his warm hand, his thumb moving back and forth across her palm.

"Tell me," she said.

"We're taking a big package of goodies to a man named Harley Schafer from Pilot Mound. He found the accident and called for help. He'd been an Army medic back in Desert Storm and knew just how to get you stabilized before the ambulance arrived. He did the same for the kid."

"What's the kid's name?" Polly asked.

"Some little stoner punk named Rudy Pierce."

Polly knew something was up with that name, but she couldn't make sense of what it meant. "I'm supposed to know something about that," she said. "I'll come back to it later. So, what happened?"

"The dispatcher got hold of Aaron and he knew right away it was you, so I think he called in everyone. While you were en route to the hospital, he called me."

"I'm so sorry," Polly said. "I didn't mean to scare you."

"Yeah. Don't you ever do this again." He brushed a lock of hair back from her forehead. "Oh, Polly. I love you. I want to say that to you every single moment of every day. When he told me what happened, I was afraid I'd said it the last time."

"I love you too," she whispered.

"Everyone was here this evening. Rebecca is staying with Sylvie and Eliseo tonight."

"Jessie?"

"She's fine. Mom was going over to make sure she knew you were safe. I wouldn't be at all surprised to find that she was safely ensconced in my old bedroom tonight."

"Jeff?"

"He was here earlier. He'll stop by in the morning on the way to Sycamore House."

"The animals?"

"Doug and Billy are taking care of them tonight. Obiwan is going up to their apartment and if Jessie is staying with Mom and Dad, the cats will be fine until tomorrow morning."

Polly took a deep breath. Everyone was where they were supposed to be. She wondered how Jason's first day back at school had gone.

"Jason!" she said abruptly.

"He's fine. I think we're all glad he wasn't in the truck with you this time."

"So am I, but he's why I know that name. How many Rudys do you think there are at Boone High School? That's one of the kids that was harassing him last week."

Henry slowly nodded his head up and down. "I'll tell Aaron about that when he shows up in the morning."

"Does he know about the black SUV and the silver Infinity? Those were the other two cars that tried to kill me today."

She felt a shudder pass through Henry's body. "He didn't say anything about that. You saw the silver car before, right?"

"Yes, but this time it was the SUV that was ramming my back bumper."

"They had better have those kids behind bars by the time I find out who they are," Henry said, his voice low and grim.

"If it's the same Rudy, I'll bet Jason will know who the other two are. Aaron shouldn't take him out of school to ask the question, though. It will make Jason nervous. He hates being a snitch. He hates it so much he won't answer the questions right." She gripped Henry's hand. "You have to tell Aaron early tomorrow morning so he talks to Jason before school. Please promise me you'll talk to him early. Lydia gets up at six o'clock every morning. Call her and don't let them embarrass Jason any more. He's having a hard enough time as it is."

"Calm down, Polly. I promise to deliver the message."

"You can't let them mess with him again. He's been through so much."

"I love you, Polly."

"I love you, too, but promise me again?"

"I promise. We'll protect Jason through this as much as we can."

"That's not enough. He will just shut down unless he knows that he's safe. He doesn't talk to people very easily."

"He talks to you."

"Because he trusts me to have his back."

"This time I think it's important for Jason to have your back, honey. How do you think he'll feel when he realizes that it was his friends who hurt you this badly?"

"They're not his friends. They're horrible kids who think that it's fun to terrorize a lone woman in a pickup truck." Polly fell silent, her mind going back over the events that had landed her in the hospital bed.

"Dad's leather gloves," she said.

"You mentioned those earlier. What about them?"

"Could you ask Aaron if he can save them from the truck? They still smell like Dad. I was trying to retrieve them from the glove compartment before everything happened."

"It's on my list."

"The truck is totaled, isn't it? Have you seen it?"

"Not yet. I don't know if I could look at it without falling apart."

"It kept me safe, Henry. It did everything I asked it to do and when I flipped end over end, it was like a metal cocoon, holding me in place until I stopped. That was Dad's last gift to me."

"And to me," he said. "He kept you alive."

CHAPTER TWENTY-ONE

Opening her eyes, Polly responded to the knock on the door. "Come in," she called out.

"Are you ready for all of us?" Sylvie asked, followed by Rebecca, Jason and Andrew.

"I'm so glad to see you. All of you. I can't wait to go home." Polly wanted to hitch herself up in the bed, but realized she couldn't use her arm. This was going to be annoying.

"You can't do anything," Andrew said grimly. "I remember that. It stinks."

She chuckled. Andrew had broken his arm earlier that summer. At first it had been fun and interesting. He soon got tired of it, though. "That's right. Well, at least you are all put back together now that I need you."

He sat down at the end of her bed. "I'll do anything you want. Maybe Mom won't make us go to school so me and Rebecca can take care of you."

"Rebecca and I," Polly corrected him.

"Whatever. Can we, Mom?"

Sylvie ruffled the hair on his head. "Whatever," she echoed.

"You have a black eye," Rebecca said. "Does it hurt?"

"Honey, everything on my body hurts right now. I don't think I can identify which hurt belongs where. Did you see your mom?"

"I'm going down there right now. Sylvie says we have plenty of time."

"How is she?"

Rebecca nodded. "Okay, I guess. She says that I might have to move upstairs with you. There are nurses that might be moving into her room. I don't want to leave her yet, Polly."

Polly patted the bed on her left side and Jason moved back so Rebecca could sit down. "Come here, honey," Polly said and pulled the girl in for a hug, trying to hide the grimace on her face. "I know you don't want to leave her and you can spend as much time there as possible, but she's your mom and you still have to do what she asks you to do. And who knows, once they get her diabetes straightened out, she might start feeling better."

"Okay. It will be fun to hang out with Jessie."

"Yes it will be. Now go on and spend some time with your Mom. Do you know how to find her room?"

"I'll walk down with her," Sylvie said. "Andrew, you can come with us. We'll be back in a little while. Is there anything you want, Polly?"

"I'd give anything for a Diet Dew. I know they're in the vending machines around here."

"We'll take care of you," Andrew said, popping up and opening the door for his mom.

"This might take a few minutes," Sylvie said, gazing at Polly knowingly while Jason was paying attention to a game he carried.

"No hurry."

Once they were gone, Jason dropped into the chair beside Polly's bed. She waited for him to finish whatever level he was playing and then he put it down.

"How is it being back in school?" she asked.

"It's fine. They aren't around this week."

"Who isn't?"

"The guys who were messing with me."

"What happened to them?"

"You know." He gave her a stricken look. "They tried to kill you."

Polly nodded. "When I heard that it was Rudy Pierce in the hospital here, I wondered. But no one has told me anything else yet."

"I didn't know that was them when I was in the truck with you. I would have told you, you know that, right?"

"Of course I know that," she said. "It didn't occur to me at all. You were the one who gave Aaron an idea of the cars in the first place."

"I didn't want you to think that I would lie and protect them."

"Do you know who the other two were out there?"

"Logan Miles and Seth Davis. They're in jail right now. The Sheriff says it's attempted murder."

Polly wasn't surprised. "You talked to him this morning?"

"Yeah. He was out at Eliseo's house before we came into town. He said he wanted to ask me some questions before I had to go to school. Mom was really scared. She thought I'd done something bad again."

"Are you okay?"

He shrugged. "I guess. Now that they're gone, the rest of the guys kind of faded into the background. Seth was like their leader or something."

"He was the one in the SUV?"

"Yeah. It was his dad's and boy, was his dad pissed. He came to the school when Sheriff Merritt was there. You could hear him yelling at Seth all the way down the hall."

"What about the rest of the kids?"

"What do you mean?" Jason asked.

"I mean, how did they act toward you when you went back on Monday? We never really got a chance to talk, did we?"

"You were right. It was fine. Like nothing ever happened. Well, except that Logan and Rudy tried to follow me around again. I just waited until there wasn't any time between classes and ran to the next room. But they weren't there today, so it was better."

"And every day will keep getting better."

"I guess." Jason looked at the floor. "Polly?"

"Yes, Jason."

"They didn't do that because of me and you, did they?"

She reached out and said, "Look at me, Jason."

He did.

"Give me your hand."

He put it on the bed beside hers. Polly covered it. The poor kid was clammy.

"You have got to quit taking responsibility for things that you can't help. They've been chasing cars for weeks and when Seth got involved, it grew out of control. It could have been anybody out there on that road. I just happened to be their first target."

He looked down again. "They were talking about it at school."

"What?" She tried to sit up, the muscles around her ribs protested and she relaxed back into the bed. "They were talking about it? Was it a specific plan or just random? Did you tell the Sheriff about it?"

Jason nodded. "I told him. They were going to be out there on that road, but Logan knew I was in your truck."

"I still think it's random, Jason." Polly gave his hand a squeeze. "You do know that all of this gives you a fresh new chance to make better friends and better decisions. It isn't often that your nemesis gets stripped away from the situation."

"I'm going to try," he said. "Did you know that my Dad is moving to Fort Dodge?"

"I heard that," Polly replied. "Did your mom tell you about it?"

"She doesn't know I know. He put another note for me in our mailbox." Jason pulled the envelope out and handed it to Polly. "Why is he doing this?"

"Have you showed this to your mom?"

"Nah, it will just upset her. She's got enough to worry about right now. She was scared last night. Really scared when Henry called her."

Polly leaned on her left arm and tried to shift a little in the bed, so she was turned more toward him. "Jason. I love that you confide in me. I will always be here for you. You know that, right?"

"You're cool."

"Okay, I'm cool. But you have to talk to your mom. She's the one who can work this out for you."

"She won't tell Dad not to see me. He'll hurt her. I have to figure out how to do this."

"Jason, she isn't scared of your dad any longer. See, she's figured something out that you haven't yet."

"What's that?"

"That there are people around who will protect you guys. If he threatens her, she can call Eliseo or Aaron or Ken Wallers. If he tries to scare her, she has me and Sal and Joss. Heck, wouldn't you be afraid of Lydia, Andy and Beryl?"

Jason nodded wildly.

"There are all of these people in your mom's life that love her and won't tolerate him and his abusive ways. You need to understand that too. Every single one of those people I named will do the same for you."

"I'm just a kid."

"You're a great kid and the thing is, you're Sylvie's kid and that means something to us. So you give that note to her and tell her that it isn't the first one you've gotten. Tell her. Let her make Anthony go away. That's her job as your mom."

"It doesn't seem fair. I'm old enough and big enough to take care of some things."

"You're getting older and bigger, but she's still your mom."

Noise at the door stopped the conversation and Andrew rushed in. He put a bottle of Diet Dew on the bed beside Polly and opened a little brown sack he was carrying, dumping the contents on the bed.

"You two are nuts and I love you," Polly said. She handed the bottle to Jason. "Would you open that for me? I'm lamed."

He gave her a weak grin and twisted off the top, then set it on the table in front of her. Polly picked through the candy bars and handed him a bag of M&Ms. "Can you open these too, please?"

Jason ripped the top, spilled a few on the table and placed the bag beside them. Polly ate them, took a drink of the soda and sighed.

"Ahhh," she said. "I'm going to heal right up now. I promise. Thank you guys."

"Sarah is planning to go home tomorrow," Sylvie said. "Evelyn is working it out to be with her."

"We'll just call Sycamore House 'Invalid Central,'" Polly said. "I'm supposed to go home tomorrow too if everything works out."

"Really?" Andrew asked. "Can we still come upstairs and play games after school?"

She gave him a look. "Of course you can. I want my life to get back to normal. That includes you running around my apartment after school."

"I'm glad. I didn't want to have to sit downstairs all afternoon while Mom works."

"Are you busy this week, Sylvie?" Polly asked.

"A little. I have two afternoon meetings. One with a bride and one with a very organized woman who is planning her Christmas party." Sylvie waved her hand at Jason to get him up and out of the chair. "You two go do something. Take your game and book and sit in the main lobby. I'll be down in a while."

The boys didn't seem to fully understand why they were leaving, but Sylvie had spent a lifetime training them to do what she asked, so they left.

"What's up?" Polly asked.

Sylvie stood up and checked the door, waited a moment and came back to sit by the bed.

"Okay, really. What's going on?"

"He kissed me," Sylvie whispered.

"He what? Who what? Who kissed you?"

"Shh. Be quiet. Don't say it out loud." Sylvie voice grew even quieter. "Eliseo. He kissed me."

Polly let out a little squeal. Just a little one that barely carried past the bed. "He kissed you? When? How did it happen? Why aren't you squealing yourself?"

"Because it was just one kiss and it freaked both of us out. We didn't talk about it or anything after it happened."

"So, a man kissed you and both of you are ignoring that it happened," Polly said in her regular tone of voice.

"Shh. Please. Not so loud. I don't want the boys to know."

"Okay, no one knows but you, me and Eliseo. Tell me how it happened."

"We were downstairs in the kitchen after Henry called me about you. I was washing pans in the sink and I just started crying. It felt like everything was coming apart. First I had it out with Anthony and it was Jason's first day back at school and then you were nearly killed."

"Yee haw. A crying woman does it every time. What happened?"

"I thought I was out there all alone. The boys were in their rooms upstairs, supposedly working on homework."

Polly didn't want to interrupt her, but the fact that the rooms now belonged to her boys was a big deal. She stayed quiet, a wicked glint in her eyes.

"Anyway, Eliseo totally snuck up on me. He put his hand on my back and I jumped and nearly knocked him over. He grabbed me so that we both didn't fall and then, he just kissed me. Right there in the kitchen."

"What did you do? Did you kiss him back?"

"Well, I, uh," Sylvie dropped her head. "Of course I did. I haven't had a man kiss me in a long time."

"What was it like?"

"Do you mean because of the scars? Those were interesting, but it was okay."

"No. I meant, what did you feel? Was it more than just a kiss?"

"Maybe. But you can't say anything to him."

Polly sat back. "Why would I say anything to him? The two of you aren't acknowledging that it happened. I'm not getting in the middle of that."

"You can't tell Joss or Sal or Lydia or anybody."

"I'm telling Henry."

"No! You can't. Not yet."

"I tell him everything."

"Just not yet. Can you swear him to secrecy?"

"Oh, for heaven's sake, Sylvie, it was just a kiss. People do that all the time." Polly leaned over on her left arm and pecked Sylvie's cheek. "See, I just kissed you. The world didn't end and you weren't swallowed up in a sinkhole."

Sylvie brushed her cheek off and glared at Polly. "You'd better be good or I won't tell you if it happens again."

"I'll be good. I'll be good. So what happened after the kiss? Did you guys talk like normal people or was it uncomfortable?"

"It was pretty uncomfortable. He went outside and after I finished in the kitchen, I went upstairs and called around, trying to find out what people knew about you. I spent the rest of the night on the phone in my room. And then this morning, Aaron came over and then I went to work and now I'm here. And I texted him to tell him that we were going to eat out tonight, so he was on his own."

"So in essence, he thinks he screwed up by kissing you."

"No!" Sylvie slapped her hand on her forehead. "He wouldn't think that. He didn't screw up. I just don't know what to do with this."

"You hid from him last night. Do you always go up to your room after supper?"

"Well, no."

"Then you've avoided him all day today and you're hiding from him again tonight. He thinks he screwed up with you."

"Crap. What am I going to do?"

"You're going to talk to him. And you're going to do it soon before he develops some big immense story in his head about why you don't like him."

"But I do like him. He's been wonderful to us."

"I suppose you talked to him about moving back to the apartment."

"Yes. This morning. Oh no," Sylvie said. "I talked to him about that this morning. I'm an idiot."

"Yes you are, my friend. You have to fix this. When did you tell him you were leaving?"

"I don't know. I just told him we'd get out of his hair. He's put up with a lot from us. What should I do?"

"If it was me, I'd text him and ask if he wanted to have supper with you somewhere. He'd come down here to Boone. Or maybe you go to Davey's. Just make it casual."

"I promised the kids McDonalds. He isn't going to want to eat McDonalds."

"You're assuming. So, do you want him to kiss you again?"

"What? I don't know."

"You're trying to tell me that you didn't think about this all night long? Come on, Sylvie. You're a girl. You've been obsessing about it since the moment it happened. You've thought through every single twist of your lips, you've imagined his touch. Everything."

"Maybe a little bit."

"So, do you want it to happen again?"

Sylvie took a breath in and when she exhaled, she said, "Yes. I think I do. Even if it's just to know that it wasn't a fluke. I don't want to marry him or anything, though."

"Then just take it slow, but don't kick it to the curb."

Another knock came at the door. As it pushed open, Lydia, Andy and Beryl came in.

"Are you ready for more company?" Lydia asked. She gave Sylvie a smile, "Hi sweetie. I saw your boys in the lobby."

"I should get going. I'm taking the kids to McDonalds and then we have to get home so they can work on homework." Sylvie stood and bent over to hug Polly. "I'll text him," she whispered.

"We didn't mean to rush you out," Lydia said. "Please stay."

"We've been here long enough. It's time to go. The boys have been patient and I don't want to push that." She hugged each of the women as she headed for the door and waved back at Polly before walking out.

"When are they releasing you from this prison?" Beryl asked, pounding lightly on the windows of the room.

Lydia held her hand out to Polly, who took it in hers and said, "Tomorrow, if I'm a good girl."

"We'll break you outta here, chickie. All ya gotta do is give us a sign," Beryl said.

"I think I'll let them give me drugs and take care of me for one more night."

"Someone is taking care of you." Andy chuckled and pointed at the candy on Polly's bed.

Polly pushed it away. "Sylvie and Andrew thought I needed sustenance beyond what the nutritionist here gives me. I begged for the Dew, but they did the rest on their own."

Andy poked Lydia. "Go ahead. You might as well."

Lydia took her hand back and opened her bag so Polly could look inside. "I couldn't help myself either. Do you want me to take these to your office or leave them here?"

Polly reached in and took out a bag of chocolate covered donuts and two Diet Dews. "You're the best. I can make sure these get home with me."

"You just don't want to let that caffeine out of your sight, do you?" Beryl asked.

"They aren't very generous with it, that's for sure." She took Lydia's hand again. "Has Aaron told you anything? What about my truck?"

"Your truck is gone, honey. Surely you know that."

Polly's shoulders dropped. "I was afraid you'd say that. I didn't want to believe it. What about the kid I hit? Is he okay?"

"He's lucky to be alive. Especially after what he did to you. It's a good thing Aaron rounded up those other two boys. A whole lot of people in Bellingwood were ready to string them up."

"That certainly wouldn't help things," Polly said.

"Who does that? And who are the parents that have kids who think forcing cars off the road is a good idea?"

"It sounds like there are some parents who have to hire good lawyers."

"That Seth Davis's parents have a lot of money. They're already scrambling to figure out how to get rid of the charges."

"He kept ramming me," Polly protested. "I didn't know what to do."

"I know. It's going to be a mess. He's a senior. Was supposed to go to K-State to play football next year. That's why his daddy's so upset. He had a scholarship and everything."

Polly sat back and flinched as her ribs adjusted to the movement. "Stupid kids."

"We're really here to see if there's anything we can do at your house before you get home."

"I don't think so. Henry and Jessie are there."

Andy put a notebook on the table in front Polly. "You are supposed to write down your favorite meals in here. Everything from entrees to side dishes to desserts. I'm organizing all of the people who want to do something for you."

"That's nuts. Henry's perfectly capable of cooking and so is Jessie. And if we don't cook, we order pizza or sandwiches. And besides," Polly said, waving her fingers weakly, "this doesn't work very well."

Lydia sat down and looked Polly in the eyes. "There are a lot of people who were scared to death last night and you have to let them ... you have to let *us* do something for you. If the only thing we can do is make a meal, you have to tell us what you like and then say thank you. Do you understand me?"

"Umm, yes?"

"I'm not kidding. This is how people tell you that you are loved. You are responsible for writing all of the thank you notes when it's finished, though. You can't believe the number of calls Jeff has been fielding today. That doesn't include all of the people who called me and those who were contacting Henry."

"He didn't say anything."

"Because he's as embarrassed about accepting this kind of love as you are. So the two of you are going to smile and say thank you and that's just the way it's going to be. Got it?"

"Got it. And I love you." Polly picked up the notebook and handed it back to Andy. "In between the hourly checks tonight, I'll talk to my note app on the phone and tell it what food we like. I promise." She glanced surreptitiously around the room. "Check it out. I'm wide awake and there isn't a nurse around. But as soon as I fall asleep, they'll tip toe in and need to take my temperature and check my pulse. They're the nicest girls on the planet, but wow it's hard to get any good sleep in a hospital."

Henry stood in the doorway. "Well, this is a scary looking group. Are you three trying to break her out of here before the doctor releases her?"

Beryl sidled up to him. "I tried, but she whined. Something about needing more drugs. I think you might have an addict on your hands."

"Yep that's me," Polly said, rolling her eyes.

"You come sit beside your pretty wife," Lydia said. "We just dropped in to check on her. Let me know when she's settled at home. I have dinner tomorrow night. Am I right to think that we should have enough for Rebecca and Sarah and Jessie too?"

"Evelyn Morrow is going to be staying with Sarah for a while," Polly said.

"She's wonderful. That's a great connection to have made. We'll tell people they should generally prepare for six people." Lydia waved Andy and Beryl to the door. "I love you sweetie," she said and blew a kiss to Polly.

Henry bent over and tried to kiss Polly's forehead. She touched his face and drew him to her lips. "I missed that last night," she said. "I've gotten really used to sleeping beside you."

"The animals kept me warm, but they weren't nearly as much fun." He picked up the bag of donuts. "What's this?"

"Don't tell the coppers," Polly hissed. "Do you want one?"

"Do you?"

"Of course I do. It's not an ice cream sandwich, but a girl has to have something."

"Has your afternoon been busy?"

"Not too bad. Sal called. She's in Massachusetts. Joss called and said that she talked to Jessie about babysitting sometime so she could come over once I got home. Sylvie was here ..." Polly stopped, then pursed her lips.

"What?" he asked.

"I'm not supposed to tell you because you have a big mouth."

"I do not!"

Polly leaned forward and whispered, "Eliseo kissed her. She made me promise not to tell you, but I had to, didn't I? Because we're married?"

"Sure," he said, chuckling. "Because we're married. What are they going to do with that?"

"Apparently, they're ignoring it right now. She was emotional and vulnerable. That's her story."

"Poor guy. When I think he's had enough of dealing with a crazy woman, I'll sit down and have a talk with him."

"Because it worked out so well for you."

"Exactly."

CHAPTER TWENTY-TWO

"Dishes are done and everything is put away," Jessie announced. "Rebecca was a lot of help. Is there anything else we can do for you?"

Polly leaned back on the stack of pillows Henry had brought out to the sofa. "No, thank you girls. I appreciate everything. The apartment looks great."

Jessie dropped into a chair. "It will be good to be back in my room. I finally got everything up here and then I was gone again."

"What do you mean?" Polly creased her brow. "You weren't staying here?"

Henry sat under Polly's feet and idly rubbed her toes. "Mom, smart woman that she is, said that since you weren't here and Rebecca was with Sylvie, Jessie should stay with them. She's had the full-on Sturtz experience for the last few days."

"Oh. I suppose that makes sense. Do you have everything back where you want it?" Polly asked Jessie.

"Almost. I have two more bags in the car to bring up, but I'll do that tomorrow." She pulled a phone from her pocket and swiped it open.

"Where'd that come from?" Polly asked. "I thought yours was destroyed. I'm so sorry I didn't have time to help you."

"It's fine. Mrs. Sturtz and I went down to Boone to buy this. She says that if I'm going to work for them, I need to be connected to the world. We put it on my regular plan and she's taking it out of my paycheck a little at a time."

"Oh, that's nice," Polly said. "It sounds like things are working out well for you over there."

"She's really good to work for. Your company is really busy, Henry. I can't believe how many projects you have going on. And Mr. Sturtz and Mr. Specek are talking about bringing on another person for the shop."

Polly chuckled and nudged Henry with her foot. "She knows more than I do about your business. I'm a bad wife."

"Yes you are. Don't you forget it."

"Are you done with your schoolwork, Rebecca?" Polly asked. "Are you working on anything interesting?"

"I'm done. I was just drawing Leia's face. Ms. Watson says I should draw whenever I don't have something else to do."

"I'm so glad you had a good time with her."

"She wasn't scary at all."

"Beryl is pretty wonderful," Polly agreed. "So are all my friends. Now tell me what is happening tomorrow. Where do I need to be? What do I need to do?"

"You don't need to do anything or be anywhere," Henry said. "I'll take Rebecca to school and Jessie is on her own for work."

"I'm not going to be good about having all of these people feed me, no matter what Lydia says."

"Be good," Henry said. "They want to help you."

"Yeah, yeah, yeah."

He stood up. "Rebecca, isn't it time for you to take a bath and get ready for bed?"

Everyone looked at him in astonishment.

"What? I can't watch a clock? Polly, do you even know what time it is?"

"No. I guess not." She giggled. "Who knew he was such a dad!"

"I can be responsible when I have to," he said. "I'm going to take the dog out one last time and you all can quit laughing at me."

Rebecca closed her books and put things in her backpack. "Will you still be awake when I come out, Polly?"

"Sure, sweetie. Go get started. I'll be here."

Jessie and Polly watched the little girl go to her room and then run across the floor to the bathroom while Henry left by the back door with Obiwan.

"First no one was here with us and now it feels normal having you all back where you belong," Polly said. "Do you like working with Marie?"

"She's wonderful and she told me that if you couldn't go next week to Oelwein for Dennis's trial, she'd go with me."

"That's why I love her son."

"Polly?"

"Yeah, Jessie."

Jessie leaned forward and said, "I have something else I need to talk to you about."

Polly's heart sunk. She really couldn't take one more thing this week, but oh well. "What's that?"

"I think I'm pregnant."

"That seems really fast. Are you sure?"

"No, not from Troy. From Dennis."

"And you're sure?"

"Yeah. I'm sure."

"Honey, we need to get you to the doctor. Tomorrow."

"You're not mad?"

"Oh, Jessie. Why would I be mad? How long have you known about this?"

"I didn't pay any attention. Everything was just so weird and upside down and then last week when I was in South Dakota, I started thinking about how I hadn't had my period and then I bought a pregnancy test. I've done it like five times."

Polly chuckled. "Of course you have. That's exactly what I would have done." She sat up a little and swung her legs off the edge of the sofa, then clutched her chest. "That is gonna hurt for a while."

"Can I help you? Are you trying to get up?"

"No, I just want to be able to look at you more directly. Because I want you to hear this."

"Okay, you're sure you aren't mad?"

"Not at all. Jessie, you are an adult. Your decisions are yours to make, and I will be here to help you do the right thing whenever you ask. But you need to realize that from here on out, those decisions of yours don't just affect you. If you keep this baby in your life, all of your decisions affect the child. You need to start taking care of yourself and you need to accept this for what it is. Don't be ashamed, don't be afraid. If you want to stay here, Henry and I will help. If you want to move out into your own place, we'll help you with that, too. Tomorrow you need to talk to Marie and then you should call Doc Mason and schedule an appointment. Sweetie, you're through your first trimester and your baby needs you to be healthy. Are you ready for this?"

"I don't think so," Jessie's voice shook as she spoke.

"Have you told anyone else yet?"

"No, I've only known for a few days."

"What about your parents?"

"Mom won't care and Dad can't do anything."

"You need to tell them. Don't hide this. It's better that they know now rather than having you show up with a little kid in tow."

"I can't believe you aren't freaking out about this."

Polly shook her head slowly back and forth. "With all that's been going on the last week or so, I'm pretty much just taking it all in stride. Have you given any thought to what you want to do?"

"I definitely want to keep it."

"Then I'm proud of you. You do know that there is going to be some more legal stuff you have to go through with Dennis now. We'll need to talk to your lawyer."

"I don't have to do that right now, do I?"

"No, let's get Dennis locked into a jail cell before springing something like this on him." Polly sat back and clutched her side again. "Dang, you'd think I'd learn. No moving."

Obiwan came tearing into the room and jumped up beside Polly on the couch. She moaned as her body bounced. He dropped his butt into a seated position and reached over to lick her on the face.

"Thank you," she said, laughing. "I missed you, too. You were gone so long!"

He dropped his head into her lap and rolled over onto his side, then to his back, his belly up for rubbing. Polly obliged. "You know, Jessie. It's all going to be okay. I'm sure this seems like the worst thing that could happen to you right now, but in a few years, you'll have a child who loves you and these days will be but a dim memory."

"I'm kinda scared and I can't believe that creep is the dad."

"It might not be ideal, but it's what you have."

"Sometimes I worry that I'm going to be like my mom. I don't want my kids to hate me and run away to all the corners of the country so they don't have to be around me."

"I always tell people that our lives are made up of choices and consequences, Jessie. Every choice you make from this point forward will decide the consequences you deal with down the road. If you are loving and kind, gentle and firm, you will raise a child who loves you and respects you."

"Don't let me screw this up."

Polly smiled. "I don't know that I'll have that much impact, but I suspect you will be just fine. You'll make horrible mistakes and you'll have glorious successes. It's kind of the way normal people live." She looked up at Henry who walked in the room carrying a plastic bag. "Isn't that right?"

"Of course it is," he said. "You're always right."

"What do you have in there?"

"Guess."

"You love me that much?" Polly attempted to stand up and put her hand out to Jessie. "Help me? Just be strong while I stand up."

"Stay there," he admonished. "I'll bring you plenty of napkins."

"I was going to hug you. I can't believe it's a chore for me to even come hug you."

Rebecca came out of the bathroom, her hair wet and her cheeks bright pink. She was dressed in a pair of pajamas that were much too big.

"Where did you get those?" Polly asked.

"Sylvie said I'd grow into them. I tried to tell her what size I wore, but I don't think she heard me."

Polly started to laugh, "You poor thing. Well, you're absolutely adorable. Come over here and sit beside me. Henry brought us ice cream sandwiches."

Rebecca stood in front of the dog and finally Polly gave Obiwan a push and he moved off the sofa. "You get to sleep with me later," Polly said to the dog. "Give the girl a break."

Once Rebecca was settled in beside Polly, Obiwan jumped right back up, this time, his head on the little girl's lap. Henry handed out ice cream sandwiches to everyone.

"Ahh, this is the life," Polly said, handing hers to Rebecca. "I'm going to make all of my body parts work tomorrow, but would you rip this open for me now?"

"I like it here," Rebecca said. "I'm glad you're home."

"Me too. However, if Henry could figure out how to put a fireplace in this room, it would be even better, wouldn't it?"

"Right here in the middle of the floor," he said, pointing to the rug. "We'll just keep everyone toasty warm."

"My friends had fire pits back in Colorado. Those are all the rage right now," Jessie said.

Polly shook her head. "My luck, Henry would build a beautiful fire pit and I'd come down one morning to find a toasty body in there. Not happening."

She felt Rebecca's body shake with laughter beside her.

"Well, that would be horrible, wouldn't it?" Polly asked.

"Andrew would think it was great."

Horrible pounding echoed through Sycamore House and up the steps to the apartment.

"What in the world?" Polly asked, lurching to her feet.

Everyone was moving by the time she was finally upright. Obiwan stood at the front door of their apartment, growling as more pounding and shouting came from the front of the building.

"I'll go see what's happening," Henry said. "The rest of you stay here. Come on, Obiwan. You're my guard dog tonight." He patted his leg and the dog stepped forward to stand at his side.

Before Polly could protest, he was out the door. She followed him and when he turned around and gave her a glare, she stopped.

"Be careful," she said.

The pounding continued and when Henry opened the main door, Polly heard a man's voice yelling for her.

"Polly Giller, do you have any idea what you've done? This is your fault! You've ruined my son's life and I won't stand for it."

She didn't hear what Henry said, just the low tones of his voice as he attempted to placate the man.

"I want to see her face and I want her to know exactly what damage she has done to our family, to the community and to my boy."

"No, you are not allowed to go up those steps. You are way out of line," Henry's voice grew louder and Obiwan let out a short bark.

"I'm not leaving until I have some satisfaction. Women like her shouldn't be allowed in public."

Polly shook her head and took out her phone, then dialed the police station.

"Bellingwood Police, how may I help you?"

"Hi, this is Polly Giller and we might need someone to drive by."

"This is Mindy, do you need them right away?"

"There's a man downstairs screaming at Henry about me. I'm guessing it's a dad of one of the kids who ran me off the road. He sounds pretty drunk. Henry's trying to calm him down ..."

"You!" Polly looked up from her call to find Seth Davis's father towering over her, his finger pointing into her face. She was absolutely right, he was quite drunk and very out of control.

Henry had chased the man up the steps, and watched closely as he held Obiwan back, which wasn't easy because the sounds coming from the dog's throat were warning that he wanted to lunge and destroy.

Instead of stepping back into the apartment, Polly decided she couldn't hurt any more than she already did and stepped into his finger, confusing the man.

"Me what?" she spat out. "I did what?"

"You got my boy arrested. He's sitting in jail tonight and it's your fault." He took a step back, rethought his words and ramped up again for another rant. "Do you have any idea what is going to happen to the football team without him? And now his scholarship is out the window! Everything is ruined!"

Polly shook her head slightly at Henry, who was looking around the tall man standing in front of her. He was asking if she was truly fearful of being hurt. She wasn't. Then she realized she was still holding the phone.

"Mindy?" she said. "Have you sent someone over here?"

"Bert is on his way. Are you okay?"

"So far I'm fine. Just a moment." Polly tilted her head up and shuddered as everything in her body relaxed from the tension she'd put it under when this man had jumped into her face. "Sir, an officer of the Bellingwood police force is pulling up to the front door right now. I've been on the phone with dispatch since the moment you entered this building. I hurt all over because of the choices your son made Monday evening. I didn't make those for him and I'm not responsible for his stupidity."

"Don't start with me, missy," he yelled, spittle splattering her face. Henry stepped in closer and Obiwan barked and growled, pulling against the hand holding his collar.

"That was gross," Polly said and took another step forward. "You are not welcome here. You are about to be escorted out and I really hope I don't have to see you again until the day I meet you and your boy in court. This is not my fault and I'm appalled that none of you are willing to take any responsibility for his actions." She took another step and then leaned into Henry.

"You are drunk, you're disgusting and you have interrupted my evening the night that I arrived home after nearly being killed by your son and his friends."

Bert Bradford came up the steps and absorbed the situation. He gave Polly a slight grin and then took the man's arm. "Sir, it is time for you to leave. You've said your piece."

Mr. Davis flung Bert's hand off his arm and turned on him, "Don't you start with me, punk. Do you know who I am? I will have your badge and your job. In fact, I will own this entire town if I have to."

"Tell me that you're resisting me and are about to make a scene," Bert said calmly.

"Hell yes, I'm resisting you. You have no rights here." The man raised a hand as if to strike Bert.

In a flash, Mr. Davis's hands were zip-tied behind his back. The shocked look on his face was priceless.

"We'll take care of this from here, Miss Giller," Bert said as he pushed the very surprised man to the side, then tugged his arms enough to gain control, effectively sending him down the steps.

"Always nice doing business with you, Officer," Polly called gaily and sagged.

"Come on back inside," Henry said, pushing the dog into the front door.

"I need to wash my face. That was horrid and ... whoops." She pulled the phone back to her ear. "Mindy, are you still there?"

The woman chuckled a little on the other end of the phone. "I'm playing that for everyone tomorrow. You're a riot!"

"Yeah. I'm a hoot. Thanks for sending Bert. I got a little bolder when I realized he was on the way. I'm pretty sure that if Henry had given that man a push, he was so drunk he would have toppled down the stairs, but I didn't want to have to be responsible for another dead body."

"We're glad that didn't happen as well. Ken will want to see you tomorrow."

Polly took in a deep breath. "Of course he will. At least this time I'm not the one who is in trouble."

"You certainly do seem to see a lot of it."

"Thanks for your help tonight."

"Take care of yourself. I hope you feel better soon."

Henry was standing in front of her again, this time with a warm, wet washcloth. "Woman, you are fearless and you scare me to death," he said. "Here, let me do this for you." He gently wiped her face with the cloth.

"You know what I love about you, Henry Sturtz?" Polly asked.

"I'm a handsome, hard-working man?"

"There's that. But I love that you don't have to out-macho me."

"That would just be foolish. You're tough as nails."

"You know what I mean. You let me fight my battles and don't have to prove that I'm the cowering princess and you're the brave knight."

"Honey, you don't cower and I love that about you. If you had needed me to be in the middle of that, I'd have taken care of it."

"And that's the main reason I have all of the courage I do, because I know you've got my back."

He leaned in and whispered. "I have all of you, let's not forget that, okay?"

Polly blushed. "There are kids here!"

Rebecca had gone back to the sofa and was holding two crushed and melted ice cream bars. "You dropped yours," she said to Polly, "and I forgot to eat mine."

"Let's go into the kitchen and clean ourselves up. Did you buy a whole box?" Polly asked Henry.

"Of course I did. I expected them to make it a couple of nights, but I can buy more tomorrow."

"Are you okay, Jessie?" Polly asked the girl, who hadn't said a word.

"You're awesome. He was mean and you called the cops on him."

"That's exactly what I did," Polly said. "There's no reason to put up with a drunken idiot who is threatening me. He needed to go away. Come on. Let's have some ice cream."

CHAPTER TWENTY-THREE

"Oh, it all hurts." Polly tried to get out of bed without moaning, but didn't succeed.

"Do you need something?" Henry asked quietly.

"Just the bathroom. And I'm going to take some ibuprofen. No more of those painkillers. I'm okay."

When she came back, the bed looked really uncomfortable. "I'm going out to the couch for a while," she said.

"Without me?"

"Yes. I think I can sleep without you. I just want to prop up."

"But I can't sleep without you," he protested, sitting up. The cats came out of their hiding spots as he turned the light on.

"You did for two nights while I was in the hospital. You'll be fine."

"I didn't either. This is the first night I fell asleep without pacing the entire building."

"Shhh. Go back to sleep. I'll be right out here."

"At least let me help you settle in." Henry jumped out of bed, much to the surprise of all of the animals. Obiwan leaped to the floor and the cats ran off the bed and up to the cat tree.

"I'm going over to the media room. I want to watch television or a movie until I fall asleep."

"You start walking. I'll probably beat you there with blankets and pillows."

Polly went through the living room and veered into the kitchen. There had to be something to eat. She was sure Lydia had sent plenty of food so there should be leftovers. With her left hand, she opened the refrigerator. Rolls. And butter. And ... no, that was perfect.

"What are you doing?" Henry asked when he walked in.

"I'm hungry. I've heard it takes a lot of calories to heal."

"Where did you hear that?"

"Probably on the internet. Where I get all of my good information."

"Do you want some help?"

"Please. I'm not an invalid. I can warm up a couple of rolls and spread butter on them."

He dropped the blankets on the sofa and came back to the dining room and watched as she fumbled with the zipper plastic bag, finally getting it open. When she dropped a roll on the floor, he sat down in the chair.

"You're just going to watch that happen?" she asked.

"You told me you weren't an invalid and that you could do it. I'm watching you do it."

Polly kicked the roll toward him and he scooped it up before it flew past. When he lobbed it back at her, she let it sail over her head and into the cupboard door behind her. "What are you doing?" she asked.

"Nothing. You have me up in the middle of the night and you're being all independent. I'm being supportive."

She put three rolls on a plate and popped the door open on the microwave, set the timer and turned it on. "You really are a brat."

"Imagine that," he said.

"You know that I'll be fine. It's just going to take some time."

"I know. I'm trying to live with it, too. But that doesn't change the fact that I've been scared out of my mind the last few days."

The microwave dinged and she popped the door open. One by one, she took the plate to the table and then the butter dish. She looked back at the cupboard, desperately wanting something to drink, but the butter was cold and she wanted to melt it in the warm rolls before doing anything else.

"What do you want to drink?" Henry asked, with mocking disgust.

"Milk? And maybe a piece of that chocolate pie Lydia brought?"

He laughed. "You really are hungry. Anything else?"

"Not right now, but don't you want some pie, too?"

"Sit down and I'll take care of you."

Polly sat and gave him a big, toothy, goofy grin. "I lub you, my hero."

He brought everything out and sat down with her, slicing two pieces of pie and putting them on plates. "This is strange. It never occurred to me to eat pie in the middle of the night," he said. "Mom would have had my head."

"Isn't it fun to have our own place where we can do whatever we want? Sometimes I still feel like I'm a little kid getting away with murder. Then it hits me that I'm an adult and have all these responsibilities. Do you suppose Aaron and Lydia ever get up in the middle of the night and just eat pie?"

Henry chuckled. "I don't want to think about what they do in the middle of the night." His face turned a little red. "See? You made me think weird things about the Sheriff."

"Hey! I was only talking about pie. I don't know how you got there. You're a perv or something."

"I am not. It's because Lydia is always teasing him. I don't know how he puts up with that. I'd be embarrassed all the time."

"I think it's her way of humanizing him. People always see him as just the Sheriff, so she reminds us all that he's a man and he's her husband and the father of their kids."

"I suppose." Henry put the fork in his mouth and drew it out slowly, his eyes wandering off to gaze at a point on a far wall.

"What are you thinking about?" she asked.

"What?" He snapped back to attention. "Oh, nothing."

"That wasn't a nothing look. That was a something look."

"I love our life together, Polly." He reached across and put his hand on hers.

"Me too. I can't believe how wonderful it is, but what just got in your head?"

"Something Mom said the other day."

"What's up?"

"That woman makes me crazy. It's like she's psychic. She's always been this way, but sometimes it is worse than others."

"What did she say?" Polly chuckled a little at him. She knew what he meant. Marie Sturtz was pretty intuitive.

"She told me that it was okay if we didn't have babies. That she and Dad had decided long ago that while grandchildren would be great, Lonnie and I should be able to make that decision for our lives without any pressure from them. She promised that they would never ask when we were having children. I don't know where that came from, but it was just out of the blue."

Polly felt the air get sucked out of her lungs. "Are you thinking about kids? Because if so, we need to really talk about things."

"Oh, good heavens, no," he said, dropping her hand. "That's not what this is about at all."

"You had me a little worried." Polly felt like she could breathe again. Babies were the last thing she wanted right now. There were too many people and children and other things that needed her attention. "Things will change next year when Rebecca lives with us permanently, you know. And I'm not the girl who gets giddy about cuddling babies. I love Joss and her kiddos, but I'm glad to walk away from the chaos. I'll be ready to take care of them when they turn four years old. That's when they get fun."

"I know, I know. And I'm on the same page. And apparently, so is Mom." He set his fork down. "I wonder if she ever had this conversation with Lonnie. That would have been fun to watch."

"Do you think Lonnie wants kids?"

"Maybe someday. Oh, I don't know. It's not like we've ever talked about it." He shrugged and took another bite of pie.

Polly put her left hand on her cheek, "I can't believe I forgot to tell you. Jessie's pregnant."

His fork clattered to the plate. "You just now think to tell me this? How long have you known?"

"She told me tonight while you were out getting ice cream. I really haven't had time to say anything. I wasn't going to tell you while Rebecca was awake. Anyway, she's talking to your mom tomorrow and they'll call Doc Mason and make an appointment. Now, you can't be mad about this."

"Give me a little credit. I won't get mad at everything she does. If she's pregnant, there's no changing that. The damage has already been done. I assume it's that guy from Oelwein?"

"Yes. And she wants to keep it."

He gave her a wry grin. "So even if I don't want babies around here, I'm going to get them, is that right?"

"Well, maybe. She isn't sure what is going to happen. Maybe she'll move into an apartment."

"You and I both know that you won't let her until she's way past ready to be on her own. I guess I'll start working on a crib."

"You're such a softie."

"Don't get me wrong. She's made some really stupid mistakes, but Mom had a sit-down with me. I'm supposed to be generous with my extra chances. I had to hear one more time that she and Dad lived through my entire freshman year at college and didn't slice and dice me. That woman is never going to let me forget that. It's her go-to whenever I get short-tempered with someone."

"It's a pretty good story."

"So have you considered just hiring a full-time nurse for all of the strays you keep rescuing?" he asked.

"Now you're just being mean." She looked at him coyly. "I did tell you that Evelyn Morrow is going to be spending time here with Sarah, didn't I?"

"You mentioned that she was going to go see Sarah at the hospital. I assumed they would work something out. I think it's a good idea. You and Rachel can't handle all of the work that she's going to require this next year."

"Hopefully Sarah can gain control of the diabetes and return to some semblance of normal. I can't believe that this hit her on top of everything else."

He reached out and took her hand. "You know I will always support you when you decide to help someone, but one of these days it's going to be too much for one person to handle."

"That's why I talked to Evelyn Morrow. For the most part, Sarah's care is out of my hands now. You aren't going to try to stop me from doing things like this, are you?"

"Well, that would be crazy, now, wouldn't it," he said, chuckling. "I figure that if your job is to take care of the world, someone has to take care of you and I'm more than glad to be that person. But first I need you to trust me and let me do my job."

"Sometimes I feel like I sucked you into my vortex and it isn't fair for you. I can handle everything I take on. I promise. I just keep surrounding myself with more and more good people and as long as they do their jobs, I can do even more. But you didn't ask for this life when we met."

"I asked for it when I asked you to marry me. Trust me, I knew what I was getting into. And I wouldn't have it any other way. But when your face is all bruised up and you can't laugh because your ribs hurt and you can't get up and down easily because you've been broken, it brings out all of my protective instincts."

"Henry Sturtz, I love you."

"It's a good thing, because I love you too."

"Don't ever leave me. Especially when I get stupidly independent and try to pull away from you."

He looked at her and shook his head. "I'm not touching that one. You and your independence aren't something I plan to mess with ... ever."

"You're so smart." She pulled the goofy grin on him again. "And that's why I lub you."

Henry got up and carried the dishes to the sink and put the food away. "Now, come on. Let's get you comfortable and see if we can get some more sleep. I'm taking the next couple of days off, so after I take Rebecca to school, I can help you."

"That isn't necessary. It's not like I'm going to do much around here. I can manage."

He snatched the roll up from the counter where it had landed. "I have a roll that says otherwise. Don't argue with me, you independent thing, you. I'm allowed to hover over the woman I love after she was nearly run off the road, been through surgery, and then listened to the father of the miscreant threaten her."

"If you put it that way ..." Polly walked to the sofa and waited while Henry picked up the pillows and blankets. She sat down and he stuffed pillows behind her and shook out blankets to lay across her. Obiwan jumped up onto the other end of the sofa and looked at her forlornly. When she stretched her legs out, he tucked himself in behind her and settled down.

"Miscreant?" she asked.

"What?"

"Miscreant?"

"I'm not allowed to use big words? I'm a smart man." He sat down in the chair beside her and stroked the back of her head.

"You are a smart man. I'm just not used to you showing off."

"It was the first word that came to mind. I used it."

"You should go back to bed," she said to Henry.

"You relax and I'll sit here for a few minutes." He picked up one of the comic books and slid it out of the plastic sleeve.

" I thought those were supposed to be at your dad's place?"

"Who even knows that we have them? I thought maybe if you feel a little better tomorrow or the next day, we might run over to Ames. There's a guy in a shop there who will tell us what they're worth. I did some checking and I'd like to just get a good number on these things before we decide whether to sell them or put them in a safety deposit box."

"Okay." Polly turned the television on and began flipping through channels. When nothing looked interesting, she turned it back off. "That's boring."

"Are you really going to stay up for a while?" he asked.

"I don't know. Maybe I should read something. That always puts me to sleep."

Henry put the comic book he was reading on the table and walked over to the bookshelf. "Tell me what you want."

She shut her eyes, imagining the bookshelves and their contents. Without opening them, she said, "Second shelf from the top. Right side. "Count of Monte Cristo."

"That was kind of impressive," he said, pulling the book down. "This is heavy. Are you sure?"

"Would you hand me a couple of those throw pillows? I'll just put them on my lap and make a table."

~~~

The next thing she knew, Henry was saying her name quietly and stroking her hand. "Polly. Polly. Please wake up."

"What? What time is it? Did I oversleep?" She looked around and the only light in the room came from the soft glow of a lamp beside the bookshelves. The book and throw pillows were on the table in front of the sofa and the blanket had been pulled up over her shoulders. Polly tried moving her neck and it hurt. "What's going on?"

"Honey, you were moaning. Why don't you take a pain pill and try to come back to bed. You'll be much more comfortable there."

"I wanted to be done with those. They make me thick-headed."

"I know, but it's only three days after the accident. You can have one if it will help you sleep." He held a pill out and a glass of water. "Please? I hate knowing you hurt."

Polly gave him a small smile. "Okay, if you insist. But I'm only doing this for you, you know."

"I know that. And I love you for it." He waited while she took the pill and then a long drink from the glass. "Can I take you back to bed?"

"That's probably a good idea. How long was I asleep?"

"Only about an hour and a half. I wasn't going to let you stay here all night anyway. The couch is comfortable, but not all night, especially when you hurt."

Polly let him help her and she stood still for a moment, trying
~~~

to stand erect. "I feel really old right now," she said. "You can't let me fall down when I'm ninety years old. This stuff stinks."

"Got it. Padded cell when you turn eighty-nine. It's on my to-do list."

She held on to him as they slowly crossed through to their bedroom. "Have you been awake all this time?"

"No, I drifted off for a while, but there was no way I could sleep through those sweet little moans of yours. The only time I want to hear those is when ..."

Polly bumped her hip into his. "Stop it. I can't even think about that right now. And look at me, I'm a mess. I don't know how *you* can even think about that."

He helped her sit down on the bed and pushed the cats out of the way so she could lean back. Once she was settled, he pulled the blankets up and went around to the other side and crawled in.

"I don't care how many black eyes you have or what you look like. I don't care if you are bent over because of age or pain from a terrible accident. You will always be my Polly and I will always want you. And by the way, I will always think about *that* with you. No matter what and no matter when."

She started humming, badly, as the pain pill began to do its work.

"What are you singing there?" he asked.

"Apparently I stink at melodies."

"Well, not usually. Are you sure you know what you're doing?"

"Will you still need me, will you still feed me when I'm sixty-four." She mangled the melody and then said, "Will you still love me?"

Henry stroked her cheek. "I will always need you and I'll even feed you. But more than anything I will always love you. Now let yourself go to sleep. Tomorrow's another day. I'll be here tomorrow and the next day and every day after that. I love you more than you will ever know."

CHAPTER TWENTY-FOUR

"Hey there!" Polly yelled, "I'm bored! No one will play with me."

Henry came into the living room from his office, chuckling. "Do I need to call your friends?"

"I thought you were staying at home to help me. Isn't part of helping me keeping me entertained?" Polly knew she was whining and wasn't quite sure how to make it stop. She felt like whining.

"Your book isn't doing it, eh?"

"No. I've read it before. I know how it ends."

"Maybe I should call Joss and have her bring you some books from the library."

Polly got up from the couch. She felt a little better today than yesterday, but she still ached. "I'm used to having people around. And if I don't have people around, I go out and see the animals or bug Jeff or Sylvie."

"So go bug Jeff and Sylvie," he said. "You aren't an invalid."

"They're probably busy," she whined again.

A knock at the front door made her light up and smile. "I've got it," she said.

"Thank goodness. I hope it's for you and not for me."

She opened the front door to Rachel and grabbed the girl's arm. "Come in. Are you here to tell me that you desperately need me downstairs for some big decision?"

Rachel looked at her and then at Henry, creasing her brows in confusion. "Uh, no?'

"Well come in anyway. I'm going stir crazy. Do you want some coffee or brownies or pie or ice cream?"

"No, I'm fine. I just wanted to talk to you about tonight."

"Tonight," Polly said. "I have no idea what is happening tonight. Henry?" She turned to look at him. "Do you know what's happening tonight?"

"Yeah. It's Sylvie's graduation party."

"That's tonight? I didn't get her a present. I haven't done anything. Henry we have to go get her a present!"

"You ordered chef's knives for her three months ago. They're in the closet."

"Oh. I was going to give them to her at the ceremony, but I guess tonight will be good enough. There's a party tonight?" Polly took Rachel's arm and led her into the dining room. "I've missed out on all the planning for this and now here it is. Tell me what's happening."

"It's no big deal. Jeff, Hannah and I took care of it."

"I remember you talking about it, but I don't think I knew the date."

"We had to do it on a Thursday because we're busy on the weekends."

"Okay, so what did you want to talk to me about?"

"I was hoping you might say something tonight."

Polly chuckled. "If you give me any of those fun pain pills before I go on, I'll say a lot of things, none of which might be appropriate, but I doubt that's what you're looking for."

"It would be funny," Rachel said. "Here, let me do that." She jumped out of the chair at the table and rushed into the kitchen to fill Polly's coffee mug.

"I'm not an invalid," Polly protested, "but thanks."

"I know, but if you spilled, I would have to clean it up."

"You all are one step ahead of me these days. Okay, so you want me to say something. What about?"

"Oh, just about Sylvie working here and going back to school and that kind of stuff."

"How long should I talk? Twenty minutes? Or longer."

There was silence.

"I'm kidding," Polly said. "Like three to five minutes?"

"That would be perfect. Are you sure?"

"Absolutely."

"We were worried that you wouldn't be here for this and we couldn't have done it without you." Rachel stood up to leave.

"I will always be around. You'll never get rid of me," Polly said. "Wait. You're leaving? You can't leave yet. You haven't had any pie or coffee."

"I have to get back to work."

"Noooo," Polly whined. "Then I'll have to go back to being bored."

Henry came back into the dining room and stepped in between the two. "Let her go back to work, Polly. The poor girl doesn't know how to tell you to be quiet."

Rachel gave him a grateful look and trotted to the front door. "I'll see you tonight, Polly. Thanks!"

"Thanks for nothing, you treacherous traitor, you," Polly said to Henry. "You wouldn't let me keep my prey. She walked into my house and was fair game."

"She didn't know you had lost your mind. It was an unfair advantage on your part," he said, bending over and kissing her forehead. "I'll get out the knives and you can tell me what wrapping paper you want to use. Then you can figure out what you're wearing tonight."

Polly stuck her tongue out at him. "That will only take a few minutes. It's not a dressy affair, is it? And why don't I know more about this?"

"Because most of the plans have been made this week and you've been kinda out of it. Give it a break. The girls wanted to do something special for Sylvie and it wasn't actually necessary for you to be involved. They've done a great job."

"How do you know all of this?"

"Because I've been running up and down stairs with the dog for the last few days. We talk downstairs sometimes."

"My friends have forgotten all about me." Polly stuck her lower lip out. "I got home and they decided I was going to live and they all went back to their busy lives and don't have time for me. My life stinks."

Henry opened the freezer door, took out an ice cream sandwich, unwrapped it and handed it to her. "Eat this. Drown your sorrows in ice cream and then call someone or something."

"It hurts to hold the phone. I always transfer it back and forth between my arms and I can't do that right now."

"Oh good heavenly days," he said. "You're going to be impossible, aren't you?"

"Maybe. I hate this."

"Fine. Let's get your butt downstairs. You can sit on a stool in the kitchen or spend time in your office. If you want to go down to the barn and torture Eliseo, I'll even take you to see him. I can't take this anymore."

She grinned at him. "Now you're talking. If you park me somewhere for a while, you might be able to get some work done."

"I think I'm going to sue that kid for wrecking your truck. He's endangered my life."

Polly was already heading for the back door. "Come on, come on," she said. "I have people to see."

"Slow down. Don't you go down those stairs without me. If you fall and hurt yourself, it only means that much more recuperation time and I can't live with that."

She waited for him at the top of the steps and they slowly made their way down to the back hallway and into the kitchen where she walked in on Hannah, Sylvie and Rachel laughing at something. As soon as they saw her, they stopped talking.

"Were you laughing at me?" Polly demanded.

"What are you doing down here?" Sylvie asked.

Polly walked over to the three of them and said, "You were laughing at me. Rachel told you I was insane and desperate, didn't she?"

"Maybe a little." Sylvie looked away, but Polly caught a grin before she had fully turned her head.

"I am desperate and bored out of my mind. Can I hang out here for a while?"

Henry said, "I'm leaving her with you. In fact, if you think you can handle her, I'm going out to a couple of the job sites."

"You go away," Polly said. "You can serve me later."

He shook his head and left the room.

"I've been torturing him, I think. I don't like being stuck in the apartment," she said. "Now all of you have to tell me what's going on in your lives and what's happening down here and anything else you think I should know. Because ... help me!"

Sylvie took a stool out from under the front counter and pointed at it. "Sit. You can watch us work. If you need anything, just say so and we'll take care of you, but no whining."

Hannah went back to work, battering chicken, letting a small giggle escape every once in a while.

"Y'all think this is funny," Polly said. "It's not."

"But you are," Rachel muttered.

"Well, there's our Polly," Jeff said as he came into the kitchen. "It's good to see your face. It's a little bit of a scary face, but it's good to see it, at least."

"Oh, I forgot!" Polly said. "Rachel, what were you thinking? I'll scare everyone tonight."

"Jessie said she'd help you with makeup," Rachel replied. "You don't look that bad."

"I saw myself this morning. I look that bad. Between the black eyes and the bandage on my forehead, I look awful. Do I really have to do this?"

"Yes you do," Jeff said. "You're one of her best friends, isn't that right, Sylvie?"

Sylvie put a full mug of coffee on the counter beside Polly's good arm. "Yes you are, and everyone who is coming tonight already knows what you've been through. They'll just be glad that you're here at all. Now don't be a baby and drink your coffee."

"Got it. So did you invite Anthony?" Polly said, laughing a little at her evil side.

"Of course I did," Sylvie flung back. "I want him involved in everything I do now that he's back in the area."

Polly peered at her friend's face, waiting for the woman to break. Nothing. She was never playing poker with Sylvie. "You're kidding, aren't you?" She turned to Jeff. "Tell me she's kidding."

He shrugged. "I don't know. She can invite whoever she wants. I'm just setting up tables and decorating the hall."

"Tell me you're joking," Polly said to Sylvie.

"Of course I am. He's probably still mad at me for Sunday night."

"She was ferocious," Polly said. "I was proud of her. Told him off and told him to go away. I think the whole restaurant wanted to applaud, but they were too polite."

"Crap," Sylvie said. "Why does this keep happening?"

Everyone stopped what they were doing, realized that she was looking into the main hallway and turned to follow her eyes. Of course it was Anthony Donovan.

"Good morning, Sylvie," he said. "You really don't go anywhere without an entourage, do you?"

"What do you want, Anthony?"

"Wow, what happened to your friend?" he asked, pointing at Polly. "What did the other guy look like?"

"He's still in the hospital," Polly retorted. "They're not sure if he's going to make it."

His eyes grew big, then he laughed. "Right. Whatever."

She winked at Jeff, "Whatever is right. Call the Boone hospital and ask for Rudy Pierce. They'll tell you."

He gave her no more than a passing glance and said, "Sylvie, could we talk for a few minutes. I would like to straighten some things out with you. I haven't been drinking and if we're going to live in the same state, we need to settle this."

"There's really nothing to settle, Anthony. I'm done with you. I was done with you seven years ago. Now I just have the courage to say so without having the sheriff around."

"Look, I don't want to discuss this in front of everyone. Come on. Let's go for a ride or something."

"I'm not going anywhere with you. I don't trust you. You've never given me a reason to and I'm not about to start now. Especially not after Sunday night."

"I had a few beers. Give a guy a break. I was just hanging with my buddies."

"Uh huh."

"Okay, then. If you want to talk about this here, we will. I want to see my boys."

"That's not happening."

"They're my boys and I have a right."

"Anthony, you gave up all of your rights when you beat the hell out of me and threatened Jason."

He flinched and looked around at the others in the kitchen a bit sheepishly. "Sylvie, stop it. Don't be airing our dirty laundry in front of everyone. I done my time."

"You didn't do enough and I'm not about to have you influencing Jason and Andrew."

"I said stop it." His face became red and his voice grew louder.

Polly stepped off the stool and moved closer to Sylvie. She glanced behind her and saw Rachel and Hannah had suddenly become very involved in what they were doing, trying to avoid watching the confrontation escalate.

"Anthony," Sylvie warned.

"No. I asked you to walk away from these people so we could talk, but you want to trash me in front of them. They don't even know my side of the story."

"You don't have a side," she said. "Don't make me say it again."

"I have a better lawyer now. If I want to spend time with my sons, he and I will make it happen. You can't stop me. I'd have preferred to do this with your approval, but he says that if I can show good behavior, a judge will let me see them again. I got out early because of it and my parole officer knows everything that I'm doing and will put in a good word for me. So will my boss."

Polly felt Sylvie wilt beside her and took her friend's hand.

"Why do you want to do this?" Sylvie asked. "You didn't want anything to do with them when we were married, why do you want to see them now?"

"Because they're growing up and I want to make sure they become men. That little one is a pansy-assed baby, running on about his books and writing and some stupid girl who likes to draw. Is that all he does, play with girls? Are you raising a fag on me, woman? Because I'll fix that, first thing. He needs to get some dirt under his fingernails and learn what it means to be a man."

A quick look at Jeff's face and Polly was barely able to contain her laughter. This was the most ridiculous thing she'd ever heard and Jeff's demeanor told her that he was hearing the same thing.

Sylvie looked back and forth at the two of them in panic. "I'm sorry," she said to Jeff. "He doesn't know what he's saying."

"Hey," he remarked. "I hate dirt under my fingernails. That one doesn't sting."

"God, what a joke," Anthony spat. "All of these women and a fag in the building and you think you're raising my boys? I'm going to put a stop to this if it's the last thing I do."

Things were beginning to get out of control now and Jeff bit his lower lip, as if to keep from blowing up. Sylvie put her head down, not knowing what to say next.

"Well, I guess it's up to me," Polly said, dropping Sylvie's hand. "Do you have anything more you want to say to him, Sylvie?"

Sylvie shook her head. "No. I'm done. I don't know why I even allowed it to continue this far."

"Anyone else have anything they need to say? Jeff?" Polly asked.

Through gritted teeth and slitted eyes, he simply said, "No. It's not worth it."

"Fine." She turned back to Anthony Donovan. "Then, I will politely ask you to leave my property. You aren't welcome here."

"Little thing like you going to make me?" he asked.

"Do I need to? Are you going to hit me? Look at me," she said, gesturing to her face and shoulder. "I'm an easy target and I'm on so many painkillers right now, I don't know that I'd even feel it. But I can promise you that if you hit me, you'd better make it permanent because I will come after you with every law enforcement person I know and you will pay in ways that you have never even imagined. So, I'll ask you one more time to leave." Wow, she was kicking bullies out at an alarming rate.

"I'm going to see my sons, Sylvie Donovan. And I'm going to be involved in their lives. Just you wait and see," he said and turned to go. Then he stopped and spun back around, shaking his finger at Polly. "Just so you know, I'm not scared of you."

"That's fine with me," she responded. "But you need to know that I'm not scared of you, either. And I'll thank you to never step foot in here again."

He left and she waited to breathe until the front door slammed shut. Jeff walked out and in a few moments, returned, saying "He drove away. What a jerk."

"I'm sorry, Jeff," Sylvie said, her face red and eyes brimming with tears. "I'm so sorry. I can't believe he said those horrible things to you."

"Stop it. I've had worse things said to me by people I cared more about. If I reacted every time someone called me a fag, I'd have wasted most of my life away. He's not worth it."

She dropped onto the stool that Polly had used earlier. "What if he really does take my sons away and what if he tries to mess with Andrew? He's such a good kid. He'll never be able to withstand that man's abuse. And Jason, I feel like we're just starting to get him back after a very weird summer. If he spends time with his dad, he'll become someone none of us likes very much."

"Rub her back for me, will ya?" Polly asked Jeff, smiling. He chuckled and obeyed.

"It will be okay," Polly said. "Do you have a good lawyer?"

"Not any longer. I can call the guy who did all of the custody stuff when I divorced Anthony. I don't even know if he's still around, though."

"Call him. The next time you see Anthony, tell him you won't have any more conversations without your lawyer present."

"I can't believe he's decided that he needs to be in their lives. He didn't care about them at all when they were little. He hated being a dad." She looked up at them. "Do you think it's because he's trying to hurt me or does he really want to do this?"

"It's probably a little of both," Jeff said.

"Look at me." Sylvie held her hand up so they could see it trembling. "I can't believe I'm shaking again. I felt so confident after that confrontation at Pizzazz on Sunday. Like I'd finally gotten it all together and could hold my own against him. But I can't do that if he threatens to take my boys away."

"Honey, you're being ridiculous," Polly said. "No judge is going to let him take them away. You've been a great mom and he's been ... well ... in jail. For nearly killing you. You are letting his big mouth scare your little heart. Don't forget about that whole kidnapping thing. And after all of this harassment, you can probably even get a restraining order against him. He doesn't know what he's talking about and probably doesn't even have a lawyer yet. The only one that would take a case like his is one who just wants Anthony's money."

She stopped and thought. "And speaking of that, how does he even have any money to hire a lawyer?"

Sylvie shook her head. "I don't know. He never had any when we were married. I had to pay off a ton of his debt after we were divorced." She looked at Polly and jumped off the stool. "Oh, I'm sorry. I wasn't thinking. Here. Sit back down."

"I'm fine. Really. My legs aren't broken. Now I know this is going to be impossible for you to do, but you have to let this go."

"He's threatening my kids this time. I can't."

"Just for the rest of today. We're celebrating your graduation tonight. People are going to tell you how proud they are of you for doing what most women your age would never dream of doing. You have changed your whole life and shown your boys that dreams can come true. You can worry about all of this tomorrow."

"No," Sylvie said. "If you don't mind, I'm going to use your office and call that lawyer. Tomorrow's Friday and I'd like to talk to him before the weekend. I can't stand the thought of having this hang over my head."

"We've got this," Hannah said. "Don't worry about us."

Sylvie nodded and left the kitchen, heading for the offices.

"She's going to really need us now." Jeff gave Polly a smirk. "I have friends back in Ohio who could deal with this once and for all."

"You do not. Stop that," Polly said.

He laughed an evil laugh. "Actually, I do. But we don't talk about it very loudly. You didn't hear it from me."

"You're a scary man, Mr. Lyndsay."

"And don't you forget it."

CHAPTER TWENTY-FIVE

"Are you sure you girls have this?" Sylvie asked, taking off her apron.

"Of course we do," Hannah said. "Go on, get out of here. We'll see you tonight. Dress pretty!"

Polly walked with Sylvie out the back door. "What did the lawyer say?" she asked.

"He's going to pull up the old files and look at the custody agreement. He didn't seem too worried." Sylvie shrugged. "I don't know. I just want things to go back to normal."

"It will. You'll see. What are you doing this afternoon?"

"I'm moving back to the apartment. At this point, Anthony can't do any more harm and I want my own bed."

"What does Eliseo think of you moving out?"

Sylvie blew air through her lips and forced a short laugh. "I don't know. Why would he think anything of it? He was just doing us a favor."

"So, the kiss? Did you guys talk?"

"I told him that I'm not ready to be in a serious relationship. I like him a lot, but my life is too out of control right now. Gah,

Polly. I don't want to have to take care of someone else. It's enough that I'm dealing with two boys. Jason has been about more than I could handle these last couple of weeks."

"Okay." Polly shrugged and put her hand on the door leading up to the apartment.

"That's all you're going to say? Okay?"

"Sweetie. I'm not going to tell you what to do with your love life. If you don't want to be in a relationship with someone, that's your business."

"So, you aren't going to tell me that I couldn't have handled Jason without Eliseo?"

"Hmm. It doesn't seem like I need to."

"Damn it, Polly. I don't want this right now."

"Then don't do this right now. I mean it. You'll know when it's right. And if it's never right, you'll know that too. Good heavens, Sylvie. You have to trust yourself."

"I'm not very good at that. Especially when it comes to relationships. Anthony really messed me up."

"Look, you have two boys that need you to be sane. If that means you can't be in a relationship of your own, then so be it. Eliseo is a big boy. He'll understand."

"I hope so. He means the world to me and the boys both adore him. I just don't want the rest of it."

"And you told him that, right?"

"I suppose. I hope I didn't hurt him."

"Well, you probably did. That's what rejection does, but he'll get over it. How will the boys feel about moving off the farm?"

"I think they'll be fine. I told them it was happening this week and today seems as good a time as any. I don't have anything I need to do this afternoon and Hannah and Rachel both told me I shouldn't be in the kitchen at all. They've got the party covered tonight." Sylvie started to walk away, then turned back. "You think I'm a fool, don't you."

"Absolutely not. But I also know that it took me a long time to realize that my life wasn't going to be over just because I married Henry. I was so worried about losing myself that I didn't realize what I was gaining. I'm not sorry that I spent all of that time living alone and building this place, but sometimes I wish I hadn't wasted time fighting with him about it. He was always so sure and confident. I should have listened to him."

"But everyone knew that the two of you were supposed to be together."

"I didn't," Polly said. "And honestly, I was the only one who counted. When I figured it out, then things started to make sense."

"Do you think I should be with Eliseo?"

"I think that if you find you love him, he will make you very happy. And honey, you will never have to worry about him hurting you or your boys. He'd sooner walk back through fire than do something that would hurt you."

"Maybe that's what I'm so scared to find out. Men in my life have never been what you'd call 'good.' There was always something in them that made them want to be in control. I never want to live with that again."

"Do you think that the animals in the barn would respond to him like they do if he was mean and controlling? They love him and do what he asks because of his gentle nature. In all of the horrible situations we've been in around here, the only time he was violent was when he was trying to protect me."

"Yeah. Down in the barn. I remember that."

"If that's what is stopping you from giving him a bit of your heart, you need to take some time to think about what you know of Eliseo. If it's something more - if you just don't have feelings for him, then be honest about it and we won't talk about it ever again."

"I honestly don't know. How's that for useless?"

"You'll figure it out. Once things settle down with Jason and you work through the process of custody with Anthony and his lawyer, you'll find yourself again."

"It's funny. I thought that once I finished with college and had my dream job, everything would all of a sudden be sunshine and rainbows." Sylvie huffed. "Not so much. I have more stress today than when I worried about how I was going to pay the rent."

"It will get better, I promise."

"I hope so. Much worse and you're going to find me in a lump, surrounded by empty Pringles cans and candy wrappers."

Polly chuckled. "Is Eliseo helping you pack up your things?"

"No. I'm just going to go deal with it. I'll tell him later that we're gone."

"He doesn't even know you're leaving today?"

"No. I don't want to get into it with him. And if he finds out that Anthony was threatening me again, he'll find some way to convince me to stay longer. I need to get out of there before he knows that or I'll never leave. It will just be too easy to stay."

"I'm sorry, Sylvie." Polly said quietly.

"For what?"

"That things stink right now. You should be able to pursue a relationship or not without all of life crumbling in on you."

"That's the thing. Life is always going on, isn't it? If all of this hadn't happened, Eliseo might never have gotten the courage to kiss me and I wouldn't have had to start thinking about things."

Henry came in from the garage. "Thinking about what things?"

"Getting ready for tonight," Polly quickly responded. "I'll talk to you later. Sorry I can't help this afternoon."

"It's probably better that I take care of it myself. Give me time to think. Thanks for hosting this tonight. I'll see you then." Sylvie turned to leave and Henry followed, opening the door for her.

He came back to the door going upstairs and opened it. "Would you like me to walk with you?" he asked.

"I think I have it. Would you take Obiwan for a walk?"

"Send him down. We'll make it a quickie." He winked at Polly. "So what was that all about?"

"Girl stuff. I'll tell you later." Polly opened the door and looked up the steps. Obiwan was wagging his tail madly at the top. "Come on down, you goofball. It's better to have you out of my way on the steps." The dog ran down and she dropped her hand for him to lick.

"We'll be back in a bit. Are you sure you don't need me to go up the steps with you?" Henry asked.

"If I hadn't been chatting with Sylvie out here, I would have long since been upstairs and you wouldn't have been there to help. Quit worrying."

"Not happening." He put his hand on the dog's collar and waited.

"What?" she asked.

"Go on. Get started. I just want to make sure you have a good sense of equilibrium."

"Not with you staring at me. Take the dog and leave."

"You're going to be like that?"

"I absolutely am. Now go."

Henry leaned in and kissed her cheek. "If I find you sprawled on the steps, I'm going to be really mad."

"I know. I know. I'll be fine."

Polly waited for him to go out the back door and then, putting her left hand on the railing, started the seemingly insurmountable trek up the steps. Dang, everything hurt. She'd been downstairs much too long this morning and standing in one place for the last fifteen minutes or so talking to Sylvie hadn't been helpful. All she wanted to do was collapse somewhere comfortable.

She finally got to the top of the steps, taking them one at a time and stood in front of Henry's desk, wondering if she could just lie down on top of his things. This had already been a long morning. Polly turned around and rested her bottom on the edge of the desk and shut her eyes. Maybe no one would notice that she hadn't gotten any further.

The sound of the downstairs door got her moving again and she was in the media room trying her best to look nonchalant in front of the television when Henry walked in.

He gave her a look and said, "What would you like for lunch? I saw sandwich makings in there."

"That sounds fine," Polly said. "I'm going to just sit down over here and watch something on television."

"Why don't you do that. There are extra pillows behind the sofa if you want them." He went on through to the kitchen and opened the refrigerator door.

"Henry?" Polly asked.

He looked over the top of the door, "Yes, Polly?"

"Could you help me?"

He chuckled and shut the door. "Of course I can. I just didn't want you to think that I was coddling you. What do you need?"

When he got close enough, she swatted him. "I need pillows and I think I need another pain pill. This one wore off and I hurt all over."

They got her situated on the sofa and he put the remote control in her hand. "Don't move. I'll be right back."

"I'm going nowhere and I feel better already. That was a lot of work this morning."

"Every day will get easier."

Both of them were startled by a knock on their front door. "Who's here?" she asked.

He pursed his lips and said, "I'm supposed to know? Sit still. I'll find out."

Polly leaned back and heard him say hello. Before she could identify the other voices, Sam and Jean Gardner had rushed past Henry into the dining room.

"There you are," Jean said. "I've been so worried about you. I wanted to give you plenty of time to get back on your feet before we showed up, but I thought today would be a perfect day to bring lunch. You don't already have a meal prepared, do you? We would have been here earlier, but Sam was in Boone and just got back to town. I didn't want to come over without him, he would have been disappointed to not get a chance to see you two."

"Come on in," Polly said. "I'm sorry I'm not going to jump up to say hello, but I just landed here and I hurt."

"Oh, of course you do, honey. Of course you do. Can I make myself comfortable in your kitchen? I'll get this all set up for you and then Sam and I will get out of your way. We don't want to be a bother."

Henry looked at Polly and she gave him a slight nod. "We'd love to have you two join us if you brought enough."

"Oh, honey," Jean said. "There's more than enough. Who do

you think you're talking to? It isn't a great meal if there aren't leftovers."

Sam had taken a seat in the chair next to the sofa. "How are you doing, little girl? You had us worried sick. I was over talking to your man at the barn when he got the call."

"You were? What about?"

"We talked about gardens and he introduced me to your horses. Those are some beautiful animals you have down there."

Polly smiled. "I'm so glad Eliseo is here to take care of them. They have thrived with him."

"He's a good man and he knows his stuff with the garden out back. We talked a little about what is going on in your little park, but he said he doesn't do much with that."

"No, there are several people who enjoy working out there. If they ever get tired of it, we'll have to make some other decisions, but for now, he has plenty to do with the animals and the rest of the grounds."

"I miss having dirt under my fingers every day," he said. "But that season is over. It's a different life I lead now."

Polly nearly opened her mouth to invite him to be part of the work at Sycamore House, but decided that if Eliseo wanted to make that happen, it was up to him. She might let him know that Sam was interested, but he could make the invitation. All she said was, "Life does change, doesn't it?"

Henry excused himself into the office and came back with four TV trays. "I thought it might be easier for Polly if we eat out here, rather than make her sit at the dining room table. She's already had a busy morning."

"Why that sounds perfect," Sam said and jumped to help Henry set them up.

Henry made several trips back and forth from the kitchen with utensils and napkins, condiments and glasses of water.

"Shall I just serve it up here and bring plates out?" Jean called across the room.

Polly looked helplessly at Henry, who said. "That sounds great. We like everything you've brought."

"What are we having?" Polly asked.

"It smells like pulled pork."

"And Jean's famous baked beans. You won't get anything like these between here and Kansas City. She made a big bowl of cole slaw and homemade buns for sandwiches. I made her bring a bag of potato chips. I like a little crunch in my meal."

"Wow," Polly said. "It all sounds amazing. Thank you."

Polly loved barbecue and Jean's tasted wonderful. What she really wanted to do was top the sandwich with a scoop of the coleslaw, but thought maybe this wasn't the right place or time. If there were leftovers, she'd do it on the next meal. She'd learned that trick from an old boyfriend and loved the way those flavors mixed. The baked beans were heavenly, lots of pork and bacon and just a hint of smoky flavor.

"This really is terrific. Henry was going to have to serve me a cold meat sandwich," Polly said, chuckling. "Either that or leftovers."

"You're going to have lots of people bringing food by," Jean said confidently.

"I am?"

"Lydia Merritt and her friend Andy are organizing the whole thing."

"Oh, that's right. They talked about that when I was in the hospital."

"I called her right up and told her I wanted to be on the list for today. We just had to come over and make sure you were doing okay. It looks like you got pretty beat up, though."

Polly unconsciously touched her cheek. She avoided mirrors right now and consequently forgot how bad she must look to others.

"Don't you be fretting about your bruises," Sam said. "Those are just a sign of strong character. You take a lickin' and keep on tickin.' It's good to know that even this isn't getting you down. You should wear them proudly."

"I don't know about that. But it is what it is." Eating with her left hand was a bit of a challenge. Fortunately, Henry had brought her a spoon. It made it much easier to scoop food into her mouth. "I will be glad to have my right hand back. I feel like a fool trying to do things without it."

"You were very lucky, Miss Polly," Jean said. "Very lucky. When we heard what happened, I nearly dropped right to my knees to pray for you, but I don't do that much anymore." She laughed out loud at her own joke. "You know. Old knees and all. If I got down, it would take God and all of his angels to bring me back up. I can't imagine what those boys were thinking, trying to run you off the road."

"They weren't thinking," Sam said with disgust. "That's one thing I don't miss about being around kids these days. Too many of them don't think through things and mess the world up for those who are doing the right thing. It's just ridiculous." He slammed his fist on his thigh. "They could have killed you."

Polly glanced at Henry. His face had gone white and he was clenching his teeth so tightly, she was afraid he might explode. "Fortunately, it's over and I'm fine. The boys have been caught and now it's up to their lawyers and the courts to decide what to do." She wanted to reach out to him, but he was too far away.

"How's Sebastian doing?" Polly asked, changing the topic.

"He's sleeping and barking. It's what old boys like him do," Jean said. "Can I get anyone another sandwich?" She stood up with her plate and stopped in front of her husband.

"I'd like to say yes, but my stomach says I should quit," he said. "And besides, didn't you bring something sweet, too?"

Jean smiled. "I made chocolate cupcakes. I thought those would be easy for Polly to eat." She took her husband's plate and smiled at Polly. "You can have as many as you like. No one is going to count today."

Henry took up Polly's plate and carried things to the kitchen, following Jean. He came back with a tray of cupcakes while Jean opened cupboard doors. "I'm just looking for glasses," she said. "We like to have a little milk when there's that much chocolate. How about you?" She glanced back across the room and then said, "Oh, here they are. Polly? Henry?"

"That sounds terrific," Polly said. "Thank you." She smiled. "I feel a little strange letting you all hover over me like this, but right now I'm not complaining. And Henry, would you mind getting my pill?"

"Oh, I'm sorry! I forgot. You must be hurting."

"I'm okay. Don't worry."

He and Jean both returned from the kitchen and sat down again.

"This has been so nice," Jean said. "You have a lovely home here. Did you do all the work, Henry?"

He nodded and handed Polly the pain pill. She popped it in her mouth and swallowed it with the last of her glass of water. "I did. Polly had an idea of what she wanted, so that made it easy."

"The bookshelves are lovely and the floors are beautiful. Is the wood from an old barn?"

Polly nodded. "Down south of Boone."

Sam ran his hand across the table beside him and then picked up one of the comics. "Do you like to read these?" he asked.

Henry nodded. "I've read comic books ever since I was a kid. I just came across these, though. It's taking me back to my childhood."

"That looks like it's from the set that was given away at that card night," Jean said. "I only remember that because I'd never seen the *Silver Surfer* and it was in a plastic bag like that. I suppose that means it's probably worth something."

"Someone put these up as a door prize?" Henry asked.

"Yes, there were two of them that night. I didn't see who the winner was, though. And Sam, do you remember who brought them?"

"It was someone new. She'd never been there before. And honestly, I don't think she's ever come again. She was a guest of ... let me think." He scratched his head and then turned to look at the floor, his brows creased in thought. "That's been such a long time ago. She was an older woman. Hill or Dill. No, what was it, Jean?"

"I don't remember her name. She ended up at your table for a while. Wasn't it Ruth Benscoter who brought her?"

"Yes, that's it. But now what was her name. Edith, I think that was her first name. Edith Diller or Miller. No, it wasn't Miller."

Polly sat back with a sigh. "Willard. Edith Willard."

"That's it!" he exclaimed. "Edith Willard. I remember her saying that she'd gotten the invitation earlier that day and didn't know what to bring for a door prize, but found these in an old trunk. But she left before they were handed out. Remember, Jean? Ruth got sick and they had to leave early."

Then it hit him. "How did you know it was her?"

"Oh, just a hunch," Polly said. "Henry and another friend of ours just bought a couple of old Woodies from her. They're going to restore them."

Sam grinned across at a very confused Henry. "You're a car guy too? I'd like to see these old heaps. How much work do you have to do on them?"

Henry nodded. "They're just rusted out shells right now. But my buddy, Nate ... you know, the pharmacist? He assures me that we can bring those babies back to life. We have everything we need to get started."

Polly felt the pain pill begin to take effect and she relaxed into the pillows, letting the sounds in the room float around her. What had Edith Willard done?

CHAPTER TWENTY-SIX

Rousing from sleep with Henry's hand on her leg, Polly jumped and said, "What?" She looked around the room and realized they were alone. "Oh no, I'm so embarrassed. Did I snore?"

He grinned at her. "No. You were quite polite in your slumber. Sam and Jean watched you fall asleep and after she cleaned the kitchen and rearranged the refrigerator so there would be plenty of room for all of the meals that would be arriving, they went home. She wanted me to tell you that if you need anything when I go back to work, all you have to do is call and she'll come right over."

"That's sweet. But I seem to remember something about a cupcake and I didn't get a chance to finish it."

"It was really yummy."

"You ate my cupcake?"

"Well, you weren't going to. I didn't want it to get stale."

She pushed her lower lip out at him. "Did she leave any?"

"Of course. Do you want another glass of milk?"

"That would be awesome. What time is it?"

"It's four o'clock. I woke you up because I didn't know how

long it would take you to get ready for tonight." He went to the kitchen and rummaged around in the refrigerator.

"Where are the kids?"

"Rebecca is downstairs with her mother and Sylvie picked Andrew up at school. Apparently, they're moving back into the apartment today. Jason's bus should be here soon and he already knows he's supposed to go over to the apartment rather than down to the barn. Jessie will be home in a little bit. Mom says that they had a good conversation with Doc Mason today."

"Wow, with you in charge, who needs me? You're managing all of this quite well."

He put a plate with an unwrapped cupcake on her lap and the glass of milk beside her. "Let's not get too carried away. I figure I can pull this off for a day or two and then I'm turning it back over to the master."

Polly took a bite. "I knew this would be good. Are there more of these?"

"Yes there are, you chocoholic. I have a feeling that before you are completely recovered from this experience, our refrigerator is going to be filled with treats."

"I feel a little guilty about that. I can eat pizza. People don't have to do this."

"For that matter," Henry said, "I can cook. It does feel a little odd."

"But Lydia yelled at me, so I can't say anything." Polly's eye caught the comic book on the table. "So, what do you think about that?" she asked.

"What?"

"Do you think that Loren won those comics from Mrs. Willard?"

"Maybe he did. It seems like a really expensive door prize, though."

"Maybe she didn't know. I'll give her a call tomorrow and see what she says."

"Polly, that's crazy. Uncle Loren could well have collected them over a lifetime. Who knows what he was into?"

She shook her head. "You're right. I'm just making things up in my head." Polly took a last drink of her milk and set it back on the table. "I'm feeling better. That nap helped, though I should probably call Jean and apologize."

"Don't worry about it. They understood." He smiled. "In fact, I think it made them feel really good that you were comfortable enough with them in your house to fall asleep."

"I'm glad they felt that way, but honestly, I didn't have a choice. I just went out."

Noise from the back steps announced Jessie's arrival. She came bouncing into the media room, full of smiles. "Hi there!" She dropped into the chair that Sam had vacated earlier. "How are you feeling today, Polly?"

"Pretty good. Henry says you went to see Doc Mason."

"I did." She turned to him. "Your Mom is wonderful. She didn't think I was a bad person or anything."

"You're not," Polly said. "I'm glad she was there for you."

"I'm going into a clinic next week for an ultrasound. That will be so cool. Then we'll know for sure how far along I am and when the baby is due."

Polly smiled. She was so thankful Jessie was excited about this. "We're going to have to look for some maternity things for you one of these days. We'll take Sal. She loves to shop."

"Can you believe I'm going to have a baby? This is crazy!" Jessie bounced in her chair a little, then sat back. "I still haven't called Mom and Dad. I don't know how to tell them."

"You just have to say it."

"Mom's going to think I did this on purpose."

Polly didn't want to hear about that woman and her emotional abuse of Jessie. It made her insane that people were so intent on screwing up their kids' lives. "Well, your mom isn't out here to do anything about it. If she wants to get involved in your life and the life of your child, she can come out and spend time with you."

"I know. You're right. Dad won't be mad, though, so I'll call him this weekend." Jessie sat forward in her chair and peered at Polly's face. "You're going to need some serious cover up tonight and maybe I can do something different with your part to make your hair cover that bandage. Fortunately, I have everything in my room. Do you know what you're wearing?"

"Not yet," Polly sighed. "I probably need to figure that out. How long is this makeover going to take?"

"I'm going to take a shower and get myself ready," Jessie said. "Then we can do your makeup and hair. I'll bet you can't even put mascara on."

Polly let her left hand swing limply in the air. "Not with this awkward hand. I'm afraid I'd poke myself in the eye. It's going to be au naturel for a while unless you're here to help me."

Jessie giggled and said to Henry, "You'd better make sure I'm aware of any big dates you two are planning to take, unless you want to put mascara on for her."

"I'm going to leave you two alone." He picked up the plate and glass. "Jessie, if you want cupcakes, Jean Gardner left some in the kitchen."

"I'm good. Your mom and I made muffins today, then we took them out to a couple of the job sites so I could meet people."

He shook his head. "Muffins on a job site. Welcome to my world." Henry walked back through and said to Obiwan, "Come on, dog. We need to escape the estrogen zone, at least for a while."

Obiwan jumped off the couch and looked back at Polly, then followed Henry to the back steps. Polly put her feet on the ground and tried to lift herself off the couch, but she'd been in one place for far too long and nothing worked. The first heave made her ribs hurt and she sat back down, panting heavily.

"Can I help?" Jessie asked.

"Put your arm out and let me hold it for balance," Polly said. "Just give me a little support, that's all." She put her left hand on Jessie's forearm and felt the girl stiffen up to hold it in place, then pulled herself into a standing position. "Thanks."

"No problem. Do you need help changing clothes or anything?"

Polly was still trying to shake off the drowsiness from the nap. She was a little afraid that if she got into her bedroom, she'd drop down onto her bed and fall asleep, but this evening was happening whether she was there or not and she really wanted to be there.

"I'm sorry, what did you ask me?"

"Do you need help ..."

"Oh, with clothes. No, I'll manage and when Henry gets back, he can help. You get ready and then you can try to beautify me."

The girl walked with Polly across to her bedroom and once Polly crossed the threshold, Jessie watched a moment longer before heading for her own room.

Polly opened the closet doors and then sat on the bed, staring at the clothes. Since she wasn't going outside tonight, she could get away with flat sandals. No one would care. There, that was one part of her body dealt with. Black pants were always appropriate. Now she was halfway there. She was thinking way too hard about this. Sylvie was the important person tonight. Polly just needed to put something on that didn't draw attention. Surely that should be easy to find. She stood up and walked over to the closet, then reached her left arm up to push several hangers and flinched. It was one thing to have a broken clavicle, but these ribs were downright annoying. She thought back to last night and the father of that boy standing in front of her accusing her of doing something awful to his privileged son. That kid had driven away, no worse for wear. He had left her and his buddy on the road, not knowing or caring whether they were dead or alive. Neither of those boys had even bothered to call 9-1-1. Her fault, hah.

She reached out and tried to pull some clothes away by tugging on the sleeve of a dress and moving it to the right. That didn't work, the dress ended up in a heap on the floor.

"Damn it," she said, tears filling her eyes. "This just shouldn't be so hard. Damn it, damn it, damn it."

"Polly?"

Rebecca stood in the doorway of Polly's bedroom.

"Are you okay?"

"I'm sorry, sweetie. I'm just frustrated. I was trying to find something to wear and everything hurts. But I'm okay."

"Can I help you?"

Polly walked back to her bed and dropped down on it. "Sit here beside me for a minute and tell me about your day. How was school?"

"It was okay. Mrs. Hastings changed the seating chart and I have to sit by Maddy Collins now."

"Do you like her?"

"She's kind of nice. She asked if I wanted to sit beside her at lunch."

"That's nice. Maybe you'll start getting to know some other kids, some of her friends."

"I guess."

"How's your mom doing? I haven't seen her since she got home."

"Fine. She's really weak and they made me leave when she got a shot. She said it was in her stomach!"

"Are you glad to have her here?"

"I can go see her anytime I want, but it's okay that I'm sleeping up here."

"I'm glad," Polly said. "Are you going to Sylvie's party tonight?"

"Mom said I should go for a while, but that I can come see her before I go to bed tonight. Is that okay?"

"Sweetie, whatever your Mom says to do is fine with me. Now, would you mind helping me pick something out for tonight? I need a top."

"Why don't you just wear that pretty blue dress?" Rebecca asked and ran over to the closet, pulling out a dress that Polly had forgotten. "That way you don't have to worry about zippers or buttons or anything. Just pull this on." She bent over and picked up the dress that Polly had dropped, hanging it back up. Then she took out a pair of black flats. "These would look nice."

"You're perfect, you know that?"

Rebecca smiled.

"That's exactly what I'll wear. Thank you. Now, you go get changed and then you can help Jessie put my makeup on and style my hair so I don't look so freaky."

"You just look like Polly to me." Rebecca approached and reached out to hug her, but stopped. "I don't want to hurt you."

Polly wrapped her left arm around the girl. "Thanks for checking on me and I'm sorry you heard me swear."

Rebecca giggled. When Obiwan rushed into the room, she bent down and hugged him tight around the neck. Henry wasn't far behind him.

"What's going on in here?" he asked. "Girl stuff?"

"Rebecca helped me decide what to wear tonight," Polly said.

"I hope that you will let me get away with slacks and a polo," he said.

"You should wear that grey shirt," Rebecca said. "I heard Sal say it was sexy."

Both Henry and Polly laughed. "Not much gets by you, does it?" Polly asked. "Now go and I'll see you downstairs later."

Henry shut the door behind her and said, "Sexy, eh? I'll wear the grey shirt!"

"You do that. Even if I can't do anything about it, I like hanging out with my sexy husband. But first, can you help me wrangle all of this so I can pull my dress on?"

~~~

"You don't look half bad," Jeff said, dropping into a chair beside Polly.

"Thanks to Jessie. She spent at least a half hour getting me to this point. I've made her promise to take it all off my face when we get back upstairs tonight. Otherwise, tomorrow morning my pillow will look like a ghoul slept there."

"How are you feeling?"

"I'm fine. And tomorrow I'll be better and the day after and the day after until this will only be a memory."

"She's quite the star, isn't she?" he said, gesturing to Sylvie.

Sylvie was surrounded by several people from town that Polly didn't know well and one or two young women that had been introduced as her classmates.
~~~

"She has a lot to be proud of. It's kind of fun to watch it happen. So, you never told me. How was your date?"

He shrugged. "It was fine. He had tickets to a show in Des Moines. I bought dinner. Come to find out we have nothing in common. He never called, I never texted. So, it was just a date."

"Okay," She looked at him to see what his face told her. There wasn't any real emotion there. "You don't seem too upset about it."

"I'm still young and fabulous," he said, laughing a little. "Someday someone will figure that out."

"You are and they will," she agreed.

"Polly, look what Mom got!" Andrew cried, running over to her with his hands behind his back.

"What's that?" She hoped it wasn't the knife set. That could get bloody.

He pushed a box into her hands. "We're going to grow mushrooms!"

"That looks like fun. And a little weird."

"Maybe we can plant them in the garden next year and have lots of mushrooms."

"Uh. Okay. Whatever your Mom wants."

"You don't think these are cool, do you?"

"I think it's wonderful. Where's Rebecca?"

"She went over to her Mom's room after we were done eating. I'm supposed to go get her when they serve dessert."

"Very nice."

Andrew ran off and Polly turned to Jeff. "I feel like such an invalid. People have been coming up to me all evening to talk and I just don't feel like wandering in and out of groups to mingle."

"Stop it, you silly girl. We all know that you're hurt. This isn't a normal night for you."

"Okay, but give me your hand. I'm going to get up anyway. It feels weird."

He walked with her over to the table where Henry had landed with Nate Mikkels.

"I'm so glad you're here," Joss said. "Look at them."

Polly looked. The two men had their phones out and were

swiping through websites that had parts for Woodies. "That's kind of sick," she said. "They can't even enjoy a social night out." She said the last a little more loudly and pointedly at the two men.

Henry looked up, not looking the least bit chagrined. "What? Nate found these sites and wanted to order parts."

"Whatever," she sighed. "Where are the kids?" she asked Joss.

"Nate's mom is in town. She's going to be here through the weekend, so I was thinking that I might come over to see you tomorrow if you're up to it."

Henry looked up again, this time his eyes lit up. "I could go out and get some work done," he said.

"I guess that's a great idea," Polly said. "Come on over any time."

"I'm bringing lunch, so maybe just a little after noon."

"You don't have to bring anything."

"Yes I do. I'm looking forward to it. You haven't had my chicken enchiladas yet."

"Polly?" Jeff said, touching her elbow. "We're going to do a couple of presentations for Sylvie. I hate to interrupt, but are you ready to say something?"

"I am." She said to Joss. "I'll see you tomorrow and thanks."

"I'm glad you're standing," he said. "That makes this part easier. We won't go up on stage since there aren't that many people here. You don't need a mic, do you?"

"No, this should be fine. I'm just talking to them. It's not like a speech or anything, right?"

"Whatever you want."

"Folks!" he called out. "If you could take a seat, we have a few things we want to say to Sylvie as we congratulate her on her achievement and welcome her to the full-time staff of Sycamore House." He waited as everyone sat down.

Sylvie sat with Jason, Eliseo, Rachel, Hannah and Andrew at a front table. It occurred to Polly that having Eliseo sit there was very interesting. She had no idea what Sylvie was doing.

"We know that Sylvie's ceremony won't happen until December, but this is such an auspicious occasion we didn't want to wait that long." Jeff nodded at Rachel, who went over to the stage and brought a package back to him.

"A graphic artist rendered her certificate for us and we'd like to present this to you as we congratulate you, our Head Chef. Sylvie?"

She came forward and the two of them pulled the paper off the sixteen by twenty frame.

"There are actually two of these, and the original has been framed as well. One will proudly hang in our kitchen here at Sycamore House and the others are for you to do with as you please."

"Thank you," she said shyly, looking at the certificate.

Hannah came up with another wrapped package and handed it to Jeff.

"Now that you're our head chef, we wanted everyone to know just how important you are to us." Jeff handed the package to her and waited while she unwrapped it. She shook out five aprons. "If you look at the front, we have embroidered your name over the Sycamore House logo. These are yours and there are plenty for as many messes as you can make in one day."

"Thank you," she said, laughing and then gave him a hug.

He looked at Polly, who began to speak. "One of the first times I met Sylvie, we were going to a party and she was carrying in this immense set of candy dishes. I don't even know what they were."

Sylvie blushed and dropped her head.

"She had made all of these little treats for five of us and then told us that the others would go to her boy's classrooms and then she was planning to take food gifts to several older people she knew who wouldn't get such fun treats otherwise. She impressed me with her care for others.

"Things happened pretty quickly those first few months here at Sycamore House. Jeff showed up and all of a sudden we had a Christmas party to prepare for. When I asked Sylvie to help, she didn't hesitate. Cooking for untold numbers of people didn't frighten her at all. She just dug in and got it done and it was wonderful. Do you remember?"

Polly looked around the room as her friends applauded Sylvie. "Then there was the barn raising and once again, Sylvie was right there, organizing meals for the workers and surprising me with her generosity. I knew she had to work here, no matter what. I was ready to hire her as our chef for any event Jeff could wrangle. But Sylvie wasn't satisfied with that. She wanted to be more than just a cook, she wanted to reach beyond herself.

"The day she ran into my office to announce that she was going to school was exciting for all of us. No matter what it took, Sylvie was going to make this happen. She has worked hard these last eighteen months. Days and evenings in class and the rest of her free time and weekends she worked here with Jeff as they developed Sycamore House into a prime location for weddings and other events. I never imagined that all of this would happen so quickly, and it wouldn't have without her skill in the kitchen and her talent for working with others.

"I'm proud of you, Sylvie Donovan. You've done something that most people would never dream of doing and I can't wait to see what you do next."

Sylvie came over and took Polly's hand as the room burst into applause. She held her hand up.

"This wasn't an accomplishment I managed on my own. My boys supported me, all of you have encouraged me and Jeff has inspired me, but you, Polly, you were my catalyst. You took care of my family, you took care of me and you gave me freedom. I will never be able to thank you enough, but for now, what I can do is this!"

Sylvie clapped her hands over her head, the lights went out in the auditorium and Rachel and Hannah pushed carts filled with flaming dishes into the room. Everyone clapped again, amidst laughter and smatterings of conversation.

"We have homemade ice cream and cherries jubilee for dessert," Sylvie said as the lights came back up. "Thank you for everything!"

CHAPTER TWENTY-SEVEN

"My mother-in-law is great. She really is and I do love her," Joss said. She and Polly were alone in the living room after lunch. Henry had grabbed the opportunity to leave for the afternoon and he took Obiwan so that the dog could have some time outside.

"But?" Polly asked. The storm that had been threatening all morning had finally hit and thunder rattled the glass windows in the apartment.

"But, he's her baby. If he's in the room, I don't exist and now that he has children, I've slipped all the way down the totem pole. It might be different if Cooper and Sophie needed me in order to eat, but since they don't, I'm just superfluous while she's in town." Joss batted her eyes at Polly, "Can I move in here?"

"I thought you said you loved her. And you know you'd miss those babies of yours."

"Like I'm going to get to spend any time with them this weekend anyway. She's come, she's seen and she will conquer."

"Sounds a little intimidating."

"She is that, but I should be good and take advantage of the time. I have work that needs to be done at the library, so I can get in there this weekend when it's quiet and I won't worry about Nate being too overwhelmed."

A knock at the front door caused Polly to jump. "Who's there?" she called out.

"Open the door, it's the bogeyman."

"I've got it," Joss said and ran to open the front door to Sal, who folded her umbrella and propped it outside the door. "When did you get home?"

"I flew in last night. Two days of my mother is more than enough. How are you doing, Polly?"

"I'm okay."

"It certainly didn't help the relationship with my mother when I found out you'd been in a terrible accident and I was flying to Boston so I could sit in a hospital while Dad had knee replacement surgery. I was so mad. If I was going to be in a hospital somewhere, I'd much rather have been worrying about you here."

"Didn't you have to host a tea?" Joss asked.

Sal dropped into a chair. "Yes, it was boring as always. Mom's club met at our house and she'd engaged a woman who spoke about handling life changes with proper etiquette. I'm not kidding when I tell you that she covered everything from having grandchildren to burying your husband."

"How's your dad?" Polly asked.

"He's fine and was going home yesterday afternoon. Mom wasn't any too happy that I was at the airport getting on a plane. She wanted me there for the whole event, but I'd already scheduled the flight and I was gone with the wind. So tell me about your face," Sal said.

Polly reached up and touched her cheekbone. It didn't hurt quite as badly as it had earlier in the week, but was still pretty sensitive. "I think I look good in multi-colored hues, don't you?"

"You really need to stop doing this, people are going to talk about Henry."

"I know, I know. I try to stay out of trouble, but it finds me with absolutely no effort. I wasn't even taking my normal way home and it found me."

"Have you seen the truck yet?"

"No," Polly said. "And I don't know if I want to. Henry and Aaron said they'd take care of it for me." She picked her phone up and then put it back down. "That reminds me, I need to ask Aaron if they've taken my things out of it. I didn't have much in there, but I don't want to lose it to a junkyard."

"You should call him while you're thinking about it. We aren't going anywhere," Sal said.

"Are you sure?"

"Do you want coffee?" Joss asked Sal. "I brought cookies and it looks like there are chocolate cupcakes and brownies, too."

Polly shook her head. "I can't go anywhere or do anything and everybody keeps bringing me food. This is going to be very, very bad for me."

"Let me help," Sal said. "But first, I'm going to freshen up." She winked at Polly. "I've spent too much time in Boston, haven't I?"

They left the room and Polly dialed Aaron Merritt's phone.

"Tell me you are still safe in your home," he said. "I don't want to hear that you are out traipsing about the county looking for more trouble."

"I'm right here, safe and sound. But I was just thinking about all of my things from Dad's truck. Do you have those and can you bring them up to me sometime?"

"In a little box on my desk. The team has finally gone through everything and they are finished with the inside. We're not releasing the truck yet, though."

"I don't need that. I don't know if I ever want to see it again," Polly said.

"That's probably a good idea. It's a sad little truck, but it certainly did its job and kept you safe."

"I said those same things to Henry."

Polly looked up when she felt a presence in the room with her. A strange man, his face covered with a ski mask, was standing just inside the front door.

"Who are you?" she demanded, loudly. "Why are you in my house?"

"It doesn't matter who I am. I just want what's mine and then I'll leave."

"I don't understand. Why do you believe I have something of yours? I don't even know who you are."

"Oh, you have it and you are going to hang up the phone right now and then you and I will gather what's mine and I'll leave."

"I have to go," Polly said into the phone. "Someone is here to see me."

"I heard everything. Is Henry there?"

"No, I have to go."

"Someone will be there soon. Be careful, Polly," Aaron said.

She put the phone down without swiping the call closed and braced herself to stand up. Joss chose that moment to come out of the kitchen with a plate filled with goodies.

"Oh!" she exclaimed. "Who are you?" Her face grew bright red and she began to back into the dining room, then looked at Polly and tried to step forward. It was obvious that a million things were processing through her brain and she wasn't sure which way to go.

The man pulled a gun from his pocket and pointed it at Joss, making the decision for her. "Don't move and no one gets hurt. Miss Giller and I just need to get a few things and I'll be gone before you know it."

"I won't move," Joss said, planting her feet.

Her hands trembled, rattling the cookies on the plate and Polly said, "Let her put the plate down on the table so that she doesn't drop it."

He waved the gun, gesturing to a small table just beside the doorway. "Fine. Put it down. Now, Miss Giller, where are those comic books?"

"The what?" Polly was confused. Then, all of a sudden, she wasn't. "Oh. The comic books. Loren hadn't collected those over the years. He was the one who won them. That makes sense now."

"Where are they?"

"Honestly, they're all over the place. You're going to have to give me a few minutes to gather them up. There are some in our bedroom and some in the media room. A friend was reading one the other night."

"You're reading them?" He was incredulous. "Do you know what those are worth?"

"I guess not. They're just comic books."

"If you've damaged them, I might just shoot you right now." He brushed his forehead with the hand holding the gun. Polly hadn't seen too many people wield weapons, but this stupid man didn't look very comfortable with it.

"Let's find them," Polly said. "We'll start in the media room. It's right through here." She sent him through the door, past Joss and gave her friend a pointed look. Sal did not need to get involved in this. Joss shrugged and stayed close to the wall.

He made a beeline for the table where three of the comics were resting, still in their plastic covers. "Thank god these are clean." He shook one at her. "This is worth eight hundred dollars! I don't know what she was thinking."

"Did you kill my husband's uncle because of these comic books?"

He spun around and pointed the gun at Polly. "Take me to the rest of them."

"You killed two men because of comic books," she said again. "That's ridiculous. So, are you planning to kill me and my friend?" Polly knew she was being rash, but she was at the end of her rope. This was the third time a man had threatened her this week and to be honest, other than the ski mask, this one looked the least likely to actually hurt her.

"Move it," he demanded.

"Okay, okay. There might be one or two on the desk in here," and she led him into Henry's office and chuckled when she realized that a bottle of pop was sitting on top of one of the comics.

"What are you people thinking?" he asked, carefully pulling it out and cradling it in his arms.

"I think you're a little overboard with your obsession."

"You don't know anything about my obsession. This is worth

sixteen hundred dollars if I can find the right buyer. I can't believe that old woman gave my things away. She never liked these things, but I knew what I was doing. My collection was worth tens of thousands of dollars before she got her hands on it. And no one had any idea that it was sitting in a barn in the middle of Iowa."

He brushed his hands across the desk, moving papers around, checking to make sure there weren't any more. "Okay, next room."

"Did you ever tell her what your collection was worth?"

"Hell no. She would have made me sell it a long time ago."

"You know she probably wouldn't have given them away if she'd known."

"Whatever. Take me to the rest of them."

"They're back here, in my room. I'll warn you, it isn't very clean, though," Polly wondered if she'd lost her mind. Worrying about her bedroom when a man had a gun in her house?

"I don't care about that. Now go."

"So why did you kill Loren?"

"The old guy in the truck? He lied to me and then he tried to run for help. I ran him off the road and when he realized I was serious, he threatened to hurt me. I don't like threats."

"So you killed him."

"Please, he was a loser old guy. He was going to die soon anyway. I probably did everyone a favor. Once they get to that age, all they do is suck the life out of everyone around them. You have to wait on them and they're not even nice. He wasn't a very nice man at all. Not as bad as my old man, but still not very nice."

"And the other man you killed?"

"I caught up to him the next day and he was going to one of the stores in Ames to sell them. He would never have gotten enough money for them. He just went on eBay and thought those low bids were the best price. I hit him over the head and then realized he would probably tell someone, so I shot him and took him back to Mom's and dropped his body in the tub. She never goes out there. No one ever goes out there but me."

Polly pointed to Henry's bedside table where he'd placed a stack of comics. "How did you even know who had gotten the comic books? Your mom left before they chose the winners."

"Old people are so gullible," he said. "I called the head person on the list at Mom's house. You know they print those things with names and addresses. Everything was right there. She was so proud of the fact that she'd kept a list of every person and what they'd won."

"Wow," Polly said.

He bent over to pick through the stack of comics and Polly looked up to see Sal tip-toeing into the bedroom with a cast iron skillet raised over her head. Before Polly could take a breath, Sal hit the guy on the head and he dropped to the floor.

The two of them looked at each other and Sal said. "We need something to tie him up. Quick. Tell me what you have."

"I don't have anything," Polly said. "I'm not a cop. Here. Maybe the tie off my robe? I don't know."

They turned the man over on his stomach and Polly handed Sal the cloth belt. She twisted it around his hands and then bent his knees and tied the two ends around his ankles as well.

"That should keep him."

" I can't believe you just did that," Polly said.

"I wouldn't trust it for very long, but I called the cops and someone should be here really soon. Apparently, your phone is still talking to Aaron."

"Henry is going to be so upset when he finds out this happened while he was gone."

"But I was here," Sal said, preening as she stood up a bit straighter.

"Yes you were. I was just trying to stall him until someone came."

"I wanted in on some of your fun, but I have to tell you, this was more pathetic than exciting."

"Except for the whole gun thing."

Sal bent over and looked at the gun and then with her toe, kicked it away from the guy on the floor. "He wasn't planning to use it. The safety is still on."

"I wouldn't even know that," Polly said. "But thank you."

Joss led Stu Decker and another deputy into the bedroom. The two men took one look at the man on the floor and did their best to withhold their laughter, but failed miserably.

"You hogtied him with the tie from your robe?" Stu asked.

"It's all we had," Sal sad. "I'm Sal Kahane."

"You're Polly's friend from Boston. Yeah. I know. And now you're caught up in her crazy world." He bent over and strapped a zip tie around the guy's wrists and untied his feet, handing the tie back to Polly.

She shied away from it. "Drop it on the floor. I'm not using that until it's been washed a few times."

Stu pulled the man's mask off. It was obviously Edith Willard's son, John, but he wasn't familiar to anyone.

"Wake up, buddy," Stu said then turned to Sal. "You hit him with a skillet?"

"Just once."

"Come on, buddy. Wake up." Stu tapped the man's face and was rewarded with a moan. "How ya doin' there? Your head hurt?"

"What?"

Stu helped him stand up and though he was wobbly, the man came to his feet. "What did you hit me with?"

Sal brandished the pan again.

"Who are you and where did you come from?" he asked. "Where's my gun?"

"Don't worry, buddy. We've got everything we need. You do understand you're under arrest for murder and for threatening these good women here."

"I wasn't going to hurt them. I just wanted my comic books."

"There's plenty of reading material in the prison library. Let's go."

"Just a second," Polly said. "Can I ask him another question?"

"Sure," Stu said. "What do you want to know?"

"How did you know the comic books were here?"

"You can thank my dear old mother for that," he said. "She called me this morning to tell me that she'd talked to someone who talked to someone else and if I wanted to replace my old comic books, you had some very similar to what she'd given away and maybe you'd agree to sell them to me. The stupid old woman thinks it's all about the comic books. She had no idea what she'd given away."

Obiwan came running into the bedroom and stopped when he saw Stu and John Willard. He barked several times and walked over to Polly, placing himself between her and the men.

"You're a good boy," she said. "Where's Henry?"

Obiwan barked again and looked at the door. Henry came rushing in, panting as he pulled up short. "I swear, Stu, they were perfectly quiet and safe when I left them. If I had thought for a moment that things would fall apart, I would never have left and I certainly wouldn't have taken the dog with me."

"We're fine," Polly said. "And I'm a little tired of having everyone stand around in my bedroom."

"I need those comic books, Polly," Stu said, guiding John Willard out. "Can someone help Jim gather them up?"

"I've got it," Henry said. "Just get him out of our house and out of my sight. I can't believe these damned comic books are at the center of all of this."

"How did you know?" Polly asked.

"Aaron called and told me what he'd been hearing on the phone call that apparently you're still on with him. He started recording things and he says that though it's broken up in places, they have a pretty good confession."

John Willard seemed to crumple at that. "Will someone call my mother?"

"You can do that when we get you to Boone," Stu said. "Let's go."

Polly followed them out and then picked up her phone, "Aaron? Are you still there?"

"Yes Polly. Sal hit him with a frying pan?"

"It was cast iron and she's a strong woman."

He chuckled on the other end of the call. "I'm glad everything turned out so well this time. I can't even yell at you about this."

"No you can't. And please, when you tell Lydia, will you make sure that she knows I'm fine. I didn't do anything stupid. I didn't get into a fight and I told you immediately."

"I'll do that. You take care of yourself and it looks like we'll be talking to you real soon."

"I know, I know. Just one more in the long list of reasons for me to come visit you."

She hung up and Joss brought the plate of treats over to the coffee table. Polly grinned at her. "How ya doin'?" she asked.

"Being your friend is absolutely bizarre," Joss said, flopping into a chair. "How am I going to explain to Nate, and, oh by the way, his mother now, that I was at your house and a man pulled a gun on me?"

"Maybe you shouldn't lead with that," Sal said. "Maybe you should start by telling him that the murderer was caught and you got to watch the whole thing happen."

Joss gave a weak chuckle. "I don't think that will help. Actually, Nate will think it's funny and be sorry that he wasn't here, but his mother is going to lecture me on how important it is to stay safe so that Cooper and Sophie have a mommy around. Because of course, I don't know that yet." She tilted her head back on her neck, looking up to the ceiling, then looked back at Polly. "Please can I move in?"

"Even after all of this?"

There was another knock at the door.

"Who is it?" Polly called.

"It's me, Jeff. And Sylvie. And Eliseo. What in the hell is going on in there?"

Polly laughed as Henry went to open the door. "Come on in," Henry said.

The three of them stood in a line, staring at Polly. "Why did the Sheriff's department just haul a man away from here?" Jeff demanded.

"First of all," Polly said. "We're all fine. Just in case you were wondering. Secondly, that was the man who killed Henry's Uncle Loren. And you won't even believe why he did it."

She waited and they couldn't come up with a good reason.

"Comic books. It was all about comic books. Isn't that the most ridiculous thing you've ever heard?"

"To be fair," Henry interrupted. "Those were collector's items and worth quite a bit of money."

"Yeah. You should have heard him panic when he thought you were reading them willy nilly."

Joss headed for the kitchen. "I'm going to get more plates and napkins. Does anybody want anything to drink?"

"Make mine whiskey," Jeff said. "Working here is taking a toll on me."

Sylvie followed Joss. "Let me help. You have to tell me everything."

"Come all the way in," Polly said to Eliseo and Jeff. "You might as well find a seat. We'll tell you what happened. Sal is the hero of this story, though. She's got some mad hog-tying skills and can heave a cast iron skillet like nobody's business."

Sal slipped down on the couch beside Polly and patted her friend's leg. "I only did what I had to because you are the walking wounded."

"I'm just glad you were here," Henry said. "I'm never leaving her side again."

Joss and Sylvie came back into the living room, carrying trays with pitchers of tea, coffee and water. They were laughing at something Joss had said. Polly watched her friends settle in around her, chatting with each other and letting their concern float away as they ate and drank. Henry took her hand and squeezed it, then put a cupcake in her lap after peeling the paper away.

A clap of thunder made everyone jump and then they smiled at each other, a little embarrassed to have been startled. The storm wasn't letting up, but that was okay. It would soon pass and at least everyone was safe and sound.

Polly touched her cheekbone again. It had been nearly two years since bones had fallen out of the bathroom ceiling and she'd been kidnapped by an old boyfriend. In between that time and now, so many other things had happened. The events of this week would soon fade into nothing more than a memory, just as everything else had. It was people like those in front of her who made life fun, no matter what happened.

"I love you guys," she said softly and realized that most of the room hadn't even heard her.

Sal patted her leg. "We love you too," she whispered.

THANK YOU FOR READING!

I'm so glad you enjoy these stories about Polly Giller and her friends. There are many ways to stay in touch with Diane and the Bellingwood community.

You can find more details about Sycamore House and Bellingwood at the website: http://nammynools.com/

Join the Bellingwood Facebook page:
https://www.facebook.com/pollygiller
for news about upcoming books, conversations while I'm writing and you're reading, and a continued look at life in a small town.

Diane Greenwood Muir's Amazon Author Page is a great place to watch for new releases.

Follow Diane on Twitter at twitter.com/nammynools for regular updates and notifications.

Recipes and decorating ideas found in the books can often be found on Pinterest at: *http://pinterest.com/nammynools/*

And, if you are looking for Sycamore House swag, check out Polly's CafePress store: *http://www.cafepress.com/sycamorehouse*

Made in the USA
Columbia, SC
11 May 2020

96425692R00163